T H E
LAST
STAR

THE
LAST
STAR

A Novel

WILLIAM PROCTOR

A
JANET
THOMA
BOOK

THOMAS NELSON PUBLISHERS
Nashville

To Maud Proctor

© Copyright 2000 by William Proctor

Published in Nashville, Tennessee, by Thomas Nelson, Inc.

Scripture quotations are from the NEW AMERICAN STANDARD BIBLE®, © Copyright The Lockman Foundation 1960, 1962, 1963, 1968, 1971, 1972, 1973, 1975, 1977, 1995. Used by permission. (www.lockman.org)

Library of Congress Cataloging-in-Publication Data

Proctor, William.
    The last star : a novel / William Proctor
      p. cm.
    ISBN 0-7852-6810-3 (pbk.)
     1. Star of Bethlehem—Fiction. 2. Astronomers—Fiction. I. Title.

PS3566.R63 L3 2000
813'.54—dc21

00-031861
CIP

Printed in the United States of America

1 2 3 4 5 6 QWD 05 04 03 02 01 00

ACKNOWLEDGMENTS

SEVERAL people have played important roles in helping me bring this book to publication.

First, I must recognize my friend Dr. Kenneth Boa, with whom I coauthored the nonfiction book *The Return of the Star of Bethlehem* twenty years ago. Many of the factual descriptions in this book about possible options for the identity of the Star are based on that earlier work. Ken was very gracious in encouraging me to proceed independently with this novel and has also supplied me with additional research materials that have been extremely helpful.

My editor, Janet Thoma, has played an absolutely essential role. Without her moral support and incisive editing suggestions, this book would never have been published. Anne Trudel, managing editor of Janet Thoma Books at Thomas Nelson, has been particularly helpful in moving the manuscript expeditiously through the production process.

My good friend Stuart Woodward provided an in-depth analysis and evaluation that improved the logical flow of the manuscript over the original draft. Also, I'm grateful for some early research guidance from Gregory Benford, the fine science fiction writer, who also happens to have been my high school classmate.

In addition, I want to thank my son, Mike Proctor, who provided special encouragement and his unique brand of infectious enthusiasm after reading some of the initial pages I had written. Mike also inspired some of my references to Amherst College, where he is now an undergraduate. Finally, as always, I'm grateful to my wonderful and talented wife, Pam

Proctor, who diligently applied her editing skills and provided plenty of loving support.

But even with all this high-powered help, I must add that ultimately, I chose to go my own way with this effort—and to follow the peculiar directions in which my characters led me.

William Proctor
Vero Beach, Florida

 # ONE

Lㅇㅇ к out your window, Dan. Up in the sky. Toward Cambridge."

Irritated by the phone call, which had broken his chain of thought, Professor Daniel Thompson turned away from the op-ed piece he was writing for the *New York Times.* He anchored the cell phone under his chin and reached over to push aside the shutters that blocked his view of the clear, starry western Massachusetts sky.

In the last few days he'd been so overwhelmed with grading final papers and his own writing projects that he'd cut off all contact with the outside world. *No radio. No TV. No regular phone calls. Leftovers in the fridge. Lousy way to spend May in western Mass. But sometimes, there's no choice.*

Professor Skidmore Kirkland had gotten through to him because he was one of the few who had Dan's cell number. If the caller had been anyone other than Skiddy, Dan would have cut him off immediately. He didn't have time right now for interruptions of any type.

But Dan knew he had to humor Skiddy—and not just because he was a prominent Harvard psychologist. The man had incredible connections with the money people, the kind who fund research projects. Dan had benefited often from those grants, and he wasn't about to jeopardize future opportunities.

"So what am I looking for?" Dan asked.

"Use your eyes. Look to the east."

Dan looked—and dropped his cell phone.

He could hear Skiddy yelling in the distance as it rolled around on the floor. But he couldn't take his eyes off the object that was

1

glowing up there in the sky. It was larger than anything else except the moon. Finally, still watching the thing out of the corner of his eye, he picked up the phone. "I see something."

"I guess you do!" Skiddy shouted. "Are you trying to wreck my eardrums, throwing that phone around?"

"What is it?"

"Where have you been for the last twenty-four hours?"

"Grading essays. Writing. What is it?"

"Nobody knows—that's the point! Try turning on your radio or TV every now and then."

Good idea.

Still craning his neck to keep the light in sight, Dan reached for his TV remote and began to channel surf.

Click.

CNN: "The strange light can apparently be seen from any location in the world . . ."

Click.

FOX: "It looks the same in South America, China, Africa . . ."

Click.

CNBC: ". . . no commonsense explanation. Some suggestions have included a weather balloon, experimental aircraft, or an errant satellite. All have been disproved . . ."

"This is really crazy," Dan said, shifting his attention to the TV, to the sky, and back to Skiddy. "What do you think? Any ideas?"

"You've got an attention problem," the Harvard psychologist said in the snide, sarcastic tone that Dan knew so well. "Are you at all interested in why I called?"

"Sure, sure," Dan replied.

Click.

THE WEATHER CHANNEL: "Telescopes don't help. Neither do high-altitude reconnaissance flights. The object looks the same, no matter how close you get to it . . ."

Click.

ABC: "In Israel, a woman has claimed that when the light focused on her, a persistent case of scaly psoriasis immediately disappeared from her skin . . ."

Click.

CBS: "Wild theories and rumors abound. Antiwar groups are

certain that a cover-up is in the works—perhaps a new super-weapon in space, or some breakthrough in spy technology. UFO enthusiasts suspect first contact with an alien civilization. Religious gurus see an apocalyptic scenario and warn that the end of the world is near . . ."

Skiddy's voice broke through the TV chatter. "You're not listening!"

"Sure I am, sure I am."

Click.

CNN: "Mass hysteria in unlikely places—Cuthbert, Georgia . . . Vero Beach, Florida . . . Bryan, Texas . . . Missoula, Montana . . ."

Click.

ENTERTAINMENT CHANNEL: "Parties to welcome alien visitors break out in the Bahamas, Cancún, L.A. . . ."

"Dan, if you don't shut that TV off, I'm hanging up—and you lose a research stipend."

Now Skiddy had his attention. Dan pressed the Off button on his remote.

"Sorry. Go ahead. What's up?"

"Finally!" Skiddy said, thoroughly exasperated. "Now listen carefully. I only want to say this once. I've got enough foundation money to help us study this thing all summer in the Middle East—mainly Israel. Are you packed?"

"Why over there? Why Israel?"

"Because that's where the UFO performs its weirdest tricks. The only substantiated report of a healing came from there. The religious gurus are gathering in Jerusalem. That's where the action is."

Dan Thompson liked the idea immediately. It meant adventure. It meant publication possibilities—an essential consideration for any academic type. And it meant money.

Sometimes he earned more from these summer schemes than from his regular salary as an Amherst College religion professor. His regular "summer job," he confided to his academic colleagues with just a touch of cynicism, was to satisfy the curiosity of gullible religious millionaires about spiritual healing, prayer power, exorcisms, and "miracles" of various types.

Religion was big business these days—and you didn't have to believe a thing to get the bucks. Dan had learned long ago that Skiddy was a spiritual chameleon at heart. He changed his surface religiosity on cue in pursuit of big foundation grants. Pentecostal today. Hindu tomorrow.

His blatant opportunism sometimes offended even Dan—who placed himself somewhere between lukewarm agnostic and bored, morning-prayer Episcopalian. But Dan never felt quite offended enough to walk away from the generous stipends Skiddy dangled in front of him.

"Who's on your research team?" Dan asked.

"I'll direct the research, of course."

Of course, Dan thought, though he didn't dare verbalize his sarcasm.

"And the main astronomer will be Dudley Dunster, from the university."

For Skiddy, the "university" or the "college" always referred to Harvard, as though there were no other comparable schools of higher learning. Somehow, Dudley, a Harvard astronomer who was about ten years Skiddy's junior, and even more arrogant and sarcastic, always managed to be included in the older man's work and social life. The two men, both of whom had recently gone through bitter divorces, played off each other like some Ivy League sick-comedy act.

"And there's that astrophysicist from the University of California, Geoffrey Gonzales, the one who writes about time and new universes and such."

The first truly qualified choice.

"And we have to include a Christian fundamentalist, because that's where the money is coming from. Our benefactor is a Baptist billionaire. Very deep pockets—and that's great for us. Fellow named Peter Van Campe. He runs a huge foundation, Panoplia International. It's based near Chicago, where a lot of those evangelical groups have their headquarters."

"The evangelical Vatican," Dan said under his breath.

"What?"

"That's what some people call the area—the evangelical Vatican—because of all the evangelical Christian ministries that are based there."

"Whatever. If this thing goes well, I might even become a Baptist myself. Anyhow, I had to agree to this Van Campe's suggestion that we include a teacher from Wheaton College, the religious school out in Illinois."

"What's the Bible-thumper's name?" Dan asked.

"James, as I recall. Professor Michael James."

The political choice.

"And that's where you come into play—as the rational religionist from Amherst College. Our northeastern skeptic. You'll be the counterbalance to Professor James. If he starts getting out of hand, I'll rely on you to keep him in line. It's essential that our conclusions be intellectually acceptable. No sectarian wackiness. You may even be able to contribute something independently. This thing may have some sort of religious angle."

"What do you mean?"

"A lot of right-wing religious people—some of those TV preachers, especially—already have the ear of politicians here and in Israel. It's amazing. Within just a couple of hours, CNN, FOX, and even the BBC were broadcasting interviews with some of these fundamentalist leaders. If we don't come up with a rational, scientific explanation for this thing pretty quickly, they may upstage us—and that wouldn't help my future fund-raising efforts."

With Skiddy, funding the bottom line was always at the top of his agenda. His lavish lifestyle—a new Mercedes every other year, a second home on Cape Cod that was more than just a vacation home, and expensive cruises every summer—depended heavily on the grant money he siphoned off for his personal use. Dan found himself wishing that once, just once, he could get involved in a summer research project that placed the simple search for truth before all else.

Unfortunately, these days it seemed that some ulterior motive backed up by big money always lay behind scientific or scholarly investigations. You were out of luck if your findings didn't enhance the profit potential of a major corporation. Or promote the belief system of some eccentric millionaire or biased foundation board. Or make headlines in the *New York Times*.

"Who else is going on the trip?" Dan asked.

"Nobody else," Skiddy replied. "Don't want to dilute the grant money any more than we have to."

"Can you fit Joanna into the program?"

"A touch of nepotism?"

"So she's my wife. So what? Besides, you need a woman to round things out."

"I'm one step ahead of you," Skiddy said. "I already have one woman lined up for the team—an Israeli archaeologist and expert in ancient languages. Dr. Yael Sharon. She'll also be our project manager. Comes with high recommendations as a hands-on administrator. And I understand she's solid with the Israeli government. She should be able to cut through the red tape. So we already have our female representative. Besides, my Christian billionaire isn't hung up about meeting some sort of gender quota."

Dan thought he could sense some of Skiddy's hostility toward women seeping through his words—a trace, no doubt, of that tough divorce. But the Amherst scholar wasn't about to give up.

"Your billionaire may not care about gender quotas, but your Harvard colleagues might. One woman isn't enough for this sort of project. Also, Joanna has credentials you could use—Yale prof, history of science, degrees in physics and electrical engineering. Expert with equipment I don't begin to understand. Who knows what skills may be required to figure out that light?"

"Okay, Danny boy," Skiddy sighed. "We'll sign up your wife. But I expect some sort of discount. Maybe we can put her on part-time. And you owe me for this."

Good ole Skiddy, Dan thought with an inward sigh. *He could have held his own at the business school.*

At least now, he and Joanna would be able to spend the summer together. That was a real accomplishment—and might help their marriage, which had been heading on a steep downhill course since Christmas. Even before that, the long periods of separation hadn't helped their relationship, as she spent most of each week in New Haven focusing on her Yale teaching duties, and he was stuck an hour and a half away in Amherst.

To make the deal more attractive for his wife, Dan would insist that he and Joanna be paid equally for this project—even if they were both put on some sort of part-time status. Joanna had insisted from the very beginning, and Dan had agreed, that they would be equal partners in their marriage. Her choice to keep her family name, Hill, had symbolized the parity, and there were also practical implications.

For one thing, she had let him know early on that her career had to be given a priority, even if it meant that they might have to live apart for a good part of each week. Whenever they discussed the future, their jobs, possessions, and vacation plans dominated the conversation. Family and children weren't part of the picture at all.

Joanna's fierce independence sometimes put extra strains on their marriage, to the point that Dan had begun to wonder if they would make it as a couple at all. He felt that he was the one who was always making the adjustments and concessions, while she was arranging everything for her own benefit. During the past year tensions had intensified so much that when they were together, they seemed to spend more time arguing than enjoying each other's company.

But maybe this project can bring us together again. Maybe we can turn it into a nice holiday. Do a little touring. And earn good money besides. She's certainly suited for this assignment.

As Dan reflected further on Joanna's expertise and technical background, he strongly suspected she might actually be a better choice than he was. Most likely, he and this James fellow from Wheaton would just be extra baggage. Religion was almost certain to take a backseat to science because after all, you could actually see this light in the sky. He expected it would be only a matter of time before the scientists came up with a reasonable explanation.

But now he turned to his immediate task—which he knew could prove formidable. He had to convince his strong-minded spouse to put aside her own summer research, which she was finalizing at this very moment. Instead, he would argue, she should join him on a wild-goose chase to the Middle East. Funded by a billionaire Midwesterner and fundamentalist. A hard sell indeed. Seemed sillier the more he thought about it.

Still, this wild-goose chase apparently involved a goose that laid golden grant-money eggs. And the expedition would be exciting. Mysterious.

As Dan speed-dialed Joanna's number, he finalized his strategy. He needed a hook. He would emphasize that Skiddy's largesse would give them the down payment they needed for that little beach cottage on Cape Cod—the one that was supposed to be coming on the market not too far from Skiddy's place. Surely she would agree that her lower-paying research could be put on hold for another summer.

And let's face it. What could possibly go wrong? Who could ever regret an all-expense-paid second honeymoon in the exotic Middle East?

 # TWO

"Y o u ' r e irrelevant," Joanna Hill said to her husband as they boarded the El Al airliner at JFK International Airport.

She obviously wasn't kidding.

"Thanks," Dan retorted, smarting at the crack.

Ignoring his sarcasm, she pushed ahead on the same track: "This James person is irrelevant too. The one from the fundamentalist school—what's it called?"

"Wheaton College."

"The only Wheaton I know of is in Massachusetts."

"Yeah, well maybe, just maybe, you don't know everything," Dan muttered. "This one is in Illinois, near Chicago."

"Anyhow, I don't know what either of you is doing on this team. This is a scientific investigation."

Dan had to force himself to hold his tongue. He was on the verge of reminding her that *she* wouldn't have been included if he hadn't gone to bat for her with Skiddy. But he thought better of it. From past experience, he knew that pointed repartee could easily anger his wife, and he just didn't want to deal with that right now. The extensive airport security procedures had put them all on edge, and he wasn't in any mood to aggravate matters further.

As he followed Joanna down the aisle of the crowded aircraft, she chattered on about why she was certain a scientific solution to the strange light was inevitable.

"Number one, I can see the light with my own eyes—and with my telescopes," she said, holding up a thumb to stress the point.

"Number two"—holding up her index finger—"news reports in the papers and on TV show that photographic equipment can record it.

"Number three"—holding up another finger—"it's virtually certain that one of our scientific instruments—a spectroscope or simple photometer or something—will at least point us toward an answer."

"Spectroscope?" Dan said, obviously not keeping up with her.

"It measures the relative intensity and nature of light across the entire spectrum," Joanna explained, obviously laboring to be patient. "The method can tell us a lot, such as the temperature of the object and whether it's moving toward or away from our position."

Without pausing for a response, she swept her long auburn hair away from her flashing brown eyes and shrugged matter-of-factly as they took their seats.

She always does that when she knows she's one up on me. When she's the expert on an issue and I'm not. It's like we're competitors on a playing field—and she's just scored the winning goal.

"The conclusion is inescapable," Joanna concluded with a condescending smile. "This light must exist in some identifiable, physical form—and that means we'll soon have a down-to-earth, scientific explanation."

So that's that. The problem is apparently solved before we even get started.

Joanna's steel-trap mind and smug manner often irritated Dan. He could deal with her intelligence if she'd just be nice about it. He wasn't even sure she was conscious of how she was coming across. At times, she could become so logical and rational and sure of herself that she forgot to take into account people's feelings. Dan knew that from firsthand experience.

He shook his head. *I'm not sure we're going to make it. This is definitely not a marriage made in heaven. How old am I? Forty, and not getting any younger. Why spend the rest of my life starring in* The Taming of the Shrew?

As the El Al airliner soared across the Atlantic, Dan leaned against the window and gazed out into the night sky. His tall, lanky frame never fit well into these airline seats, so he held out little hope that he would get much sleep on the long flight. But maybe that was just as well. He needed to do some thinking about the challenges that lay ahead.

Dan had an unimpeded view of the mysterious, glowing object through the relatively clear aircraft window. Occasionally, he peeked at it through a pair of binoculars he had packed. But as various news reports had suggested, the light looked the same, whether you were thousands of feet in the air or on the ground.

Glancing back at the row of seats behind him, Dan could hear Michael James, the Wheaton Bible scholar, talking animatedly with Geoffrey Gonzales, the astrophysicist from the University of California. On one level, James—who appeared to be about his own age—seemed the epitome of the cloistered library scholar. His pasty-white, cherubic face didn't suggest much outdoor activity. And the somewhat goofy grin and large horn-rimmed glasses seemed more suited to the ivory tower than a rugged scientific expedition.

But there was something about this unimpressive facade that didn't quite fit the egghead image. As James peppered the shorter, more relaxed Gonzales with question after question about the Californian's work in time warps and parallel universes, he exuded pent-up energy and excitement.

"But do you have any solid basis for thinking this light may be extradimensional?" James pressed, his eyes locked onto Gonzales's. "And what does 'extradimensional' really mean here? That's a mathematical construct, isn't it? What would that mean if somehow we could approach or pass through the light? Would we enter another universe?"

Gonzales was temporarily speechless, apparently unsure which question to tackle first. And he was obviously impressed by the Wheaton man's grasp of the issues.

Though only of average height, probably a good three or four inches shorter than Dan, James's bearing and dominant manner made him seem taller than he was. Also, as Dan looked more closely, he concluded that the Wheaton man might actually be in pretty good shape. The rather sinewy forearms, which protruded from his rolled-up sleeves, didn't quite match the rather wimpy face.

He might even pump iron.

There was also something about the way the Wheaton man moved his hands and body that made Dan think of varsity athletes he had known in college.

Somehow, something just doesn't quite mesh here. Something about this guy just doesn't register right.

Skiddy Kirkland, on the way back to his seat from the rest room, paused in the aisle and listened for a moment to the conversation.

"Sounds as though you know something about theoretical physics," he said to James.

"Just general reading," James replied. "Theologians are getting into this area more and more, and I find it fascinating. Theology and science seem to come together at this point."

Yes, Dan decided, *the Wheaton professor did give the appearance of being reasonably intelligent and broad-minded, at least for a fundamentalist.* Also, as far as Dan could tell, James had made no move so far to impose his religious views on anyone. There was no obvious dogmatism. No attempt to proselytize. Apparently not even a defensive or judgmental remark.

Even Skiddy seemed somewhat positive as he moved back toward his own seat.

"Seems open-minded and reasonable," Skiddy said, leaning across Joanna and whispering in Dan's ear. "But keep an eye on him. That's your assignment. Can't have this fellow making us look silly."

Dan still didn't know quite what to make of the "Bible guy," as he had dubbed James. But he was confident that he would eventually get a firm handle on him—and would then be in a position to neutralize him quickly if he started to cause any trouble.

Dan had yet to meet a Bible-wielding evangelical Christian who couldn't be put down rather easily as a narrow-minded, predictable prig. A verbal thrust here, a pointed remark there, and this Michael James character would soon be dismantled.

Through incisive, subtle articles in the *Times* and other liberal publications, Dan had eviscerated more than one conservative religious opponent. So it was with quiet yet confident pride that he now prepared once again to live up to that affectionate nickname that had been bestowed upon him by some of his colleagues—"the Amherst fundy-fighter."

Dan glanced over at Joanna, who was now sound asleep on the seat next to him. Her shiny auburn hair cushioned her head like a liquid, flowing pillow, partly tumbling over her face and partly spilling over the back of her seat, where it dangled as a backdrop for the James–Gonzales discussion. As always, she seemed considerably younger than her thirty-eight years.

Too good-looking to be a Yale professor.

He'd never tell her that, of course. She would skewer him as hopelessly sexist if she heard him utter such a remark.

Too bad she's so intense. Too serious. No sense of humor.

It hadn't been easy to convince his wife to forsake her precious research and join the team. But as he had expected, when he played the Cape Cod house card, she began to listen seriously. Though a serious scholar—and a leading expert on the history of solar energy and the study of light—Joanna was a thorough pragmatist, and not at all averse to a high-paying assignment.

The pragmatism carried over to her work. She was at her best with projects that demanded hard research and held out the promise of firm, no-nonsense conclusions. Theoretical or speculative thinking didn't appeal to her. And religious or spiritual issues simply didn't register on her intellectual radar.

It sometimes amazed Dan that, given his own fascination with spirituality and comparative religions, Joanna had been interested enough to marry him. His standard line when anyone commented on their divergent interests was: "It was my body, not my mind, that got her."

Dan peered over the seat in front of him to check on Skiddy. The project director and his younger associate, the astronomer Dudley Dunster, were huddled in an intense whispered conversation—undoubtedly exploring new ways that they might wring additional funds out of their latest benefactor.

Not quite ready to take a nap, Dan decided to join them for a few minutes, so he climbed over Joanna's outstretched legs and stood in the aisle next to them. They nodded to him but then turned back to finish their conversation, which had something to do with the setup of the team's research area in northern Israel.

As Dan studied the pair, he was struck that it would have been hard for any two people to have been more unlike in appearance.

Skiddy, in his mid-forties, was the senior partner in this Mutt-and-Jeff duo. He was tall, angular, and skinny—at least six-feet-four and surely no more than about 170 pounds. Yet his steely handshake, along with his remarkable ability to handle the group's heavy telescopic and photographic equipment, suggested that he was considerably stronger physically than first appearances might suggest. Rawboned. Wiry. But not your typical Mr. Nice Guy.

A prominent, beaklike nose and a tendency to lean forward with a slight smirk on his thin lips betrayed an in-your-face attitude. The aggressive effect was magnified by small, wire-rimmed glasses, which gave his slightly bulging eyes a perpetually hard, penetrating stare.

In physical appearance, Dudley Dunster, a nontenured assistant professor in his mid-thirties, was the polar opposite of Skiddy—so much so that he sometimes reminded Dan of a human cream puff. But he was definitely a cream puff that had gone sour at the center.

Short, pudgy, and oozing mild, sugary platitudes, Dudley turned an almost boyish and unthreatening face toward Dan and commented, "So it's really nice that you and Joanna can be together on this outing. You're separated a lot, aren't you?"

"Yeah, too much. But we cope."

"Well, I hope you have better luck than I did with my former wife. Sometimes I think I wasn't quite sensitive enough. She had her career and I had mine, and I'm afraid I didn't always take her feelings into account."

Dan looked back at Joanna to be sure she was asleep and then confided in a low voice, "You know, I have some of the same thoughts, Dudley. Am I really taking her career into account enough? Should I try to get a position at Yale so I can be near her? I worry about such things."

Dudley shook his head sympathetically. "Hard decisions. Very hard. Your career or hers. I know the problem. I understand."

"And I worry about her safety," Dan said, now unburdening some worries that he had shared with no one up to this point.

"Her safety?" Dudley said.

"Yes. New Haven's not too safe, you know. Bad area. Lots of crime. I'm always worried she'll be mugged—or worse."

"Unsafe New Haven," Dudley echoed.

"Yeah."

"Terrible, mean old Yale," he said, his tone changing.

Dan now looked at the Harvard astronomer and saw the glint in Dudley's eye that he had seen too many times before.

Here it comes. What have I done? How did I fall into this trap?

"Poor little Danny boy," Dudley cooed sarcastically. "Poor little Amherst guy. You really think a grown woman can't handle herself? Are you living in the nineteenth century?"

"Well, I . . ."

"By the way, are you henpecked, Dan?" Dudley asked, now changing the ground of his attack.

"Look, I . . ."

"How about it, Dan?" Dudley said, as Skiddy looked on with a gleeful grin. "A man or a mouse—which is it? You'd actually think about leaving your professorship, giving up your career for a woman?"

Dan glanced back nervously at Joanna, but thankfully, she seemed to still be asleep.

How did I open this Pandora's box? Why do I do this to myself? I know these two. They're the evil twins. So why don't I keep my mouth shut?

Dan was far too familiar with Dudley's modus operandi to allow himself to fall for this trick, but once again, he had been tripped up. Dudley was so predictable. First, he'd encourage intimate conversation. Then, if you revealed you were wrestling with a personal problem, he could come across as so solicitous and compassionate that you might wonder if you had actually encountered a priest in disguise, ready to listen to your confession.

But when you really began to open up or allowed yourself to become emotionally vulnerable, Dudley would more often than not turn on you—partly out of pure meanness, and partly out of a desire to get an approving laugh.

Sometimes, it almost seemed that Dudley's main purpose in life was to employ cutting humor to entertain those above him in the academic hierarchy—especially tenured, well-connected professors like Skiddy. In many respects, Dudley was the caricature of the insecure academic who lived in constant fear that he would never be selected by the senior faculty for tenure—and thus never become a permanent, full-fledged member of the university establishment.

As far as Dan could tell, Skiddy had become one of Dudley's main mentors for one overriding reason: the full professor's ability to secure research grants. Skiddy's extensive web of funding contacts, which on more than one occasion had benefited Harvard's scientists—including those in Dudley's astronomy department—had provided the younger man with opportunities to publish and enhance his academic reputation. So long as Skiddy continued to fulfill this career-building function, Dudley seemed ready to die for him, to take any measures necessary to ensure Skiddy's dominance over all comers.

So as unlike as the two were in appearance, they soon made it clear to anyone who got to know them that their personalities could work in agonizing synergy to make others miserable, with verbal barbs and condescending sarcasm. They seemed caught forever in a sophomoric time warp—a kind of *Lord of the Flies, Part Two*—where the power of two perpetual adolescents combined to wreak more devastating havoc than one of them could ever achieve alone.

Finally, as the conversation turned away from Dan to other matters, he extricated himself and slipped back into his seat.

"I can't understand why you put up with those two," Joanna said. The discussion had evidently awakened her.

I wonder how much she heard. Well, nothing I can do about that now. Water under the bridge. Over the dam. Whatever.

"The pain lasts only a moment," Dan sighed quietly in her ear. "And what I earn on Skiddy's summer boondoggles can heal almost any wound. Besides, they're still bitter about their divorces. They have problems with women."

"And you don't?" Joanna said, closing her eyes and turning her head away from him before he could reply.

Great. Just great. First Dudley. Now my wife. What am I doing here? The money and the prestige. I guess that's what it's all about. The money and the prestige.

In fact, Dan had almost reached the point where he was ready to sever ties with Skiddy. He had actually toyed with the idea of trying to find something else to do this summer. But he knew that the key to heading in another direction was to find his own sources of funding and research support.

Seething inside, he turned his face toward the window and found himself gazing at the strange light again. After a while, the glow seemed to soothe him, and he could actually feel his anger ebbing a little. He glanced down at his watch and was surprised to see how much time had passed. By now, the flight attendants had collected all the meal trays, and the in-flight movie was a bland memory. The lights in the plane had dimmed, and most of the travelers, including those on the research team, were dozing. Despite the unsettled thoughts still swirling through his mind, Dan, too, began to drift away into a fitful sleep.

The last thing he remembered just before he lost consciousness was the disturbing sight of Skiddy's angular face—certainly a dream, but the impression was so real. As the Harvard professor moved closer and closer, the penetrating, vulturelike eyes peered intensely into Dan's own, as though probing for something deep inside his psyche. At the last moment, the eyes merged into a single orb, an exact replica of that strange light in the sky.

Then, Dan slept.

 # THREE

T H E plane touched down in Tel Aviv in the early morning, about two hours before dawn.

But this time, unlike other trips Dan Thompson had made to Israel, there was no delay at customs or security. A stern-looking Israeli army sergeant, who obviously knew the team members by sight, met them at the gate and guided them and their baggage and equipment quickly through all the checkpoints. Before they knew it, they were on the street, where a van and a truck were waiting for them.

"We should always travel this way," Dan whispered to Joanna, who responded with a somewhat strained smile but then turned away to watch her scientific equipment being loaded into the truck.

"If any of this stuff gets lost, I might as well go home," she muttered. "And that army guy makes me nervous. He didn't say two words. Just fiddled with his pistol."

She was obviously preoccupied and anxious as she checked and rechecked her cases containing sophisticated equipment for measuring light and energy emissions. Other scientific instruments had already arrived and were waiting for them at the site. Joanna expected the apparatuses would provide a definitive identification of the light—and she wanted to be sure all her "gadgets," as Dan called them, were ready to go when they finally arrived at their research compound up in the Galilee hill region of northern Israel.

Dan sensed that at this point, he and Michael James might be the only two laid-back members of the team. Everybody else seemed to grow quieter and more intense as the sergeant and a corporal loaded the van and truck, and then climbed into the driver's seats.

"Uh-oh, look over there," Dudley said, pointing at a small crowd milling around a line of vehicles a short distance away.

"Who's that?" Dan asked.

"The Caltech group," he said. "And some other people I don't recognize. The competition."

"Back in a minute," Geoffrey Gonzales said as he hurried over to the crowd. "Just want to say hello."

"How many others do you figure will be coming over here?" Joanna asked no one in particular as she watched the other investigators preparing to board their trucks and vans.

"Too many," Skiddy replied. "That's why we have to hit the ground running when we get to our compound. Israel is the center of the action, at least for the foreseeable future. Probably until someone comes up with a solution to that thing in the sky. We have to be first. There's no second place in this deal."

A heavy sense of the importance of this mission now began to register with everyone, even Dan. The overall mood was clearly shifting from boondoggle to serious business. Increasingly, the investigation had taken on a higher profile, as newspapers like the *Wall Street Journal* and *New York Times* had reported on the Israel preparations. More publicity was sure to come.

To increase the tension, the aura of a scientific race had settled on the project. They were well aware that many other research teams were heading into Israel and other parts of the Middle East to investigate the light. The entire world seemed to be watching to see who would be first to discover the identity of the strange light—and who would get the main headlines in the *Times* and other major newspapers.

A prevailing assumption was that victory would bring significant rewards. Certainly, there would be plenty of research opportunities for everyone associated with the project. They could also expect offers of prominent positions or professorships in major universities.

"And if the light turns out to be some major scientific breakthrough, who knows?" Skiddy remarked. "Maybe even a Nobel."

So it was understandable that Dan's colleagues were starting to look as focused as a team of bobsledders on an Olympic starting line, about to take their one big shot at the gold. Yet Dan felt more like a spectator, and he wasn't quite sure why. Maybe he just wasn't taking this whole thing as seriously as the others because he regarded his role as peripheral at this point.

After all, he wasn't even a scientist, and this outing seemed ready-made for astronomy, physics, or some other "hard science" field that had always caused Dan to run in the opposite direction. He was in the "mushiest" of the humanities—religion—as Dudley Dunster had pointed out condescendingly more than once.

He looked over at the other teams of scientists and saw Geoffrey Gonzales talking intently with two men he had pulled to one side.

Probably California colleagues. These scientists are so incestuous. Hope he remembers whose side he's on.

"So, you seem to be enjoying yourself," Michael James said, tapping Dan on the shoulder and jerking him abruptly out of his reverie.

Realizing that he had been smiling as he watched Gonzales, Dan quickly composed himself and replied rather brusquely, "So what's not to enjoy? I don't have much to worry about at this point. You and I are backups, aren't we? A couple of insurance policies. If by some remote chance the scientists can't figure this thing out, then they turn to the witch doctors."

"Maybe," James said with a wry smile. "But I'm not so sure that the scientific method is going to work here. I'm all for exhausting the natural possibilities first. But I suspect that our talents may be needed sooner than we think."

As if you know, Dan thought, but he nodded politely. This know-it-all definitely could get on your nerves because he was always thinking. The more Dan was around him, the more he realized that if he was going to keep up with James, he had to maintain his own mental edge.

"Geoffrey, let's go!" Skiddy yelled at Gonzales. "We've got to get moving!"

"Who was that?" Dudley asked when the California astrophysicist had rejoined them.

"A couple of astronomers I know," Geoffrey said. "Experts in SETI. Their team will set up close to us, in northern Galilee."

"SETI?" Dan asked.

Dudley rolled his eyes and patted his soft belly impatiently.

"Search for Extraterrestrial Intelligence. Don't you read anything but religion?"

"Is that legitimate?" Dan said, ignoring the gibe. "Sounds a little over the edge to me. They're looking for little green men?"

"Some scientists do think SETI research is a waste of time," Joanna said.

"I'd rather see grant money go elsewhere," Dudley added.

"But the research is still quite legitimate," Gonzales said. "And who knows? They may be in just the right field for this venture. For all we know, extraterrestrials could be involved with that light up there."

And they think I'm *in an oddball field,* Dan thought. *This thing gets wackier by the minute.*

As they were speeding northward up the coastal highway, Dan, who had a window seat, studied the night sky. Even though he had made numerous trips to Israel, the country always fascinated him. He didn't really accept most of what was presented in the Bible as history. But somehow, when his feet actually touched the soil of the Holy Land, something changed inside him. Almost mystically, he sensed he was in touch with a force beyond himself, something unspeakably old, even eternal.

Then Dan's eyes drifted up toward the light, which was still shining in the eastern sky, in exactly the same spot where it had been when he first saw it in Massachusetts—even though now they were practically on the other side of the earth.

"It's intriguing," the astrophysicist Gonzales observed, as if reading Dan's mind. "That thing is always in the same place. Never goes up or down. No rising or setting, as with other stars and planets. Yes, quite intriguing."

Dan reflected on Michael James's prediction that science probably wasn't going to provide an answer to this puzzle. Then he shrugged off the thought. He couldn't bear the idea that James might actually be right. Besides, the Wheaton professor almost certainly knew as little about astronomy and astrophysics as he did.

"It seems bigger than it did back in the States," Joanna said.

"Probably because the sky's clearer here," Dudley said. "Fewer lights along this road to interfere with our view."

"Still, it does seem bigger," Joanna insisted.

"Yes, it does," Michael agreed.

"Also, is it my imagination, or is that thing pulsating or shimmering?" Skiddy asked, rolling down his window to get a better view.

Everyone looked quietly into the sky for a moment, some using binoculars. Then Geoffrey Gonzales responded, as though thinking out loud. "We can't really say at this point," he said. "At least not when we're looking at this with the naked eye, or even through binocs. We need powerful telescopes and other instruments. And it will be essential to observe this thing above the atmosphere."

"Subspace flights are already under way," Joanna said, relying on some of her government connections information.

"The SOFIA operation?" Dudley asked.

"That's one example."

"What's SOFIA?" Dan asked, feeling quite ignorant but determined to gather as much information as he could in as short a time as possible.

"The Stratospheric Observatory for Infrared Astronomy," Dudley said with a sigh. "I feel like I'm back in Astronomy 101 with you, Dan. Anyhow, all you need to know is that this involves a Boeing 747-SP aircraft that's been modified to carry a 2.7-meter reflecting telescope. Flies at just above forty thousand feet—high enough to avoid the water vapor, dust, and other parts of the atmosphere that interfere with infrared waves."

Noticing Dan's blank look, Dudley explained further. "The infrared range on the electromagnetic spectrum is a very long wavelength that's invisible to the eye. You can feel infrared radiation as warmth, such as when you put your hand over the coils on a stove just before they turn red. But you can't see it. The SOFIA will help us tell if that light is putting out any infrared radiation—and that could be evidence that something is going on up there that we can't observe directly with our eyes, or by looking through our telescopes."

"The plane also carries sophisticated spectrometers and other devices for measuring other types of radiation," Joanna said.

"Yeah, the SOFIA could help—especially if the light is nearby," Geoffrey said.

"There are also some other NASA flights that'll be going up, using modified F-18 jets," Joanna said. "But those are under wraps. Top secret."

"And a shuttle launch is scheduled for next week," Dudley said. "We're hitting that thing with everything we have. I think we'll be getting some answers pretty soon."

"Maybe, maybe not," Michael James said.

Joanna and Dudley looked at the Wheaton professor as though he were from some other planet. But apparently deciding that because he wasn't a scientist, his views weren't worth commenting upon, they didn't respond.

What's with this guy? Dan wondered. *Does he really have some inside information, or is he just the most arrogant person I've ever met?*

After the van reached the city of Hadera, which, as Dan recalled, lay close to the Mediterranean coast in the Plain of Sharon about thirty miles north of Tel Aviv, they turned northeast onto a highway that led into the Valley of Jezreel. In answer to a question that someone put to him, the taciturn army sergeant who was at the wheel explained that early Jewish settlers had established Hadera as a cradle of modern Zionism in 1890. They had bought an old Arab inn, or caravansary, also known as a "kahn," for their home and headquarters, and made Hadera the center of the country's citrus industry.

As the lights of Hadera faded in the distance, Michael James remarked: "Now we're heading toward Megiddo and the Valley of Jezreel—perhaps the site of the last battle of history, Armageddon."

There he goes again, Dan thought. *Can't wait to flaunt his Bible knowledge, or whatever.*

Joanna, who had never been to Israel before, irritated Dan further by treating the Bible guy's observations on prophecy seriously. "What evidence is there that this is the spot? What makes you think Armageddon will be here?"

"Of course, no one knows for sure," Michael replied. "But the reference to Armageddon in some translations of the book of Revelation—chapter sixteen, to be precise—is thought to be derived from a Hebrew term, which could mean the 'hill or mound of Megiddo.'"

"Fascinating," Joanna mused. "So for Christian prophecy, this is sort of ground zero?"

"You might say that."

"How about you, Michael?" Joanna pressed. "What do you think?"

"Personally, I believe history's coming to some sort of culmination. And this valley that we're driving across may well play a key role."

"This really is fascinating," Joanna said again. "I don't think I've ever met anyone who took the Bible so seriously."

Dan shook his head. *What is she thinking, humoring the guy this way? I thought she said Michael was irrelevant to this trip, like me. What's going on?* The way Dan saw it, the more you responded to such people, the more you encouraged their nonsense.

Dan looked over at Skiddy, who was also watching James intently, but this time with a decided frown. *Yes indeed*, Dan mused. *Harvard seems to be getting less and less kindly disposed toward Wheaton.*

Skiddy then glanced at Dan, with an expression that seemed to say, "You'd better get ready to put this fellow in his place. We can't let the others get too interested in his fundamentalist craziness, or he could take us completely off track."

But Dan's mind was fuzzy after the flight. As hard as he tried, he couldn't think of anything intelligent to contribute about prophecy or the Bible that would counterbalance James's comments.

He considered throwing out something completely obscure as a distraction or conversation stopper. Something like, "We really can't be definitive about eschatology because there's no scholarly consensus on hermeneutics, the Parousia, or even ontology. Are our texts preterit or not? That's the question."

Dan suspected that, despite the stellar array of scholars around him, few would have the foggiest notion what he was talking about. Probably only James would know that he was referring to the principles of biblical interpretation relating to teachings about the end of history, the Second Coming, and the nature of God. Certainly Joanna wouldn't.

But even if he sidetracked the discussion for a moment, Dan had no idea what he would say after that. Fortunately, he was saved the effort. Everyone seemed to grow groggy at once. Silence and sleep— hastened by fatigue, jet lag, and the steady, lulling roar of the wind rushing by outside—soon settled over the van.

When Dan awoke, the sun was already shining in the eastern sky. He rubbed his eyes and swallowed a couple of times to try to rid his mouth of that early-morning cottony feeling. Then he scanned the interior of the speeding van and noticed that Michael James, Dudley Dunster, and Geoffrey Gonzales were awake too. But they were shading their eyes, looking in the direction of the sun.

"Incredible," Geoffrey said.

"It doesn't make sense," Dudley remarked. "We shouldn't be able to see an astronomical body that close to the sun."

"But there it is," Geoffrey said. "The light is right there, almost as clear as the sun itself."

Dan looked up, and sure enough, when he put up his hand to block out the sun, the light was close to it, glowing prominently.

They drove on in silence and soon arrived in Tiberias, the capital of Galilee, which is situated on the shores of the Sea of Galilee, or Lake Kinneret.

"Let's eat some breakfast at the hotel," Skiddy said, pointing toward a luxurious-looking building down the street. "Then we'll drive north up the coast. Our research site is not too far from Kiryat-Shemona, about thirty-five miles from here, just north of the Sea of Galilee."

"Isn't that getting pretty close to the Golan Heights?" Dudley asked nervously. "At the Lebanese border? Where the Israelis are always getting shelled by the Arabs?"

"Yeah, but don't worry," Michael said. "Things have been pretty peaceful up there lately. And I imagine the shooting will stop for the time being because all sides are distracted. Everybody is obsessed with this light."

Although speculation about the light continued during breakfast, Joanna managed to turn the conversation toward the spectacular scenery that surrounded them. Mountains rose dramatically over the far coastline, five or six miles away. In between them and the mountains, the morning sun glistened on the calm water.

"Look at those boats out there," she said. "Are those sightseers?"

"More likely fishermen coming back with their morning's catch," Michael said.

"Just like Saint Peter," she reflected.

"Yes, and James and John and Andrew," Michael replied. "Sometimes it strikes me that things haven't changed much in two thousand years."

"Was Tiberias here when Jesus and the disciples were sailing around out there?" she asked.

"As a matter of fact, it was," Michael said, settling into what Dan feared would be another full-blown lecture. "Herod Antipas—or Herod the Tetrarch as he is sometimes called—was the Roman-appointed ruler over Galilee at the time. He inherited the province from his father, Herod the Great, and began construction on this site in A.D. 20 or so. Tiberias replaced an older town, Rakkat, and was named in honor of the Roman emperor at the time, Tiberius. By most dating methods, Jesus didn't begin His ministry here until at least the late twenties. So He and the disciples were almost certainly around here when the city was quite new."

Yes, Dan thought, *this guy could really drive me crazy.*

Before long, the team was back on the road again, but now they grew quiet. Their brief tour of Israel and Galilee was about to end, and hard work with an uncertain outcome lay before them.

With the sun higher in the sky, the strange light had become more prominent than ever.

Maybe that thing really is bigger over here, Dan thought.

And the more he gazed at the light, the less confident he became that the scientists would easily find the answers they were seeking.

 # FOUR

YAEL Sharon hunched over her notebook computer screen, hurrying to finish her real-time contact with her Mossad control in Jerusalem.

The driver of the van had just radioed that the scientific team would arrive in a few minutes, and she wanted to be waiting at the parking area to greet them. She certainly didn't want to have to bother with explanations about her work this early in the game. Her mind was already spinning, anticipating the innocent questions that could trigger suspicion if she failed to respond with convincing answers:

Question: So what's your connection with the government?

Answer: Nothing real formal. But as an archaeologist I have to keep in close touch with different agencies. And like everybody else, I've had some military training. *Be vague. Boring. Undistinguished.*

Question: Are the government people still on board?

Answer: Sure. You got through customs okay, didn't you? *Be positive. Distract by throwing a question back at them.*

Question: You do a lot of e-mailing, don't you?

Answer: Every scholar I know does. Don't you? And remember, I have to keep everything going smoothly for you. *Toss back a counterquestion. Make them feel a little defensive.*

Yael knew that the more successful she was at diverting attention from herself—and keeping others away from her files—the more safely she could pursue her covert operations. In any case, she had too many things on her mind now to have to make up elaborate cover stories to conceal her intelligence connections.

She shook her head in frustration as she looked back at the computer screen. It didn't help that her Mossad control—the supervisor in Tel Aviv who monitored her every movement—had insisted that they set up additional top secret procedures. It took half a minute just to get on-line with him, as she threaded her way through multiple passwords and computerized encryptions, not to mention a layer of traditional linguistic encoding devices.

But the control was paranoid. He had insisted that all communications be executed over a super-secure line that would appear only on-screen, not by voice. Then the messages had to be erased immediately after the completion of the interchange. He was afraid that any spoken discussions might be overheard or intercepted too easily, or that someone might stumble onto one of their written messages and begin to ask questions.

"This may be the most important single event in the history of Israel and the Middle East," he had told her. "The repercussions could be worldwide. We can't afford to take any chances."

Although Yael was certainly aware of how important the pending investigations were, she thought the man was going a little over the edge with his precautions. But he was her superior.

And who knows? she concluded. *Maybe he's right. Maybe spies and counterspies are looking over my shoulder right now—and I don't even know who they are.*

Just as she signed off and watched the main computer menu come back up on the screen, the guard stationed at the gate to the compound radioed: "They're here. Should be parked in front of your office in a couple of minutes."

Yael stood up, buckled on her pistol, reached for her army fatigue cap, and headed toward the front door of the hut that had been erected as the team's headquarters. She knew she might look a little too "military" for these Americans, but they would quickly get used to it. Besides, when you were operating out in the countryside, that was the Israeli way—the fatigue-khaki-bush look, with a weapon close at hand.

"Dr. Sharon! Yael Sharon!"

It was Michael James, whom she already knew, waving at her from about thirty yards away. The others were piling out of the van and turning to look in her direction.

"Come here, let me introduce you!" James said. "First, this is Professor Skidmore Kirkland. You've already been in touch with him by e-mail, I believe."

"Call me Skiddy," the professor said, looking the archaeologist up and down with a curious smile.

As Dan Thompson watched Skiddy's reaction, he could tell that this Israeli bombshell was obviously not quite what the Harvard psychologist had expected. In previous discussions with the team, Skiddy had emphasized Yael's academic and professional credentials. He said he expected her to be a tough, no-nonsense project manager for the investigation.

"I'm sure she wears army boots," Skiddy had joked. "But who cares, so long as she does her job."

Clearly, the glamorous, swashbuckling young woman standing before them didn't fit the image that had been in Skiddy's mind. From the look in his eye, it almost seemed that he could take an interest in her that might extend well beyond their professional relationship. But Dan also sensed that the Harvard director would treat Yael Sharon with kid gloves because of her reported connections with the Israeli government. One of her main functions, as Skiddy had told him, was to keep them from getting their wires crossed with the bureaucrats in Tel Aviv or Jerusalem.

"If we start running into red tape, that could finish us," he said. "Dr. Sharon is our ticket through any government thicket. She's a sabra, a native Israeli who was born just after the 1967 Six-Day War. She apparently has all the academic and political connections we need to pull strings for us."

But as Yael Sharon stood before them—flashing a dazzling smile and turning on a confident charm—it was evident that she had more going for her than an archaeology degree, expertise in several ancient Semitic and modern languages, and the ear of a few official functionaries. The rumpled khaki shorts, bush shirt, and floppy cap—and the inevitable army boots, which extended a few inches up her well-tanned calves—couldn't conceal the fundamental fact that the woman was truly stunning.

Each attribute seemed to enhance the whole. Her shiny,

medium-length jet-black hair was pulled back and secured efficiently at the nape of her neck with a simple leather loop. The lithe, athletic frame and well-defined muscles suggested many hours of rugged outdoor exercise.

Dr. Sharon was definitely not the usual "your-mother-wears-army-boots" military type. Not by a long shot. Her magnetic personality and casual self-assurance in greeting this group of prominent foreign scientists and academics suggested that she had plenty of experience dealing with important people—as well as people who *thought* they were important.

Dan could easily picture her playing several quite different roles. In one scenario, she was a tough, pistol-packing gunslinger on the wild West Bank. In another, she was a popular, brainy professor in the most civilized sector of academia. In still another, she was swirling about on an elegant dance floor, the center of attention at a formal diplomatic ball.

"Put your eyes back in their sockets," Joanna purred softly, tugging him toward the headquarters shack, where the others were now heading.

"Impressive project manager," he said.

"Yeah, sure. Just remember, she carries a gun."

The two were the last to enter the headquarters building, which was really a prefabricated three-room shack. Obviously Israeli army issue. The front room where they were gathering was the largest and was sparsely furnished with metal desks, a few chairs, and several computer terminals. An old sofa against one wall seemed the only concession to comfort.

Yael identified the back room on their right as the office of the project director, Skiddy Kirkland. Her office, as project manager, was the one on the left.

She proceeded with a well-organized orientation describing the layout of the compound. The site covered several square miles of high ground not too far from the Golan Heights, where Israel leaves off and Lebanon and Syria begin. The area designated for their research project was bounded on all sides by an electrified barbed-wire fence. The team had also seen a couple of guards armed with rifles patrolling the perimeter as they drove up to the gate.

"Several other research teams are in the vicinity," she said. "In fact, you can see one of them about a quarter mile to the south. That bunch specializes in SETI research."

Looking for aliens, Dan thought. *Must be where those guys Gonzales knows are working.*

"Are the barbed wire and the guns really necessary?" Dudley Dunster asked, pointing with a slight smirk to the weapon on her hip. "Aren't we getting into overkill here? A little paranoia?"

"This is wild country, Professor Dunster," Yael replied dryly. "Anything can happen this close to the Lebanese and Syrian borders. We don't take chances around here. Also, the government regards your work as extremely important, and for all we know, someone might try to disrupt it—violently."

She paused, patted her semiautomatic, and smiled back at him. "And this is a pistol, not a gun, Professor. The four guards assigned to the twenty-four-hour security detail carry fully automatic AK-47 assault rifles. Those aren't guns either. They have rifling in the barrels, while guns are smooth. The officer in charge has access to an arsenal of other weapons, including a few real guns. Shotguns, I believe."

Dan was now enjoying himself immensely, as he watched Dudley squirm and turn several shades of red.

Then the Harvard astronomer tried to recoup a little of his lost dignity. "Well, if you're so obsessed with security, I wonder why that guard who was driving us up here didn't have more to protect us with than that peashooter he was carrying."

"That 'peashooter' was a semiautomatic, magazine-fed Beretta pistol," Yael replied smoothly. "He's a crack shot—several championships in combat course competitions. With the extra magazines he was carrying, he could have nailed an enemy between the eyes at thirty meters or more—with several dozen rounds in less than a minute."

The room grew very quiet.

"And I guess you didn't notice the rifle," she added.

"What rifle?" Dudley said meekly, now thoroughly chastened.

"The AK-47 under the wrap on the floor, just next to the driver's seat. You can rest assured that you've been well protected since you stepped off that plane in Tel Aviv, Professor Dunster."

"This is really sounding like an armed camp," Geoffrey Gonzales remarked. "Are we really in that much danger, Dr. Sharon? Should we start looking over our shoulders for snipers?"

She smiled that dazzling Miss Israel smile again. "Of course not. As I said, we just believe in being prepared for anything. You should feel perfectly safe as you go about your work."

"Good, good," Skiddy said, patting his hands together rather nervously, Dan thought. "So now we want to hit the ground running. We're all a little tired, I think, but let's take a minute or two to go over our preliminary work plan before we get some rest."

"If I may, Professor Kirkland?" Dr. Sharon said, raising her hand to interrupt.

"Not so formal, not so formal," Skiddy said. "It's Skiddy, Yael. All first names from now on. So what's on your mind?"

"We know a lot about jet lag here in Israel," she said. "We have so many visitors coming through our little country. So—Skiddy—I'd suggest a recovery strategy that's worked quite well for us. And it's backed up by the latest medical literature."

"Fine, let's hear it," Skiddy said.

"Studies have shown that when you cross several time zones, it's best not to go to bed immediately, but rather to exercise vigorously for an hour or so," Yael explained. "That can cut the usual jet-lag symptoms down to one day from three or four. After all, time is of the essence in your investigation."

"So what would you suggest for exercise, Yael?" Dan asked, well aware of the daggers Joanna was glaring at him from the side. "Maybe you could lead us in a hora? Or some aerobic dancing?"

"No, Professor Thompson, ah, Dan," Yael said, ignoring his attempt at humor, but at least remembering his name. "Just a good jog or run will do. Something to get your heart rate up—and produce the aerobic training effect. I plan to run twelve kilometers after we finish here. Any of you who'd like to join me are welcome."

No takers.

"Then, after the workout, it would be advisable to pursue your research for a couple of hours and have an early supper. You may choose to make a few final observations of the light at dusk, but you should retire as soon as possible after that. You'll want to be up again around 2:00 A.M., so that you can conduct further studies while the sky is still dark."

She stood up. "Now, let's get ready to run. Please meet back here in your workout gear in ten minutes."

Dan had to put a hand over his mouth to cover an uncontrollable grin. Dudley was now looking as though he was going to be sick. The astronomer clearly hadn't done any vigorous exercise in years—if in his entire life. Probably his worst nightmare would be trying to keep up with this Israeli firecracker on a five-mile run across the rough terrain in this area.

But Skiddy saved Dudley, as well as some of the others who were looking extremely uncomfortable at the prospect of a demanding P.E. routine.

"Interesting idea, Yael, but we'll make the exercise optional," the Harvard psychologist said. "On the other hand, I do think we should get some work in today before we go to bed. And we will have to wake up very early in the morning from now on—2:00 A.M. sounds about right. We're under some pressure with this investigation, and it's important to make the fastest progress possible and come up with some answers quickly."

With that, the group dispersed toward the living quarters that had been assigned to them. Dan and Joanna got settled in a one-room shack with a small window on one wall, which gave them a view of the unisex shower stalls and the flimsy latrine building. No air-conditioning, of course, and not a breath of air.

"Not too much privacy," Dan said.

He rubbed his sweat-drenched neck, looked over at the primitive toilet facilities, and then glanced back at Joanna to get her reaction.

"No, but I've checked—it's like the freshman dorms at Amherst," she said, tweaking her husband. "Curtains on the shower stalls, and individual latrines, with doors of a sort. Probably built that way to satisfy my modesty. I doubt if our sassy sabra really cares."

"You're sounding sexist," he said, making a lame attempt at a joke.

"I'm a woman. I can be sexist with other women."

Definitely an edge to that remark, Dan decided.

Sensing that fatigue was about to overwhelm them both, he asked, "Are you interested in taking a run now?"

"No, not a run," she said, talking to him over her shoulder as she unpacked her clothes and toilet articles. "But I do believe she was right about the physical exercise. Before I take a nap, I think I'll try a brisk walk around the compound to check out our new home."

Then she stopped, turned around, and stared a hole through him. "But I must say, the more I see of this place, the more I wonder what you've gotten us into. Dust, heat, guns, unisex toilets. Let's just hope you're right—that this uncomfortable little military exercise is going to produce enough money to buy a little slice of Cape Cod. Otherwise, you owe me big time!"

Not exactly a win-win deal for old Dan, he thought and sighed. *But she does have a point. What have I gotten us into?*

 # FIVE

A s Captain André Rothchild reached the desired altitude, forty-one thousand feet, he picked up his intercom transmitter.

"Dr. Hodges, we're ready," he said. "You can start your work whenever you like."

Then he turned over the controls to his copilot, nodded to the navigator, and went back into the main part of the 747-SP where the research was to be conducted.

Not exactly your average airliner, he thought as he surveyed the scientific equipment spread out before him. Scientists and technicians scurried about, making their calculations. Rothchild had been chosen as one of the first pilots to work on the SOFIA project when it went airborne just after the turn of the millennium, as a successor to the old Kuiper Airborne Observatory, which had been discontinued in the mid-1990s.

Astronomer Everett Hodges had already mobilized his ten-person SOFIA crew into action and was standing near the cockpit door, surveying his little high-altitude empire, when Rothchild walked out.

Some of the technicians and scientists were laboring over the huge infrared telescope, the largest airborne telescope in the world, with a 2.7-meter primary mirror. The opening pointed out the left side of the plane's fuselage—directly toward the strange light that hung in mysterious silence in the dark sky, against a backdrop of glowing stars and planets.

Other experts were working with a "far-infrared" spectrometer and camera, which measured and recorded infrared radiation at the outside or longest end of the wave spectrum. In addition, there were teams who were manning near- and mid-infrared equipment in an effort to capture shorter waves that were closer to visible light.

"So what do you think it is?" the pilot asked Dr. Hodges.

"If that thing puts out any infrared, we'll nail it," the head astronomer replied. "But I've got a funny feeling. You see how it looks the same up here as it does back on earth?"

"Yeah, well, I figured that was just because I'm looking at it through the cockpit window," Rothchild said. "But it does look the same. In fact, the copilot brought some binoculars, and we don't see any difference through them."

Hodges nodded and pointed toward the 20,000-kilogram reflecting telescope that was protruding through the fuselage. "So far, that monster—forty-four thousand pounds of the latest equipment—has given us nothing. No results. The object isn't putting out any infrared at all."

"No radiation?"

"None at those wavelengths. If there is any, this equipment should tell us. After all, at this height we're above 99 percent of the atmospheric garbage and water vapor that absorb most infrared before it reaches the earth. But we're not picking up anything."

"Oh well," Rothchild said. "We're still in the preliminary stages of our research. Maybe something will turn up."

"Maybe."

The SOFIA crew continued with their tests and observations on every infrared wavelength for the full six hours of observation allowed on the flight. But there was nothing to report. The instruments all registered no infrared radiation at all from the object.

"A big goose egg," Rothchild muttered as he settled down in the cockpit and prepared to take the 747 back to home base at the NASA Ames Research Center in California. "And I wanted us to be the heroes. Maybe next flight."

But somehow, he wasn't optimistic.

 # SIX

As Dan watched Joanna bending over and peering intently through a strange-looking tube—which he assumed was a telescope of some sort—he knew she was completely unaware of his presence.

She had already created her own little scientific fiefdom, even though they had now been on the compound in northern Galilee for less than twenty-four hours. A half dozen configurations of glistening equipment were sitting on separate tables. Some of the machines were churning out jagged graph lines and other shapes on paper rolls, and others lay dormant, as though awaiting a command from their mistress to spring into action.

The machines were in the open under the dark, early morning Middle Eastern sky. But Joanna's work area was organized in such a way that if rain clouds began to threaten, she could quickly pull waterproof covers over the devices. At the same time, a couple of technicians who had been assigned to the team would cover the area with a makeshift tent that could be erected in seconds. Each of the scientists had also been assigned a small trailer that housed computers and the other sensitive electronic equipment used with their outdoor apparatuses.

As far as Dan could recall, this was the first time in their five-year marriage that he had actually seen Joanna in action, involved directly with a hands-on project. Sure, she had talked about what she did on the job. And he visited her laboratory at Yale. But this level of intensity was something new to behold.

Then she straightened up, looked around as she took a moment to stretch, and saw him.

"Come on over," she said.

"Don't want to interrupt. I can just watch."

"No, you might as well take a look," she replied, pointing to the sea of specialized equipment that extended out from her for yards in every direction. "I finally got it all set up. Took a full day, but now I'm ready to go."

"I'm glad this is your job and not mine," he said. "I wouldn't know where to begin."

"You're not supposed to. I'm the scientist. You're the man of the spirit. Want a tour?"

"Sure. Since I'm on the team, I might as well get some idea about what's going on—but don't expect too much from me."

"I won't," she said in her usual direct manner. "But I'm not sure that anything you learn here will be helpful anyhow. Here's the deal. It's already become obvious that if we get any readings from the light, any at all, we'll be ahead of everybody. The preliminary work we've done—Dudley, Geoffrey, and me—shows absolutely nothing on our instruments." She stopped and stared at him. "Do you have any idea how incredible that is?"

"Well, no, not exactly . . ."

"*Everything* puts out some kind of radiation. Some electromagnetic wave. Something. This rock"—she picked up a loose stone off the ground—"the moon, the sun, the stars up there. *Everything.* That's what these instruments around me here are designed to do—pick up the natural radiation that objects put out in different wavelengths. That's what all of us, and that includes the scientists in the sky—on the SOFIA plane that Dudley told you about—are set up to do. Monitor and analyze this electromagnetic activity."

She sighed in frustration and pointed at the strange light that was in full view in the sky. "But that thing registers nothing. It's just not right. Not natural."

He smiled, but before he could say anything she raised her hand to stop him. "But I'm not saying it's *super*natural!" she said. "Just that our normal instruments don't show anything. At least not yet. Let me explain what I'm trying to do."

Joanna took a sheet of blank graph paper over to an open table and began to draft a word diagram. Dan was only vaguely familiar with some of the terms.

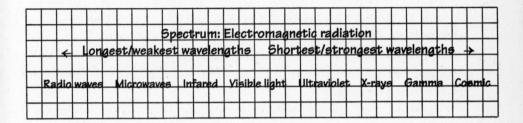

"Okay—these are the general categories in the radiation spectrum we're trying to study. Practically every object, here on earth or millions of light-years away, in the farthest stars, puts out some type of radiation."

She tapped the left side of the list with her finger. "The longest wavelengths, which are also the weakest, begin over here on the left, with the radio waves. The shortest wavelengths—these are the most powerful—can be found on the right. Gamma and cosmic rays are the strongest."

She then pointed to one of the middle categories, "Visible light."

"You can actually see a limited range of electromagnetic radiation with your eyes. So when you look at the stars or the reflection of sunlight off the moon, you're observing radiation in this middle, visible-light range."

Shifting back to the left side of the paper, she underlined the "Infrared" category with her finger.

"You'll remember that Dudley gave you that nasty little lecture on infrared radiation when he was talking about the SOFIA scientists who fly for NASA?"

He nodded.

"Their instruments are specially designed to pick up a wide range of infrared, which consists of longer and weaker wavelengths than visible light. You can even feel radiant heat from the near-infrared, which is closest to the red you can actually see. But the far-infrared can only be picked up with instruments."

Then she indicated the "Ultraviolet" term, which was just to the right of the "Visible light" category.

"This involves shorter and stronger wavelengths. You know all about this from your sunblocks and sunscreens. They keep ultraviolet rays from the sun from harming your body. You can't see that UV radiation, but boy, you know what it can do to your skin! Now we're getting into the very powerful part of the spectrum."

She paused to let this information sink in. Seeing that her husband seemed to be following her, she framed the "X ray" designation with her fingers.

"These are very strong forms of radiation. That's why, when you go to the dentist and have a picture taken of your teeth, the technician puts a protective covering over you and stands behind a wall. A lot of the most distant celestial phenomena—such as the Coma Cluster of galaxies—can be pictured by using equipment that measures X-ray wavelengths."

"Does any of your equipment here measure X rays?" Dan asked.

"No. We're relying on the Chandra X-ray Observatory up in space for that. Dudley gets regular reports from scientists who specialize in the Chandra."

Moving a little farther to the right on the rough diagram she had made, she pointed to the "Gamma" category.

"Scientists also have sophisticated instruments that can pick up these incredibly potent gamma rays at the right end of the spectrum. For example, there's the GRIS—or Gamma-Ray Imaging Spectrometer—which goes up by balloon from a base in Australia."

As she paused a moment to look over the equipment she was using, he studied her even profile and flowing hair.

Beautiful. I have a brilliant, beautiful wife. If we can only work things out. The very fact that Joanna was taking time to bring him up to speed with this mini-lecture was encouraging. It would have been easy to abandon him to his scientific ignorance. To be embarrassed that up to this point, he looked like a fifth wheel on the team. At least she hadn't given up on him entirely.

"Obviously, this stuff I'm working with isn't nearly as sophisticated as what you'll find in the main earth observatories or up in space," she finally said. "But frankly, we don't know what's going on up there with that light. For all we know, basic, relatively crude equipment in this part of the world may turn up something that the

Keck Observatory in Hawaii or the Chandra X-ray Observatory in space will miss."

She pointed to the instrument she had been working on when he had interrupted her. "See this? It's a very simple prism spectroscope."

It didn't look so simple to Dan. The device stood on a solid tripod-like base with three horizontal tubes protruding from the top.

Fingering each tube in turn, she explained, "This is a telescope. That's what we use to magnify light from the stars and planets—or in this case, the weird light. And this cylinder sticking out the other side is called a collimator. It's a device with a slit at the outer end and a lens at the inner end, which concentrates the light and directs it into the prism." She pointed to a glass object at the center of the apparatus.

"This other tube is a micrometer, which helps us make spectrum measurements. So the light comes in through the collimator and is dispersed into different colors of the spectrum through the prism. Then the colors can be observed in separate wavelengths through the telescope. We can also turn the thing into a spectrograph by fitting a camera onto it and photographing the lines of the spectrum."

Dan shook his head. "It's all a little beyond me."

"All you have to know is this," Joanna said, sitting down on a wooden bench near the spectroscope. "This device, and several of the others sitting around here, are supposed to be able to pick up radiation of electromagnetic wavelengths from that light in the sky. But so far, nothing shows up."

Joanna stopped and shrugged helplessly. Her uncertain expression contrasted sharply with her usual air of competence. Dan couldn't remember the last time his wife had appeared stumped.

"But we can *see* it up there," Dan protested. "We know it has colors. And visible light is part of this electromagnetic spectrum, right? That's what you just said."

"Right, we can see it with our eyes. But for some reason, none of my instruments pick up any electromagnetic radiation. *Nobody's* instruments pick it up. Not the equipment Dudley is working with—which is similar to mine. Not the instruments of the SOFIA scientists in that 747 airplane. Not even the orbiting telescopes and other radiation detectors in space."

"So what does this mean? That the object emits light that's not really light?"

She frowned. "That might be a good way of putting it. It looks like light but doesn't behave like light, or any other electromagnetic radiation."

"So what do you think?" he asked.

"Frankly, I don't know what to think," Joanna said. Dan was particularly struck by how much more tentative she was now than just a couple of days ago. When they were boarding the plane, she was certain that science would quickly provide some solid direction, even if it took a while to arrive at a definitive solution. But her early confidence had disappeared completely.

"We have to be able to take electromagnetic measurements to figure out the properties and characteristics of an object in space," Joanna continued, almost seeming to be talking to herself. "That way, we can tell if it's moving toward us or away from us. Or what its chemical makeup is. We can tell a lot about even distant stars and gases if we can get a radiation reading. But this thing leaves us with nothing but questions. Where exactly is it? Is it moving? What's it made of? No answers at all."

For some reason, Dan remembered Michael James's remark just after they had arrived in Tel Aviv—that he doubted science would provide the answer to the light. His apparent cockiness had annoyed Dan at the time. But now, he wasn't so sure.

Either he's the luckiest guesser in the world, or maybe he's onto something. Whatever, the man will bear watching.

SEVEN

BAFFLING—the thing is totally baffling."

Dudley sat shaking his head, murmuring his puzzlement to no one in particular. The others just slumped in their chairs, staring at the floor. After forty-eight hours of intense research, using a wide variety of scientific instruments and relying on data being collected by colleagues at various research sites around the globe, they had come up with nothing. Zero.

This report—or the lack thereof—wasn't music to Skiddy Kirkland's ears. In fact, as he stood before the group, he was getting downright testy.

"This is absurd!" he barked. "You people supposedly represent some of the best scientific minds in the world. Astronomers, astrophysicists, whatever. And you're sharing your research with scores of other experts all over the earth. Yet you're telling me we have nothing? Ridiculous! There must be *something* to report. You don't put this much effort and money into a research project and come back with *nothing!*"

Dan, who was sprawled in a chair at the back of the room, chuckled to himself.

He's definitely on the verge of losing it, Dan thought. *Skiddy's been handed a small fortune by this foundation, and now he can't deliver. All this might really be funny—that is, if I didn't stand to lose as well.*

"Relax!" Geoffrey Gonzales said with a smile. "No other research groups have an answer either. We know that for a fact. This is just not your usual heavenly body. We'll have to be patient and try some other lines of inquiry. Maybe go beyond the bounds of normal scientific research."

"Okay, okay," Skiddy said, waving him off. "Let's go over everything again. Maybe some detail will trigger something in one of your brilliant minds. First, Joanna."

Joanna took a deep breath before summarizing her report for a second time. Her impressive assembly of expensive equipment—including a variety of spectroscopes—had become her daily accusers. She could almost hear the devices admonishing her, reproving her efforts at every turn: *Unimaginative! Incompetent! Failure!*

It seemed incredible to Joanna that these scientific apparatuses, worth millions of dollars, had produced nothing. There was no indication whatsoever that the light, which they could see clearly up there in the sky, emitted any energy, any particles, anything at all that would register on the spectrum of light.

"I simply have nothing to report," she said. "Something should show up on my instruments. But there's nothing—as though the light we are looking at with our eyes, and through our telescopes, isn't a light at all. At least, it doesn't seem to have the usual qualities of light."

Skiddy shook his head impatiently and turned to his Harvard colleague. "Dudley? Do you have any more for us?"

"Like I said, my telescopes show a light that seems to shimmer or undulate slightly, and the colors are washed-out, or pastel. Mostly greens and blues and white. No prominent details or features. From the colors we can see, the thing should be hot. It should show up that way on the spectrum. But my spectroscopes, even my radio-telescope array, confirm what Joanna is saying. Nothing registers!"

Skiddy was now looking tired and defeated. "Yes, I know all about your array," he growled, referring to the series of miniature but extremely expensive dishes that had been set up to help Dudley pick up any tiny radio wavelength images that might be emitted from the light. "That cost us a small fortune—money that could have gone into salaries."

But Skiddy knew there had been no choice if they hoped to find an answer to the light. Dudley's miniature array was the latest thing for astronomers on the go in out-of-the-way locations, where they didn't have access to the more extensive equipment in the main observatories, such as the one in New Mexico, where twenty-seven huge, linked dishes scanned the skies.

Skiddy shifted his long, angular frame toward Gonzales. "Think, Geoffrey! You're the theoretician. Where do we go from here?"

The California astrophysicist pursed his lips and tipped his chair back on two legs, twiddling his thumbs as he folded his hands across his chest. He actually seemed to be enjoying the mystery.

Strange fellow, Dan thought. *Doesn't quite seem to fit the image of the great scientist. But then most of these geniuses are eccentric.*

"Remember that our findings are entirely consistent with what's been found at the big astronomy sites in California," Geoffrey said. "Such as the Owens Valley Array and the Berkeley-Illinois-Maryland interferometer at Hat Creek—not to mention many other major research facilities around the world."

Then, in an apparent attempt to assuage Skiddy's financial anxieties, he allowed his chair to return to all fours and leaned forward with what Dan interpreted as a concerned expression—or at least an attempt to project a concerned expression. "Certainly, we *are* spending a lot of money here, Skiddy. But the cost of our operation is nothing compared to what's being allotted by some of these permanent facilities—like the centers in California or the Keck Observatory in Hawaii."

"And don't forget the orbiting observatories," Dudley chimed in. "NASA's Hubble Space Telescope, the Chandra X-ray Observatory, and the like."

"Yes," Geoffrey continued. "And of course, the SOFIA operation. With all these pricey programs, who could criticize our modest little operation? I think we should just proceed on our present track. If our benefactors decide to pull the plug, so be it. Given the concern about this phenomenon, I have a feeling we could get somebody else to pick up the tab in a flash."

"I wouldn't worry about the funding," Michael James said, without elaborating. "At least not at this point."

All eyes turned in his direction, some clearly filled with skepticism. The looks seemed to be saying: *What does he know about it? After all, he's not even a scientist.*

But Skiddy understood the Wheaton professor perfectly. He took Michael's comment as a reassuring sign. Though he wasn't sure of the exact nature of the relationship, the Harvard professor knew that Michael had close ties with Panoplia and Peter Van Campe. He wasn't convinced that James could actually speak for Panoplia. But he did suspect that the Wheaton man would know better than anyone else on the team what Van Campe's reaction to the state of their investigation might be.

So Skiddy breathed a small sigh of relief and pointed toward Geoffrey, who clearly wanted to continue speaking.

"We have to remember that this light is really weird and perhaps unique," the California scientist said. "We may be having trouble with our earth-based instruments, but the same thing seems to be happening in space. The Hubble is recording essentially what we see—though it's supposedly much closer to that light and there's no atmosphere to obscure or distort the view."

"Of course, we really don't know the location of the light," Joanna reminded him. "It could be far away, light-years beyond us in space, or it could be just a few feet out of reach. We just can't tell."

"And the Chandra, which registers X-ray emissions, shows nothing," Dudley added. He reminded them again that he had been in close touch with NASA scientists, as well as with astronomers and astrophysicists from other sites and organizations.

"The very fact that nothing registers on the light spectrum or in any other way on our instruments may be significant in itself," Geoffrey said. "It seems clear that we aren't dealing with a normal physical phenomenon."

"Also, don't forget that the light always appears the same to our eyes, whether it's viewed from here on earth or in space," Joanna reminded them. "That's not natural or normal either. A powerful telescope here on earth should reveal more than a weaker one. And certainly a space telescope should provide a clearer picture still. But the pictures are all basically the same. Incredibly, even the earth's atmosphere seems to make no difference."

"So none of our usual methods of observation or testing seem to produce the expected scientific results," Dan summarized, evidently wanting to clarify the situation in his nontechnical mind. "Is there any scientific precedent for this?"

"As a matter of fact, there is," Geoffrey said. "Back in 1996, a team of Caltech astronomers stumbled upon a mysterious light in the constellation Serpens, in the northern sky. They tried all sorts of spectrum and radio-emission tests, much like those we're conducting. But they couldn't figure it out. They couldn't tell if the thing was close to earth, or very far away. The spectrum didn't fit any known patterns at the time.

"Their preliminary evaluation was that it wasn't a regular star. It wasn't a distant galaxy or known type of quasar—which, for you nonastronomers, are cosmic entities that are extremely bright and put out powerful radio waves. And it wasn't a supernova, or exploding star."

"So what was it?" Dan asked, sensing that something akin to a science-fiction thriller might be unfolding.

Geoffrey, obviously enjoying the attention, was happy to spin out the story a little longer. "About three years later, in August of 1999, scientists at Hawaii's Keck Observatory determined that the thing was putting out a pattern of hydrogen emissions, which are characteristic of quasars. So they concluded that it was a very rare type of quasar."

He paused and shook his head slightly.

"You don't seem entirely convinced," Michael James interjected.

"Perceptive, Professor James," Geoffrey replied. "A number of responsible researchers—myself included—were dissatisfied with the quasar answer because of the lack of strong radio emissions. You see, most quasars do put out very strong radio signals. The explanation just didn't quite fit."

"So why rush to a conclusion?" Dan asked.

"Many traditional scientists begin to get nervous when they can't give the public an immediate answer that fits into a recognizable scientific category," he explained. "Speculation begins. UFO and religious theories may even begin to pop up—and establishment scientists can't stand to contribute to such an atmosphere. They believe they are expected to have scientific answers for every important question about the physical world. And heaven forbid that intellectual honesty should increase the risk of extra-terrestrial or apocalyptic speculation. In such a situation, many scientists often would rather shut off public discussion, rather than be straightforward and keep a question open."

"The public can't be trusted?" Dan said. "Only elite, highly educated specialists are truly reliable?"

"Exactly," Geoffrey replied. "At least, that's a common attitude."

"Seems to reflect a high need to control public opinion and attitudes," Dan said.

"Right again, I'm afraid."

"Well, I think you're going a little too far, Geoffrey," Dudley objected. "Good scientists do tend to have more of a sense of responsibility than most people about how information is to be disseminated."

"And after all," Joanna added, "we can be fairly confident that all these mysterious objects will eventually be explained in scientific terms."

"But is that really true?" Geoffrey replied—with rather surprising skepticism, Dan thought, at least for a scientist who was definitely part of the "establishment."

"I'm not so sure," the Californian continued, answering his own question. "And we certainly haven't made any headway on our present puzzle. In any event, I downloaded and printed out some newspaper articles on this bizarre, quasarlike phenomenon, which were written by reporters from the *New York Times*, the Associated Press, and other media outlets in August of 1999. You can look them over and make up your own minds."

Skiddy, who had been listening with growing agitation to this interchange, was becoming afraid that the others might just give up after hearing Gonzales's comments.

"You're not suggesting that we abandon this project, are you, Geoffrey?" he asked, fairly sure of the answer he would receive.

"Of course not," Geoffrey replied. "I just want us to be realistic—and also not fall into the trap of thinking in conventional scientific terms. It's clear that the usual tests, analyses, and observations are producing nothing. We have to put aside our current mind-set and find other categories."

"Think outside the box," Michael James said.

"Yes, that may be a cliché, but it's what we have to do," Geoffrey said. "We must try to find entirely new and unexpected ways to look at this problem."

Michael had been uncharacteristically quiet and noncommittal during the discussion, so when he spoke, the others immediately cocked an ear. They still didn't quite trust him because of his known conservative Christian religious views. But so far, he had said and done nothing that would make anyone feel that he was trying to influence the investigation or their own beliefs in any way.

In some respects, as they explored all the scientific options, Michael actually seemed more open-minded than many of the others in the room. Even the suspicious Dan Thompson had to admit that. Furthermore, Skiddy Kirkland now was beginning to believe that Michael had the potential to be his solid ally in pushing for continued support of their efforts by Panoplia International. For Skiddy, the acid test of friendship was the degree to which you supported his fund-raising.

"Okay, this is progress," Skiddy said with some relief. "Let's move outside the box, as you say. Any suggestions?"

"Try this," Geoffrey said. "We've been thinking of this as an astronomical body or object—something in near space or deep space. We've been looking for radio emissions, X rays, redshifts, and the like. Right?"

Most of the group nodded. By this time, even the nonscientists knew that "redshift" referred to the tendency of the light photons emitted by an object to grow longer and be displaced toward the red end of the spectrum, as the object moved farther and farther away. For distant objects, redshifts could indicate that the universe is expanding. But with the strange light, there was no indication of a redshift or any other usual astronomical signal.

"Well, let's assume that we're not dealing with an astronomical body at all," Geoffrey suggested.

"What are you getting at?" Dudley replied with some concern seeping into his voice. He knew quite well the implications of his question. If the light had nothing to do with astronomy, he would have nothing to publish. And if he emerged from this venture without any additional journal articles, he wouldn't be a bit closer to his ultimate goal—tenure in the hallowed halls of Harvard.

"For example, could the object be man-made?" Geoffrey asked.

Everyone was silent for a moment, but then Yael Sharon offered her first comments of the meeting. "I'm in close touch with our government people, and they're in contact with the Americans and other authorities. If they have any information that this is some sort of aircraft, or surveillance or weapons system, they aren't letting on at all."

"So what do *you* think?" Dan asked, looking closely at the young woman. He figured that if anyone knew about weapons, Yael would.

"Again, no, I don't think so. The thing has none of those characteristics. The astronomers have apparently already determined that it looks the same from space or the earth. And it seems impossible to get close to it. A human device wouldn't behave like that, any more than a normal celestial body."

"Makes sense," Skiddy said. "So we can eliminate aircraft or human spaceships. It's not earth-made. What else could it be?"

"Let's try your field—psychology," Dan suggested, turning to Skiddy. "How about mass hysteria? Or some sort of illusion?"

Skiddy shook his head. "I've considered that," he said. "But there are too many levelheaded, rational people who have seen this thing in the sky. If we were dealing with one person, then we might consider some sort of psychosis. Or a group of people under heavy stress—that might produce a belief that something was up there, when it really wasn't. A variation on the placebo effect, where belief becomes a kind of reality unto itself. But again that's not our situation—where every observer on earth, regardless of emotional state, sees substantially the same thing."

"So you'd say definitely no—it's not a psychological or emotional phenomenon?" Dan pressed, trying to nail down the Harvard project director.

"Correct," Skiddy replied. "In some way, that thing up there is an objective reality. It's really above us, somewhere up there, outside our minds."

Again, they lapsed into frustrated silence. Several jotted notes on the pads or computer screens in front of them.

"Two other possibilities come to mind," Geoffrey finally said. "It could be a phenomenon from space that we are sure exists but that we've never seen up close—such as a black hole."

"Can you actually *see* a black hole?" Joanna asked. "After all, we can see that light up there."

"Good question," Geoffrey replied. "We don't really know what black holes actually look like, or if they have normal visual qualities at all, because they're so far away. We only see what they seem to do—eat up galaxies at a great distance, or pass like a giant shadow between us and other bright star clusters in space."

"Geoffrey, just to bring us nonastronomers up to speed, could you give us a quick refresher?" Michael asked.

"Sure. Black holes are remnants of stars—stars that explode as huge, bright supernovas and then collapse back on themselves. The black holes that result are so dense, light can't escape from them. They may vary in mass from a few kilograms to a mass that is millions of times greater than that of our own sun. Nothing escapes from them, and when you get to the center, they may consist of what is known as a 'singularity,' where normal space and time are completely distorted. We believe that the main emissions from black holes are X rays."

"Sounds dangerous," Dan said.

"Yes," Geoffrey agreed. "You wouldn't want to get too near a black hole."

"But also, this is all theory," Dan said.

"Much is theory. Still, we're virtually certain they do exist in some form."

"But light doesn't escape from black holes, and that object overhead does seem to emit some sort of light—even though we can't measure it yet," Dudley objected. "Also, black holes put out X rays, and we've detected none of those. So our light doesn't quite fit the bill, does it?"

"No," Geoffrey agreed. "It doesn't. But a second possibility might be . . . a wormhole."

"Now we're really getting over the edge," Dudley said, becoming somewhat annoyed that this theorist, this astrophysicist, was getting all the attention. He preferred to return to the hard, known observations of his field of regular astronomy.

"Hear me out," Geoffrey said. "Dudley is correct that wormholes are highly theoretical. They may not exist at all. But remember, we're thinking out of the box now. None of the usual explanations have worked, so we need to extend ourselves."

Before Dudley could object further, Geoffrey stood up, waving a single piece of notebook paper in one hand and a ballpoint pen in the other. Though he was rather short, his solid, fireplug build projected a physical strength that demanded attention.

"Let's reflect for a moment on wormholes," he said. "Many feel they are a kind of rip or tunnel in the space–time continuum, which would allow us to travel in the blink of an eye from one end of our universe to the other. Or they may even be entrances to an entirely different dimension of reality. Perhaps to another universe."

He then bent the paper over into a curved shape and poked holes through the two curved-over ends with his pen. Finally, he suspended the bent-over paper in front of them, with the pen protruding through it in the two separate locations.

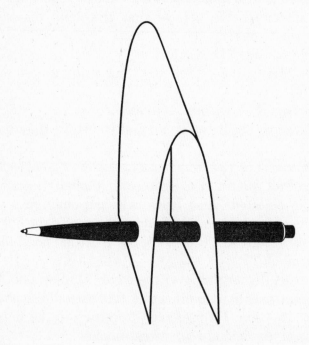

"Okay, now what you're looking at is a rough model of what many theoretical physicists think space might look like," Geoffrey said. "It's a curved surface, a relatively thin fabric or pad. Our earth may sit over here on the left, where one end of the pen is poking through, and some distant star system may be on the right, near the hole caused by the opposite part of the pen. If you're going to travel around the fabric of space to get from the earth to that star, you'll have a very long trip. But if you go along the route traced by the pen, you'll have a shortcut. The pen becomes a kind of tunnel or path that connects one part of the surface of the paper to another. Or in terms of astrophysics, it becomes a wormhole that can be a shortcut from one part of the universe to another."

"Raw speculation," Dudley sniffed. "And even if wormholes do exist, we have no idea what they look like."

Ignoring his colleague, Geoffrey picked up two other pieces of paper and another pen. "Here's another possibility," he said, as he poked a hole in the middle of each sheet and connected the two sheets with the second pen.

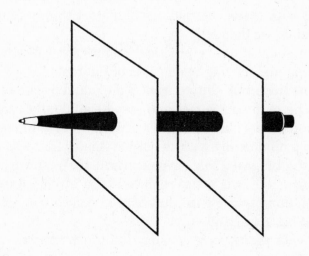

"In this case, the pen still represents a wormhole or passageway," he explained. "But now you have two universes, represented by the two sheets of paper. The wormhole might enable beings in one universe to pass through to the other universe."

"So you're saying that the light up there may actually be the opening to a wormhole?" Dan asked.

"Possibly."

"And that means the light may lead to another part of our own universe—or even to another universe?" Dan pressed.

"Again, it's possible," Geoffrey replied.

"Your imagination is running away with you!" Dudley said. "Don't forget my point—nobody has ever seen a wormhole. And we don't even know if they exist."

"I'm the first to admit that," Geoffrey replied. Then he stopped and pointed upward. "But who knows? That thing up there might just be our first look at a wormhole—or one end of it."

Again, there was silence.

Then Skiddy vented his building frustration: "Fine, fine, you could be onto something with your wormholes, or rabbit holes, or whatever. But what can we do about it? How can we evaluate or measure it? This is all entirely too theoretical. We have to get off dead center with these abstractions and start thinking more practically. What do we do next?"

"I have a suggestion—a practical suggestion," Michael James said, standing and moving to one side of the room.

All eyes immediately shifted from Skiddy and became riveted on Michael as he planted his feet and stood confidently before them. He had taken off his glasses and was twirling them in one hand as he gestured emphatically with the other. Again, Dan was struck by the easy, athletic grace that characterized the man's movements. The cherubic smile was gone, replaced by a strong, fixed jawline and a direct, unrelenting gaze that bore into each team member as he surveyed his small audience.

Definitely not your typical cloistered fundamentalist.

Then Michael uttered the words that would change the course of their lives:

"The Star of Bethlehem."

 # EIGHT

ﬀ т е r a few seconds of stunned silence, Skiddy threw up his hands, his frustration now spilling over into outright anger.

"This is too much!" he shouted, now putting aside any attempt to be polite or deferential—even though Michael was the team member who seemed to have the strongest connections to the precious grant money. "Do you people have any sense of responsibility at all? We have a serious job to do, Michael. So I'd suggest that we quit telling bad jokes."

"I'm not joking," the Wheaton man said in a relaxed, quiet tone. "I'm suggesting a very practical line of investigation—the Star of Bethlehem."

Dan figured the time had finally arrived for him to weigh in. Employing the strongest and most condescending professorial tone he could muster, he looked the Wheaton Bible guy straight in the eye. "Michael, this is not a Bible course at your college," he declared. "And it isn't some half-baked Sunday school class. I enjoy religious speculation as much as the next guy. I do it for a living. But this is a serious scientific investigation. Let's face it, that thing up there in the sky really could be important for all of us—maybe for the entire world."

Then, pulling out all the stops, he jabbed an index finger in Michael's direction. "So I, for one, agree completely with Skiddy. I think you should get with the program, and keep your personal religious views to yourself."

But his wife wasn't impressed. Joanna knew from her previous conversations with Michael that the man wasn't stupid. Furthermore, he seemed as interested in getting to the bottom of the mystery as anyone. So she decided that he must have something in mind that Dan and Skiddy were missing.

"I'd like to hear more about this," she said, dismissing with a sweep of her hand the decisive, dominant image Dan had tried to project. "Go ahead, Michael. What are you getting at?"

James, who had remained quite calm and unflustered despite the vociferous objections from Dan and Skiddy, bowed slightly in her direction and began to pace slowly in front of them as he proceeded with his unorthodox suggestion. "All the scientists here have pointed out the limitations of their usual methods of observation and analysis—correct?"

A few heads nodded.

"And Geoffrey has suggested that we consider theoretical astrophysics—black holes, wormholes, and the like. Right?"

Again, the heads bobbed slightly.

"So I'm suggesting we continue with his line of thought, but add a historical and theological twist to it."

"How could theology add anything to scientific speculation?" Skiddy objected.

"Wait a minute," Geoffrey said, raising his hand. "It's true that there've been some productive discussions between physicists and theologians in recent years. Experts from each discipline use similar language when they talk about such things as time and multidimensional reality. Some even feel that the two fields might actually merge at some points. But why the Star of Bethlehem, Michael?"

"First of all," the Wheaton man said, "if we pursue this line of inquiry, I think we may discover exactly what you're suggesting, Geoffrey. We may discover a link between theoretical science and theology that will help us solve our problem. In other words, the Star of Bethlehem could in some way be the key to our current puzzle."

"You mean you think that the Star of Bethlehem may have returned in some way—and it's sitting up there in our own sky?" Dan asked, trying to put the issue in the most absurd language he could imagine.

But Michael James wasn't biting. He laughed and replied, "Dan, let's just say that's your idea, not mine. But I do think that any previous reports of strange lights should become part of our investigation. That's where the history part comes in. I know you've done considerable research into the history of religion, and I'd encourage you to check your files and sources. Also, Joanna should check her materials on the history of science. We're not making any headway with the usual methods of investigation, and your skills and knowledge may become as important as the traditional scientific method."

It's hard to argue with a guy who is complimenting you for being smart and an expert in your field, Dan mused, lapsing reluctantly back into silence. He felt strangely like a chess player who had just been checkmated.

Then Michael looked directly at the project director. "But that brings me to my most important point, Skiddy. I'm concerned because we've reached an impasse—a total dead end in our investigation. You're not the only one who feels we're going nowhere. I'm entirely sympathetic to your feelings."

Michael paused in case there was a comment or objection. But Skiddy's failure to respond encouraged the Wheaton professor to continue.

"I know from my previous experience with team building and focus groups that if we allow ourselves to become irritated, or if we get at one another's throats, that won't help foster creative thinking. So what I'm suggesting is that as a team, we make a radical shift in the framework of our discussion."

Then Michael flashed his engaging, boyish grin—*the goofy grin,* Dan thought.

"I'm the first to admit that we may *never* find out much about the Star of Bethlehem. But at least if we use it as a reference point, we might begin to brainstorm more effectively."

"But the Star of Bethlehem is almost certainly pure fiction!" Dudley objected. He had been fuming silently at the turn the discussion had taken, and now he seemed unable to bear it any longer. "That thing up in the sky is *fact*. We can all see it. What evidence do you have that there was even any such thing as a Star of Bethlehem?"

"It's true that the only written evidence we have about the Star is the Gospel of Matthew. But if we proceed with this approach, you'll see that there have been plenty of theories about the Star that relate to objects in the heavens. Bolides, comets, conjunctions—many things we haven't really discussed seriously up to this point. Also, there are some interesting extradimensional explanations for the Star that may dovetail with what Geoffrey has been suggesting about theoretical physics."

Dan, who had now recovered fully from Michael's flattery, noticed that Skiddy was sending him rather obvious head signals, which clearly said, "Now is the time to attack!"

Dan could see that serious interest was indeed building in James's notion about the Star. If the "Bible guy" was allowed to proceed unchallenged, they might all end up in a pointless fundamentalist quagmire.

Yes, Dan determined, *now is the time to pull out the heavy theological guns. Objective: Blow the man and his wacky ideas out of the water before he goes any further!*

"Michael, you're not being entirely forthright with the group," Dan interjected, deciding to launch his counteroffensive obliquely, rather than as a frontal assault. "You're assuming that the biblical account of the Star is accurate. But as you know, most reputable scholars think the Gospels are a bunch of fairy tales. Certainly, that was the conclusion of the Jesus Seminar scholars, who determined that practically nothing in those accounts actually happened. Why should we waste our time considering bedtime stories?"

"As *you* know, Dan," Michael replied pointedly, "the Jesus Seminar view is quite biased against the supernatural—or as Geoffrey would say, against the extradimensional. And really, those people represent a radical minority view on the theological scene. In fact, most scholars, liberal or conservative, would at least hold out the possibility that something strange really did happen when the Magi visited the infant Jesus. In fact, the most secular, nonreligious planetarium programs still treat the identity of the Star as a serious issue."

"But what evidence can you offer that the Gospels have any historical value?" Dan pressed. "Why should we treat them as accurate, factual accounts?"

Michael looked around at the others. "I do have some evidence—but are the rest of you interested in pursuing this? I don't want to create divisions among us. I'm just trying to jump-start our thinking in new directions."

Joanna responded with enthusiasm that Dan didn't quite understand or expect. "Go for it, Michael!" she almost shouted, sounding more like a college cheerleader than a scientist. "Make your case. We're not getting anywhere anyhow."

What's gotten into my wife? Dan thought, shaking his head.

When they had set out on this trip, she had been openly irreligious, a committed skeptic. Why, she didn't think Michael and Dan should even be on board! With her, it had been science or nothing. But now, it seemed that Michael James could do no wrong.

Maybe she's just frustrated because her experiments have produced nothing. Or maybe it's something about James . . .

"Yes, let's hear more," Geoffrey responded, seconding Joanna's suggestion. He was obviously intrigued by the direction the discussion had taken. "We need some stimulation!"

Michael looked over at Skiddy, who nodded grudgingly for him to proceed.

"I'll make it brief," he said. "Let me say at the outset that I don't expect to convince any of you that the Bible is divinely inspired. All I want to do is suggest that there's sufficient evidence to warrant our accepting the truth of the Star as a historical hypothesis. In other words, I'd like to assume it actually occurred in some form until we find we can't support that assumption from the evidence."

Then he turned to face a white melamine writing board, which was attached to the wall behind him, and used an erasable green marker to jot down a series of points.

"Here's a brief summary of some of the evidence that the Gospels are history, not fantasy. First, on its face the Matthew account purports to be history or a factual narrative—not poetry or fiction or some other literary form. In other words, there are no signals in the text to suggest that the writer's intent was to give us anything other than a straightforward narrative. So I say we should take the narrative for what it purports to be—in effect, a first-century news or history account—until we can bring forward evidence to the contrary."

Dan raised his hand. "Are we allowed to comment as we go along, or do we have to wait for the end of your lecture?"

Michael smiled patiently. "Please feel free to say whatever you like."

Dan stood, straightening his lanky frame to full height, hoping that the extra inches he had on the Wheaton professor would give him an advantage. "The author, Matthew or whoever, was clearly biased," Dan said. "He wanted to convince his readers that Jesus was the Messiah. He was also convinced that miracles occur—that God intervenes actively in history, and so forth. It seems to me that all those preconceptions make for an unreliable, nonobjective account."

"Yet every historian and news writer today is also biased," Michael replied, striding a step toward Dan and gesturing forcefully toward him. "Any working historical writer or journalist will tell you there is no such thing as objectivity. Never has been."

Michael then turned and pointed at his open computer screen, which evidently contained some notes he had made. "For example, we accept the *History of the Peloponnesian War* by Thucydides and the *History of the Greco-Persian Wars* by Herodotus—both written in the fifth century B.C.—as substantially accurate, even though each had a strong political point of view.

"Also, they included the action of the Greek gods in history. In other words, they mixed spiritual and earthly action. And no student of American history would throw out Bradford's *History of Plimoth Plantation* simply because the writer believed that God intervened in the affairs of mankind, or that God could answer prayer."

Michael then turned and looked Dan directly in the eye. "Again, I'm not asking that you accept Matthew's account as true—at least not at this point. But let's be fair. For now, let's give him the same benefit of the doubt that you'd give Herodotus or Thucydides or Bradford. Okay?"

Dan shrugged, smiling wryly, and sat down again. *This guy's definitely no pushover.*

"Second," Michael continued, scribbling his second point on the board, "leading scholars such as the late British New Testament expert, F. F. Bruce—who was no fundamentalist, by the way—have ranked the New Testament, including Matthew, among the most trustworthy of all ancient records.

"For example, about five thousand early Greek manuscripts of the New Testament have survived, and fragments actually have been dated as early as the first part of the second century—or less than a century after Jesus walked the earth. But consider Caesar's

Gallic Wars, which, again, any reputable historian would accept as completely authentic. Am I right?"

Several heads nodded.

"Yet Caesar's work is based on only ten decent manuscripts!" Michael said. "Furthermore, even though Caesar wrote his original account back in about 50 B.C., the earliest manuscript of his work that's now in existence has been dated *nine hundred years after he wrote*—or about A.D. 850!"

Michael paused again and surveyed the room to see if there were any responses. But everyone was looking intently at the melamine board.

"Third," he said, noting his next point with the marker, "most Bible scholars agree that Matthew was written sometime between A.D. 65 and 90. In fact, there are many references and lengthy quotations from Matthew in the last part of the first century by Clement, the Bishop of Rome, as well as other church leaders. So Matthew's manuscript—including the Star account—would have been written while many eyewitnesses were still alive. As you know, the presence of eyewitnesses makes it much less likely that lies would have been published. It's hard to stretch the truth when some live witness can contradict you."

Michael went on to enumerate other points to substantiate his argument for the reliability of the Gospel accounts—such as references to Jesus in early non-Christian literature, including writings of a Jewish–Roman historian, Flavius Josephus.

Finally, Dan piped up again. "All this is interesting, Michael. But it's not proof that the Star of Bethlehem was real."

"Remember, I never claimed I would provide definitive proof," Michael replied, still maddeningly calm and self-assured. "You've got to distinguish between proof and evidence. I'm only introducing some evidence that has caused many people, including scientists, to want to inquire further into the truth of the Gospel accounts— including the Star of Bethlehem."

Then he looked directly at Joanna and next at Geoffrey, evidently choosing them as his most receptive listeners.

"Obviously, I'm no scientist," the Wheaton professor said. "But it seems to me that if I *were* a scientist—and felt I'd reached a dead end in an important investigation—I might try to formulate an alternate hypothesis, which might lead me to an answer."

"So what are you suggesting?" Geoffrey asked.

"Just this," Michael replied. "Perhaps there is enough evidence supporting the Gospel accounts to warrant our taking the next step. Maybe we should take a closer look to see if the Star of Bethlehem might actually have occurred—and if so, what it was. If we determine there really may have been such a phenomenon, we might find ourselves a little closer to solving the identity of the strange light over our heads."

Geoffrey raised his hands palms upward and gave a slight shrug. "Why not?" he said. "What do we have to lose? We're not getting anywhere on our present course. So why not give this a try?"

"My better judgment says this idea will probably go nowhere," Joanna said. "But I tend to agree with Geoffrey. We need to take a radical turn and begin to think more creatively. We may lose a little time, but we've wasted plenty of time already. And who knows? We might even learn something. Crazier ideas have produced important scientific breakthroughs in other situations."

By now, Dudley was beside himself with anger. "I can't believe what I'm hearing! I didn't sign on with you people so that I could ruin my reputation as a scholar. If we do this, and the press gets hold of it, we're dead ducks back home."

Skiddy nodded vigorously. "I agree with Dudley. As far as I'm concerned, this is getting us completely off track. We haven't been commissioned to explore fantasies! What would our university colleagues say if they heard we were investigating some Bible tale?"

Skiddy, unlike Dudley, wasn't at all concerned about tenure. He was already a full professor. But he was worried about damaging his hard-won reputation as a person who led serious, highly financed research projects.

As he looked around the group, he expected to pick up some signals that other team members were on his side. After all, the serious scholars were in a clear majority—he had planned it that way. But it quickly became apparent that only Dudley and Dan favored junking the Star idea. The others—Joanna, Geoffrey, Yael, and Michael—indicated that they were ready to proceed with the absurd suggestion. And they constituted a majority!

Of course, this wasn't a democracy. He could always exercise his prerogative as project director to mandate a change in direction. But that could be dangerous, especially with such strong-minded intellectuals. On projects like this, you had to build a consensus. If you didn't give these academic prima donnas some leeway, you could lose control of them altogether. And he certainly didn't want to provoke a mutiny.

In an exasperated, last-gasp effort to bring someone else over to his side, Skiddy looked at Yael Sharon, who administratively was his second in command. She was tough-minded, but Skiddy figured he might be able to pressure her to change her mind.

"I'm *very* surprised that you are prepared to go along with this nonsense, Yael. What would your government officials say? Would they approve of your voting to investigate this Christian . . . *thing*?"

"They couldn't care less," Yael retorted peevishly. "Most of the people I work with are not particularly religious. All they want is results. They don't care if the Dalai Lama put that thing up there in the sky. They just want to know what it is and whether it poses any danger. And they want us to recommend what, if anything, they should do about it."

Her words seemed the final blow to Skiddy's opposition.

"Okay, okay," the Harvard psychologist finally conceded, looking thoroughly deflated. "But it's essential that we set up some protocols so that our research strategy doesn't disintegrate completely."

He stood in front of the group and gestured for Michael to take a seat. "To begin with," Skiddy said, "I insist that we continue with our regular research as we have our discussions about this Star thing. We'll allocate plenty of time to talk about the theological theories—probably more than most of us really want. But we can't neglect the scientific instruments. We would really look stupid if the light began to change rapidly and we missed the event because we were sitting around talking about Jesus and the three wise men."

Seeing that everyone seemed to agree with this limitation, Skiddy turned to his next point. "Also, we must set a strict time limit on Michael's suggestion. We'll stay on this topic no more than twenty-four hours. If we don't see any forward movement by that time—or if it becomes evident sooner that we're on a wild-goose chase—we'll try something else. Agreed?"

Everyone, including Michael, went along with this limitation.

"Another thing," Dudley said. "We have to keep this Star thing quiet. If we can't agree to keep our mouths shut, you can count me out. I can't afford to have something like this leaked to my colleagues."

Everyone nodded agreement. Dudley then settled back sullenly in his chair, obviously not happy with the new plan, but apparently willing to put up with it for a short time.

"Okay, Michael, against my better judgment, I'll give you the floor," Skiddy barked, looking at his watch as though he were already starting to count the seconds. "Beginning right now, it's in your lap. Show us how you think the Star can provide some answers. But I caution you, if you can't make this thing relevant pretty quick, you'll get the hook."

 # NINE

D A N was amazed at how hard it was to rattle Michael James. The man seemed unflappable. You got the impression he had faced every imaginable challenge and had developed such confidence that he could survive any attack—including those from an arrogant, overbearing intellectual like Skiddy Kirkland.

Where does the confidence come from? Dan wondered.

No overt pressure that Skiddy put on Michael seemed to have any effect. Having been given the reluctant go-ahead, the Wheaton professor apparently intended to proceed at his own pace and in his own time. And he wasn't about to be tempted to make any sweeping claims about what his approach could accomplish.

"I'll be satisfied if we can just move forward a step or two," Michael said mildly. Then he picked up a folding chair and pointed toward the door. "Why don't we move outside for the remainder of our discussion today. It's getting a little stuffy in here, and I think it may help to have our mysterious light in plain view."

Soon they were all seated outside, most on folding chairs on a knoll just next to the headquarters building. The rotund Dudley looked quite uncomfortable, frequently shifting his position and constantly slapping at insects that seemed to have honed in on him.

"You're quite the outdoorsman, Dudley," gibed Dan, who was sitting next to the astronomer. He found that he was actually enjoying the cool afternoon breeze that had just started wafting over the compound.

Geoffrey, who was sitting squarely in front of where Michael would be speaking, was already typing something into his computer. *Seems to send more e-mail than anyone, except maybe Yael,* Dan reflected.

Symbolically, Skiddy had picked a chair on the end of the row, as far away from Michael as he could get. His body language—tightly crossed legs and arms—fairly screamed, *"I'll put up with this, but don't ask me to like it!"*

Joanna decided to curl up on a soft, grassy spot on the ground up front, near where Michael would be leading the discussion. Her computer was resting lightly in her lap, and she set up a small, portable telescope nearby—"just in case something starts to happen," she explained.

As for Yael, she chose a large flat rock a few feet away from the rest of the group where she could keep an eye on the patrolling guards. In the distance, she could see another research team setting up their equipment. *The SETI people. Geoffrey's friends. I'll have to check them out.* She smiled to herself. *See if they've discovered any aliens.*

Some extra chairs placed here and there served as makeshift desks to hold computers and notes. The barbed-wire fence was now in full view, and a couple of the armed guards who were patrolling the perimeter looked over curiously at them.

The strange light, as always, glowed serenely in the sky overhead, apparently unchanged. Their eyes automatically locked on it. All they could see was the same mildly undulating blue-and-green mass, with slivers of dull white appearing here and there. It seemed to remain the same size as when they arrived in Israel—or about a quarter the diameter of a full moon.

"Looks like one of the big marbles I used to play with when I was a kid," Dan commented.

"Or a jawbreaker," Joanna said, looking through her telescope. "An astronomical jawbreaker."

"Okay, here are seven copies of the Bible, one for each of us," Michael began, bringing their attention back to earth.

"Are you kidding me?" Dudley protested. "A Bible study? You've got us in a Bible study?"

"We all have different English translations so we can get a flavor for the variety of renditions of the text," Michael said, smiling good-naturedly at the pudgy Harvard astronomer's sarcasm. "My New Testament is in Greek, by the way. So is Yael's, since she reads the original. I wasn't sure about you, Dan, but there's another Greek version for you as well if you'd like to use it."

Dan took the Greek New Testament, but he also held on to his English translation. He hadn't looked seriously at the Greek version since his graduate school days.

Sounding more and more like an old-fashioned Sunday school teacher, Michael said, "Let's turn to the book of Matthew, chapter two."

When he saw that most were hesitating or looking for the table of contents, he said, "That's the first book of the New Testament, the first of the four Gospels."

When they all had the passage in front of them, Michael explained that the Greek word for "star" was *aster*—which was used four times in Matthew 2:1–10.

"But contrary to what you might think, the word has a much richer meaning in the Greek than our English translations suggest," he said. "For example, in the ninth chapter of the book of Revelation, *aster*, translated 'star,' actually seems to refer to the fallen angel, Satan. And again, in chapter twelve of the book of Revelation, 'stars' appears to refer to a multitude of fallen angels."

"The Hebrew use of the word translated 'star' is also interesting," Yael said, pulling out her well-worn Hebrew text. Knowing that she was an expert in both Hebrew and Aramaic, the others listened respectfully.

"I've just noted that my database says *star* is used only thirty-seven times in our Hebrew Scriptures," she said. "But there are a lot of meanings. It's true that the main use of the word refers to a celestial body. But in one of Joseph's dreams, eleven stars represent his eleven brothers. Also, in the book of Numbers, chapter twenty-four, verse seventeen, the prophet Balaam predicts that a star will come out of Jacob and a scepter out of Israel. Some feel this is a reference to the coming of the Hebrew Messiah."

"So where is all this taking us?" Skiddy asked impatiently.

"Here's the point," Michael replied. "When we try to determine the identity of the Star of Bethlehem, we shouldn't limit ourselves to thinking only about a physical object you see with a telescope in the sky."

"Same principle of interpretation applies to that light above us," Joanna said.

"Correct," Michael agreed.

"Okay, okay," Dan said, trying to exhaust this line of inquiry as quickly as possible. "So where does that leave us?"

"It leaves us with the specific movements and other characteristics of the Star of Bethlehem, and quite honestly, I must admit there are some problems with our comparison," Michael said.

"What do you mean?" Skiddy asked eagerly, obviously looking for any excuse to end this line of inquiry and move on to something more productive.

"I mean this," Michael replied. "There are at least three main characteristics that I've identified for the Star of Bethlehem. First, the Star apparently failed to catch the attention of the general public. In fact, biblical reports suggest that knowledge of the event may have been limited to the Magi. It's not at all clear that Herod the Great or his advisers saw it, because they had to ask the Magi about the time of the light's appearance. In fact, the Bible doesn't even indicate that Mary or Joseph saw the light."

"But our present light is probably known to everyone on earth right now," Joanna said.

"Exactly," Michael said. "So that could be a difference—though it remains to be seen just how important a difference. For example, others may very well have seen this ancient starlight—but just misinterpreted it."

"Okay, what's number two?" Dudley said, pushing the discussion along as quickly as he dared.

"Second, the Star of Bethlehem may have appeared, disappeared, and then reappeared," Michael said. "At least that seems to be the implication, because the Magi followed it to Jerusalem. But then they had to ask Herod the Great where the King of the Jews was. After they left Herod, they caught sight of the light again and followed it to Bethlehem."

"Possibly, possibly," Geoffrey said, studying the Gospel text closely.

"Then third, the Star apparently moved across the sky and emitted

68

some sort of directional beam, so that the Magi could identify the house where Jesus and His family were living."

Dudley tossed his Bible aside. "You're being so literal about this, Michael! Why so literal?"

"Remember, we're following a hypothesis here," Michael replied. "We're assuming that this account"—he raised his Bible in front of them—"represents an accurate reporting job. We're taking the text at face value, for what it purports to be. That is, we're taking it as an accurate piece of first-century journalism. Okay?"

He took their silence to be at least grudging agreement.

"So if we assume for the time being that this report is accurate," he continued, "then we should read it very, very closely, so as to wring every possible detail out of it. For all we know, the Star of Bethlehem—if it really did occur—may provide a precedent that will help us understand the mysterious light in our own skies. We must leave no stone unturned. Okay?"

"Fine, so what about this third point?" Dan said.

"Well, we haven't seen any movement across the sky," Michael replied. "In fact, this thing seems to be more stationary than any other astronomical object we know about. Stars move. Planets move. The sun and moon move. But this light doesn't. It's just stuck up there in the east, in the same spot."

"But perhaps it really is moving," Joanna suggested. "After all, it may seem to stay in the same spot, but that depends on your vantage point. You might argue that when you move, the light must also move if it's going to stay in the same spot, regardless of where you're standing or flying or whatever."

"In other words, it's in the same spot positionally for each observer," Geoffrey mused. "It's in the east for me on this side of the world, but also in the east for the Keck astronomers in Hawaii, and in the east for the guys up in the SOFIA plane. And it's as near to me as it is to the people high above earth."

"This is a really interesting point," Joanna said, now showing some excitement. "One that we haven't explored. You know there are theories that some subatomic particles may actually change shape or position when they are observed. Maybe we're seeing the same thing here on a much larger scale."

Michael paused for a moment to let this new insight sink in. He was encouraged to see that both Geoffrey and Dudley were taking notes. The others stared up at the light, temporarily lost in thought.

"There have also been reports of some sort of directional beam," Michael finally said. "You remember that Israeli woman who said she was healed of a disease after the light shone on her?"

"There were a couple of initial reports along those lines," Skiddy admitted. "But they remain unsubstantiated."

"And I really don't think the movement of the Star in the Bible fits any movement that might be occurring with that thing overhead," Dudley said. Then he displayed a self-satisfied smirk. "On the whole, my dear Michael, I think you may be providing a good argument for dropping this Star business altogether. You've described several features of the Star. Yet when you compare those to the characteristics of our current object, it's hard to find any that apply. Seems to be one, two, three strikes you're out, wouldn't you say?"

Dan knew that look. On more than one occasion, the Harvard astronomer had led off with the same sneer before ridiculing him mercilessly.

But Michael James wasn't an easy mark in verbal repartee.

"Actually, Dudley," he said without missing a beat, "I wanted to put the weaknesses in the Star case before you clearly at the very outset. There certainly are differences in the two phenomena—at least, as things now stand. But there are also some possible similarities—such as the report of a directional beam. And we're at an early stage in this game. We don't yet know what future changes may occur in that light up there."

"Pure speculation," Dudley sniffed. "I think we should move on to something else."

"No, no," Joanna objected. "Our main purpose here is not to research the Star of Bethlehem. It's to get our thinking processes unstuck. I'm already starting to consider other possibilities. We hadn't thought of that idea of movement in relation to observation. Let's stay with the program."

Then she turned to the Harvard project director with a sardonic look. "Besides, Skiddy, we're still operating on Michael's clock, right? He still has close to twenty-four hours."

The Harvard psychologist nodded, not particularly appreciating

Joanna's thinly veiled sarcasm. But he knew he was outnumbered. From their sympathetic body language, it was obvious that Geoffrey and Yael were also still interested in pursuing Professor James's approach. "Yes, yes," Skiddy conceded reluctantly. "We'll just have to be patient, Dudley, and let this thing play itself out. All right, Michael, proceed with your Bible study."

Ignoring the cut, Michael turned back to his introductory remarks. "Before we plunge into the actual possibilities for the Star, I need to mention a couple of historical guidelines we should keep in mind. These may provide clues to the identity of the Star.

"First, there is the question of dating. In other words, we need to know the approximate time range when the Star possibly appeared so we'll know what clues to look for in the skies of that period."

He placed two dates on a small melamine board he had brought outside—4 B.C. and 1 B.C.

"These are the main candidates for the death of Herod the Great," he said. "We get them by interpreting certain historical reports in the writings of the Jewish-Roman historian Josephus. He said that Herod died just after a lunar eclipse—which may have occurred in either 4 B.C. or 1 B.C."

"The date's that important?" Joanna asked.

"Extremely important," Michael said. "According to the Gospel account, Herod was alive when Jesus was a young child and the Star appeared. In fact, Herod plays a major role in the events described in the second chapter of Matthew. So the Star must have appeared prior to 1 B.C., and perhaps prior to 4 B.C."

He contemplated both dates for a moment. "For our purposes, we really don't have to worry about which date is correct. I'll just assume it was the later date—1 B.C. So we'll consider astronomical and other phenomena before 1 B.C., which may help us identify the Star."

"What's the earliest date you'd consider for the Star?" Yael asked.

"Probably about 8 B.C., just to be on the safe side," Michael replied. "According to Matthew, just after the Magi left, Herod killed all children in Bethlehem and the vicinity who were two years old or younger. The reason was that he wanted to murder Jesus and eliminate any claim He might have to kingship."

Joanna, who had been typing notes on her notebook computer as

Michael spoke, stopped him. "Let me be sure I've got it right. The time range we'll be looking at for the Star of Bethlehem is 8 B.C. at the earliest, and 1 B.C. at the latest. Right?"

"Exactly," Michael said. Then he picked up his computer and turned it around so that everyone could see the screen. In full color there was a Christmas card–type picture that depicted the shepherds, the wise men, Joseph, and Mary, all looking down at the baby Jesus. An exploding star shone brightly in the background.

"We know the approximate year range for the appearance of the Star," Michael said. "But we also know that the usual crèche scenes or Christmas card depictions, such as this one, are inaccurate. In fact, those who saw the Star—the Magi, or 'wise men,' as they are sometimes known—didn't arrive at the same time as the shepherds mentioned in Luke, chapter two."

"How's that?" Geoffrey asked, now becoming quite intrigued with the history lesson.

"Luke says that the shepherds saw the infant Jesus in a 'manger,' or a feeding trough for livestock, which was just outside an inn," Michael explained. "But Matthew says that the Magi saw Jesus in a 'house.' So it would seem that the family moved to better quarters after the shepherds' visit, and that would mean that the visit by the Magi came later. Besides, there is no textual evidence that the two groups saw Christ at the same time."

"Who were these three Magi?" Joanna asked.

"Actually, there's no evidence that there were three of them," Michael replied. "Traditionally, we infer there were three because of the three gifts they brought—gold, frankincense, and myrrh. But for all we know, there may have been two or four or ten."

"How about 'We Three Kings of Orient Are'?" Joanna said, somewhat facetiously.

"Again, that's just tradition based on the three gifts, which inspired the Christmas song," Michael said. "But the question of their identity is more interesting, and there is some disagreement on that score. The best interpretation seems to be that they were Zoroastrian priests, possibly from as far away as Persia, or present-day Iran."

"What makes you say that?" Dan asked, intent on challenging his adversary every step of the way. "That sounds like pure speculation. What evidence do you have?"

Dan did have some remote recollection that there were reasonable arguments for the identity of the Magi, but he didn't really care about that. He was now in a debating mode, trying to fluster James and, if possible, discredit him before the group.

But Michael dealt with the objection effortlessly. "There are a number of fairly strong arguments for a Persian and Zoroastrian link, but here are two.

"First, the Greek word for 'magi'—*magos*—which is used in the Greek text of Matthew, means a sorcerer, wise man, or even scientist from the East. The Magi were a priestly tribe of the Median people, or Persians as we also call them. We know this from the Greek historian Herodotus, who, as I already mentioned, wrote back in the fifth century B.C.

"The second point is that the dominant ancient Persian faith centered on a belief in Zoroaster, a prophet whom some historians have identified as the founder of the Magi caste around 1000 B.C."

Then Michael leaned toward them and delivered what he knew would be a zinger.

"But the really interesting thing about Zoroastrianism is *what* they believed. For one thing, they taught that there was one supreme God, but two creators of the universe, one good and one evil. According to their doctrines, these two would fight it out for control of the universe, and finally the good spirit would win. But to achieve the final victory, the good spirit would have to send a Savior—or 'Sosiosh.' This Sosiosh would be born supernaturally of a virgin, heal the world of all strife, and reign for a thousand years."

Michael paused to let this information sink in. "Sound vaguely familiar?" he finally asked.

"So the Magi who visited the infant Christ would have believed all this?" Joanna asked. "And they had this tradition and prophecy well before the birth of Christ?"

"They wouldn't have believed it just intellectually," Michael replied. "Their beliefs would almost certainly have been the motivating force that caused them to trek hundreds, maybe thousands of miles to find the person they believed to be the Sosiosh."

Joanna was now thoroughly absorbed. "So they apparently believed that the Sosiosh they had sought for so long was . . ."

"Jesus of Nazareth," Yael said, finishing Joanna's thought.

Everyone looked up at her in surprise. She had been sitting rather quietly during this discussion, and most had assumed that as a Jew, she was merely tolerating the direction the discussion had taken. But obviously, she had been listening—and listening closely.

"I'm sure you find all this to be quite convincing, Yael," Skiddy said rather snidely.

"It is rather fascinating," she replied, causing the Harvard professor to do a double take in her direction.

"Fascinating, but is it relevant?" Dudley asked in an annoyed tone.

"Actually, yes," Michael replied. "You see, among other things, the Magi would have been trained in a combination of what today we call astronomy and astrology. The two fields merged in ancient times because most people, including the best educated, believed that somehow, the stars and other heavenly bodies could influence human affairs and provide answers to human questions and dilemmas, including insights into the future."

"So we come full circle," Geoffrey said. "The Magi were studying some sort of strange light in the sky, looking for meaning and perhaps a message—and so are we."

"Exactly," Michael said.

"Well and good," Geoffrey said. "But where does that leave us, Michael? Where do we go from here?"

"I'd suggest a systematic plan of attack—which we should be able to cover at least in cursory fashion in the remaining hours that Skiddy's allotted for this exercise," Michael replied. "First, let's go through all the possibilities for the Star of Bethlehem, as a kind of checklist. As we talk, we should be alert for any new thoughts or insights about our lightbulb in the sky. If something promising pops up, we can then pursue that line of inquiry."

"Okay," Skiddy said, standing up to signal that this particular meeting was finished. "Let's get something to eat."

As they gathered their materials, he reminded those who were monitoring the spectroscopes and other instruments to check for any changes in the light. After that, he said, they'd get some sleep and arise again at 2:00 A.M. to take some more readings before they proceeded further with the Star discussion.

Dudley Dunster lingered behind after the others had started moving toward their living quarters.

"I really can't believe this," Dudley whispered to Skiddy when the others were out of earshot. "I feel like Alice in Wonderland. If I believed in prayer, I'd be on my knees asking that nobody at Harvard would find out about what we're doing."

Skiddy shrugged. "I think the situation has been nicely contained. We have a definite time limit for James's approach. And we can always justify our involvement because Geoffrey and Joanna— both good scientists and solid atheists, as far as I can tell—have outvoted us. And who knows? The exercise may even trigger a productive new idea."

"Not too likely," Dudley said, still not convinced. "But at least the Bible scholar seems to have put himself at a decided disadvantage. None of the criteria he suggested for the Star of Bethlehem seem to apply to this light. It certainly hasn't moved about or disappeared yet."

"I really don't think there's a thing to worry about," Skiddy said confidently. But he stopped short as he began to move toward his living quarters. The other members of the team had also stopped and seemed to be milling around, craning their necks up toward the sky.

"What are you doing?" he called out to Geoffrey, who was standing closest to him.

"It's gone," the California astrophysicist said. "The light has disappeared."

⁂ TEN

T H E team's site was located on a high plain in northern Israel, with relatively unimpeded views in every direction except the northeast, where the snow-covered peaks of Mount Hermon punctuated the horizon. But as the researchers scanned the sky, they saw nothing except the rays of the setting sun and a scattering of high clouds. The strange light had indeed disappeared from the sky.

"This is remarkable," Geoffrey said, his voice edged with wonder. "Where did that thing go?"

"Did anyone see it leave?" Skiddy asked, looking from face to face.

Every head shook "no."

"Were our video cameras running?" he asked again, pressing to find some clue to what had happened. "I hope we have a record of this."

"Yes!" Dudley replied. "Two sets of videos have been focused on the thing all afternoon."

"Maybe we even have recordings this time from our spectroscopes or other instruments," Joanna said.

A hurried check of the equipment gave them an answer of sorts—but at the same time left them with even more of a mystery. The cameras had indeed recorded the glowing object, but as before, the spectroscopes had detected no radiation or electromagnetic waves. Also, according to the videos, the thing vanished without warning. There had been no movement in another direction. No fading away. Just an abrupt disappearance. One moment, the light was there; the next, it was gone.

"Can we do an analysis of that film?" Skiddy asked. "Is it possible to examine it inch by inch, or frame by frame, to see exactly what happened?"

"It can be done," Dudley said. "But we don't have the facilities here to handle it."

"I can send the film and any other records to one of our labs in Tel Aviv or Jerusalem," Yael volunteered. "They should be able to turn it around pretty quickly. In a day or so."

"Good," Skiddy said. "But can we be sure they won't pass the information on to anyone else? We have a proprietary interest in this, and I want to be sure we have the first shot at interpreting it for the public."

"I'll do my best," Yael said. "I'll assign one of the guards on this compound to take it in and instruct him not to let it out of his sight. I'm reasonably confident we'll be able to maintain control. But as I've said, there is a sense in the Israeli government that this thing may be a threat to national security. I can't guarantee what will happen to the film after it leaves our hands."

"We don't really have a choice, do we?" Michael asked.

"Not really," Geoffrey replied. "Besides, other groups undoubtedly saw the disappearance and recorded it as well. I don't think this presents us with an overwhelming problem."

"Okay, Yael, get started with the analysis," Skiddy said. "And be sure all our instruments are still running. If that thing appears again, we don't want to miss the show."

As they were breaking up, Joanna turned to Michael James and within the hearing of everyone, she said: "Looks like one of your three criteria for the Star has just been met. Congratulations."

As Dudley glowered and Skiddy frowned disapprovingly, Dan looked away in exasperation. But Michael just removed his glasses, locked his eyes onto hers, and shook his head modestly. "This disappearance is an interesting turn of events. But forget the congratulations. I meant what I said before. I have no vested interest in establishing that this thing is a recurrence of the Star of Bethlehem or anything else. I just want to learn the truth."

Dan, watching the interchange closely, actually felt himself becoming jealous as he studied the way Joanna looked at Michael.

They say that the most attractive men are those who can look at a woman and make her feel as if she's the only other person in the world at that moment. Is that happening with my wife?

Dan was still irritated when he and Joanna finally found themselves alone in their one-room hut after supper.

"Why do you keep playing up to that guy James?" he asked. "You've really changed your tune. Before we got here, you were saying he and I didn't even belong on the team. Now, you seem to think he should be in charge of it!"

"He's not quite what I expected," she said. "And I do think his approach may help us make some progress. Besides, it can't hurt, can it? Why are you so uptight?"

"I'm not uptight," Dan said, feeling exceptionally uptight.

"Not much," she said.

"I mean, you seem really taken with him. I've never seen you consider religion so seriously. You never do when I bring it up."

"A little jealous?"

"I just don't get it," he said, growing angrier by the second. "But yeah, why shouldn't I be a little jealous, when my wife starts fawning over another man? He's spouting the same kind of spiritual stuff I've been tossing at you for years—but do you listen to me? No way!"

"It's not quite the same."

"Oh?"

"No," she said, trying to draw a careful distinction that would be honest, yet wouldn't make her husband even more defensive than he was already. "Granted, he's from a conservative Christian tradition, and I don't like that. But you must admit, he knows his stuff. And there's a quiet certainty about his faith. A confidence in his convictions. That's rather appealing."

"Appealing to you?"

"To anyone," she said, actually thinking, *to any woman,* but not daring to use those words with her husband.

Over the years, Joanna had become convinced that self-assurance and self-confidence in a man were profoundly appealing to practically any female. And she certainly knew she was no exception. She had initially been drawn to Dan because of his intellect.

But he was always searching for the meaning of life—like some perennial college sophomore. Even worse, he seemed far too ready to accommodate his views on morality, God, and other spiritual or social issues to the views that were in fashion that year at Amherst.

Dan was like many men she had known who were either students or teachers in the elite American university system. He liked to free-associate with his peers and play intellectual games. But he couldn't bring himself to make firm personal commitments about what was really right and wrong in his everyday life.

It seemed to Joanna that in their marriage, she was always the one expected to take the definite stand on such matters as the existence or nonexistence of God, having children or undergoing an abortion. She was supposed to make final decisions on the direction of their relationship, and typically, Dan was content just to follow her lead.

Will our marriage make it? she wondered.

That thought had been nagging at her for months now. And the more time that passed, the more she began to suspect that divorce was the only answer to their problems.

What could save our relationship? She asked herself that question again and again. The same answer kept haunting her. She felt increasingly that she needed someone who was stronger than Dan, someone with a clear sense of purpose in life. In short, despite the confident image she projected to the world, Joanna wished that sometimes Dan would take the lead on the big decisions in their family and remove some of the burden from her shoulders.

It wasn't religion she was looking for. As far as she was concerned, there was no God—or if He was there, He was irrelevant to her life. But still, it was refreshing to encounter a man like Michael James, even if he was deeply religious. Certainly, he was highly intelligent and well educated—qualities that were prerequisites in a man, as far as she was concerned. But even more important, Michael seemed to know exactly where he stood on the important issues of life.

You get the idea that he's wise and totally reliable. That he'd lead you the right way if you were faced with an earth-shaking decision. Or if you were forced to deal with a life-or-death situation.

Just being around Michael gave her a sense of security that she lacked with Dan. She looked over at her husband. As hard as she had tried to avoid hurting him, he was now clearly miffed. Once again, she realized with a resigned sigh, her need to be forthright and truthful had caused her to trample on Dan's feelings.

I should just keep my mouth shut. He doesn't need to know the details of how I might respond to Michael James. Just keep it zipped, Joanna!

They had been assigned two cots, and earlier, Dan had made motions to push them together to form a double bed. But now he dragged his bed farther away, muttering something about getting nearer to the evening breeze coming through the window.

Even as we try our best to come together, we grow farther and farther apart, Joanna thought as she began to prepare for bed.

When the lights were finally turned out and darkness and quiet settled on the camp, Joanna lay awake, staring up at the prefabricated ceiling. For a while, she had continued to berate herself for the way she had mishandled the "Michael matter," as she had come to think about it. But Joanna was not one to dwell long on her own missteps. After resolving to do better the next time, she pushed the matter out of her mind.

Soon, thoughts about the strange light replaced her concern for Dan. While listening to his steady breathing in the other cot, she kept playing over mentally the exit of the "Star"—as she had privately come to think about the phenomenon.

How did I miss that? I was looking at it through the telescope just before it disappeared! Why didn't I wait just a little longer before I packed up?

She remained pessimistic about their scientific instruments. *Are they simply too primitive to record what's actually happening? Will the Israeli technicians come up with a completely unexpected answer? What might it be? Or could we be dealing with something in a completely different category—something "extradimensional," as Geoffrey calls it?*

The questions swirled around in her mind in a confusing jumble until finally, she drifted off into a fitful sleep.

Joanna wasn't sure what it was that woke her. Perhaps it was some random noise out in the wild country surrounding them. Or the voice of one of the guards. Or Dan's light snoring.

But she did know for certain that she was sitting bolt upright in her bed, wide-awake and alert to every sight and sound around her.

And she also knew that the brilliant white figure standing at the foot of her bed was definitely not a dream, nor a figment of her imagination.

# ELEVEN

JOANNA was too petrified to say a word as the shining figure stood—or floated—in front of her.

The entire room had filled with light—if, indeed, the room or its walls were still there. She was aware of nothing except this apparition before her. Then the figure seemed to gesture or beckon, and she followed, or floated, until she realized she was outside, enveloped by the light, but also by warm, soothing night air.

For some reason, Joanna felt compelled to look up into the dark sky. There it was once again. The strange light had returned.

But now it was larger, perhaps twice as large as before, half the size of a full moon. And the colors emanating from it now included deep reds, reminding her of glowing embers from a fire.

"Joanna, the time is near," the figure said clearly, in a voice that resonated not in her ears or head, but throughout her entire body, a voice that seemed neither male nor female. The words were more impressions than sounds. But they were clearer than human language, and conveyed in an inner tone that exuded authority and would brook no argument.

"The time approaches when you must decide."

"Who are you?" Joanna asked, now quite frightened and confused. "What do you want from me?"

"I am a messenger," the figure answered, *"but not of this world of shadows and reflections."*

"I don't understand."

"You shall. Soon you shall understand fully. Just continue to

watch and wait. Look up and listen. The Star will guide you."

"But . . ."

Suddenly, Joanna was standing alone, not far from the barbed-wire fence. The light and the shining figure were gone, and the air whipping through her khakis now seemed quite cold. The rocky ground, which she had not even noticed before, felt like dull spikes pushing hard against her bare feet.

Khakis—I'm wearing khakis. But I was wearing a nightshirt when I went to bed. Bare feet—I can't stand to walk outside without shoes. How did I get this far from our quarters in bare feet?

"Stop where you are! Who goes there?"

The booming voice, the sound of a barking dog, and a blinding light all hit her at the same instant. She automatically raised both hands above her head.

"It's just me! Don't shoot!"

"Who . . . Dr. Hill? It's Dr. Joanna Hill," the voice yelled.

Soon two guards, a growling canine, and an officer had surrounded her.

"What are you doing out here, ma'am?" the officer asked. "This is no-man's-land. Our safeties are off. You could have been shot."

"I . . . I'm sorry. I guess I was just taking a walk," she said lamely.

The officer looked at her with his head cocked to one side, obviously not satisfied by her response, but he didn't probe further. He'd let others take care of that. Still, his questions and observations about this strange incident would definitely be included in the report he filed before he went off duty.

"We'd better get you back to your room," he finally said. "But you could hurt yourself with those bare feet. These sharp rocks and thorns around here—I don't know how you made it this far. Corporal Maoz will be happy to carry you back."

Joanna complied without argument. But as the guard picked her up and lugged her back toward her quarters, she lapsed into an embarrassed silence, avoiding any eye contact.

How am I ever going to explain this absolutely bizarre incident to Dan, much less to the other team members—who will certainly hear about it?

When she was safely back in her room, sitting on her cot, Joanna checked the time. *Still two hours before reveille.* Dan was sound asleep, and it seemed that, mercifully, none of the other team members had been roused by her adventure.

Did it really happen? she wondered. *Did I actually see some ghost? Or was I sleepwalking for the first time in my life?*

Then the really important question hit her—the one that might confirm or deny the reality of her experience.

Did I actually see that strange light again? Is it back in the sky?

She rushed outside and looked up.

A wave of emotion swept through her. Her knees buckled, and she slumped to the ground. Sobs racked her uncontrollably, and tears flowed as if from a salty inner river, stinging her eyes and forcing her to shut them tightly for a few moments.

But that didn't matter—because before the tears had blinded her, she had seen what she needed to see.

The Star was back in the sky.

But it was larger and redder.

It looked exactly the same as when the shining figure had served as her guide.

TWELVE

JOANNA was the last to walk into the predawn meeting at the headquarters building. She was painfully aware that all eyes were turned on her—except Dan's. He was staring at the floor.

They all know. And they probably think I'm sick or crazy. She glanced over at Dan. *He's probably mad as a hornet. Or embarrassed to death. Mortified. I should have told him.*

Skiddy, who was standing at the front, cleared his throat and glanced down at a thin folder he was holding in his hands.

The report. The guards' report. Okay, here it comes.

"Umm, you doing okay, Joanna?" Skiddy began, looking up at her and then back at the folder. "I guess you had a rather upsetting night."

"Actually, that report you're looking at doesn't tell you how upsetting. What exactly does it say?"

"Just that the guards found you wandering around in your bare feet next to the perimeter fence. Dangerous business, you know. They could have shot you."

Joanna took a deep breath and prepared to give them an account of her entire experience. But first she asked, "What do you think about the Star?"

Silence.

Then Dudley responded, "What Star?"

"The light. You've seen it, right?"

"Not when I walked in here," Dudley said.

85

"There's no light in the sky, Joanna," Dan said, now getting up and walking over to put his arm around her shoulder.

But she brushed him aside, ran to the door, and flung it open. The light was gone. She rushed out into the parking area so that she could see the entire horizon. Nothing. In a daze, she slowly returned to the building and pushed past the others, who had crowded around the doorway.

"I don't understand," she said, a sense of panic now creeping over her as she plopped into her chair. "I saw it last night. I know I saw it. And it had changed. It was a lot bigger, and almost fiery red, and . . ."

Dan patted and hugged her into silence. "Obviously, you had a disturbing dream. This whole thing's been very stressful. And you may still not have recovered from the trip and the jet lag."

"Perhaps a physician could help," Skiddy suggested. "We don't have anyone on-site, but I'm sure Yael could arrange for someone to drive you into Tiberias or even Jerusalem."

"I'm not sick, and I'm not crazy!" Joanna retorted, pushing Dan away and standing up. "I may be a little stressed out, but something happened to me last night that is not in that report and that I don't understand at all."

She was on the verge of tears, and Skiddy looked at a loss about how to proceed. Finally, Michael James stood up and walked over to her.

"We're dealing with extremely strange phenomena, and your experience may very well relate to it in some way," he said soothingly. "So I, for one, would like to hear all you have to say. Besides, I believe it's about time for me to pick up where I left off yesterday. So why don't I give you some of my time. Is that okay, Skiddy?"

"Of course, of course," the Harvard psychologist answered. *Besides, the more time we allocate to Joanna's problem, the less time we'll have to devote to James's Bible nonsense.*

"Okay, let's continue in here since it's still quite dark outside," Michael said. "You have the floor, Joanna. Tell us what happened."

Joanna walked to the back of the hut and leaned against one of the windows so she could gaze out into the night sky—just to assure herself that the light was still missing. Then she proceeded to give a detailed account of the strange white figure, the almost blinding light, and the view of the transformed object in the sky.

"I even went back outside to check on it after the guards brought me back to the room," she said. "And it was still there, looking larger and redder. When I woke up this morning, I was in such a hurry running over here—and so preoccupied with what I would say to all of you—that I didn't think to look up and check it out again. That's why I was so stunned when you said the light wasn't there anymore."

"Probably a vivid dream," Dudley said.

"Or maybe a form of hysteria," Skiddy added. "No offense, Joanna. It's just that there are many cases in medical literature of strange illnesses—fainting and other emotional reactions—when people are under tremendous stress. Mystical experiences are sometimes linked to these events as well."

"I'm convinced that this was different," Joanna said, trying to remain calm in the face of the skepticism. "Granted, I was frightened when this figure first appeared. But mostly, I was fascinated, even reassured by its presence. I felt wonder and excitement—not stress."

"But you also were quite wrought up," Skiddy said. "You said you cried, experienced intense fear, were confused."

"And you don't even remember putting on your khakis or walking barefoot over to the fence," Dan added.

"All signs of heightened emotionalism," Skiddy said. "Again, Joanna, no offense intended. You're a rational person, and we're just trying to sort through this thing. How do you feel now?"

"A little silly and quite embarrassed," she replied. "Especially since there seems to be no way to convince any of you that what happened to me was anything more than a dream or hallucination."

Michael paced thoughtfully in front of the group for a few seconds and then turned to face her.

"I'm inclined to think your experience *was* more than a dream," he said.

This guy is obviously making a move toward my wife, Dan thought. *She's vulnerable now, and he's going to tell her exactly what she wants to hear—and maybe step into a vacuum created by an unsympathetic husband. Well, not if I can help it!*

"Michael, do you really have Joanna's best interests in mind?" Dan asked, resolving to lay his cards on the table. "I think we should focus on her well-being right now rather than on any theological

agenda or other personal interest you may have. I take it you're trying to say this was some sort of mystical vision—consistent with
your belief system, of course. And her vision was somehow triggered
by the light, which, by the way, isn't even visible anymore."

But in a manner that had become maddening to the Amherst
professor, Michael once more came up with the unexpected.

"No, not a vision," he said. "And I really don't have any theological preconceptions about the light. I'm open to anything."

Michael looked over solicitously at the Harvard project director.
"For example, I don't want to discount completely what Skiddy's
said about hysteria. We're all still tired, and we *have* been under a
lot of stress. We're frustrated because we haven't come up with any
answers. The pressure could work on anyone's mind. But from
what Joanna has told us, her experience sounds more like something that really happened, rather than an alteration of her consciousness through a stressful event. You correct me if I'm wrong,
Skiddy. But isn't it true that the typical responses to stress usually
involve temporary illness, such as nausea or headaches, rather
than personal encounters of the type she's described?"

"So what are you saying?" Skiddy asked—realizing that Michael
had a point, but reluctant to admit it publicly. "That she really did
see some figure in a shiny white robe? And that the light up there
really did reappear, even though nobody else saw it? And it looked
different?"

"We can't discount those possibilities," Michael said. "At least not
until we come up with a better explanation. And frankly, Joanna's
interpretation of her experience—that it actually happened—is the
simplest explanation, and the one most consistent with her own
perceptions."

"Occam's razor," Geoffrey interjected.

"Exactly what I had in mind," Michael said.

"What are you talking about?" Yael asked.

"Occam's razor is a philosophical principle—also called the 'Law
of Economy,'" Geoffrey explained. "The idea is that the simplest
theory or explanation of a phenomenon should be preferred over
those that are more complex. I might also add this: Even when the
simplest answer seems unlikely or conflicts with our expectations
or philosophical presuppositions, it may still be the best choice."

"So what do you think about all this, Geoffrey?" Yael asked.

Geoffrey rubbed one of his broad shoulders for what seemed an interminable time, and then said, "I think that Joanna's experience may have been real. But we need to know more. I'm not buying it completely just yet. But let's be patient."

Dudley, who now seemed to have finally been pushed over some emotional edge, began to gesticulate rather wildly. "We're moving farther and farther astray! I'm certainly sympathetic to Joanna's condition. She's upset. But we can't assume that some unearthly being just appeared out of nowhere. This is all so absurd! Are we scientists, or members of some cult?"

"Remember, we have a time limit for this line of discussion," Skiddy said, looking at his watch.

He was apparently calculating the precise number of hours that still remained for Michael's Star discussion. His rather satisfied expression seemed to say that he was pleased they had been dealing with Joanna's hysteria on Michael's time.

"Unprofessional," Dudley muttered. "It's all so unprofessional."

At that moment, the officer in charge of the guards burst through the door.

"Yes, Baruch?" Yael asked, obviously somewhat annoyed by the intrusion.

"Sorry for the interruption, but I thought you'd want to know. The light is back in the sky. But it's different. Very different."

THIRTEEN

THE team rushed out into the dark, early morning coolness and stood speechless, staring up into the night sky.

The light had indeed returned. In the few minutes that had elapsed since Joanna had run out into the parking lot, it was back. And the object now seemed to fit Joanna's description in every detail.

"It is considerably larger than before," Dudley said in a near whisper.

"And there are clear red streaks running through it now," Geoffrey said. "Seems to be more active as well. Reminds me of some pictures of Jupiter. Let's check our instruments."

Dudley and Joanna were already hurrying toward the sites where they had set up their telescopes, cameras, and spectroscopes. But after about a half hour of fruitless adjustments and readjustments of their detection equipment, and fresh attempts at computer analysis, they returned to the headquarters building.

"I simply don't understand this," Dudley said. "There is definitely something going on up there. That thing clearly is putting out some sort of light. There should be radiation or light waves. Something. But nothing registers."

"Now, Joanna, tell us again," Geoffrey said. "This figure you say you saw said something about a 'star.'"

"Yes, the words were simple and clear. I'll never forget them. This . . . figure or person, I don't know if it was male or female, or what . . . said to keep watching and waiting and looking up and listening. And the final words were, 'The Star will guide you.'"

"You're sure that was really the word?" Yael asked. "The figure actually used the word *star*?"

"That's right," Joanna replied.

They were quiet for a moment, and then Skiddy broke the silence.

"Could be just subliminal suggestion. We've been talking about the Star of Bethlehem and almost nothing else for the past day. Don't misunderstand, Joanna. I'm not saying your report is unreliable. It's just that all of us had the word *star* on the brain, perhaps subconsciously as well as consciously. The stress of unproductive research, and perhaps a night of fitful sleep, might have caused you to hear the word in a half-awake state."

"Occam's razor again," Geoffrey said quietly.

"What?"

"The simplest solution is not some convoluted psychological interpretation," Geoffrey reminded Skiddy. "The simplest thing is that she actually heard those words. It may not be logical, and it may not conform to our expectations as hardheaded scientists. But now we have more reason than ever to accept her account at face value. Think about it. The light has actually come back. And it looks exactly as she said it did in her encounter with it."

"With all due respect, Geoffrey, I really don't think you are the expert on psychological theory or analysis," retorted Skiddy, smarting from Geoffrey's implied rebuke.

"Psychology is hardly precise science," Geoffrey replied, not at all intimidated by Skiddy's attempt at a rebuke. "And you certainly don't have to be an expert in any academic discipline to evaluate what seems like good common sense and what doesn't."

The argument was cut off when the officer in charge of the guard detail burst through the door and handed Yael several official-looking papers. He whispered a few words to the Israeli, who then turned to the group.

"These are reports we've received from several of the other research sites," she said. "They all saw this thing in the sky. And they describe it the same way we do."

"Any explanations from the other researchers?" Skiddy said with some trepidation, obviously afraid that their team might be behind in the race to find an answer.

"None," Yael answered, studying the reports. "There are a lot of theories. But so far, no scientific instruments register anything—other than video camcorders and other cameras. And they show nothing more than we see with the naked eye or telescopes."

After the guard had left, Dudley heaved a sigh of relief. "At least no one else is ahead of us."

"True, but I'm still at a loss to know what we should do now," Skiddy said.

Joanna waved her hand. "The shining figure told me to listen," she said. "That was one of the main commands. And I don't know anyone to listen to at this point other than Michael. He's the only one who's been saying anything of substance about the Star."

That answer wasn't particularly satisfying to Skiddy. Dudley and Dan also made their displeasure obvious by frowning and shifting noisily in their seats, but they knew they had no rebuttal.

"Okay, we'll proceed as planned," Skiddy finally said, resigning himself to more of the Star of Bethlehem distraction. "You have the floor again, Michael."

But even as he sat down, Skiddy couldn't avoid anxious thoughts about the potential impact of Joanna's "vision." Given the most recent turn of events, there was every reason to believe that the group might want to continue with James's approach past the twenty-four-hour deadline that had been established.

That must not happen, Skiddy thought, fighting off a growing sense of panic, mixed with simmering anger. His anxiety made the spare headquarters room where they were meeting seem claustrophobic—though only a few hours before, the space had seemed roomy enough for the seven team members.

Professionally, I simply can't afford to become part of some religious quackery. Dudley can't either. But what's going on with Joanna and Geoffrey? They're entirely too interested in all this. Isn't this supposed to be a scientific investigation? It's looking more and more like some sort of prayer and testimony meeting.

But Skiddy felt he had no option other than to let Michael James proceed. Michael, now seeming almost like some biblical juggernaut, was already in front of the group, spreading out his notes and adjusting his notebook computer screen.

I'll just have to bide my time, Skiddy decided. *But my time will come—I'll make absolutely sure of that.*

As the Harvard psychologist looked around the room, he could see that he was facing a tough, uphill battle—that is, if facial expressions were any indication. If frowns meant anything, Dan was certainly still on his side, and so was Dudley. Both were working hard at avoiding eye contact with Michael.

But Joanna and Geoffrey seemed even more attentive and interested than ever. Geoffrey was rocking his stocky body back and forth, ready to interrupt with a question or sympathetic comment every time Michael made a new point. As for Joanna, she was hanging on the Wheaton professor's every word, as though he was the only one who could help her understand her emotional lapse. Even Yael was riveted on the speaker.

The guy has become a Svengali! Amazing what a difference one disturbing dream can make. Finally, Skiddy settled back into a quiet stew of frustration.

"This morning, we'll begin to look seriously at some of the theories for the Star," Michael was saying.

Using his erasable marker, he jotted a list on the melamine board in front of them:

1. Nova/supernova
2. Meteor/meteor shower
3. Bolide/fireball
4. Comet
5. One star or planet
6. Conjunction
7. UFO/extradimensional phenomenon

The Wheaton professor then stepped back from the board and surveyed the list. But the challenges began before he could launch into his presentation.

"We can already eliminate most of those—at least as far as the current light is concerned," Dudley said brusquely. "Our instruments aren't registering a supernova, or meteor, or comet, or the like."

"True, but bear with me," Michael replied. "Given Joanna's experience, I think it's become more important than ever to try to distinguish the Star of Bethlehem from the object we're dealing with. If we can't make such a distinction, then it's at least possible that we may be dealing with the same or a similar phenomenon. After all, that figure she encountered did make reference to a 'star.'"

He glanced over at Skiddy. "And don't worry, Professor Kirkland, I still plan to finish well within the time frame you originally set for me. We should know by tonight whether or not this line of inquiry is going to be fruitful."

Michael then underlined the first item, "Nova/supernova."

"This is one candidate for the Star that's been mentioned frequently—probably because it's a burst of light and has been the inspiration for many of our Christmas cards. Because I'm not an astronomer, I'd prefer to rely on our scientific experts in that field, Dudley and Geoffrey. Dudley, can you tell us what novas and supernovas involve?"

Dudley cleared his throat and shifted uncomfortably. He obviously hadn't expected Professor James, whom he had begun to regard as his adversary, to recognize him as an authority for this part of the discussion. In Dudley's suspicious mind, the ploy was probably designed to blunt his own opposition to the Star inquiry. Still, he felt he had no choice but to respond.

"Let me pull up some data on my computer here," he said, injecting an appropriately irritated tone in his voice, "and then I'm sure I'll be able to give you more than you probably want."

He watched his notebook computer screen for a few moments, and then nodded with obvious satisfaction. "Okay, let me begin this way. You can think of novas and supernovas as explosions of ordinary stars in deep space. Basically, a nova is a small explosion, and a supernova is a huge explosion. You may not even be able to see a nova with the naked eye. But a supernova, which is a rare event, may flare up to hundreds of millions of times the star's original brightness. It's been estimated that if a star a hundred light-years away from earth became a supernova, it would be brighter than the full moon in our night skies."

"What causes them?" Yael asked.

"A supernova is a star, like our sun, that has used up its nuclear fuel and then collapses into a highly concentrated state. Finally, it explodes in one last big burst of energy. The star's particles and gases are ejected at incredible rates of speed—up to three thousand miles per second. The final result is an expanding cloud of luminous gases, called a nebula."

"How often do they occur?" Yael asked again.

"Many novas have appeared over the years, but there are records of only a small number of 'big blast' supernovas in our galaxy. The earliest, and perhaps the brightest, occurred in the constellation Vega several thousand years ago. The event was recorded on an ancient Sumerian tablet—and the explosion became an important feature of Sumerian mythology."

He examined his computer more closely and toyed with his mouse and keyboard. "I see from my database here that another striking supernova appeared in the eleventh century, A.D. 1054. Yes, that was the Crab nebula, in the constellation Taurus. Chinese and Japanese astronomers of the time kept rather detailed records of the event. They said that the exploding star was visible during the day for about twenty-three days, and at night for about six months."

"So what about the Star of Bethlehem?" Joanna asked. "Could that have been a supernova?"

Dudley shrugged. "There's no record of a supernova around 4 B.C. That's the date you suggested for the Star, right, Michael?"

"Yes, though we should probably be looking at a range of dates from about 8 B.C. to 1 B.C."

"No record for that entire period," Dudley repeated, obviously with some satisfaction.

"And I must concur that my investigation of this—as a layman, of course—confirms the lack of evidence," Michael said. "I believe there were a number of novas—or much dimmer stellar explosions—in March of 5 B.C. and April of 4 B.C. These 'guest stars,' as the Chinese called them, were noted in Chinese records. But I agree with you. Novas and supernovas don't seem likely candidates."

Dudley was clearly a little disconcerted that Michael knew so much about this subject, but he quickly recovered and tried to take the initiative again.

"I might also add," Dudley said, "that supernovas and novas definitely don't explain that strange light overhead. For one thing, they look completely different. And for another, you can measure them with our instruments."

"Good!" Skiddy said, almost leaping out of his seat with what he immediately realized might be interpreted as a little too much glee. He had learned years ago that anyone as tall and thin as he was had to move more deliberately to project a serious, dignified image.

"So let's move on," he said in a more businesslike tone as he eased back into his seat. "What's next, Michael?"

But there was nothing to restrain Skiddy from exulting to the maximum in private. *If we can dispose of the other items on James's list this quickly, we could be back on track with our regular investigation in a matter of an hour or two!*

Michael, seemingly oblivious to the fact that he was giving his opponents such encouragement, turned back to the board and underlined point number two: "Meteor/meteor shower."

"You can mark that one off too!" Dudley blurted, glancing around in triumph at the others. The Harvard astronomer plainly felt he was now on such a roll that he should be able to rush this annoying Professor James offstage and into the background where he belonged.

"Well, you may be right," Michael replied in such a disturbingly quiet tone that Dudley looked back at him with a start.

Is it possible to get a rise out of this guy? Dudley wondered.

"But let's at least take a couple of minutes with this," the Wheaton professor continued. "Remember, our discussion isn't really just about the Star of Bethlehem. We want to keep our minds open to any new ideas about that object in our own skies."

Geoffrey Gonzales was about to offer a comment, but Dudley butted in again before the California scholar could open his mouth. "Okay, okay," Dudley said, "I can dispose of this meteor business in short order." In his enthusiasm to single-handedly banish Michael from the driver's seat in the discussion, Dudley seemed more than ready to ignore the fact that Geoffrey had achieved renown as an expert astronomer, in addition to the fact that he was regarded as one of the world's leading astrophysicists.

"Fine, Dudley," Michael said patiently. "Fill us in on meteors."

"Meteors are also called 'falling stars' in popular parlance," the Harvard astronomer began. "In effect, they're rocks that fly through space at dizzying speeds, between eight and forty-five miles per second."

Dudley was now warming to his topic, and it didn't hurt that everyone in the room was hanging on his every word.

"These flying rocks are called *meteoroids* when they are still in space. Then they become *meteors* when they enter the earth's atmosphere and begin to burn up, at an average height of about sixty miles above us. Large meteors may actually make it all the way to the ground, and in that case, their physical remains are called *meteorites*."

"Obviously, we're not dealing with a meteor overhead," Geoffrey said dryly.

"No, and by Michael's standards the Star of Bethlehem couldn't have been a meteor," Dan said, happy to jump in on what he perceived as the anti-James side of the discussion.

"Explain," Yael said.

"Well, a meteor flashes across the sky once," Dan said. "But if the Bible is to be believed—and I still have serious questions about that—the Star kept reappearing over a relatively longer period of time."

"You're absolutely right, Dan," Michael agreed. "On the other hand—as I'm sure Dudley will tell us—there are other variations on meteors. For example, there's the meteor shower, which may involve thousands or even hundreds of thousands of meteors that rain down from the sky, sometimes over a period of hours, or even a day or two. I believe there were two major instances of this in 1833 and 1866. And many people today can remember dramatic meteor showers in 1933, 1966, and 1999. I believe those were part of the Leonid shower in November 1999, when the earth crossed the path of the Tempel–Tuttle comet. Right, Dudley?"

Again, Dudley was somewhat taken aback at Michael's knowledge on the subject.

"That's right. But I still don't think a meteor shower, even a long-lasting one, would meet your criteria for the Star of Bethlehem," he finally said.

"Absolutely correct," Michael agreed. "No directional beam to indicate the house where Jesus and His family lived. And the limited time period for these meteor showers isn't long enough to fit the bill."

"And as I recall, in ancient times there were many fears linked to such events—even concerns that the world might be ending," Dan said.

He was happy that he could at least remember something relevant from his readings on apocalyptic fears and expectations.

"Yes, another good point," Michael said. "There were negative associations with meteor showers, while the Magi had positive expectations about the Star."

"Of course, you haven't mentioned bolides," Geoffrey said.

"Fireballs," Dudley echoed, giving the popular name for very large meteors. "One of those would have made quite an impression. Certainly a bolide would have caused enough of a stir to cause someone to make a record in China, Iran, or somewhere. Probably bolides were responsible for the huge craters and massive prehistoric devastation we see in Arizona and Siberia. People couldn't ignore a bolide. But there's no record of one between 8 B.C. and 1 B.C. So I think we can assume there weren't any during that period."

"Agreed," Michael said. "And besides, huge meteors are subject to the same objections as the smaller ones."

"Well, Michael, I'm afraid you're still barking up the wrong tree," Dudley said, obviously trying to rub in the inadequacy of the Wheaton professor's methodology.

But again, Michael ignored the implied criticism and proceeded to his next point. "Comets," he said, pointing to the fourth item on his list.

"Same problem as meteors," Dudley said quickly. The Harvard astronomer could now see light at the end of this irrational tunnel, and he was in a headlong rush to push Michael James out of the picture.

"Perhaps," Michael said. "But let's take at least a couple of minutes with this. Geoffrey, would you like to give us an explanation this time?"

"Interesting phenomenon, comets," Geoffrey said. "Known as 'sweeping stars,' or *hui hsing*, by the Chinese. The reason for the name, I suppose, was the bright trail they can leave across the skies, on occasion for a year or more at a time."

Joanna, who had been deferring to the astronomers up to this point, was particularly taken with Geoffrey's description.

"So unlike a meteor, a comet could have been in the sky during the Magi's entire journey from Iran to Israel," she noted. "And that would have been possible even if they were on the road for many weeks or months."

"That's true," Geoffrey said. "And there are some other arguments that could prove interesting here. Here's one. According to my data"—he peered closely at his computer screen—"a comet was identified by Chinese astronomers in 5 B.C., in the constellation of Capricorn. That one was visible for more than seventy days. Also, in 4 B.C., they recorded a *po hsing*, or a 'comet without a tail,' which appeared in the constellation Aquila. But many experts feel this second, tailless object was actually a nova, or an exploding star."

Michael, referring to his own notes, again showed he was capable of keeping up with the scientists. "Halley's Comet has also been mentioned as a candidate, but that came too early—11 B.C. was the nearest pass. Remember, our date range for the Star is 8 B.C. to 1 B.C."

"As I recall, public response to comets was negative," Dan said, trying to close out the discussion. "They were an evil sign, weren't they? Sort of like meteors."

"True," Michael replied. "Josephus, for instance, regarded the appearance of a comet before the destruction of Jerusalem in 70 to 72 B.C. as a bad omen.

"On the other hand," he added, "comets have communicated mixed messages over the centuries. Sometimes the messages were more positive. For example, a comet is supposed to have announced the birth of Mithradates the Great, king of Pontus, in 134 B.C. Chinese records indicate that a comet did appear in that year, and one was also seen in 120 B.C, the year he took over the throne."

"So what do you conclude from all this?" Dudley pressed, again becoming agitated with what he regarded as irrelevancies. "What do you suggest about comets?"

"I'd say a comet would certainly be a better candidate for the Star than a meteor," Michael said. "Comets move across the sky over a fairly long period of time. I suppose they appear and disappear, according to the density of the cloud cover. And they have a tail—which one might argue can 'point' in a sense."

Then he shook his head. "But the tail always points away from the sun. It's not particularly directional. So it doesn't seem too likely that it would have pointed toward Jesus' house in Bethlehem."

"So you would conclude . . . " Dudley said.

"I'd conclude that a comet by itself isn't enough to qualify as the Star. But when we consider conjunctions later, we may find that we want to return for another look at comets. In other words, ancient observers may have received the first part of a message from a comet and shortly afterward, another part of the message from a conjunction."

"Good!" Skiddy said. "That seems to wrap up comets, and we now only have three items left on your list—a single star or planet, a conjunction, and the extradimensional thing. Maybe we can finish your presentation by brunch!"

Dudley, who was rubbing his hands together, also seemed enthused that they were close to leaving this embarrassing topic.

"I might add something else about comets that most of us already know," Geoffrey said. He was obviously not in as big a rush to leave this line of thought as his colleagues. "Unlike the light in the sky over our heads, a comet would have shown up on our instruments. So we know that thing in our own sky is not a comet either."

"Wait a minute," Joanna said. "I just thought of something. We're eliminating all of these astronomical phenomena as possibilities for the Star of Bethlehem. But at the same time, we're eliminating them as possibilities for our strange light."

"So?" Dudley said.

"Don't you see? It's starting to look more and more like there may be some relationship between the Star and the strange light. Neither can be a supernova or nova. Neither can be a meteor or meteor shower. Neither can be a bolide. And neither can be a comet."

Dudley had turned slightly pale, and Skiddy was becoming visibly agitated. "So what are you trying to say?" Skiddy finally asked, though he didn't seem to really want an answer to his own question.

"That maybe we need to be more open to the idea that the light overhead could in fact be the same phenomenon as the Star that was seen over Bethlehem," Joanna replied.

"I thought you were supposed to be a scientist, Joanna!" Dudley almost shouted. "Don't be ridiculous. We're not even close to such a conclusion."

"Your logic is totally flawed!" Skiddy replied. Then he muttered some crack under his breath about "problems with clear thinking at Yale."

"And remember," Dudley said, "we don't have any idea if the Star of Bethlehem—provided it even existed—would have registered on our instruments or not. That's all speculation."

"Still, an interesting thought," Geoffrey said, evidently enjoying the consternation and near panic that had gripped his scientific colleagues.

"Easy for you to say, Geoffrey," Dudley almost shrieked. "You don't have much to lose except a summer's work. And you've got tenure. I don't. If the Harvard faculty learned I was investigating the Star of Bethlehem, I'd be dead meat at my next review."

"Relax, relax," Michael said. "Nobody's saying that the Star of Bethlehem has reappeared. Remember, we're just brainstorming. We still have a ways to go before we start trying to formulate any conclusions. But I'm sure we all appreciate the fact that Joanna is stepping back from this discussion and trying to put some of our many thoughts together in a new way."

The hostile looks coming from Dudley and Skiddy signaled that not everyone appreciated Joanna's observations. Even her husband was frowning at her and shaking his head. Michael decided that some of the ill feeling might be defused if they ended the session quickly. So he glanced down at his watch and signaled that he was finished.

"It's about time for our brunch break," he announced. "Also, it's starting to get light outside. Why don't we eat, and then the scientists can check their instruments. If you like, we can reassemble in about an hour and a half."

As the group was leaving, he signaled to Yael. "Could I speak with you for a moment, Dr. Sharon?" he said, in a formal tone loud enough for all to hear. "I understand you may have some historical or linguistic data that could be helpful to me. Do you have a few minutes?"

"Certainly," she replied, also quite formally. "Why don't we go into my office so that I'll have access to my computer."

When the others had cleared out of the headquarters building, Michael peered through a window to confirm that they were gathering near the makeshift mess hall.

"We're alone," he said. "Things are getting a little tense."

"Dudley is almost over the edge," she replied. "And Skiddy's not far behind. Even Dan Thompson sometimes seems ready to lose it. I think he's jealous of you."

"Me? Why?"

"Joanna," she replied, smiling slyly. "She's quite taken with you."

He shrugged. "It's more than that. She's desperate to find some answers. That experience she had was clearly genuine, though I don't pretend to understand it."

"The others may be skeptical," Yael noted.

"But not Joanna," he said. "She's been affected quite deeply. Seems to have softened considerably since we got here. Not such a hard-nosed rationalist."

"What do you make of her dream?"

"I think it was more than a dream," Michael said. "Reminds me of the experience Paul had on the road to Damascus. I believe that was a very real light he saw. A real voice he heard, an actual conversation with Jesus—who had already ascended into heaven. That wasn't any dream."

"And you think Joanna experienced something similar?" Yael asked.

"Wouldn't be surprised."

"But what's the meaning?" Yael asked.

"Clearly, God is involved. And somehow, we really are dealing with a 'star'—perhaps the very same Star seen by the Magi. Finally, I feel affirmed that Joanna was told by that bright figure to continue to 'listen.' Since I'm the only one talking now, that has to mean I'm saying something worthwhile."

Yael looked a little nervous. "I'd suggest that you hold off mentioning any of these conclusions to the others—at least at this point."

"Of course," he said. "Dudley and Skiddy would freak out. Probably Dan too. The possibilities have to unfold gradually for them. They have to come to an understanding of that strange light themselves. And besides, I really don't know for sure what it's all about. I could be completely wrong."

"But you think we're making progress?"

"No doubt about it."

"I'm so proud of you," she said.

"I just have to keep reminding myself that God is running this show, not Michael James. That keeps me calm when the attacks come."

She moved closer to him and put her arms around his neck. "I've been desperate to be alone with you," she said softly, gazing steadily into his eyes. "I want this business to end as soon as you do. I'm ready to come in out of the cold—as they say about us spies. I want to marry you, and settle down in front of a fireplace. And have a child or two, just to keep us laughing."

They kissed and then pulled away, each looking quietly into the other's eyes. What they failed to see was Joanna Hill, who was standing dumbstruck at the open headquarters door.

✦ FOURTEEN

J OANNA was seated on the edge of her cot, shaking and rocking back and forth when Dan found her.

"What's wrong?" he cried, running over to her. "Are you sick?"

Tears were running down her face, and she was sobbing.

"What on earth is the matter?" he asked again.

She shook her head silently. For one of the few times in her life, Joanna was completely confused, unsure what to say or do. She also felt totally alone.

She knew she had experienced a powerful encounter with something or Someone beyond herself. She sensed she had been given a glimpse at a world beyond this world—a startling experience for someone who had always assumed that all reality could be explained by the principles of natural science.

But now her fundamental assumptions were crumbling. She had no idea about how to understand or interpret her experience with the figure and the light—and she was at a loss about where to turn for answers.

To make matters worse, the only person she thought might have been able to help her, Michael James, was apparently carrying on a secret love affair with their Israeli project manager. Was this any way for a prospective spiritual guide to behave?

Joanna's childhood as a member of an obedient, observing Catholic family had given her the impression that priests and serious Bible teachers were celibate—or at least discreet. How could she expect Michael to be the main source of insight into all the confusing events going on around her?

To upset matters even more, she suspected that Yael was more than just their team's formal contact with the Israeli government. Suspicious and nosy by nature, Joanna had looked over the sabra's shoulder several times when she was working on her computer screen. Also, she had slipped into Yael's office once or twice when the office was empty and had surveyed the Israeli's equipment.

Joanna had done enough work with the American government, including assisting with several top secret projects, to know sophisticated military communications gear and encryption devices and software when she saw them. Up to this point, she had said nothing about her discoveries, mainly because she wasn't sure what they meant.

For all I know, I'm just being paranoid, she had decided.

But Yael's connection with Michael James was muddying the waters. Although she had hoped to discuss her experience with the shining figure and the strange light in private with him, she suspected now that there was considerably more to his role here than met the eye.

Joanna needed to talk to someone. That was clear. And despite his flippant and negative attitude toward the strange light, Dan seemed the only reasonable possibility.

"I want to mention a few things to you, so that maybe you can help me get some perspective," she began. "But you *must promise me* you'll keep this just between us for now. Okay? What I'm about to say must be kept strictly confidential because there may be nothing to it. We could hurt people, alienate them, really poison the atmosphere around here even more if we act too hastily. Will you promise?"

"Sure, sure," Dan said. "Now what's the matter? Did somebody try to attack you? If one of those guards . . ."

"No, no, it's nothing like that. It's just some things I've noticed in the last couple of days. I want you to help me sort through them."

Then she told Dan about the communications equipment she had seen in Yael's office. She also described the passionate embrace between the sabra and Michael James, which she had witnessed less than an hour before.

Dan dismissed the communications gear as something you'd expect an Israeli government person in the field to have. But he smiled slyly as she finished describing the romantic incident.

"Well, well, a hidden side to the good Christian, Professor James!" he said. "So the two of them have a little something going on the side!"

"That's not the point!" Joanna said with a flash of anger.

She wondered if she should even continue. *He's totally insensitive. But who else can I talk to over here?* So against her better judgment, she forged ahead.

"Look, I'm upset because I was starting to trust him," she said. "Can you at least understand that? But now I don't know where he's coming from. I thought he was a reasonably objective scholar—that he had his mind on that light."

"But now you have doubts," Dan interjected, feeling more than a little satisfaction with this development.

"Yes," Joanna said. "Wouldn't anyone? I mean, what's going on with him? What are his connections with the Israeli government? Is this just a secret love affair, or are the two of them working together in some way?"

Dan pondered her words, realizing that she was raising issues that had never entered his mind. Suddenly, he felt very naive. He realized that subplots upon subplots could be going on right under his nose, and he would be completely ignorant of them.

"Maybe we should mention this to Skiddy," he suggested.

"Absolutely not!" she hissed, tears of frustration coming into her eyes. "Are you completely dependent on him? Skiddy and Dudley are totally hostile to Michael. And they're totally closed to any nontraditional interpretations of that light. They'd immediately use what I've told you against him. For all we know, Michael may be on precisely the right track to figure this thing out. Certainly, Geoffrey seems to be responding positively to his approach—and I respect his scientific credentials as much as anyone's on this team."

Reluctantly, Dan agreed to keep Skiddy in the dark about these new revelations, at least for the time being. "Okay, I'll keep quiet—is that okay?" he asked, hoping she was done with her crying. "Does that make you feel better?"

"Not entirely," she replied, realizing that as usual, she had to be extremely explicit in trying to help her husband understand her feelings. It wasn't that he was stupid. He just seemed incapable of comprehending her emotional responses without considerable help. He always wanted to fix things, like emotions, that couldn't be repaired with a toolbox.

"You see," Joanna continued, "I simply have to find some way to figure out the meaning of the experience I had with that bright figure—and I thought Michael, with his religious background, might help. The whole thing has been very upsetting to me. Because I know, beyond any doubt, that what I saw was highly unusual."

Then she looked him in the eye. "Listen. You're the religion expert. You tell me. Are there any precedents for this sort of thing in spiritual literature? Could I have seen an angel? Could it have been God Himself? Do you believe there are such things as supernatural visitations, or even miracles?"

Her questions threw him off guard. Although it was true that he was a religion scholar, he had consistently kept his academic disciplines at arm's length from his inner life, for what he felt were very good reasons. Dan had always assumed that if you got too involved in a particular philosophy or theology—if you started to believe too strongly—you might become sectarian and lose your detachment. It was okay to study others who became immersed in mysticism, or social and moral movements. But scholars and intellectuals needed to stand apart so they could observe and analyze more effectively.

Still, somewhere down deep he wasn't particularly satisfied. After studying the great mystics and religious thinkers of the past, he couldn't help but wonder if maybe he was missing something by sitting perennially on the sidelines. Now, Joanna was really putting him on the spot.

Finally, because he didn't have any good answers for her questions, he decided it was best to try to get her to drop the subject. "I think that experience of yours was just a vivid dream," he said. "All in your head."

"But I was standing barefoot out near the perimeter fence when it was over!"

"So you sleepwalked."

"I never sleepwalk."

"There's always a first time."

"And I saw the light just before it returned. And I was able to describe the changes exactly as they looked when it reappeared for the rest of you."

"The light could have returned for a short time while you were outside," Dan insisted. "You might have seen it when you were half awake. Then it could have disappeared again."

The explanation was too pat to convince Joanna—and she wasn't willing to let him off so easily. "So you're saying that there's no chance it could have been a supernatural encounter? There's no possibility at all that God could have been involved?" Now she was getting angry. "By the way, Dan, do you even believe in God?"

"I don't know what I believe," he said defensively.

"Well, that's weird," she said sarcastically. "A religion prof who doesn't believe in God. Reassuring."

"Why are you always on the attack with me?" he asked, not quite aware of what he'd said to offend her. "You've always said you didn't believe. Why should it bother you if I have doubts? What's with you—getting religion all of a sudden?"

He half expected an explosion in response, but she seemed worn out, tired of the discussion. "Actually, I'm not so sure anymore," she replied. "I just thought you might be able to help."

"Look, I guess I think anything's possible," he said finally, relenting a little. "But I'd need to see more to be convinced that anything supernatural was involved."

"You'd insist on shaking hands with the shining figure yourself, I suppose. And maybe having a formal report signed by God."

He smiled. "That would help. But I might still have as many questions as you do."

After sitting silently for a moment, she asked, "So what do you think about Yael?"

"She still looks pretty good to me."

"Come on! You know what I mean. What do you think her role here really is?"

"I have no idea," he said. "But I wouldn't be surprised if she had all sorts of secret missions and assignments that we know nothing about."

Dan turned the thought over in his mind and then continued, "For all we know, she could be a spy stationed here to monitor our every movement. In fact, I think that's probably more likely than not. After all, if you were running the Israeli government, wouldn't you want to know exactly what a bunch of foreign scientists were doing on your soil? And wouldn't you be particularly concerned if they were studying some weird object hanging ominously over your country? I'll bet they have some agent planted with every research group in the country right now."

"So what do you think Michael's role is in all this?" Joanna asked. "After all, if she's a spy, it wouldn't be very professional to get romantically involved with one of the guys conducting the investigation."

"Not unless she's James Bond's twin sister."

"That doesn't happen in the real world. So what do you think about Michael?" Joanna asked again.

"I think your imagination's running away with you," Dan said, standing up. "Despite my disagreements with him, I don't think Michael's an Israeli spy. That just doesn't add up. Why would the Israelis assign some guy to lead Bible studies on the Star of Bethlehem when, for all they know, that weird lightbulb overhead may explode any minute?"

But his attempt at an explanation didn't satisfy her. "She apparently knew him before we started this investigation," Joanna said. "You remember they didn't have to be introduced when we first arrived here? They obviously had met before."

"No, as a matter of fact, I don't remember that. But I wouldn't read too much into that kiss. That's their business. All I know is I get irritated by James and his Star speculations—and I'd prefer that we drop the Bible study."

"Because you feel a responsibility to back Skiddy up?" Joanna said, a cynical tone creeping into her voice.

"That's part of it," Dan replied defensively. "After all, he was nice enough to include us in this project, and I think we need to support him."

"But there's more to this thing than a summer's worth of grant money," Joanna said, rising and starting to get ready to leave for their next discussion session. "Loyalty to Skiddy is fine. So is a well-paid summer project. But the really important thing is that we can't compromise our investigation. Some really strange and disturbing things are going on up there in the sky. Not to mention down here on earth. We might be on the verge of witnessing events that could totally change our future. So I wouldn't be too concerned about Skiddy."

As Dan and Joanna left their quarters and headed toward the mess area where they would be having brunch, an added dose of their usual unresolved tension separated them. So they said little.

Joanna in particular retreated into her own thoughts. Though a rational scientist who had initially looked to her instruments to provide a quick solution, she now found herself contemplating non-scientific explanations. She had trouble believing that her husband—the airy-headed religion scholar—was still depending on science to give them answers.

This really is an Alice-in-Wonderland world, she thought. *Without warning, things go from right side up to upside down.*

She had no idea just how topsy-turvy the world she had entered was actually becoming.

 # FIFTEEN

I N that brief but vulnerable moment, Yael Sharon and Michael James had eyes only for each other. Their guard was down, and their well-honed professional wariness returned a split second too late. So they missed seeing Professor Joanna Hill hurrying away from the headquarters door.

When they looked up, no one was there. It was only then that they thought to check very carefully to be certain that they were alone. Then, comforted by a false sense of security, they settled down on chairs in Yael's office behind a closed door. Yael even brought up a CD of traditional Israeli music on the audio player in her computer and adjusted the volume to cover their conversation. With these precautions in place, they began to talk quickly and intensely in the softest of tones, barely above a whisper.

"You're in touch with your Mossad control?" Michael asked.

"Yes," she replied. "But we must refer to him indirectly, in case we should ever be overheard. Call him my 'colleague.' And never, ever mention Mossad. Remember, you're not supposed to know a thing about my Israeli intelligence connections."

"We're always careful."

"I know. But this time, security and secrecy are even more essential than usual. We have reason to believe that outsiders are trying to eavesdrop on us. Saboteurs may even be on this very compound."

Michael appeared startled. "You mean we may have a mole on board our team—an actual spy?"

"Perhaps. All your team members have been checked thoroughly by our security people, both here and in the States, and we've turned up nothing so far. But rumors continue to circulate among our informants, so one can't be too careful. This investigation could be of supreme importance to Israel—not to mention to our ultimate objective."

"Yes, the ultimate objective," Michael said.

"We mustn't talk in those terms," Yael reminded him. "The Mossad would arrest me immediately if they knew. Let's refer to our mission in some other way—perhaps as the 'administrative matter.'"

"Yes, 'administrative matter' will do. Do you think the Mossad suspects your true identity?"

"No. But if they knew I was a Jewish Christian, they'd go berserk. Might assassinate me on the spot and ask questions later. As you know, Jewish believers are outcasts over here. Our kind are barely tolerated. And for someone in my profession, the designation could be an automatic death sentence. Especially if they learn I've in effect been operating as a double agent."

"You'd better stay alive," Michael replied, his voice edged with new concern. "I couldn't stand to lose you."

"The ironic thing is, my faith could ultimately work in Israel's favor. But I don't relish the thought of trying to convince them of that with a cocked automatic in my face."

"Have you been limiting your contacts with other believers?"

"I never talk to other Christians here in this country—at least, not unless I'm directed to by Tel Aviv," she replied. "It's not easy. The only believers I seem to have any extended conversations with are you and Peter. And that's allowed only because the Mossad wants to cultivate and use Panoplia International to strengthen Israel's connections with American evangelicals."

"So your assignment remains the same?"

She nodded. "Yes. I watch you and Panoplia closely, and feed you our propaganda to be sure you stay on Israel's side. Then I report back regularly to the Mossad on your activities and movements."

Michael nodded with a sardonic smile. "You're our fox in the chicken coop."

It was meant as a joke. But both realized that if the words reached the wrong ears, the attempt at humor could be deadly. They lapsed into silence, with Yael's responsibilities weighing heavily on their

minds. Michael worried frequently about her complex and potentially explosive undercover work. The Mossad was bad enough. But
she would be flirting with disaster if they ever found out she was a
double agent—even if the "other side" was a pro-Israel American
organization like Panoplia.

As the main visionary and financial resource behind Panoplia
International, Peter Van Campe had developed the shadowy
Chicago foundation into one of the most extensive international reli-
gious intelligence operations in history.

Michael, who had advised Peter almost since Panoplia's incep-
tion, recalled the group's secret mission statement—a four-point
"prime directive" that was on paper in only one location, a locked
vault in Chicago. The words had become branded into his memory
long ago:

Our primary mission: to spread the gospel into those parts of the
world that are hostile to Christianity—especially where the faith
has been outlawed or restricted—and to protect or rescue believers
who are persecuted or in harm's way.

Our secondary mission: to gather intelligence to further our primary mission and to provide early warning of events that may signal the second coming of Christ.

Our moral imperative: to operate always in a manner that is consistent with the Bible and the direction of God's Spirit.

Our modus operandi: to be aggressive—and if necessary, unconventional—in employing every moral means at hand to accomplish
our primary and secondary missions. Because of the potential dangers to innocent Christians and our own operatives, we resolve to
use appropriate stealth, concealment, and other covert tactics to
ensure the secrecy and safety of our activities.

As a young Wheaton professor with a conservative Bible
scholar's intellectual caution—but a secret swashbuckler's thirst
for high-risk action—Michael had helped Peter formulate the
mission statement years before. He had studied it and meditated
on it so often that the words were now second nature.

But as they were drafting the document, he had expressed certain qualms. "What we're talking about seems almost too sneaky or underhanded to be acceptable for a Christian," he argued—and Peter agreed that this was a basic difficulty they had to resolve.

However, as they had researched and then drafted the "four Ms," as they now called the affirmation, they had found there were plenty of precedents. For one thing, the Bible was filled with legitimate secret operations.

Michael could still recall one rapid-fire brainstorming interchange, during which he and Peter had rattled off biblical illustrations to support their case for deception and undercover methods while doing God's work:

Peter: "Gideon's surprise guerrilla attack on the Midianites!"

Michael: "Moses' assignment to Joshua, Caleb, and others to spy on the promised land."

Peter: "Joshua's spies—who plotted with the prostitute Rahab in Jericho!"

Michael: "David's secret observations of King Saul."

Peter: "Jesus' commands that His disciples and others keep quiet about His identity or activities."

Michael: "That included keeping their mouths shut about the Transfiguration!"

Peter: "Paul—a stealthy guy on occasion."

Michael: "When?"

Peter: "Sneaking out of Damascus when his life was threatened—remember, he was lowered through the city wall in a big basket."

Michael: "And receiving intelligence from his nephew about the assassination plot when he was imprisoned at Jerusalem. That saved his life!"

The two men had also discussed the many semisecret evangelistic forays and missions of mercy of their own day, including Bible-smuggling operations into the old Iron Curtain countries. In addition, there were plenty of instances of low-profile preaching and teaching missions in places where Christian missionaries had been officially outlawed—such as Islamic cultures in the Middle East and Africa, as well as hostile Communist regimes in the Far East.

And these cases were just the beginning. Michael couldn't count the number of times when, as a member of his church's mission committee, he had received bulletins or notices describing aspects of these operations. Typically, the communiqués warned: *"Confidential! Do Not Post!"*

"Helloooo!" Yael's voice echoed somewhere in his consciousness, bringing him back to the present. "Are you still with me—or off somewhere else?"

"Yeah, I was just thinking about Peter—and how incredibly far-flung our operations are now," he replied.

"Don't get distracted," she cautioned, always acutely aware of the need for discipline as a professional spy. "What's going on right here may well be the biggest thing we've ever encountered. So we have to keep focused. There's also a practical consideration. Staying alert has kept me alive more than once. Our enemies are all about. We can't trust anyone—not the other team members, not my Mossad contacts, no one."

Even though he was well aware of the dangers, Michael couldn't help himself—he loved the cloak-and-dagger stuff.

"If they only knew," he said, lowering his voice confidentially.

"Let's pray they never find out."

Seeing the anxiety in Yael's face, Michael remembered that for her especially, this was no game. Her life might hang in the balance.

He covered her hand with his. "I'd never forgive myself if something happened to you."

Their eyes met. She squeezed his hand, leaned over, and kissed him softly. "I love you," she replied. "But I know the risks. And I've made my own decisions every step of the way. I know I'm first and foremost a citizen of the kingdom of God—and second, a citizen of Israel. But our relationship must remain on hold—at least for now, until this present matter is resolved."

Her words cut Michael to the quick, but he knew she was right. And he was fully aware of how incredibly far she had come since she had first caught his eye in the Chicago offices of Panoplia almost four years before.

✦ SIXTEEN

Yael Sharon's life had taken an entirely new and extremely tangled turn after she was assigned by the Mossad to infiltrate Panoplia International in Chicago. Her assignment: Take as long as you need to check out the organization and assess the group's potential impact on Israel. If possible, become part of their organization so that you can watch them from the inside.

"We don't like the idea that they may be proselytizing among our people," her control had said. "Also, they are more shadowy in their operations than most mission organizations. We don't quite know what they're about. But we have to balance those negatives against their apparent support of Israel over the Arabs. We want you to determine the pros and cons of their operations—and tell us what's really going on with them."

The assignment was a little out of Yael's line. She was basically irreligious, though she had been trained in a number of biblical languages, including Old Testament Hebrew, Aramaic, and even a little New Testament Greek. Politics and patriotism defined her personal spiritual center, as she affirmed a strong Zionist commitment that had been passed on to her by her mother. Her father had died in battle during the Six-Day War in 1967, and her mother, who had been pregnant at the time with Yael, had never let her daughter forget that heritage, not until the day she had died of cancer just five years before.

Of course, as for many other Israelis, the Bible was always a presence in her life. Experience on several archaeological digs had made her realize that some hard, scientific evidence was available to support parts of the Hebrew Scriptures. But at heart, Yael remained an agnostic who was highly suspicious of anything that smacked of serious faith, especially fundamentalism.

At the very outset of her new assignment, Yael became concerned when she noted that the operative word in Van Campe's organization, *panoplia,* was a Greek term meaning "full armor."

"Ominous-sounding name for a group that's supposed to be spreading a message of love and compassion," she remarked cynically to one of her Mossad contacts.

She readily acknowledged that she fully expected to find the group was up to no good. Maybe a CIA front. Or a bunch of arms dealers. Or right-wing, anti-Semitic terrorists. They seemed far too secretive for an ordinary missionary operation. So before she traveled to Chicago to evaluate the group firsthand, she resolved to prepare even more thoroughly than she usually did for a normal assignment.

First and foremost, she realized that she needed to figure out what conservative American Christianity was all about. It would be essential to familiarize herself with contemporary evangelical movements and theological views so she would have some basis for comparison as she evaluated Panoplia.

During this period of preparation, Yael learned that at least one first impression she had of the group had been wrong. It turned out that *panoplia* was indeed a Greek term, but one used by the apostle Paul in his letter to the church at Ephesus. It referred to the "full armor of God," which the believer was instructed to put on as protection against evil.

Despite this explanation, she remained suspicious of the group's motives and told Israeli intelligence about her continuing concerns. So they proceeded with the original game plan.

First, the Mossad gave her a well-documented background with connections in Canada and even a Canadian college degree, which could be confirmed at the school's alumni office. But she retained her real name and her Israeli passport.

"These Chicago people will like the idea that you have an Israeli background and know a lot of languages," one of her intelligence colleagues told her. "It'll make you more attractive when you apply for a job. But you can't stay Jewish. You'll have to become a Christian," he said with a wink.

So after she moved to Chicago, Yael faked a conversion experience in a local independent Bible church. Then she engineered an opportunity to give her "testimony" as a newly minted "Jewish Christian" or "Messianic Jew" to a couple of Panoplia staff members. With her new identity and credentials, she had little trouble securing a low-level position with the mission organization.

Gradually, with her academic background, language abilities, and social skills, Yael moved up in the organization until finally, she got her dream job—at least from the Mossad's point of view. She was offered a position as one of four people in Peter Van Campe's executive office, where she had access to many of the organization's key files.

But during those first months in Chicago, as she was becoming involved in Panoplia and feeding preliminary information to the Mossad, Yael also started to wrestle with deep inner questions and doubts. Even though she wasn't religious herself, she found she increasingly harbored certain qualms about hoodwinking people who seemed to be perfectly nice Christians and no apparent threat to her government. Also, exposure to the spiritually committed staff at Panoplia was causing the cynical, skeptical spy to consider more seriously some of the New Testament claims of Christ. She actually allowed herself to toy with the possibility that Jesus might have been the Messiah whom her people had awaited for so long.

Finally, one night in her bedroom, lights seemed to go on in her mind as she read silently the prophetic account of the "suffering servant" in the fifty-third chapter of Isaiah.

". . . our griefs He Himself bore . . . our sorrows He carried . . . He was pierced through for our transgressions . . . crushed for our iniquities . . . by His scourging we are healed. All of us like sheep have gone astray . . . But the LORD has caused the iniquity of us all to fall on Him . . ."

"This *does* sound a lot like Jesus Christ," she said out loud.

Then some quick thumbing through cross-references in the New Testament revealed that the Hebrew prophet's words were indeed quoted or alluded to in many parts of the Gospels and Epistles.

She caught her breath as she realized the implications of her thoughts.

What might this mean for my friends and family? I know the answer. And the Mossad? I don't want to think about it!

Yet somehow, Yael couldn't put on the brakes. Finally, she realized that she had only one option—go with the flow that was carrying her into unknown waters. In a brief moment of great inner anguish, followed by a sustained sense of ineffable peace, her feigned conversion became a genuine rebirth.

As part of this transforming revelation, she also suddenly understood that Panoplia's international mission was far different from that of the Mossad. She would have to make difficult personal decisions about her role as a spy.

What do I do now?

What's my responsibility to Israel?

Should I resign from the Mossad?

Should I reveal my real identity to other Christian believers?

Finally, she understood that at the bottom of all these concerns lay one fundamental question: *Where does my real allegiance lie?*

For many days, Yael was in spiritual and emotional agony every waking moment. She thought back with guilt and fear on the life she had chosen as a spy. Fortunately, she had never been ordered to kill an enemy. But she knew she might be given that sort of assignment any day because she had been trained in many of the deadly martial arts.

She also knew that, in a way, it was beside the point to dwell on the fact that she had never pulled the trigger or slipped the blade between an enemy's ribs. Even though she regularly tried to block out her darkest memories, when she was lying in bed at night, alone with her thoughts, she knew only too well that her work had paved the way for others to kill.

Finally, she decided she had no choice but to take a major risk and break Mossad protocols. With great trepidation, she resolved to reveal her true identity to Peter Van Campe, who was not only her boss at Panoplia, but was also becoming her spiritual mentor.

SEVENTEEN

P E T E R Van Campe always dressed in handmade or top-of-the-line designer clothing. It was his major weakness.

Sometimes, he felt a slight pang of guilt when he thought about the simple attire of his missionaries, who were stationed at far-flung posts around the globe. Or when he reflected on the poor that his organization was ministering to in Third and Fourth World countries—families who could have lived for years on what he had paid for his Rolex or Guccis.

Peter rationalized that he needed to maintain a prosperous "power look" to enhance his ability to raise the money that would help those missionaries and peasants. More than once, he'd told his wife that his impressive mane of steel-gray hair, his square executive's jaw, and his fit, fifty-year-old frame needed an extra touch.

"Clothes do make the man" was a cliché he had used more than once with her.

She put up with his extravagant tastes good-naturedly, but she usually let him know she was never quite convinced by his attempts to justify this or that expenditure. And down deep, in his heart of hearts, Peter knew he was rationalizing. He could make all the excuses he liked, but he wasn't fooling himself. He knew he had a weakness for fine, expensive suits, shirts, and shoes, Armani and Gucci being the preferred brands.

Someday, I'll give all this up, he thought that morning as he sat behind his desk, contemplating his new linen shirt and silk tie. *But not now. Not today.*

"Yael Sharon is here, Mr. Van Campe," his executive secretary said over the intercom. "Can you see her for a few moments now?"

He looked at his Rolex. Yael wasn't scheduled to see him for another hour. "I'm supposed to talk about that Italian matter with her later this morning," he said.

"She says this is about something else. Can you see her?"

He hesitated. *Full day. Inconvenient. Well, it must be important.* "Sure, sure, send her on in."

Peter noticed that Yael was shaking when she walked into his office for the unscheduled appointment. But her nervousness became the least of his worries when she began the meeting by swearing him to absolute secrecy.

"On your faith in Christ and the Bible, you must promise me that nothing I'm about to tell you will go beyond this room. If word of this gets out, both our lives will be in danger. *Extreme* danger. I almost certainly will die or spend the rest of my life in prison."

Peter's mouth sagged open, and for a moment he was speechless. Death and prison weren't quite what he had on his agenda this particular morning.

But he recovered and assured her, "Of course. Confidential. Totally confidential. Nothing goes beyond these walls. I promise." He raised his right hand, as though taking an oath. "Now, what's up?"

"First of all, I'm not who you think I am."

The statement seemed to disconcert Peter further, as he bumped his coffee and sloshed part of it on his desk. *Not starting out well,* she thought. But feeling that now she had no choice, Yael took a deep breath and plunged ahead.

"I work for Israeli intelligence. I can't tell you anything about my work, but I need your advice because I'm not comfortable about many of my duties. So I think maybe I should quit. But I want you to advise me about how to find God's will in this."

She went on to summarize her spiritual journey, the genuine spiritual rebirth she had experienced, and her inner struggle to find the right course of action now that she had become a believer.

For the second time that morning, Peter found himself speechless. He had come to trust and respect this young woman as one of his executive assistants. But now she was sitting in front of him, trying so hard to control her emotions, and yet confessing that she was, in effect, Judas redux. She had insinuated herself into his inner circle and had learned many of Panoplia's secrets—and apparently had passed some of them on to the Mossad. But now, unbelievably, she was confessing her misdeeds and asking for his help.

Thought after anxious thought tumbled through his mind:

What does she know about us? Everything. She's one of my top assistants!

Did I suspect her? Not at all.

Did I check her background thoroughly enough? Obviously not.

What has she told the Mossad? I have no idea—but I shudder to think.

Have any of our workers abroad been placed in danger? I must find out—fast!

Swallowing hard, he tried to appear as calm as he could, but it wasn't easy. He was in total inner turmoil. Finally, Peter managed to bring himself under control enough to begin to ascertain from Yael exactly how much she had disclosed to the Mossad about Panoplia and its sensitive overseas work.

Her initial explanations didn't satisfy him at all. She said she had to avoid giving him too many specifics, to protect both of them—and that sort of response wasn't designed to generate confidence in a chief executive who needed to feel in control. Also, he still didn't entirely trust her. Things were moving too quickly for him to make a reasonable judgment at this point.

Is this another trick? Is she "confessing" to me so that I'll disclose even more information—which she can then pass on to her fellow spies in Tel Aviv?

Peter was absolutely adamant about protecting his overseas workers from further exposure to danger. But after continuing to question the Israeli for more than an hour, he finally decided that she could be telling the truth. Also, he was relieved when she assured him that so far, she had passed on only information that was relatively innocuous or publicly known.

"I should also tell you that I haven't passed on the names of any of your operatives in the Islamic or Communist nations," she said.

He nodded calmly and greeted this news with an impassive expression. But it took a lot of control. Inside, he was releasing the greatest sigh of relief of his life. *Thank You, Lord, thank You, thank You!*

After mulling over her disclosures for a few moments, Peter finally said that for the time being, he would allow Yael to retain her title as his executive assistant. But he would have to cut off her access to the organization's most sensitive files and operations.

"For now, this arrangement will protect both you and us," he explained. "There will be no outward change in your responsibilities from the Mossad's perspective. But at the same time, we won't be putting ourselves at further risk."

She agreed with this assessment and his short-term solution. "But that still leaves me with my ultimate decision," she said. "What should I do about the Mossad?"

"You asked about finding God's will. Well, I think God is the only One who can answer your question. I know I can't."

They spent a few minutes discussing how prayer and meditation might help her move toward a solution to her problems. But even though Yael seemed to hang on his every word, Peter felt he had entered some strange, surreal new world where every concept and fact was fluid and inconstant, and nothing was what it seemed.

Are You still solid, God? I can still rely on You, can't I—even if everything else is in flux?

"As you begin to meditate on your decision, I want to mention an idea that's been nagging away at me in the last few minutes," Peter finally said. So many conflicting thoughts were whirling around in his mind, he was reluctant to bring up anything that he hadn't thought through thoroughly. But somehow, he sensed that the time was right to put a tentative proposal on the table.

"I'm not quite sure how I feel about this," he continued. "But it's something to consider as you're trying to make your decision. In your present position, you could be a very valuable contact for us. Of course, if you do decide to help us and also stay with the Mossad, the danger to you would escalate significantly."

He paused and tapped his fingers on his desk for a moment before proceeding. "I only raise this possibility because here at Panoplia, we're in the business of courting danger. We have plenty of missionaries out in the field who have been killed or are languishing in prison. Many more could sacrifice their lives today or tomorrow. So you would be taking a big personal risk. But you'd also become part of a team that believes in trusting God totally as they operate daily in harm's way."

He stopped again and looked her in the eye: "In the end, though, the choice is entirely up to you, as you feel God directing you."

In her profession, Yael had always been taught to think several steps ahead of her current situation. That was the way you lived a nice long life in the spy business. But for some reason, Peter's suggestion hadn't crossed her mind.

A double agent. In effect, I'd be a double agent.

As Yael turned the idea over in her mind in the hours after she left Peter, she became intrigued. Then excited. After all, any way you cut it, she was already at odds with the Mossad. They'd go ballistic if they found out about her conversion and disclosures to Peter. And she could kiss life good-bye if they learned she was a double agent. But you had to trust somebody sometime. So long as Peter could keep a secret, she'd probably be okay.

Besides, I didn't get into this business because I wanted to play it safe. And what better way to serve the needs of her new faith than to employ the undercover and intelligence-gathering skills that she knew so well?

It took a full two days of reflection. But finally, Yael contacted Peter and said she was ready to explore—just explore—the possibility of operating as a double agent for Panoplia. "But only under certain ground rules," she cautioned.

The most important was that no more than two people besides herself could know about the arrangement. Obviously, one would be Peter. In addition, there could be one other, who would be her field contact. But she insisted on the right to interview and choose that person before he—or she—was apprised of her real identity.

The only candidate Peter even considered for this sensitive and potentially dangerous role was Michael James, who had been instrumental in helping Peter start and build Panoplia. But tragedy had struck and prostrated him emotionally a year before, when his young wife, pregnant with their first child, had been killed by a drunk driver.

Michael had tried, rather unsuccessfully, to bury his grief in his teaching responsibilities at Wheaton and his overseas work with

Panoplia. But he rarely smiled anymore and seemed to have settled into a permanent state of mild depression.

As Peter thought further about it, Michael seemed the perfect fit for this assignment. He was looking to recapture the meaning of his faith. Also, like Yael, he came without messy personal encumbrances. No spouse or children . . . no other family responsibilities that would prevent him from working closely with a young single woman on a dangerous long-term assignment . . . nothing that could keep him from traveling abroad on a moment's notice.

So Peter suggested Michael as Yael's field control.

She immediately proceeded to research his background and got to know him on an informal basis. Within a month, she approved Peter's choice. Shortly afterward, the assignment was offered to Michael and he accepted.

Over the next two years, Yael and Michael developed into one of the most effective Panoplia teams. But gradually, they also became much more to each other. First, the best of friends. Then soul mates. Finally, they fell in love.

Before this incident involving the strange glow in the sky, Yael and Michael had been talking seriously about getting married. But with the advent of the light, their lives became unimaginably complicated, even for an undercover evangelical operative and an Israeli double agent. For one thing, Peter decided that it was essential for Yael to be on the Harvard research team.

"But the Harvard people mustn't know you work for us," he cautioned. "And somehow you also have to convince the Mossad that it's a good idea for you to be assigned over there. If they get nervous about your returning to Israel, they might pull the plug and then we'd lose you entirely."

"Don't worry about the Mossad," she said. "They trust me implicitly. I'll just tell them I'm their best ticket to learn more about Panoplia, *and* to solve the mystery of that light."

She stopped and smiled. "And that's really true, isn't it? I am their best ticket!"

Peter thought a moment and nodded his agreement. "The Harvard bunch won't be a problem either. So long as they get the grant money, they won't ask any questions. And they'll never see you here, as part of our operation, because they won't have any reason to come to Chicago. I'll just tell them that we've approved the presence of an Israeli woman with government connections. One who'll grease the skids for them when they arrive on site in Galilee. They'll be overjoyed."

But even though the master strategy had worked to near perfection, all the components remained in delicate balance. They couldn't afford any distractions. Romance was out. Personal matters had to be put on hold until the matter of the mysterious light was resolved—as much as Michael might hope or desire otherwise.

So as he sat there with her in her office, he pushed his emotions aside, cleared his throat, and returned to business. "Now tell me," he pressed her. "Exactly what precautions are you taking to maintain secrecy?"

"I have my people sweep this room and my living quarters for bugs every day," Yael said. "Also, we have access to global satellite surveillance. And we run periodic security sweeps of the surrounding countryside, just to be sure no one is camping out there, listening to us with a parabolic microphone."

"No security measures are ever perfect," he said. "There's always a way to break them."

"Yes, but maybe by the time someone figures out what I'm all about, our mission will be accomplished."

"We can hope . . ." Michael began.

". . . and pray," Yael finished, echoing his deepest thought.

# EIGHTEEN

D UDLEY Dunster, who was late for the next session, was shaking with rage as he entered the headquarters building.

"Look at this! Just look at this!" he screamed, almost in tears.

Everyone crowded around the paper that he was waving about—an e-mail printout that contained the lead story that day from the front page of the *New York Times*.

**BAFFLED SCIENTISTS
TURN TO STAR OF BETHLEHEM
Harvard Team Working in Israel
Switches from Science to Theology**

"My worst nightmare!" Dudley ranted. "Absolutely, my worst nightmare! Who leaked this? Who's responsible for this?"

By now, Skiddy, who was reading the story as though his life depended on it, was shaking like a leaf on a blustery fall day in Harvard Yard. His face was as pale as Dudley's was red. "I don't believe it," he seethed. "Everybody sit down. Right now!"

The members of the team found seats, though not as quickly as Skiddy would have liked. He actually began to point them into their chairs, as though they were a first-grade class.

"This is completely irresponsible!" he hissed. "Completely unethical! Now I want to know—who did this?"

He looked slowly and accusingly around the room from face to face, but no one confessed. The more aggressively he jutted his sharp nose and chin in their faces, the steadier their gazes seemed to become. The lack of any response made him even angrier.

"You might as well tell me now!" he shouted. "I'll find out! I promise you, I'll find out. I have ways. I have sources."

"Perhaps no one from this group talked to the paper," Geoffrey finally offered quietly. "After all, what motive would any of us have?"

"The information in here is too detailed," Skiddy said. "The source had to be right here. Had to know what we were talking about."

"But we want this investigation to succeed as much as you do," Joanna said. "And we certainly don't want to look stupid in front of our colleagues or the public."

"That's understandable because you two are scientists," Skiddy said darkly, glancing at Joanna and Geoffrey. "But let's hear from the others. Dan, for instance."

Dan was stunned that Skiddy would suspect him.

"Are you serious?" Dan asked, spluttering as he searched his mind to piece together some defense. "I've been part of your past research projects—and I hope to participate in others in the future. Why would I shoot myself in the foot by trying to sabotage this one?"

As Skiddy contemplated Dan's response, Dudley intervened. "Dan's right. He wouldn't do something like this. What would he have to gain?"

Skiddy, seemingly mollified, turned his attention to Michael.

"That brings us to you, Professor James," the Harvard professor said sternly, using Michael's formal title just to make it clear how serious he considered this infraction. "Can you satisfy us that you're not the source of this leak?"

"I don't have to satisfy you, Skiddy," Michael retorted with such unexpected force that the Harvard man actually staggered back a step. "And I won't submit to any implied accusations or interrogation on this or any other matter. My participation in this project doesn't depend on you. I was asked to join the study by the foundation."

For once, Skiddy was speechless. He seemed well aware that he had overstepped his authority by challenging Michael on this issue.

Satisfied that he had made his point, Michael continued in a more conciliatory tone. "But to set your mind at ease, let me say this. I regard our work here as so important that I would probably be the last one in this room who would do anything to jeopardize it. As far as I'm concerned, what we're doing is confidential, at least until we come to some defensible conclusion about this light. Furthermore, I regard this *New York Times* article to be totally ill-timed. It's premature, by any measurement. So if you must have a culprit, please look elsewhere."

"Fine, fine," Skiddy responded, clearly wanting to change the subject as quickly as possible. "And I suppose there's no point in raising this issue with you, Yael. Unless you can think of some reason your government might want to disclose what we're doing."

Yael shook her head. "Certainly not. Israeli officials connected with scientific projects get involved with the press only when they have to. We definitely have no interest in premature publicity. That would just lead to undue speculation. Maybe even panic."

"Of course, of course," Skiddy said, obviously giving up on the idea of unmasking any press leak. "But we've all got to be careful to say nothing, absolutely nothing, to outsiders. Somebody has obviously found out what we're doing. As for damage control, I don't know what to suggest. I suppose we can expect a horde of reporters at our gate shortly."

"I was wondering what that was all about," Yael said with a distracted look out the window.

"What's that?" Skiddy asked.

"Several reporters tried to get onto the compound earlier," she said. "It must have been this story. They were turned away, but I'm sure we can expect more shortly. Let me notify the guards." As she hurried out the door, barking through her handheld radio, the others turned their attention back to Skiddy.

"Now, we have to decide where we go from here," he said.

"I can tell you exactly where we should go," Dudley said. "We should drop this Star thing like a hotcake. Issue an announcement that the *Times* story was all wrong, and get back to serious research. Then we might save our reputations."

"I don't see any problem continuing with Michael's checklist for a little longer," Geoffrey said, again surprising Dudley and Skiddy with his openness to this religious line of inquiry. "We're moving along rather quickly, and I'm reluctant to let a news story dictate our research plan. Besides, I'm particularly interested in the extradimensional point he has up there on the board. I'd insist on exploring that, regardless of whether we use his Star methodology."

"The longer we pursue this nonsense, the more vulnerable we become to the ridicule of our colleagues!" Dudley objected.

"What do you think, Joanna?" Skiddy asked, hoping that the attitudes of the group were shifting more in his direction.

"I don't know," she said tentatively. "This whole business is so strange and confusing."

"So, an abstention!" Dudley exclaimed exultantly.

As Yael reentered the room, Skiddy turned to her. "We're polling the team about the next step in our investigation," he said. "How do you stand?"

"I thought we'd already decided," she responded. "Michael hasn't finished his part yet."

"Yes, but the news story . . ."

"Let's stick with our plan. We've got to be disciplined."

"And I assume you still want to continue, Michael," Skiddy said to his Wheaton nemesis.

"I should be finished sooner rather than later—probably before my deadline at the end of today," he said. "And as Geoffrey said, we can segue from my last point into his wormholes and parallel universes and the like. So yes, I do prefer to continue with our plan."

"Well, that's three against three, and one not voting," Dudley said. "Unless there is a majority, I think we should shift to something else."

The room broke out into a loud argument until Yael finally called for quiet. "There's a message from the guard shack. Be quiet so I can hear what they're trying to tell me."

She listened for a few seconds as the room lapsed into an uneasy silence. Finally, she turned to face them, ready to relay the message. "It seems that we have a visitor at the front gate."

"More reporters?" Dudley asked fearfully.

"No. The man behind your grant. Peter Van Campe of Panoplia International."

NINETEEN

P E T E R Van Campe—wearing what looked like a hand-stitched bush jacket and ornate, specially made hiking boots—swept through the rough headquarters door, escorted by two of his aides and a compound guard. He looked more like visiting royalty than the head of an evangelical Christian foundation. Certainly his crisp, sartorial splendor set him completely apart from the other, rumpled occupants of the room. But as most of them now realized, Panoplia International wasn't just any religious foundation.

"These people have money growing on their money," Skiddy had confided to Dan and Dudley just before they had left for Israel. "As far as I can tell from my contacts, they are one of the five richest foundations in the United States, religious or otherwise."

As befits royalty, Skiddy saw to it that Van Campe had the most comfortable and prominent chair in the room, though that wasn't saying much, given the crude, folding-chair and metal-desk decor of the main headquarters office. The billionaire's two muscular aides, who Dan suspected doubled as bodyguards, declined an offer of folding chairs and positioned themselves so that they were standing against opposite walls. They seemed more intent on scanning the team members, the doorway, and the windows than on listening to their leader. As for the foundation director, he was obviously more concerned about the progress of the investigation than about the physical surroundings.

"Now, exactly what's going on around here?" Peter Van Campe asked, taking his seat, which happened to be the only one with a cushion. "I hopped on my jet and headed right over here when I first got word about that *New York Times* article."

Seeing a possible rebuke to Michael James in the making, Skiddy was quick with an answer. "Yes, well, we were quite upset about that too," Skiddy said solicitously. "And I've conducted a brief investigation to try to determine the source of the leak. But so far, we've come up with nothing. The Star thing was nothing but a sideline. An idea to help us break out of a rut—to think in new ways. Michael's idea, by the way."

Skiddy paused a moment to let the implied accusation sink in. "But I think it's clear we should drop that approach."

"No, I'm not suggesting you should drop that line of inquiry," Peter said. "In fact, it sounds intriguing. I was more concerned about publicizing your reports prematurely. You could sabotage your entire investigation if that happens, don't you think?"

"Yes, oh yes, definitely," Skiddy replied obsequiously.

"So where do we stand with the research?" Peter asked.

"Our scientific instruments register nothing," Skiddy said. "Weird. Really strange. Never seen anything like it. Right, Dudley . . . Geoffrey?"

"Unique situation," Dudley said, somewhat tongue-tied for once. "Unique."

"But fascinating," Geoffrey said in his most relaxed California style. "We certainly don't have any answers yet, but that doesn't mean they won't be coming—and perhaps sooner than we think. You must have heard—the look of the light has changed recently. So something is up."

Peter looked at Geoffrey intently. "And what exactly do you think may be up, Professor Gonzales?"

For once, Geoffrey seemed to become uncomfortable under the scrutiny. Something about Peter's stare was unsettling. "Uh, well, that's hard to say right now. But frankly, I suspect it's something extradimensional. Maybe even some intelligent beings from another universe. After all, if our instruments don't record anything, we must be dealing with something beyond normal perception."

"That's why I've been thinking we should drop this Star business and go directly to the extradimensional inquiry," Dudley said, not giving up on the idea that Van Campe might come around to his and Skiddy's side. "The Star thing is obviously an embarrassment. The sooner we can get back to science—even if it's theoretical astrophysics—the better."

"What do you think, Professor James?" Peter asked in such a formal tone that Skiddy began to question whether the two were actually as close as he had assumed.

"I believe there's a lot to be said for exploring the extradimensional area," Michael replied. "This object may well have entered our space from a parallel universe of sorts. But I'd still prefer to finish up the Star of Bethlehem inquiry, just to be sure we've covered all our bases. Besides, that shouldn't take much longer to complete—and one of the topics we plan to deal with is extradimensional explanations for the Star."

"Fine, sounds good to me," Peter said. Then he looked over at Skiddy. "It's always good to finish one line of thought before you shift to another, don't you think? Of course, you're the project director, Professor Kirkland. But doesn't this make sense to you?"

"Of course, of course," Skiddy said, not about to disagree with the source of his current funding, not to mention additional grants in the future. "So would you care to get some rest, Mr. Van Campe? Or would you like to join us in our discussion?"

"Actually, I'd like to join you," Peter said unexpectedly. "But would you mind taking a short break so that I can discuss a couple of matters with Dr. Sharon?"

At this point, no one was about to argue with the foundation director, least of all Skiddy.

"No, no, not at all," Skiddy said. "We'll break for, let's say, an hour—is that okay, Mr. Van Campe?"

Peter quickly assented, and the meeting broke up. As Peter joined Yael in her office, Skiddy and Dudley drifted off toward the site where Dudley was conducting his astronomical observations. After a moment's hesitation, Dan headed in their direction.

When her office door was closed, Yael pulled out a radio, tuned in a music station at a relatively high volume, and moved closer to Peter. "I'm a little paranoid about being overheard," she whispered.

"As I've told someone else"—she nodded her head so that Peter would understand she was referring to Michael James—"I suspect efforts are being made to eavesdrop or otherwise monitor our communications. There have even been reports about possible violence directed at us."

"Who?" he asked.

"I'm not sure," she said. "But our informers have reported that strangers have been asking questions about our work. And I just received word that two rather unusual snoops had to be shooed away from the brush just outside our fence."

"Reporters?"

"Maybe, maybe not," she said. "They claimed to be reporters following up on that *Times* story. But they carried photography equipment that seemed much more sophisticated than what you usually find with an ordinary news crew. And they had very advanced wireless computer transmission equipment. Much more characteristic of an intelligence operation than a news organization."

"I have some interesting news as well," he said. "About the source of that story."

"You know who leaked it?"

"We think it may have been Professor Geoffrey Gonzales."

TWENTY

GEOFFREY?" Yael exclaimed, obviously taken by surprise. "I wouldn't have suspected him at all. Are you certain?"

"No," Peter admitted. "It's hard for us, as a conservative Christian organization, to nail down anything that comes out of the *New York Times*. Running down sources that have been used in one of their stories is always a tedious business. And it's even more of a challenge to place people—'moles,' if you will—in their organization, though we do have a few."

"I imagine that would be a tough nut to crack," she said. "From what I understand, they guard the identity of their sources like Fort Knox. They'll go to jail before they reveal a name."

Peter added, "It would be about as easy for the United States to monitor Iraq as for a conservative group like ours to keep tabs on the activities of *Times* reporters and editors."

"So you're not sure about Gonzales?" she asked again.

"No. But our sources have done a good job of gathering evidence. Now, we think there's at least a possibility that Gonzales is the culprit."

"I wondered why your question to him was so pointed just now."

"Was it that obvious?" Peter said with a wry smile.

"I picked up an attitude," she said, tweaking him. "But I doubt the others noticed. Tell me, though—what on earth could have been his motive?"

"No idea," Peter replied, shaking his head so vigorously that some of his perfectly combed gray locks came loose. "Absolutely no notion. Motives that drive the others are clear. Dudley Dunster is obviously petrified that his career will be jeopardized by the disclosures. Getting tenure—that's his main reason for living. And his astronomer buddies at Harvard wouldn't exactly put the Star of Bethlehem on their front burner. As for Professor Kirkland, he's mainly worried about future grant money. So for him, this kind of publicity could hurt."

"But these concerns don't drive Gonzales?" Yael asked.

"I would have thought that the negative academic reaction to your work would have worried Professor Gonzales. But perhaps not."

"So he'll bear watching," Yael said.

"Yes, but I wouldn't jump to any conclusions. Maybe he's just a publicity hound. As my mama used to say, 'I don't care what you say about me so long as you use my name.'"

"There's another worry," she said. "I'm virtually certain we have someone on this compound who wants to sabotage our work. At least we're getting warnings to that effect from our intelligence contacts."

"Anything specific?"

"Not yet. But I don't like to take chances."

"For you, unnecessary risks could be fatal," he replied. "The only time I recall that you were really indiscreet was when you told me you had become a Christian."

She put her index finger up against her lips to silence him. "The walls have ears."

Dan Thompson hesitated before heading after Dudley and Skiddy, who were now huddled in an intense conversation near one of Dudley's telescopes. He hadn't thought this matter through as much as he would have liked. But events were tumbling along too quickly now for him to be able to justify holding back what he had learned from Joanna.

Granted, she was his wife. And granted, she had sworn him to secrecy. But he didn't feel bound by what he had said because she was obviously distraught. She was clearly incapable of making wise, discerning judgments in her current emotional condition, including the best use of what she had learned about the relationship between Michael and Yael. So things were now up to him.

Also, he was becoming increasingly uncertain of her loyalty to him. *For all I know, she could serve me with divorce papers the moment we set foot back in the States.*

When Dan came within earshot of the Harvard scholars, he heard Dudley say, "We've got to get rid of James. He's the main problem. Is there any way to turn this Van Campe against him?"

"I might know a way," Dan said, entering their circle and then looking over his shoulder to be sure no one else was listening.

"So earn your pay," Skiddy said testily. He was obviously unhappy that Dan had been unable to neutralize James's influence on the investigation up to this point.

Skiddy's crack smarted a bit but confirmed Dan on the course he had chosen. Obviously, it would help his prospects for future research assignments if he could do something to get back into Skiddy's good graces. And the information he had acquired about the secret love affair on the compound seemed made to order for his purposes.

"Michael James and Yael have a thing going between them," he said.

A shocked silence ensued, giving Dan some modicum of satisfaction. "Explain," Skiddy finally said.

"I have good information that they're romantically involved—a love affair right under our noses," he continued, choosing not to bring Joanna into the matter. He figured he at least owed her that.

"What do you mean, good information?" Dudley pressed. "You can't make an accusation like that without solid evidence. They could just deny it. Then where would you be?"

"Is eyewitness evidence sufficient?" Dan responded, more tentative now because he really didn't want to mention Joanna.

"Maybe," Skiddy said. "Depends on who saw them—and what was seen. Who's your source?"

"Uh, let's just say this is definite, firsthand information," Dan waffled.

"So *you* saw them?" Dudley said, a skeptical tone now seeping into his voice.

"I didn't say that."

"Quit the games, Dan!" Skiddy said. "This is useless information unless we know how you got it, who saw it, and what happened—specifically."

Knowing that he was trapped, Dan first swore them to secrecy—hoping they would behave more reliably than he had. Then he disclosed what Joanna had seen.

"Well, it's not as though they were caught in bed together," Dudley said. "But at least it's something. So what's to be done with their dirty little secret?"

"They're both single," Skiddy mused. "Two unmarried adults hugging and kissing isn't exactly what most people would regard as immoral."

"But remember, these evangelicals are prudes as far as sex outside marriage is concerned," Dudley said. "Michael's friends and colleagues, such as Van Campe, might not be too pleased."

"And don't forget," Dan argued, "there could be all sorts of conflicts of interest here, not to mention a public embarrassment if word of this got out. Think about it. Our Israeli project manager, with clear connections to her government, is carrying on a secret love affair with a fundamentalist Bible professor. What would the Israelis say? Is there really any room for that kind of hanky-panky here on this site, where we're trying to conduct what could be the most important research project of all time?"

Skiddy turned the thought over in his mind.

"Come to think of it, this may be exactly what we need to get rid of James," he said. "On the one hand, the whole thing is probably quite harmless. But will Peter Van Campe see it that way? He wasn't happy about the publicity on the Star of Bethlehem. Think how he might react if the *National Enquirer* or one of the TV magazine shows ran a story on this."

"I can see it now—'Love Under the Star of Bethlehem,'" Dudley said. "No, I don't think Mr. Van Campe would be at all pleased."

"If James goes, Yael would probably have to go too," Dan reminded them.

"Not necessarily," Skiddy said. "After all, she's important because of her Israeli connections."

"There's something else," Dan said—and he then related Joanna's suspicion that Yael might be doing some sort of undercover work for the Israelis.

"It wouldn't surprise me, but we have absolutely no evidence for that," Skiddy said. "Besides, this whole country is full of spies and intrigue. The romance thing has more possibilities. Yeah, I think I'll pass that on to Van Campe."

"Just keep Joanna out of it," Dan said.

"Don't worry, don't worry," Skiddy said, waving him off.

But somehow, Dan feared that he had just opened a Pandora's box that was going to be very difficult to close.

TWENTY-ONE

Peter Van Campe listened impassively in Skiddy Kirkland's office as Skiddy leaned his long, angular frame forward to relate what Dan had told him about the romantic attachment between Yael and Michael. Dan and Dudley sat to one side, watching the interchange closely.

Dan was particularly attentive because he was afraid Skiddy might bring Joanna's involvement into the discussion. But to Dan's relief, Skiddy managed to describe the incident without mentioning Joanna.

When Skiddy had finished, Peter asked, "So what do you suggest we do?"

"As much as I hate to say it, I think Michael should leave our team," the Harvard psychologist said. "We simply can't stand any more bad publicity—and we certainly don't need further distractions from our work."

"I think that's a little drastic," Peter replied smoothly, but leaving no doubt that James would stay. "I agree that emotional complications *might* get in the way of the project. But then again, they might not. Besides, it's not at all clear to me that this is a very high-profile love affair—if indeed it's a love affair at all. What would really happen if the press got hold of the matter?"

"Headlines!" Dudley interjected tersely, and then repeated the tabloid line he had used earlier: "Bad headlines, like 'Love Under the Star of Bethlehem.' The press could kill us with that."

Peter shook his head. "I think you're blowing this thing way out of proportion. After all, they're both unmarried. Their little encounter seems rather tame and might be interpreted more than one way."

"That was a passionate embrace," Skiddy responded. "Only one way to interpret that."

"Did you see it?" Peter asked.

"No, but . . ."

"So this is secondhand. Is it really a reliable eyewitness report? What are the details? Who saw them?"

Dan gulped as the room became silent at that last question. He wished he could snap his fingers and end the discussion before it went any further. But he knew what was coming.

"It was Joanna," Skiddy finally said. "She saw them, and she's about as reliable a witness as you could find. She doesn't have an ax to grind."

Peter glanced at Dan, who felt that he would shrivel up on the spot. Then the foundation chief shrugged. "I still don't see the problem. If Joanna wants to discuss this with me, I'd be happy to meet with her. Frankly, I really don't think this is a particularly important issue. But I'll talk to both Yael and Michael and tell them your concerns—and emphasize again that this investigation must come before any personal feelings."

Peter then stopped abruptly and looked steadily at Skiddy. The meeting was obviously over, and it was equally obvious that the three team members had failed in their effort to remove Michael James from the scene. Clearly, Peter Van Campe was not only planning on keeping James around, but he was expecting him to continue on this Star of Bethlehem track.

"I don't believe this," Dudley said when the three had left the headquarters building and gathered on a grassy knoll to wait for the others to arrive for the next session. "Not only is James going to stay, but I got the impression that his position is stronger than ever."

"You didn't have to mention Joanna's name," Dan said, turning to face Skiddy head-on. "You've put me in an untenable position with her."

"Oh, forget it!" Skiddy said. "Van Campe probably won't say a thing to her."

"But he'll tell Michael and Yael. Joanna is sure to find out one way or another."

"And if she does, you can tell her this thing was too important to keep under wraps," Skiddy said, turning to walk back into the headquarters building. "It's time for our next Star of Bethlehem session. Don't be late! And by the way, if Joanna gives you any trouble, blame me, if you like."

"Yeah, me too—if you think that'll save your marriage," Dudley added with a mirthless grin.

If the overweight Harvard astronomer had been a couple of steps closer, Dan was sure he would have decked the man. But he just clenched and unclenched his fists as the other two walked away, chuckling at some unheard comment.

Probably about me, Dan thought, smoldering at the uncomfortable spot he was now in with his wife. Then the irony of the situation hit him.

I really have no cause to complain about Skiddy, do I? I put myself in this situation. Skiddy may have broken a confidence. But I was the first offender—breaking a promise to my wife. What goes around, comes around.

Then he looked up at the sky and sighed.

The whole thing reminds me of a bad Restoration comedy—and I might laugh if I didn't feel like crying—or slugging Dudley.

Finally, Dan began to calm down. But he still didn't quite know how—or whether—to break the news about his indiscreet blabbering to Joanna. As he followed Dudley and Skiddy back to the headquarters shack, he found himself wondering if his marriage was going to end on this wild patch of wilderness. *Or will the God of this land, provided He exists at all, give me another chance?*

With this crude prayer still reverberating in his mind, Dan wasn't sure how he heard a thing that Michael James said as the team began to consider the next episode of the Star of Bethlehem.

TWENTY-TWO

A s Dan took his seat, Michael pointed to the fifth item on his list: "One star or planet." But when he turned back to his audience, he found himself facing a different group.

Peter Van Campe, still crisply attired and sitting in the prominent, cushioned chair Skiddy had prepared for him toward the front of the room, was watching Michael attentively. His aides, or guards, were once again stationed against opposing walls.

Did Peter bring his own valet? Michael mused, smiling to himself. *At least I have one sympathetic ear.*

Dan Thompson was looking away from Michael at nothing in particular. If anything, he looked less hostile and considerably more preoccupied. *Looks very unhappy,* Michael decided.

Joanna, wearing close-fitting jeans and a loose shirt, was making only occasional eye contact with Michael. The Wheaton professor noticed a more distant air. Her body language was entirely closed. She hugged herself tightly and wound her long legs around each other in a near-contortionist configuration. *Something's definitely wrong there. She was on my side. Have I lost her?*

The short, pudgy Dudley and the rawboned, tall Skiddy couldn't have looked more different physically. Their wrinkled fatigues were even different—with Dudley's buttoned, green-drab shirt pulling apart in the front, too small for his girth, while Skiddy's outfit hung on his skinny frame like a scarecrow's suit. Yet their facial expressions were almost identical, with similar hostile frowns directed openly at the Wheaton professor.

143

I'm lucky neither of these guys is packing a weapon.

Geoffrey Gonzales was the most pleasant-looking of the bunch. *Seems focused, interested. I like that.* But as Michael looked at the Californian a little more closely, he noticed that something about the man's demeanor seemed hard to read, as though his mind was churning, but he wasn't quite ready to disclose the precise nature of his thoughts.

Yael, as always, had on her public face. A beautiful, dark mask that revealed nothing that was going on inside. But he noticed that her right hand was resting lightly on the handle of her pistol. *An omen? I hope not!*

Realizing that he had paused for an unusually long time—and his listeners were beginning to get a little restless—Michael cleared his throat and quickly launched the next part of his presentation. "Could the Star of Bethlehem have been one star or planet?" he asked rhetorically. "That may seem the most obvious and logical solution. After all, the Greek word for 'star' in Matthew's text— *aster*—is used in the singular. And the most common interpretation of the word is one single luminous body in the sky.

"In fact, some of the most popular interpretations of the Star of Bethlehem have focused on one celestial body. A few of the ancients suggested that the Star event may have been a solar or lunar eclipse. But usually, those events were interpreted as evil, ominous signs."

"There were lunar eclipses in 4 B.C. and 1 B.C.," Dudley said, referring to his computer database. He was apparently interested in getting the facts out as quickly as possible in the hope that Michael's time before them could be cut.

"But those have usually not been associated with the Star," Michael said. "They've been linked to attempts to date the death of Herod the Great. Remember, Josephus said that a lunar eclipse happened just before Herod's death. As for solar eclipses, they were quite rare. The closest ones to the time of Christ were in 10 B.C. and A.D. 29—and neither of those falls within our time range for the biblical star, which probably occurred sometime between 8 B.C. and 1 B.C."

"How about a star?" Dudley pressed, wanting to move things along. "Maybe Sirius?"

"Yes, Sirius," Michael replied. "The so-called 'dog star,' which is located in the 'great dog' constellation, Canis Major. It's the brightest star in the heavens. And you're right, Dudley. Some have suggested this as a possibility. Another candidate might be one of the bright planets, such as Venus or Jupiter."

"So why don't we just say the Star of Bethlehem was really one of these actual planets or stars?" Skiddy said, hoping against hope that Michael might agree.

But Michael ignored the obvious impatience that was pushing the Harvard professors. Instead, he just sighed and threw up his hands. "Frankly, the appearance of these lone celestial bodies doesn't seem unusual enough to qualify any of them as the Star of Bethlehem. Not only that, they don't really meet the other criteria of that special Star, such as being able to move about or emit a focused or directed beam to guide the Magi."

"So you'd reject this fifth possibility, I take it?" Dudley said, again unable to contain his eagerness to hurry Michael along so that the group could embark on a more serious investigation.

"Yes," the Wheaton man replied. "But now, I think the stage is set for us to segue from individual objects in the sky to what might be called a 'gathering' of planets or stars."

"Sounds obscure," Joanna said.

"I'm talking about astrology," Michael said.

With that, the room erupted in a near frenzy of voices, with Dudley Dunster's protests soon overwhelming all the rest.

"Come on!" Dudley cried, standing up and moving so close to Michael that it seemed he might jump the Wheaton man. Michael James was taller and clearly in better physical condition. But Dudley projected an angry energy that made the speaker take a step backward.

"This is a total waste of our time!" Dudley cried, jabbing his finger toward Michael's chest. "I've been patient. Way too patient! I'm a serious astronomer! A scientist! And occult theories have nothing to do with science!"

He stopped to catch his breath and took a step back toward his chair, apparently realizing he was losing control. But he wasn't about to back down on his basic point. "Astrology?" he said, taking his seat again. "Absolutely not! I want to go on record! I want this written down—that I'm utterly and unalterably opposed to this approach. Somebody please write that down!"

No one moved to record the Harvard astronomer's objection. Finally, Dudley turned to his computer and started typing, evidently deciding to make his own notes about his objections.

Satisfied that things had calmed down enough for him to continue, Michael pointed at the melamine board where he had written his list and underlined the sixth item—"Conjunction."

Then he turned back to the group and looked directly at Dudley. "Let me explain myself," Michael began. "I'm certainly not suggesting that we get sidetracked into a lengthy examination of astrology. In fact, given my own Christian belief system, I may be more suspicious of astrology and the occult than you are, Dudley."

He paused to let this point sink in and then continued to speak directly to the astronomer. "But think about it this way. When we look back into the past, to the days of the ancient Magi, one of their main disciplines was astrology—which for them was indistinguishable from astronomy. This area of study or belief might seem completely strange and archaic to us. Yet our own mysterious light in the sky is at least as strange! It may just be that if we can somehow enter into the mind-set of the ancient Magi, we'll be in a better position to grasp whatever new mind-set is required to understand the current phenomenon above us."

Then he backed up and spoke to the group at large. "Again, remember our main objective," he said. "We're trying to step outside our usual thought categories. Dudley, you think in terms of traditional science—and that's one reason you're so valuable to this team. I think in terms of traditional Christianity—and that may or may not have something to do with our mysterious object.

"But that thing up there in the sky is making both of us reevaluate many of our basic assumptions. We're looking for new categories of analysis and insight—or at least more creative ways to deal with old categories."

"Makes sense," Geoffrey said. "We obviously need new ways to evaluate this phenomenon. I'd like for our group to make the breakthrough. Find the answer. But I suspect that the answer's not going to be what most of us expect."

"Yeah, but do you really want tomorrow's *New York Times* to say we're getting into astrology?" Dudley objected.

"Frankly, I don't really care," Geoffrey said, surprising everyone except Peter and Yael, who perked up as they recalled his suspected role as the press leak. "And who knows? Popular articles could easily work in our favor. After all, we're respected scientists. We're supposed to think creatively. I'll bet the public would be intrigued with the fact that we're talking about the Star of Bethlehem and maybe astrology."

"But what about the academic community?" Dudley protested.

"No single newspaper article's going to destroy us," Geoffrey said casually. "And publicity may even help. Serious investigators are beginning to realize that the usual scientific methods and procedures aren't going to provide a solution. So why not let the public and the scientific community know we're willing to take some risks?"

So that was his motive for contacting the Times? Yael wondered. *I'm not so sure. But I do have to get to know you a little better, Professor Gonzales.*

Dudley was so surprised at Geoffrey's comments that he was momentarily left without a response. Skiddy, though, just wanted to hurry through Michael's presentation, seeing it as a necessary evil that he had to put up with to pacify his benefactor, Peter Van Campe.

"Oh, forget it, Dudley!" the Harvard psychologist said. "The more we argue, the longer this is going to take. Let's just get on with it. Please keep moving, Michael."

Michael, seemingly unflustered by the arguments and charges swirling around him, calmly turned back to his notes. "The most popular theories for the identity of the Star of Bethlehem have centered on conjunctions—or a drawing together or crossing of two or more celestial objects," he continued. "And the reason I brought up astrology is that these conjunctions had meaning in the ancient world only if they could fit into some astrological interpretation."

"Define exactly what you mean by astrology," Joanna said sharply. "It's different from horoscopes in the paper, right?"

She's definitely a little irritated, Michael thought. *Not exactly on my side.*

"You're right that astrology continues today in the form of horoscopes or in the rituals of certain cults," Michael said. "But it was much more pervasive and accepted in ancient times. In a nutshell, it's the belief system that says celestial bodies influence human affairs and other events on earth. Persian intellectuals were trained in astrology. So it's virtually certain that the Magi of Matthew were astrologers."

"But God condemned astrology and divination throughout the Bible, didn't He?" Dan said. "So why would He have allowed such practices to be a key factor in leading the wise men to the Messiah?"

"Good question," Michael said. "Let me respond first by agreeing that it's true—God and His prophets always condemned the use of astrology. For example, Isaiah reported that God warned Babylon against following astrologers in Isaiah, chapter forty-seven, and Jeremiah told Israel not to be frightened by the 'signs of the heavens,' in Jeremiah, chapter ten."

Having made this concession, Michael stressed the point by writing on the board, "*Israelites—no astrology.*"

Then he turned back to Dan and zeroed in on his main point. "But that's not the end of it. God also wanted to announce the birth of His Son to Gentiles, who apparently didn't have a very clear understanding of the Hebrew Scriptures. So to communicate effectively, it was necessary to use their own idiom—Zoroastrian religion and also astrology."

That explanation seemed to satisfy Dan and the others for the time being, so Michael continued on this tack. "Let me give you a simple example of the use of astrological thinking to explain the Star—one that doesn't include a conjunction," he said. "A Rutgers astronomer, Dr. Michael Molnar, has suggested that the Star of Bethlehem may actually have been an appearance of the planet Jupiter in the constellation Aries, the Ram, in April of 6 B.C.

"Now, this event would have no meaning without an understanding of ancient astrology. As Dr. Molnar pointed out, Aries was regarded in ancient times as the symbol of Judea, and Jupiter was thought to be the regal planet. So you put the two astrological ideas together, and you have a great king being born in Judea."

"So the Magi would have seen this event in the sky and headed to Israel to find the King of the Jews, the Messiah?" Geoffrey said.

"That's correct."

"But that still leaves us short of your other tests for the Star,"

Geoffrey said. "Most important, Jupiter in Aries wouldn't guide the Magi to a specific house in Bethlehem."

"Again, correct," Michael said. "But let's stick with astrology for another minute or two before we throw it out entirely—because a lot of people have been satisfied with the astrological explanation of the Star."

He turned back to the board and began to draw a diagram of a small part of the sky, with labels for the planets Jupiter and Saturn. "Consider the operation of some conjunctions that occurred about the same time—in 7 B.C. and again in 6 B.C.," he said, and then he looked toward his listeners with an apologetic smile.

"What I'm about to discuss requires a lot of nerve because I'm not an astronomer or a scientist—and I know we have three of the top scholars in the world sitting here in this room," he said, glancing first at Geoffrey, then at Dudley, and finally at Joanna. "And I also know that Dan is an expert on unusual religious movements and cults, including astrology. But I'll take a shot at this anyhow—with the full knowledge that some of you may want to correct or challenge me."

False modesty, Dan thought. *And you can bet I'll be looking for ways to challenge you.*

"First, in 7 B.C. there was an event called a 'triple conjunction,' involving the planets Jupiter and Saturn," Michael said. "This means that Jupiter—the planet of kings—first moved from west to east and caught up with Saturn—a planet that many ancients associated with the destiny of Judea. When Jupiter passed Saturn, that constituted the first conjunction."

He drew an arrow to indicate this first movement of Jupiter.

"Then, from the viewpoint of observers on earth, Jupiter seemed to back up and actually move east to west until it passed Saturn again from the opposite direction. This was the second conjunction."

To illustrate, he drew a second arrow under the first, but this one was pointed in the opposite direction.

"Finally, Jupiter changed direction once more, resuming its west-to-east motion. It passed Saturn a third time to form the third conjunction."

He then drew a third arrow, which pointed in the direction of the first arrow.

"These back-and-forth movements occurred from May to December of 7 B.C. They may—just may—have been the signals that caused the Magi to follow the 'Star' toward Jerusalem—the 'Star' being the kingly planet of Jupiter."

He stopped for a moment and contemplated the diagrams he had drawn. "But the story doesn't end there," Michael continued. "A peculiar triangular grouping of Saturn, Jupiter, and Mars appeared in February of 6 B.C. That might have encouraged the Magi to continue on their way toward Jerusalem because it occurred farther to the west than the third Jupiter–Saturn conjunction."

He moved a couple of steps toward one side of the room to suggest the appearance of this new "gathering of planets" farther to the west.

"Finally, two conjunctions have been recorded later in 6 B.C.—one with Venus and Saturn in April, and another with Venus and Jupiter in May. This final grouping would have been clearly visible in the morning sky and would have pointed generally from Jerusalem in the direction of Bethlehem."

Michael paused and looked around at the team members, who were silently contemplating his explanation and the diagrams he had drawn on the board.

"Complicated," Yael finally said.

"Too complicated," Skiddy echoed.

"But still, interesting," Geoffrey added. "Shows how those of a completely different spiritual mind-set could perhaps make sense of celestial events in a way that nonspiritual observers might miss."

Dudley looked at the California scientist accusingly. "Are you saying that you put credence in this sort of thing?"

"I'm just thinking," Geoffrey replied calmly. "Just trying to adjust my biases to events that are hard to understand in the usual scientific terms. Events such as that object overhead."

Dudley just shook his head, as if to ask, "*Is everyone in this room going crazy?*"

"Okay," Skiddy finally said. "Does that wrap it up, Michael?"

"Not quite," Michael replied, going back to his list and underlining the final item: "UFO/extradimensional phenomenon."

"I can't take UFO's right now," Dudley said in exasperation, looking impatiently at his watch. "Can we take a break? I need to recover from this astrology lesson."

He had obviously given up any pretense of trying to please Peter Van Campe. In fact, he seemed so agitated by the course of the discussion that Dan wondered if he might be on the verge of losing control completely. Dudley had never seemed emotionally unbalanced before. But after all, these were highly unusual times, and the pressures building on the team were enormous.

Seeming to sense the inner crisis that was building in his colleague, Skiddy quickly agreed with Dudley's suggestion that they take a break. "That's a good idea. We'll adjourn, and you scientists can check your instruments again. If you like, get something to eat too. Or just relax. We'll reconvene in an hour and a half."

But then, realizing that he didn't really have the last say in such matters anymore, Skiddy looked solicitously in Peter's direction. "Sound okay to you, Mr. Van Campe?" he asked.

The foundation director, who had been sitting quietly but was clearly absorbed in the presentation, didn't answer immediately. Staring intently at Michael's notes and lists on the board, he seemed lost in his own thoughts. But finally he nodded his assent, and the meeting broke up.

As the team members headed out the door, Dan decided to try to patch things up with Joanna. They hadn't said a thing to each other since the strained discussion in their quarters. She hadn't even made eye contact with him during the meeting. He had tried to smile at her at one point, but she had just looked away.

This is not good. Not good at all.

He knew he had to get on her good side if he hoped to make her understand why he had run to Skiddy and Dudley and blurted out what she had shared secretly about Michael and Yael.

"Uh, Joanna, I . . ." he began, but she stopped him with an upraised palm.

"Not now, Dan," she said. "I can't deal with you now."

"Are you angry?"

"I've given up. I needed some help and advice, and you're incapable of providing it. So I have to work things out myself. But I don't want to talk about it now, okay?"

She walked away quickly before he had a chance to respond.

Dan stood rooted to the spot, shocked at how their relationship had deteriorated in just the last couple of days. *With a history of problems, it doesn't take much, does it? Just an ill-timed word or two, and we're teetering on the edge.*

He recalled a puzzling divorce between a couple of good friends of theirs that had been triggered by a trivial incident, a disagreement over a movie they had seen. Of course, it wasn't the movie but what came *before* the movie. The months and years of sniping and criticizing and growing apart. The movie was just the final straw.

Are we facing our final straw? I need some air.

Dan hurried outside and filled his lungs with the warm breeze that was blowing in from the direction of the Sea of Galilee. To clear his head, he decided to take a short walk along the north perimeter fence before the next session started.

As he sauntered over the rough terrain, a couple of hundred yards away from the complex of buildings, the warm Middle Eastern breeze blew steadily in his face. The only other sign of humanity was one of the perimeter guards, who nodded to him as they passed on the almost nonexistent path. The silence of the hillside was broken only by the sound of the stiff breeze whistling in his ears and the *crunch-crunch* of the guard's boots retreating behind him.

The scene was conducive to contemplation—a silence that Dan found he needed desperately as he tried to sort through ways he might handle the messy situation with his wife.

She's sure to find out that I told Dudley and Skiddy about the James–Sharon love affair. And she'll learn they told Van Campe. How would I react? Would I be ready to forgive? What would convince me to forget the mistake and move on?

As he turned the problem over in his mind, he tried to fight off the anger and lingering sense of disgust he felt at the way Skiddy had betrayed him. *I can only pray I'll get another chance.*

There it was again. Had he actually been praying? Or was this just the last, wishful gasp of a desperate husband, trying to hold on to a beautiful, talented wife who was quickly drifting away from him?

The gunshot rang in his ears before he could find the answer.

TWENTY-THREE

DAN immediately turned in the direction of the shot, which had cracked the serene silence behind him. He was horrified to see the guard he had just passed lying on the ground about thirty yards away. A fountain of blood was spurting from the center of the man's chest.

Without thinking, Dan started sprinting toward the fallen soldier—but then he dived to the ground and flattened himself against the rocky path. *What if there's a sniper out there? I could be his next target.*

Fortunately, there were no other shots. As Dan looked over at the guard, he saw that the man's rifle was still strapped to his shoulder. His pistol was out of its holster and lying beside him on the ground.

Could he have shot himself? An accidental discharge? A suicide?

Deciding he was probably as exposed lying down as he would be crawling toward the fallen guard, Dan began edging his way closer to the man. He could hear an urgent voice crackling in Hebrew over the man's portable radio.

Obviously, they want to know what's happening up here.

"Hey, can you hear me?" Dan called out to the man.

No response.

Dan realized that if he didn't stop the bleeding from that gaping chest wound immediately, the guard would die before help arrived. So he raised himself to a kneeling position and prepared to sprint the final twenty yards and do his best to administer first aid.

But he never got an opportunity. Just as he was gathering himself to run, a blinding beam of light enveloped the wounded soldier. The light was so intense and bright that Dan had to shield his eyes. He couldn't look at it directly, any more than he could gaze at the sun.

Out of the corner of his eye, though, he could see that the light was streaming in what appeared to be a solid column of illumination from somewhere in the eastern sky.

From where I last saw the strange light. From the Star.

Then, as abruptly as the light had appeared, it vanished. The day returned to normal, with the same steady breeze and the warm summer sun.

But at least one thing was very, very different from before. The guard was now sitting up, his hands testing his chest here and there. There was blood all over the front of his uniform, but no open wound. In fact, no wound at all. The man stood up, looking thoroughly bewildered and shaken.

"Are you okay?" Dan said, rushing up to him.

"I . . . I think so," the man replied, apparently in something of a daze. "But I don't understand what happened."

Dan helped the man pull his shirt open to bare his chest, and they both ran their hands up and down on the bare skin.

"There's no wound," the guard said. "I was shot. I was dying. But now there's no wound. I'm healed."

Dan stood looking at the man's naked chest. It was true. There was no chest wound. No spurting blood. Just a normal, healthy expanse of skin. Then Dan reached over and felt the wet blood on the guard's fatigue top. The redness stained Dan's own hand.

"That's blood, all right," he said absently, not quite comprehending his own words.

By now, three other guards had reached them, and Dan could see Yael running in their direction as well. In the ensuing confusion, the guard was hustled off to the first aid clinic on the compound. Yael and the officer in charge of the guard detail escorted Dan to the guard shack for further questioning.

"Okay, tell us exactly what happened," Yael said after they had settled in the guard shack and closed the door. She was perched on the edge of the officer's desk, and the officer was standing next to his desk chair, one foot propped on the seat. Dan was sitting uncomfortably on the only other seat in the room, a hard bench with no back that seemed ready-made for tough interrogation.

"It was quiet, peaceful," he began. "I passed the guard. We nodded at each other, but didn't say anything. A few seconds later, I heard a shot, so I hit the ground. The first thing I thought of was snipers. Then I looked back toward the guard, and he was lying on the ground, blood spurting out of his chest. I mean, a real stream, shooting up in the air several inches. I called out, but he didn't answer. Seemed unconscious."

Dan leaned over and held out his hands, palms down, as though acting out his next movements. "Then I started moving toward him, hugging the ground. All I could think of was snipers. But then this beam of light hit him. I couldn't look at it straight on, it was so bright. Almost blinded me. Then it went out, like somebody switched it off, and the guard was sitting up. There was no blood coming out of his chest. When I got to him, I unbuttoned his shirt, and his chest was fine. No wound at all."

"Are you sure you saw blood coming out of his chest?" the officer asked.

"Yes, absolutely!" Dan replied. "At least it was red and looked like blood. Look, I got some on my hand."

He held up his hand, palm toward them, but they frowned and glanced at each other. Dan then turned his hand around and saw the problem—it was clean. Not a trace of red.

"I don't get it," he said. "I put my hand on his shirt, and it came away wet with blood."

The officer's two-way radio buzzed, and he clicked it on and talked for what seemed an interminable time. Then he looked back at Dan with that disturbing frown again.

"That was the first aid station," he said. "Tuvya, the guard who was on the ground, was apparently completely uninjured when they brought him in. And there was no blood on his clothing. None anywhere."

Then the officer paused. "But otherwise, he more or less confirms your story. He says he was shot, and felt he was dying."

"And he was losing blood?" Dan asked.

"Yeah, lots of blood," the officer said.

"Still another mystery," Yael said with a sigh.

The officer looked sideways at Yael. "They think maybe he just stumbled and fell and imagined he had been wounded."

"But there was a shot!" Dan said. "You heard it, didn't you?"

"Yes, his pistol confirms that," the officer said. "Apparently an accidental discharge. He remembers pulling out his pistol to check it, and he thinks it went off and a round hit him in the chest."

"He *thinks*?" Dan said incredulously.

"That's another problem we have with this," the officer said. "Tuvya could have lost consciousness for a moment. Other than a vague memory of seeing himself bleeding, he apparently doesn't remember much until he saw you standing in front of him, pulling his shirt apart."

"This situation gets stranger and stranger," Yael said. "Well, let's go back to the headquarters building and see where we go from here."

As Dan walked back to the main hut with Yael, he realized he was no longer quite so worried about Joanna's reaction to his indiscreet disclosures to Skiddy. The condition of their marriage still weighed on him. He desperately wanted the relationship to work. But he sensed something was happening that was much bigger than the two of them. Or Skiddy's approval of his performance. Or future grant stipends. Or his academic reputation.

The strange light had now taken the main stage in his life, front and center. Complacency was out of the question. Finally, he could begin to understand why Joanna had been so deeply affected by this phenomenon. One way or another, he knew he had to understand its true meaning—even if that meant changing his thinking and actions in ways he could never have imagined only a few weeks before.

TWENTY-FOUR

So the plot thickens," Peter Van Campe said.

He, Yael, Skiddy, and Dan sat thoughtfully in Yael's office after hearing Dan's story. They were acutely aware that the others were waiting rather impatiently out in the meeting room just on the other side of the closed door. Everyone had now heard some version of the remarkable experience of Dan and the guard. So the pressure was building for the leaders in this room to suggest some sort of explanation for the strange incidents—and perhaps propose an action plan.

"Could be hysteria," Skiddy said tentatively, though he seemed to realize that this explanation was now wearing thin.

"I think we have to quit looking for excuses," Yael said with a dismissive toss of her jet-black hair. "First it was Joanna. Now Dan. Neither showed any particular religious or spiritual inclination before their experience. Neither has any history of emotional instability. I've checked."

Dan looked up abruptly at that.

"They are inherently credible witnesses," Yael declared.

"But the evidence is still shaky," Skiddy said. "We have their word that these events happened. But no corroborating evidence. No blood in Dan's case. And the guard's story isn't too solid. He remembers a little, but not much."

"Before this happened to me, I'd have agreed with you, Skiddy," Dan said. "But I know the facts. Regardless of the blood, I know what I saw. There was definitely a chest wound. And definitely a strong beam of light that covered that guard. I even had after-shadows on my optic nerves for a minute or so, like when you accidentally look up at the sun. I was definitely exposed to some sort of bright light."

"The brain and nerves, optic nerves included, can play tricks when you're under stress," Skiddy said.

"But I wasn't feeling any unusual stress," he said. "I was a little worried . . ." He almost said *about Joanna* but caught himself. "But I know what heavy stress is, and this wasn't it."

Peter cleared his throat. "Seems to me these two incidents are some evidence that something strange is going on. Not definitive proof, but some evidence. If we ignore these reports, or dismiss them as psychological aberrations, we may find we've missed important signals about the identity of that light. And if other research groups are experiencing things like this and they take them seriously, they could move ahead of us. Doesn't that worry you, Skiddy?"

"Well, we certainly can't discount these reports," Skiddy replied reluctantly. "And I want to use any means we can find to be the first with an answer. But these are sensitive matters. Our group is already seen as a little unusual, if not kooky, with that *Times* article on the Star of Bethlehem. I'd suggest that we withhold final judgment until we have more evidence."

"What do you recommend, Yael?" Peter said, always the consensus-seeking, task-oriented business executive.

"I think we should assume, until we have evidence to the contrary, that both Dan and Joanna had real experiences that were somehow caused by that light," she said. "Our working hypothesis should incorporate their reports. And I certainly think we have to tell everyone on the team what's happened—and how seriously we are taking these strange incidents."

Skiddy sighed and shook his head. "I suppose there's no choice. But we *must* keep this confidential. Our research team, and no one else, must know. If this gets out and we're wrong, our reputations as scientists and researchers will be ruined. We'll be a joke in the academic community. Nothing we say in the future will carry any weight."

"I think we can all agree to that," Peter said.

"Also," Skiddy said, "if you don't mind, Mr. Van Campe, I'd like for you to summarize our discussion to the team. Okay? After all, you're the foundation head, and what's been happening goes well beyond any known scientific occurrence."

What Skiddy didn't say was that he wanted to distance himself as far as possible from the direction the investigation was now taking. If, by some remote chance, it turned out that they were on the right track—and some entirely novel explanation turned out to be the correct answer to the light—then he would be the first to take the credit. But Skiddy remained convinced that these reported visions, healings, and other paranormal phenomena were either figments of the imagination or unusual symptoms of emotional stress. And if the whole business exploded in their faces, as he feared it would, he wanted to be sure he had some sort of escape route in place to help him avoid the brunt of the criticism.

With an uneasy consensus now reached, the four returned to the main room, where all eyes turned in their direction. Peter immediately proceeded to encapsulate the conversation in Yael's office and concluded with a personal affirmation of the validity of the experiences of Joanna and Dan.

"We must assume at this point that they had valid encounters of some type with that light," he said. "If you can marshal evidence to the contrary, well and good. But until you have that evidence, let's assume their reports are factual. Now, Michael, I believe you still have the floor. What's next on your agenda?"

As Skiddy watched the meeting proceed, he became more and more sullen. It had been his choice not to take the lead and report on the leadership's thinking about Dan's experience. But the Harvard psychologist could see his authority over the investigation slipping away before his very eyes. All this was quite irregular. After all, he was the project director, and for an investigation of this type to be valid, there had to be a certain objectivity. The person or organization funding the study was supposed to remain hands-off.

Of course, everyone in the academic research business knew that it was unquestionably best for the results of a study to support the funding agency in one way or another. Otherwise, you could never expect future funds from that source. If you absolutely had to conclude something that was contrary to the sponsor, that was okay—

but in such a case, don't look for any more money in that direction!

In any event, as this strange investigation proceeded, Skiddy was becoming less and less interested in having anything to do with Van Campe and his Panoplia International. He couldn't afford to compromise his reputation, regardless of the amount of money involved.

In fact, I'd be tempted to pull out right now if I had a little more money in hand, he reflected.

But they were not even three weeks into the project, and it was scheduled to last for at least eight more. If he left now, he wouldn't even have enough cash to cover the payments on his summer home or his Mercedes. He'd actually have to dip into his savings to make it through the summer! As lavishly as he seemed to live, he faced monstrous alimony payments every month. And he never managed to save a cent.

No, leaving now would be precipitous. If necessary, I'll find some other way to deal with Van Campe and Michael James.

As he focused once more on the discussion going on in the room, Skiddy noted that Geoffrey Gonzales, for once, seemed to be getting agitated.

"I tell you UFO's *are* a possibility here!" the California scientist was saying stridently to Michael, who was looking down at the floor quietly, his arms folded across his chest. "But if you like, we won't call them UFO's. We'll call them extradimensional visitors. How's that?"

"Wait," Dudley interrupted. "Now let me get this straight, Geoffrey. You really are saying there are little green men running that light in the sky, and pretty soon, they're going to invade the earth, is that right?"

"You're not listening," Geoffrey cried, thoroughly exasperated. He hopped out of his chair and began to stride back and forth in front of them, gesticulating wildly with his stubby, muscular arms. "None of you are listening to me! Now keep quiet for a minute, and I'll go over it all again."

Geoffrey was breathing hard now, and he seemed much more upset than any of them could remember. After a noticeable effort to calm himself, he said in a tone of forced patience: "Extraterrestrial visitors from our own universe are pretty much a practical impossibility. Most reputable scientists recognize that. For example, if that thing up in the sky were some sort of spaceship that we could evaluate with our scientific instruments—which we can't—the mathematical odds against its coming from our universe are overwhelming.

"The late scientist Carl Sagan suggested that we think about the problem this way. Assume there are one million separate alien civilizations on other planets in our galaxy. Also, assume that they are all capable of launching spaceships to search for intelligent life elsewhere in the universe. Finally, consider the vast distances that would have to be covered and the fact that it's probably not possible for anything in our universe to travel faster than the speed of light. In some cases, it would take hundreds or thousands of years for a vehicle traveling at the speed of light to reach us.

"So even if you make these generous assumptions—which are very optimistic—each of these one million civilizations would have to send out about ten thousand spaceships every year for even one UFO to make it to earth every year!"

"Not likely," Joanna said.

"When you consider the small number of space probes we send out, a visit from extraterrestrials seems highly unlikely," Dudley said.

"Of course!" Geoffrey exclaimed. "The idea is absurd! Impossible! That's why I'm saying that any UFO's or extraterrestrial beings— which I believe are the only logical explanations for that light— must also be *extradimensional*. That means they must come from a parallel universe."

"So we're back to your wormholes again," Dudley said, groaning audibly.

"It's the only logical explanation!" Geoffrey said, clearly annoyed that he wasn't getting an enthusiastic response. "That thing still doesn't show up on our instruments. Yet it's there. We can see it. And apparently it's interacting with us in various ways. I happen to believe that Joanna and Dan actually encountered something very real. But it's real in a way that we can't comprehend or measure. Somehow, we must find a way to make contact."

"Now let me get this straight, Geoffrey," Dudley said again, unable to contain the sarcasm that was welling up inside him. "You really do want us to assume that the light contains little green men"—Dudley knew this term pressed Geoffrey's buttons—"and we're supposed to make contact with them, like Captain Kirk in *Star Trek*. Is that right?"

"Please, Dudley, let's keep this professional," Geoffrey said testily. "I'm suggesting that we could be witnessing an intervention from another universe that has entirely different physical rules that govern it. Furthermore, there may be some intelligent beings or entities that are probing us, or trying to communicate. And they seem quite benign. Consider the reassuring words conveyed to Joanna, and the healing of the guard, which Dan witnessed."

"This is a leap, Geoffrey—a real leap!" Skiddy said. "It's all speculation. We still don't know exactly what Joanna and Dan experienced. And we'll probably never know."

"But Geoffrey does make a provocative argument," Michael said. "He might be wrong, but his theory puts all the pieces of our puzzle together. At least for now."

Everyone, even Peter, looked at Michael as though he had just landed from another planet. "You're actually buying into this?" Joanna asked incredulously. "How can this possibly fit into your Christian belief system?"

"I'm just listening and keeping my mind open," Michael said cryptically.

"But we have no precedents for this!" Dudley protested. "No solid evidence! No one's ever seen a wormhole—if they exist at all! No one's seen an object or being from a parallel universe. How can we know if this is what we're observing?"

"Does anyone have a better explanation?" Geoffrey asked, feeling more confident now that he seemed to have an ally in Michael.

"I'm thinking of a variation on your concept," Michael said. "One that may provide us with the precedents that Dudley says are lacking."

"You mean you think this sort of thing has happened before?" Dudley said derisively. "Suddenly you're a theoretical physicist, Michael? Now I've heard it all."

"No, Dudley, you haven't heard it all," Michael said so caustically that several pairs of eyes, including Joanna's, turned abruptly in his direction.

This man's truly an enigma. Who is he? Where's he trying to take us?

Michael moved back to the melamine board and pointed once again to the final item on his list, the "Extradimensional" category. "You see, I still believe the real answer to this puzzle—an answer that may dovetail to some extent with Geoffrey's suggestion—lies in the Star of Bethlehem. And in that Bible you have at your side. I still have a little time left for my presentation. So please turn with me to Exodus, the second book of the Old Testament."

TWENTY-FIVE

I can't deal with this!" Dudley shouted in exasperation as he stood up and headed for the door. "I simply can't deal with this anymore! First the Bible. Then UFO's. Now it's back to the Bible again. Have you all gone crazy?"

"Dudley, please bear with me for just a few more minutes," Michael said soothingly. "I'm going to try to tie this whole discussion together now—wormholes, UFO's, theology, everything—and I would greatly value your input. You're naturally skeptical, and we need a good dose of skepticism at this point to balance things out."

Dudley stopped in his tracks and looked at Michael as though he were seeing the man for the first time. He had regarded James as his adversary from the moment they had met, and so this apparent offer of an olive branch was unexpected.

It's a trick, Dudley finally decided. *But okay, I'm a little curious. I'll stick around for a while longer and watch him make a fool of himself.*

"Thanks, Dudley," Michael said after the Harvard astronomer had taken his seat again. "Now as I said, let's turn to Exodus 3:4-5. As you'll see, that passage contains the account of how God appeared to Moses through the burning bush. Throughout both the Old and New Testaments, you'll find this motif—God or His messengers breaking through into our space–time continuum in a burst of light. In Hebrew terms, this is known as the *shekinah* glory of God—meaning His appearance, or dwelling among humans, often accompanied by strange lights of one type or another."

164

"So you're trying to argue that the light above us is the shekinah glory—a dwelling place for God?" Dudley asked.

"I'm not arguing anything," Michael replied. "I just want to outline this idea from the Scriptures—an idea that various interpreters have had trouble explaining—and then let you evaluate it. As you'll see, the accounts of the shekinah vary, and the lights aren't always the same. Yet they're usually presented as historical events. Certainly, you can choose not to believe the writers or the text. But before you make up your minds, I'd just ask that you let me finish. Okay?"

"Fine, fine—proceed," Skiddy said, waving Michael on with a dismissive air.

With that, the Wheaton professor began to lead the team on a journey through a variety of ancient light-oriented appearances of God, including Moses' shining face when he encountered God on Mount Sinai after he received the Ten Commandments.

"One of my favorite references is the description of what Moses saw the first time he was on Mount Sinai," Michael said. "Exodus says that the glory of the Lord 'was like a consuming fire on the mountain top.'"

"What about the pillar of fire that guided the Israelites through the wilderness?" Yael asked. "Does that qualify?"

"That's one of the best examples of the shekinah glory," Michael replied. "Turn to Exodus 13:21–22. There, the Bible says that God went before them in a pillar of cloud by day and a pillar of fire by night."

Then he told them how God's "glory" filled the tabernacle in the wilderness, and how the glory of God was also mentioned frequently in Psalms and Isaiah.

"But perhaps the most significant reference in the Old Testament—at least for our purposes—is in the book of Ezekiel," Michael said.

He encouraged them to take their Bibles and turn to Ezekiel 10, verses 3–5 and 18–19. Then he asked Peter to read that passage out loud.

As the Panoplia executive read, a verbal picture emerged of strange, fearsome angels called cherubim standing next to the temple as a bright cloud filled the court with God's glory.

"What did these cherubim look like?" Joanna asked, ignoring Dudley, who rolled his eyes at her question.

"Uncertain," Michael said. "Like many of these extradimensional creatures, they may have one appearance one time, and another appearance on another occasion. Various descriptions give them two wings or four, and two faces—a man and a lion—or even four faces."

"Typical biblical inconsistency," Skiddy grumbled. "Unreliable."

"On the contrary," Michael responded. "These may well be just different human perceptions of how a certain extradimensional creature—a particular type of angel—looked in different contexts."

"Interesting," Geoffrey said. "I suppose it's possible."

Dudley just shook his head.

Seeing there were no further comments, Michael returned to his explanation of the Ezekiel passage.

"So the prophet says that in his vision, the shekinah glory rose up above the cherubim and hovered over them."

Then Michael asked Peter to skip ahead and read Ezekiel 11:22–23.

"'Then the cherubim lifted up their wings with the wheels beside them, and the glory of the God of Israel hovered over them. And the glory of the LORD went up from the midst of the city, and stood over the mountain which is east of the city.'"

Michael paused for a moment to let this sink in.

"The mountain that's referred to there is the Mount of Olives," he finally said, "just to the east of Jerusalem. So the shekinah departed toward the east. And we know from what we've read in Matthew that the Magi saw the Star of Bethlehem in the east."

Then he pointed overhead. "And that light we're seeing—that's in the east."

"So you're saying that these phenomena—the shekinah glory described by Ezekiel, and the Star of Bethlehem, and our mystery light—are one and the same?" Dan asked.

"I'm just suggesting possible connections," Michael said. "It's up to you to draw your own conclusions. But personally, I find the similarities compelling."

"A novel theological theory," Geoffrey said, apparently not overly impressed. "But I think it's a little too pat. It fits a bit too neatly into your particular Christian belief system. Besides, have you ever heard of anyone else who interpreted the Star of Bethlehem in this way?"

"Actually, there's ancient authority for this conclusion," Michael said, looking at his notes and finally pulling out a journal article. "John Chrysostom, the archbishop of Constantinople, for instance. In the late fourth and early fifth centuries, he argued—and I quote—'This star was not of the common sort, or rather not a star at all, as it seems at least to me, but some invisible power transformed into this appearance.'"

The Wheaton professor took off his glasses and paused for a moment, twirling them in his right hand. "Chrysostom came to his conclusion because of the unusual movements of the Star, which we've been discussing. He didn't explicitly say it was the shekinah. But he seemed impressed by its unusual brightness, its ability to appear and disappear, and the way it pointed out the Christ child."

Michael then paused again, and an uncomfortable quiet settled on the group. He knew they needed a moment or two to reflect. *They're resisting. But this can sound like bizarre stuff. Give them time. Plant the seed, and give them time.*

Finally, Geoffrey broke the silence. "Are you aware of other examples of this shekinah light appearing after the birth of Christ?"

"Yes, many in fact," Michael replied. "Remember when the apostle Paul was converted on the road to Damascus? Jesus appeared to him in an intense blast of light. In fact, Paul himself was blinded for a time."

He then turned to Skiddy. "As a psychologist, you know about the phenomena called *photisms,* don't you?"

Skiddy frowned and then nodded. "Dramatic bright lights, I believe. A person may see them after multiple stimulation of the senses. In other words, if you experience intense or painful touching, or a combination of things, such as loud noises, strong smells, and visual stimuli, you may also see flashes of light."

"Photisms have also sometimes accompanied religious conversions," Michael said. "For example, the nineteenth-century evangelist Charles Finney said that the glory of God surrounded him, with a light that—to use Finney's own words, which I'm reading off my screen here—'seemed like the brightness of the sun in every direction.' He said the brightness was too intense for his eyes."

"I seem to remember something about that in William James," Dan added.

"Yes, in the *Varieties of Religious Experience,*" Michael responded, again referring to his notes. "He recorded one conversion where the person said that a 'strange light' seemed to 'light up the whole room . . .'"

"You're obviously well prepared with all this, Michael," Geoffrey said. "But are you letting your preconceptions run away with your judgment? Let's back off a minute and get some perspective. Most of us here aren't Christians. In fact, you and Peter Van Campe are probably the only ones who are serious about your faith."

"Dan's a Christian, sort of," Joanna said.

"Well, he's an Episcopalian," Skiddy said, smirking.

"Episcopalians are Christians!" Dan retorted rather defensively. "But I'll admit, I haven't really thought of myself as a traditional Christian. I'm always exploring this and that . . ."

"Like I said, only two of you are real Christians," Geoffrey said. "So why should the rest of us buy into your rather narrow theological interpretation of that light?"

Michael went back to the board behind him, erased it, and drew three vertical parallel lines with his marker.

"Let me try to pull it all together this way," Michael said. "You talk of parallel universes, Geoffrey, and wormholes or some other gateway or portal to move from one universe to another. Those are the terms of theoretical physics and astrophysics. You're not positive they exist at all, but given the theoretical models you guys have come up with, you think it's likely that something like that exists. Am I on track?"

"A little simplistic, but yes. I can accept the basic outlines of what you're saying."

"Well, the shekinah glory and some of the related theological concepts we've been discussing can actually be understood in similar terms," Michael continued. "Let me emphasize—we can't rely on theoretical physics to understand God. But that kind of thinking may help us begin to wrap our minds around what heaven may be like."

He turned back to the lines he'd drawn on the melamine board. "The place where God resides is not really a place at all, at least not in terms of the space–time continuum where we exist. Rather, in a sense it's another dimension. Or more likely, many dimensions or an infinite number of dimensions, which reach far beyond our three dimensions of height, width, and length, and the fourth dimension of time."

"What do you suppose those other dimensions might be like?" Dan asked.

He was now thoroughly involved in the discussion for the first time since he had arrived on the compound. That unsettling experience with the beam of light had gotten his attention.

"Superstrings," Geoffrey said, referring to one idea theoretical physicists had suggested for a multidimensional reality.

"Perhaps," Michael said. "But superstrings, if they do exist at all, are thought to operate on the subatomic level, right?"

"Yes, they may be the ultimate, indivisible level of reality, vibrating in tiny, tightly folded configurations of ten dimensions or so," Geoffrey said.

"All theory," Dudley said. "All speculation."

"But perhaps valid speculation," Geoffrey retorted.

"In any event, what I'm suggesting is that we consider an extradimensional reality that exists on a much grander scale," Michael said. "It might begin on the subatomic level, but the end result could be another universe of sorts—a universe that is parallel to ours, and may even interact with ours. Now look back at these three lines and think of them this way."

Then he jotted down some terms in the spaces between the lines.

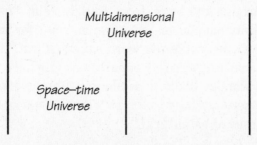

"Now, as you can see, our space–time reality exists in only one of these areas—or 'universes,' if we want to use that term," Michael said. "But multidimensional reality can exist in both. Or to put this another way, the multidimensional universe—and any beings who inhabit that universe—can overlap with our space–time universe. But unless we're given some special 'multidimensional travel ticket,' we can't do a reverse trip. We can't leave our universe and explore the realm of extra dimensions."

"But what does this have to do with the light or Star overhead?" Yael asked.

Again, Michael turned to his diagram and made another entry.

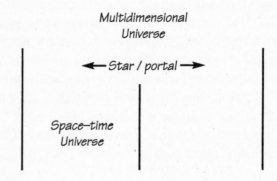

"From this, you can see that the Star or strange light overhead may actually be a portal or window that gives us an extra-special glimpse into the multidimensional universe," Michael said. "Or the Star might even provide us with the 'multidimensional travel ticket' that we otherwise lack. Certainly, Joanna and Dan and the guard who was healed seemed to step into some reality that's quite different from our own."

"Sounds like you're really trying to drag the supernatural into this discussion through the back door," Skiddy said. "You're just substituting 'multidimensional' or 'extradimensional' for 'supernatural.'"

"Personally, I don't like the word *supernatural*," Michael replied. "It implies something entirely separate from what's natural. Yet I'm beginning to wonder if the possible multidimensional reality we're dealing with here actually overlaps with the space–time arena that we typically regard as natural."

He pondered his own words for a moment and seemed to hesitate about his next point. But then he squared his shoulders and proceeded. "I'm a little reluctant to bring in Christianity here because I know some of you are suspicious of my motives. But really, Christ's incarnation is an example of what I'm talking about. That may help you picture the point. The Gospel of John tells us He was preexistent, the agent of creation. In other words, He existed in an infinite, multidimensional reality—what many might call heaven—but chose to limit Himself to our space–time world. To put this in theological terms, He was incarnated as Jesus of Nazareth. Yet while He was here on earth, He continued to be one with His Father in heaven and to participate in many ways in the multidimensional reality He had left."

"And remember what He was like when He returned to earth briefly after His resurrection," Peter reminded him.

"Yes. He had a special kind of body that could move in and out of locked rooms. That could appear and disappear. Like our bodies in some ways, but far beyond them. You might say Christ had an extradimensional body after the Resurrection."

"So in a sense, you're saying that the light up there may give us a look at the same multidimensional world Jesus came from?" Joanna said. "A look at heaven?"

Michael shrugged. "That's the precise point I want us to explore. If the light is in fact the shekinah glory, I think there's a very good chance that it will provide us with a window on the reality beyond our reality."

"So let's assume that the light is really the shekinah—and that it can tell us something about God's universe," Joanna said. "What exactly could we expect to see if we looked deeply into this portal—this Star? What would the multidimensional, parallel universe on the other side be like?"

Like Dan, she had been able to think of little more than her recent encounter with the shining figure and the mysterious light.

"Hasn't this speculation gone far enough?" Dudley asked, his frustration finally getting the best of him. "You're talking religion, not science."

"Yet science hasn't answered any of our questions," Joanna protested.

"But Michael isn't really providing a convincing answer either," Geoffrey said. "Michael, you're simply too sectarian. Too tied to one theological tradition. I'll admit that you're advancing our discussion to some extent. But I'd like for us to get away from the Bible and the shekinah glory and all that. We really must think in broader terms. Extradimensional reality—or heaven, if you want to call it that—isn't populated exclusively by beings who buy into your particular belief system. I do believe there may be extraterrestrials up there. But I think they're likely to be intelligent beings much like us—more advanced, certainly, but still like us."

"I don't pretend to have all the answers," Michael said. "But I think that the evidence we have about this light in the sky warrants further investigation into the shekinah glory. To talk vaguely in terms of extraterrestrials and UFO's might be fashionable, but it might also be a fantasy that's not rooted in solid historical research."

Geoffrey was obviously not convinced, but Michael held up his hand to cut him off. "Let me continue for a moment, and then we can return to the UFO issue if you like."

Michael then looked over at Joanna again.

"You asked what we might see if we could peer through this Star portal into the other, extradimensional universe," he began. "The answer is that, without help from the other side, we would probably see very little, and certainly nothing that made any sense. One way of thinking of this is to consider the old *Flatland* story that Edwin Abbott published back in the nineteenth century. Do any of you remember that?"

Dudley and Geoffrey were the only two who indicated knowledge of the book. So Michael provided some background for the others.

"For the benefit of those of you who aren't familiar with the story, let me summarize it this way. Abbott imagined a land where everything was two-dimensional—length and width, but no height. Like a sheet of typing paper. Furthermore, those who inhabited this land could only perceive reality in these two dimensions."

To illustrate, he held up one sheet of paper.

"Then, Abbott speculated about what would happen if a three-dimensional being, like you or me, entered this two-dimensional space."

He pointed again to the piece of paper.

"Our arms or legs or head or trunk might pass through the flat plane, but they'd be seen only as separate, straight lines by the two-dimensional creatures of Flatland—because they'd have no understanding or perception of creatures with the dimension of height."

To demonstrate, Michael drew three straight lines on the melamine board. "What they would see in their two-dimensional world—as they looked along the edge of their paper-thin reality—might look like this."

| Arm | Head | Arm |

"That's all the Flatlander would see from his perspective on his flat world if he looked at places where, let's say, your raised arms and your head had entered his two-dimensional space. It's sort of like what you'd see if you were half submerged in a very still body of water and you looked exactly along the surface of the water at another human who was wading near you with his arms raised. Suppose the surface of the water cut through the person's face and upper arms. If you couldn't see any part of that person's body except the parts that were touched by the surface of the water, then you'd see what the Flatlander sees from his world."

Then Michael drew three circles on the board.

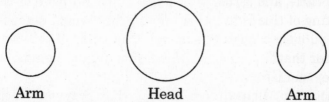

| Arm | Head | Arm |

Pointing at the circles, he said, "Next, assume the same situation. Your arms and head are still in Flatland. But now, somehow you can lift that Flatlander above his flat plane, so he can look down on the spaces where you've entered his world. He still wouldn't see all of you, because remember, he can't perceive three-dimensional space. He has no ability to see height. But looking down, he would be able to see three circles where you cut through his space."

Michael paused and looked around at the group. Geoffrey and Dudley were looking bored, undoubtedly because they had read and discussed the Flatland story in a physics class. But the others seemed enthralled—so he continued.

"But of course, if any *three*-dimensional creature happened along—you or I or our dog, for instance—that creature would immediately see the entire three-dimensional figure, with arms, legs, stomach, head, and so on."

To illustrate, he posted a complete figure from some simple Microsoft Word clip art, and then drew a straight line through the head and arms.

"The line represents the limited, two-dimensional line of sight or perception that the people in Flatland would have of this figure," Michael explained. "In other words, they would see only a small part of three sections of the body—thin slices of the two arms and the head. But of course, as three-dimensional beings, we can see the whole person.

"Flatlanders would have no idea that they were dealing with one complete figure," Michael concluded. "And even if one of them happened to be so brilliant that he suspected one entity was involved, he wouldn't have a clue as to what that entity would look like."

Although Geoffrey and Dudley immediately understood what Michael was getting at, the other team members were still wrestling with what Michael's illustration might mean in their own investigation.

"Can you give us an example of how this might work for us?" Dan asked. "How might this relate to the Star?"

"Sure. Let's go back to Ezekiel's special angels, the cherubim," Michael said. "You'll remember that some accounts say they had two faces, and others say they had four?"

"Yes," Dan replied.

"Okay," Michael continued, "these reports differ from one another. The descriptions of these kinds of angels, cherubim, may vary. But in fact, all the reports may be quite accurate. It's just that each observer is reporting the characteristics of a multidimensional creature—in this case a particular kind of angel. But each is describing it from a different vantage point in our three-dimensional universe."

He pointed back at his Flatland diagrams. "Remember Flatland. If a three-dimensional figure enters a two-dimensional world, the two-dimensional creature may see one line or two or three, depending on where the observer is and how many parts of the three-dimensional body enter the flat space. In a similar way, if a multidimensional creature enters our space–time world, we may perceive it with two 'faces' one time, and with four on another occasion."

"So what you're saying is that we, in our limited space–time universe, are possibly seeing only a part of what that Star in the sky is all about," Dan said. "Because of our natural limitations, we—and our scientific instruments—are incapable of seeing the whole picture?"

"That's exactly right," Michael said. "We're stymied—unless, of course, those who inhabit that transcendent universe want us to see more. Who knows? They may be able to give us special faculties—special eyes to see, or special ears to hear, or other senses that we're not even aware of. With these enhanced senses, we might then understand a little better what's going on up there—and what that phenomenon is all about."

Joanna, who had been lost in thought during the presentation, now perked up. "I think I'm beginning to get it," she said. "Maybe I was able to see that shining figure because I was given some sort of special insight or revelation. I was given a kind of window on another reality by whatever or whoever is on the other side of that light in the sky."

"That may be," Michael said. "In effect, you might have been given special eyes and ears, at least for a few moments."

Dan was clearly getting excited at the turn the discussion had taken. "So the beam of light I saw heal that guard, and maybe the glowing object itself—the Star, which we can't measure with our instruments—these phenomena may somehow be signals of extradimensionality?" he asked.

"Yes, I think the strange lights may in fact accompany or signal multidimensional probes into our reality," Michael said. "Certainly, such an interpretation is consistent with what we know of unearthly lights that accompany visits from another reality in the Bible, or in later Christian tradition."

"But we can't limit ourselves to Christian theology and the Bible!" Geoffrey protested.

"Why not?" Joanna asked. Now she was becoming impatient with what she was beginning to see as the limited perspective of traditional science.

"I'm not necessarily discounting the idea that these biblical references could be related to extradimensional events," Geoffrey said, backing off slightly. "But I'm virtually certain that there's much, much more involved."

As the others grew quiet, he pressed his case. "For all we know, we may be encountering for the very first time an extraterrestrial intelligence—an ETI. These aliens might have an important message for us, something that could change the course of our history forever. Why get tied down to the Bible at this point?"

Surprisingly, Dan—who might have been sympathetic to such an argument before his encounter with the light—remained unconvinced. "Frankly, Geoffrey, your views seem too speculative," he said. "I mean, I really want to find an answer to this thing. But I think I'd rather rely on historical precedent—even when it comes from the Bible—than on just one person's speculation."

"Let's face it, Geoffrey, you're going beyond even what Michael has been saying," Joanna added. "When you start dragging your UFO's out, you don't sound entirely convincing. I think I'd prefer the Star of Bethlehem rather than some variation on Steven Spielberg's *E.T.*"

Geoffrey became visibly upset at the rebuke, but he didn't reply. Instead, he glanced over at Dudley Dunster, apparently hoping for some support from a fellow scientist and astronomer. But Dudley was in no mood to come to the defense of anyone—much less a UFO advocate.

"As far as I'm concerned, this discussion is good for only one thing—an interesting tidbit in the tabloid press," Dudley groused. "Is that the next step for us? The *National Enquirer?*"

His lips were pursed with barely concealed malice that now seemed to be directed generally around the room, with only Skiddy Kirkland being spared.

"This line of thinking is a dead end," Dudley continued. "Means nothing to a real scientist confronted with an actual light shining in the sky. We're still left with zilch, as far as I can see. So forget the Bible, UFO's, and Flatland! Try some legitimate research for a change!"

To emphasize his point, he stood up and stretched, and made an attempt to smooth out his wrinkled fatigues. "If this discussion is finally over, I want to return to our real business—which is analyzing that light scientifically."

"That's fine except for one thing," Joanna said. "Regular scientific research has gotten us nowhere."

"I think we just have to keep trying," Dudley replied. "At least we should drop this Bible business."

"That seems reasonable to me," Skiddy agreed. "I think we should move on. Try to find a more productive approach."

"I'm through with my presentation," Michael said, seemingly unconcerned by the criticism. "And certainly, I didn't expect for us to come to any final conclusions. But now I hope we're at least inclined to consider more options—since traditional science seems inadequate in giving us answers to this problem."

"Just one last thing," Dudley said, ignoring the barb from Michael about traditional science. "I want to emphasize that this entire discussion must be kept within these walls. Let me be clear: I do not expect to see another article on this matter in any newspaper."

The implied threat hung over the room, seeming to demand some sort of response.

Just who does Dudley think he is? He's not exactly the leader of this team! Dan reflected. Dan was on the verge of calling the Harvard astronomer's bluff by asking him to finish his thought. He wanted to say, "*Or what, Dudley? What are you going to do if another article comes out?*"

But the look in Dudley's eyes gave him pause. There was something strange about the man, something a little over the edge.

In any case, Dan had no opportunity to act on his impulse. Unexpectedly, the officer of the guard came striding through the door with another set of papers for Yael. Everyone froze in place—even Dudley, who was already headed toward the door. These messages usually contained important news, which was almost always bad.

Yael quickly perused the e-mail message and looked up with a pained look on her face.

"You're not going to like this. The *New York Times* has done it again. They've reported now that we're looking into UFO's as an answer to the light. They even suggest that we're leaning toward that as the most likely solution."

"How did they find out about our discussion so fast?" Dan exclaimed, plainly stunned. "And they got it all wrong! We haven't zeroed in on UFO's . . ."

But the message, as shocking as it was, didn't come close to the reaction from Dudley. He turned such a deep red that Dan—who stopped in mid-sentence—thought the Harvard astronomer might have a stroke on the spot. Dudley's pent-up anger and frustration almost seemed to lift him off the ground and propel him directly toward Michael James.

The cream puff had suddenly turned into a human cannonball. With grasping, outstretched hands, he rushed headlong toward his target—the throat of the dumbstruck Wheaton professor.

TWENTY-SIX

DUDLEY barreled squarely into Michael James before anyone could intercept him. Even Peter's bodyguards were caught completely by surprise.

"You're to blame for all this!" Dudley screamed. "I'll kill you!"

But the Wheaton man recovered quickly, parried the thrust at his throat, and spun the Harvard astronomer around and over on his stomach, against one of the tables.

Holding Dudley from behind in a wristlock, which prevented any further threatening movements, Michael said almost casually, "Relax, Dudley. You're getting too excited. Calm down."

"You've been leaking these stories, haven't you?" Dudley hissed at Michael, as a flood of disconnected, pent-up venom poured out of his mouth.

"Of course not, I . . ."

"You've come up with this Star nonsense for one reason only—it furthers your career!" Dudley shouted, squirming in Michael's grip. "You're grandstanding! Well, this may be great for fundamentalists. But you know it's a disaster for me—and I won't let you do it!"

"I'm no more enthusiastic about UFO's than you are," Michael said calmly.

But Dudley was in no mood to listen. "I'll expose you for what you are, you hypocrite! Here you are, having an affair with that Israeli and pretending to be such a holier-than-thou spiritual leader. I'll get you . . ."

The accusation took Michael by surprise. Without thinking, he glanced at Yael, then quickly composed himself. *How did he know? Has her cover been compromised?*

As for Dan, he felt as if a knife had been thrust through his gut. He didn't dare look at Joanna. *Now she knows I blabbed. She knows I let her down.*

But events were now moving so quickly, there was no time for reflection on anyone's part. Dudley started squirming so furiously under Michael's grip that it seemed the astronomer's wrist might snap. Then he abruptly stopped resisting and began coughing violently. Suddenly, he went limp.

Michael immediately released him and felt the carotid artery in his neck to be sure there was a pulse. "Get him over to the first aid clinic—now!" Michael ordered.

Yael immediately pulled out her radio and called the guard shack for help. They arrived a few moments later with a stretcher and rushed Dudley over to the medical facility.

After the guards had left with Dudley, the other members of the team lingered in the headquarters building, obviously trying to regain their emotional equilibrium after the incident.

"I knew he was on edge, but I had no idea he would completely lose it," Dan said.

"His reaction is understandable," Skiddy said darkly. "He tries his best to maintain high scientific standards. But the pressure to lower them is overwhelming. So I'm completely sympathetic."

Then the project director turned his wrath toward Michael James. "If he's seriously hurt, you're responsible!"

The battle lines are drawn, Dan mused, looking around the room. *Skiddy's still openly at war with Michael. Dudley too, but he's wacko. And amazing! For once, Joanna and I may be on the same side—with Michael—even if we're at odds with each other.*

Then he thought of the California astrophysicist. *More of a loose cannon than I thought. Hard to read.*

As for Yael, Dan had never been able to figure her out. *The inscrutable Miss Israel. Will we ever know what you're all about?*

Suddenly, Dan found his attention jerked back to the headquarters room. "May I have your attention?" Peter Van Campe was saying to the group. "Obviously, the stress has gotten out of hand. I hope I'm correct in assuming that everyone still wants to find an answer to the mysterious light—even if we disagree on how to go about it. Am I right?"

The team members responded with uncertain nods, clearly puzzled about where the foundation director was trying to take them. "Good," Peter said. "As far as I'm concerned, you're doing all you can to solve this mystery. You can be confident I'll continue to support your efforts. But now, let me suggest a change of scene for a day or so. Get off the compound. Some of you should check out what's happening in Jerusalem. We should also send some representatives to another research site—if they'll let us in. Just to see if we can generate any new ideas. Then get back here and resolve this thing! Okay?"

No one seemed particularly optimistic that they'd learn anything new during the short break. "But at least it's a paid holiday," Dan whispered to Joanna, causing her to smile slightly. *First decent reaction from her in weeks. Progress!*

As the others were leaving, Peter pulled the project director aside. "Skiddy, I'll be leaving in about an hour," Peter said in low tones. "My party will drive to Tel Aviv, where the Panoplia jet is waiting for us. We'll be back in Chicago by tomorrow. But I want you to leave no stone unturned in solving this mystery—and that means all options. Regular science, extradimensional possibilities, shekinah glory, everything. Can you live with that?"

Skiddy nodded, though a voice from somewhere deep inside said, *Everything but your spiritual foolishness!*

"You're in charge," Peter continued. "But I want reports every day as to your progress, or lack of it. This thing seems to be heating up. The social and political unrest is escalating. I want to stay on top of things personally. And don't worry—you'll be given further financing as necessary. Plenty of our resources will be channeled into this project. This is our top priority now."

Skiddy liked hearing the sound of extra money jingling around back there in the background. But he now saw Van Campe as an adversary as much as a benefactor. The money was important. But the possibility that his and Dudley's scholarly reputations might be destroyed was an equally grave concern.

So we're on a high-wire act. Well and good. But I expect to be standing safely up there at the top of the big tent when this thing is all over.

And frankly, I don't care if Van Campe, James, and all the rest of them splatter their guts out on the hard, cold ground below!

As Dan and Joanna walked quietly back to their quarters, she turned to him. "How did Dudley know about Yael and Michael? Did you tell him?"

Here it comes. No point in denying anything now, Dan decided.

"Yes," he admitted, hardly able to look her in the eye. "I told both him and Skiddy. After I talked to them, I could have pulled my tongue out because I knew I'd made a mistake. But at the time, it seemed the right thing to do. I didn't understand Michael as well then as I think I do now. I was more suspicious."

He looked at her sadly. "But I know I was wrong. I've been afraid of this moment for a couple of days, ever since I violated your confidence. I love you, Joanna. I know we've been having trouble, but I don't want to lose you. I really don't. Can you forgive me?"

She gave him a long, serious look and then smiled. The broadest, warmest smile he'd had from her in a long time. "Of course. And I love you too—even though I may not always act like it."

Oblivious to a guard who was studying them curiously, they embraced and kissed. Dan held her in his arms an extra moment and looked gratefully into her eyes, this time without hesitation. "That Star does seem able to heal—in more ways than one," he said.

TWENTY-SEVEN

THE much-feared social unrest in the wake of the Star phenomenon began in earnest in the United States with a wave of terrorist attacks on various sites in Manhattan. In only two weeks' time—which began with the appearance of the mysterious light—the heart had, in effect, been ripped out of New York City.

A right-wing Aryan group, headquartered in the Montana backwoods, had hit the World Trade Center with multiple firebombs that caused considerably more property damage and personal injuries than the bombing of 1993. More than 100 people died in the new attack, and the explosions had seriously injured many more.

The images from the TV coverage were seared into the public consciousness. During the Vietnam War, the definitive picture that had highlighted the horrors of American napalm bombing was the wounded, naked Vietnamese girl, running and crying with other civilians down a highway that had come under heavy air bombardment.

In this recent violence in Lower Manhattan, the public would never forget the stark image of a young mother, a tourist from the Midwest, whose tears streamed down her soot-covered face. She was cradling in her arms the charred remains of her daughter as she pushed her way out of the wreckage.

Another blast had damaged beyond repair the odd, skinny Flatiron Building, on Twenty-third Street at Madison Square, where Broadway crosses Fifth Avenue. A group that called itself "Aliens for

International Justice" claimed responsibility. Fortunately, the explosion had occurred at night, so only a handful of night workers had been injured. No one had died.

"We'll restore it completely!" the mayor had said. "Terrorists won't win this round!"

But news features and editorials suggested average citizens were no longer so sure they could trust brave words from public officials. Especially after the most recent threat—an attempt to launch biological attacks at the busy subway interchanges at Grand Central Station and on the Lexington line at Fifty-ninth Street.

Granted, antiterrorist operatives had thwarted these attacks, which had been attempted by a cult that called itself the New Jerusalem Way. But the emergence of this group in particular signaled a new and disturbing turn in international terrorism, reminiscent of the cult attack on the Tokyo subways years before.

"These people aren't just high school graduates," one government source told the *Washington Post*. "They include scientists, scholars, people with special skills, who know how to handle deadly viruses and how to assemble tactical nuclear devices. They're true revolutionaries—and extremely well-prepared. The war against terrorism is definitely changing for the worse."

Ironically, terrorist bombings, shootings, and other threats had actually been on the decline in New York for a number of years. The attitude had increasingly become *It'll never happen here. Our security is too tight. Our local gun laws are too tough. Our cops are too vigilant.*

But antiterrorist agencies in the federal and state governments knew better. They understood that it wasn't a question of whether, but when. The mysterious light in the eastern sky had apparently been all that was needed to escalate the dissatisfaction of a number of splinter groups to violence.

As government agents bemoaned these developments in the anonymous reports they leaked to the press, the leaders of perhaps the deadliest of these organizations, the New Jerusalem Way, trickled one-by-one into their well-disguised headquarters in a remote location in the western United States. When the entire "board of elders" had finally assembled, they began to lay final plans for an ultimate series of attacks—a "purification" campaign involving tactical nuclear and biological weapons, which they believed would usher in a new era of peace and justice.

"The World Trade Center incident will pale when we strike," the chairman boasted.

"Jerusalem, New York, London, Paris—these will be just the beginning of the purification," the chief of staff promised.

"The light will be our signal," the chief spiritual guide said. "And our twelve light messengers, posted in major research groups around the world, stand ready to alert us when the final countdown begins. Most likely, the group that the cofounder has joined in Israel will be the first to know."

"The cofounder says the time is imminent," the chairman said. "The light is changing. Those from beyond will reveal themselves shortly. We're almost ready to receive their final signal. Then, we'll become their high priests. We'll be the ones to help them establish the new and better world."

TWENTY-EIGHT

A short break was exactly what Dan and Joanna felt they needed at this point. The stress of the last few days had been overwhelming, and they needed to distance themselves from their work at the compound. The destination that they had chosen was Jerusalem.

"Strange things are happening there," Dan told his wife. "Things that may have some connection with what we're going through here on the compound."

He had learned through e-mail messages he had received from several colleagues in religious studies back in the States—as well as from academic contacts in the Middle East—that splinter religious groups and cults were gathering in increasing numbers in the Holy City. Also, there had been news reports suggesting that terrorists could be targeting Jerusalem during this chaotic period.

"There's been no major violence yet, but the Israeli military is apparently preparing for the worst," he said.

"What does Yael say about the situation?" Joanna asked.

"We'll find out shortly," Dan replied. "She and Michael are driving down there with us. By the way, have you heard anything about Dudley?"

"I heard he's still in the medical clinic, though he's supposed to be much better this morning," she said, lowering her voice. "They've put him on some sort of medication. A tranquilizer, I think. He may follow us down to Jerusalem later today or tomorrow with Geoffrey."

"Yes, Geoffrey told me he wanted to try a few more tests with his instruments, just to be sure he hadn't overlooked anything," Dan said. "He also wants to check those buddies of his working at the SETI site," he added, pointing to the compound next to theirs, just to the south, where they frequently saw khaki-clad guards and other personnel moving about.

Joanna shook her head. "I still don't think any of these devices—either the ones the SETI people use to detect radio frequencies, or the ones we have for measuring light spectra, heat waves, or the like—are going to tell us anything about the Star," she said.

Dan smiled. "Funny, how we've taken to referring to that light as the Star."

"Shows Michael's powers of persuasion," she replied.

It's also funny that it doesn't bother me anymore when she refers to Michael as some sort of authority, Dan reflected. *I guess witnessing an extradimensional event can change anyone's thinking, even mine.*

A few minutes later, one of the vans pulled up to the front of the headquarters building, with Yael at the wheel and Michael James in the bucket seat beside her. Dan and Joanna piled into the seats just behind them, and they roared out of the compound and onto the highway leading south to Jerusalem.

"So you don't feel we need a guard—or a driver—with us?" Dan asked, holding on for dear life as Yael took the curves on the road at high speed. A cloak of early morning darkness still covered the countryside, and Dan couldn't understand how Yael could possibly see where she was going.

"I'm the only guard you need," she replied curtly. "And I've driven these roads more often than any of the soldiers in our compound."

Dan glanced down at the semiautomatic pistol strapped to her hip. In the space between the two front seats, he could see an inch or so of a rifle barrel protruding out from under a canvas cover.

Okay, she's prepared. And she seems to know how to drive. But can Miss Israel really shoot? We can only hope.

TWENTY-NINE

DUDLEY, the outing will do you good," Geoffrey assured the shaky Harvard astronomer. "You check out fine. Just a severe panic attack, that's all."

"I'm still a little on edge," Dudley said. "A little weak. And embarrassed."

"No reason to be embarrassed," Geoffrey said. "These are trying times. Lots of stress. Probably you care too much. But that's a strength, not a weakness."

"So what are your plans?" Dudley asked.

"First, we'll drop by the SETI compound and see some of my colleagues there. Very brief visit. Then on to Jerusalem. We should get there an hour or so after the others—Yael, Michael, Dan, and Joanna."

"I can't deal with Michael," Dudley said.

"So we'll avoid him. I've only agreed to a rendezvous late in the day just before we come back. And here, try these." He handed the Harvard astronomer several unmarked capsules. "They're a prescription I use when I start feeling anxious. Calms you down nicely."

"You use them?" Dudley asked.

"Sure. Works like a charm. Take all three. I'll carry some more with me in case you need them."

Dudley looked doubtfully at the pills for a moment, then shrugged and downed all three. "Nothing to lose, I guess," he said. "Couldn't turn in any worse performance than last night."

As their driver turned into the entrance to the SETI compound, which lay only about a third of a mile from their own site, Dudley

188

was already feeling drowsy. He seemed to be moving and thinking in slow motion. But at least the nervousness and hostility had disappeared.

The idea of examining a SETI site up close fascinated him. Though he wasn't too optimistic about finding aliens in space, he had always been interested in SETI research. Besides, the term "Search for Extraterrestrial Intelligence" had a rather exotic and exciting sound to it, even for a jaded astronomer such as himself.

As they drove through the compound, he noticed several telltale pieces of SETI equipment. On one side of the road, he saw the huge dish of a late-model radio telescope, accompanied by a version of the so-called "Targeted Search System," or TSS. He knew that the TSS was a transportable SETI system often used with radio telescopes to enhance sensitivity of astronomical observations.

On another side of the road he saw equipment that he was certain represented the latest "Follow-up Detection Device," or FUDD. This apparatus, he recalled, was also used to increase sensitivity and accuracy of space signals through special filters that eliminated much of the background noise on earth. The FUDD equipment allowed investigators to use a small antenna to search in more detail following a preliminary detection of a possible extraterrestrial signal by a large radio-telescope antenna.

Amazing, how much equipment we make available for a potentially useless purpose, he thought rather absently. But somehow, he couldn't get angry or irritated about the possible waste of money. *Having trouble focusing. But for once, it feels good not to think or worry so much.*

The van stopped about a hundred yards into the compound, and Geoffrey called out to a couple of men who were standing near some of the equipment. They picked up small bags and ran toward the vehicle.

"Dudley, see these two men?" Geoffrey said, speaking rather slowly and carefully, the astronomer thought.

"Sure."

"This is Frederick, and this is Harold. You know them. Both scientists and astronomers. You met them at a conference a couple of years ago."

"I did?"

"Yes. You knew them before I did. Maybe you forgot. But if you keep thinking, you'll remember."

"Okay." Anything Geoffrey said was all right with him.

"I think we should invite them to visit our compound," Geoffrey said. "What do you think? They could help us find an answer to the light. Good idea?"

"Sure."

"You should invite them. You know Skiddy better than I do. So you'll invite them? Okay?"

"Sounds okay to me."

"Great."

The driver was already heading out of the compound and turning onto the road that led south to Jerusalem. Dudley enjoyed the gentle swaying of the van and became mesmerized by the orange groves and foliage speeding by outside his window. Soon he drifted off to sleep.

 THIRTY

Y A E L ' S group drove in silence for a long while, enjoying the dawn vistas of the mountain country north of the Sea of Galilee. Although they had become accustomed to arising by 2:00 A.M. to begin their research, they had welcomed the opportunity to sleep a little later on this "holiday" of sorts that they were taking. The extra rest had made them all more alert.

"It should take only a few hours for us to get close to Jerusalem," Yael said. "Then the time we make will depend on the traffic. I understand the roads are a great deal more crowded these days— what with the Star and all. They've even blocked off many of the arteries leading into congested parts of Jerusalem, including the Old City. Fortunately, we have a government pass that should get us through."

"What exactly do you hear from the government about the social and political situation down there?" Dan asked.

Yael hesitated for a moment, and Michael glanced at her, knowing what was going through her mind. Just before they had left the compound, she had received word that security had been beefed up another notch because of additional terrorist threats and intensified agitation among cult members who had overrun the city.

"We must be careful and stick together when we enter the city," she said. "Security's very tight. If any Israeli officials stop you, don't argue. Just comply."

"Sounds serious," Joanna said.

"It is serious," Yael replied.

As the van sped southward, through Nazareth and Nablus, they became lost in their thoughts. Their van worked harder as they moved up the mountainsides, reaching a peak of sorts at Ramallah, which lies only about nine miles from Jerusalem.

"You can see why passages in the Bible often talk about people going up to Jerusalem, regardless of the direction they're coming from," Michael said. "Obviously, what the writers had in mind was not the direction, but the altitude of Jerusalem, which is relatively high. It's a city on a hill."

Finally, moving steadily along with the traffic on the Nablus Road, they entered the city proper. Then they passed through a checkpoint where all ordinary traffic was stopped and put on a detour route. But by flashing her government pass, Yael got them through easily and continued to drive directly toward the most ancient part of Jerusalem. The Old City wall soon appeared up ahead, with the golden-topped Dome of the Rock, the "Mosque of Omar," perched on the Temple Mount, the ancient site of Solomon's temple.

"What an incredible sight," Joanna said, viewing the historic landscape for the first time.

"I've seen the Old City many times, but I never quite get used to it," Dan said. "So much history. So many of our own spiritual roots here."

But Yael and Michael weren't taking in the sights. They were watching the road and side streets closely, looking for any activities or individuals that might bear special scrutiny.

Soon, Yael swerved into a small, gated parking area about two blocks from the Old City wall.

"The van will be safe here," she said. "Geoffrey and Dudley have directions for this place too. I told them we'd check for them after 5:00 P.M., every hour on the hour, at the southern end of the Wailing Wall."

Dan explained to Joanna that Yael was referring to the retaining wall on the western side of the Temple Mount. Also called the "Western Wall," this impressive architectural fragment, which was constructed of huge stone blocks, had encircled the temple and temple court restored by Herod the Great just before the birth of Christ.

As predicted, the crowds in the Old City were incredibly dense. Dan and Joanna agreed that they had never encountered anything quite like this, even in New York or Boston at rush hour. The four had to push and shove constantly to be sure they stayed together as they inched their way along the narrow Al Wad Road. After you passed through the Damascus Gate and entered the Old City, the walkway became more or less an extension of Nablus Road.

There was absolutely no place to stop for a breather. Dan knew that if they hesitated, the crowd behind would push them forward or might even knock them off their feet.

But the teeming throngs were only a small part of their concerns. Dan noticed that Yael, who was leading the way, often rested a hand casually on top of her pistol, which she had hidden in a holster just under her loose fatigue shirt.

"Expecting trouble," Dan whispered to Joanna, with a gesture toward the sabra.

"I'm glad she's with us," Joanna said. "Is Skiddy in that other van?"

"No—said he had some things to tend to on the compound," Dan said. "Maybe he figured he'd get more rest being away from us for a while."

"He's certainly not a happy camper," Joanna muttered, giving an elbow to a particularly aggressive pedestrian dressed in an ankle-length Arab caftan and kaffiyeh headdress. "Not much happier than Dudley, as far as I can see.

"This Star thing is not really their idea of enjoyable or meaningful research. It obviously involves categories that they're not comfortable with. They're not exactly flexible thinkers. I get the feeling they're so frustrated that it wouldn't take much to make them lose it completely, push them over the edge—that is, if Dudley is any example," she continued.

The noisy, pressing mob made further conversation impossible. So they lapsed into silence and concentrated on keeping sight of Yael and Michael, who were fighting their way through just ahead.

Dan was glad he was watching the other two fairly closely, because unexpectedly, both Yael and Michael began gesturing vigorously to the left.

"Left turn coming up," Dan said. "Ah, the Via Dolorosa."

"What's that?" Joanna shouted, trying to be heard above the din.

"Way of Sorrows. The street where Jesus is supposed to have carried the cross to Calvary."

When they had turned and begun walking down the Via Dolorosa toward the Temple Mount, both grew quiet. The crowds thinned out somewhat, to the point that they could now catch up with Michael and Yael.

"This is really where Jesus carried His cross?" Joanna asked with an almost reverent tone in her voice.

"There's good reason to think this was the area," Michael replied. "A little way ahead is Pilate's Praetorium, where the Roman procurator passed judgment on Christ. That arch over the street up there is known as the Ecce Homo arch. Commemorates Pilate's Latin words referring to Christ, 'Behold the man!'"

"I seem to recall from somewhere that the Roman emperor Hadrian erected that in about A.D. 135," Dan said. "Is that right?"

Michael looked at him in surprise. "Yeah. That's exactly right."

Dan was proud of himself for dredging that date from some buried memory connected with a previous trip.

"Of course, whatever took place here actually occurred seventy or eighty feet or more below us," Yael said, her archaeological training now coming to the fore. "That was two thousand years ago, and a lot of trash, dirt, and stone has accumulated on the city since then."

After they passed under the arch, a high wall, punctuated by the Antonia Tower, rose on their right.

"This may be the most dangerous spot in the world right now," Yael said, pointing beyond the tower. "Just on the other side of that wall are the Dome of the Rock and the Temple Mount—the holiest of sites for Muslims and Jews, not to mention Christians. A major flash point for religious conflict."

They saw TV camera crews stationed here and there. One, with the CNN logo on the equipment, gave the Americans a sense of familiarity, even though they were far from home.

Soon they had climbed a steep set of stairs and were standing on the level ground that constituted the Temple Mount. The striking Mosque of Omar—the Dome of the Rock—glittered in the sun a short distance away. Just above it, still glowing mysteriously in the eastern sky over the Mount of Olives, was the strange light that had baffled them for so long.

"Fill me in about this place," Joanna said, surveying the Mount. "I'm totally ignorant when it comes to the Bible and Israel."

"The Muslims believe that the prophet Muhammad ascended to heaven from here," Dan said. "They think his last footprint on earth is still visible in the large rock that's under the Dome."

"Jews believe that's the same rock where Abraham was going to sacrifice his son Isaac," Yael said. "Also, they believe that the Hebrew temples, including Solomon's temple, were built on this spot."

"And then there are the Christians," Michael said. "Some Christian interpreters of the Bible have concluded that when the temple is rebuilt, that will be the sign that it's time for the world to end and for Christ to return."

"And remember, there are sects of Orthodox Jews who believe the same thing—except they assume that the rebuilding of the temple will signal the *first* advent," Yael said.

They lapsed into silence, contemplating the scene that spread out before them. The activity on the Temple Mount was quite different from what Dan and Michael remembered on their previous trips, and even from what Yael had seen just a few weeks before. Now, the lame, the blind, and others with physical or emotional ailments were sitting or wandering around on the grounds, which were more crowded than any of them remembered.

Then Joanna broke the silence. "Could we go inside the Dome and take a look at the rock? I might not get another chance."

But she never got her chance. Just as they started walking toward the Mosque of Omar, the fireworks began.

✺ THIRTY-ONE

T H E R E wasn't a cloud overhead, but the sky suddenly grew dark—as though a full eclipse had obscured the sun.

All eyes turned up toward the heavens, and that was when the strange light began to pulsate and move. For a moment, it flared to at least three times its usual size, or considerably larger than a full moon. Then, the object shrank to the size of a stellar pinprick. And then, once again, it expanded in a kind of controlled explosion. Back and forth, large to small, in a mesmerizing cycle of light.

"What's going on?" Joanna exclaimed to no one in particular.

"Look!" Dan said in awe.

Now, the object was moving, accelerating, from one end of the sky to the other, from east to west.

"It almost looks like a fast-moving comet!" Michael said. "See, there's a tail!"

"Or a bolt of lightning in slow motion," Dan whispered.

"I wonder if anyone is measuring these movements?" Joanna said. "Some light waves or radiation must be showing up on some instruments somewhere."

Before anyone could answer, the light flashed back across the sky, this time from west to east. But now, it looked not so much like a comet as a slow-moving ball of fire.

Cries of terror, awe, and even worship arose from the Mount. The entire city of Jerusalem was bathed in an eerie light, as bright as the sun—which no longer seemed to be shining. But the light was completely different from anything they had seen before. Somehow, this light seemed to penetrate buildings, trees, and even human beings, so that they glowed from within.

"Are my eyes playing tricks on me?" Dan said to no one in particular. "Do the rest of you see what I see?"

But again, there was no time for an answer, for the pulsating light now seemed to hover just overhead, casting one directed beam after another toward the ground. Three beams illuminated individuals on the Temple Mount.

A middle-aged man lying on a blanket abruptly sat up and tried to turn away.

An older woman, apparently blind and carrying a white cane, held on tightly to the arm of a young woman.

And a child, about eight or ten years old, huddled ever more deeply into the comforting arms of a man and a woman, apparently his parents.

Yet there was nothing any of these people could do to escape the blasts of yellow–white light that were seeking them out. When the beams focused on these chosen three, their bodies became so bright that it was too painful to look directly at them.

Then, as quickly as it had begun, it was all over.

The sun was out once more, and the strange object had receded in size and glow, now about half the size of a full moon. It almost seemed that nothing had actually happened, that the entire show had been some kind of dream.

But then each of the team members on the Mount—Yael, Michael, Dan, and Joanna—looked around and saw that they were no longer standing. They were on the ground, leaning and looking away from the source of the light. They didn't remember being knocked off their feet, but there they were, sprawled about.

As they rose to their feet and surveyed their surroundings, they saw that parts of the Mount had erupted in shouting, and spontaneous dancing had begun. Hurrying over to the source of the tumult, they found themselves facing singing, whirling people celebrating in different languages.

"I've never seen anything like this," Joanna said. "Never in my whole life."

Then they saw the reasons for the celebrations.

The middle-aged man was up on his feet, jumping and dancing with his hands held high in the air, shouting in Arabic:

"I can walk!"

The elderly woman looked about her in wonder, saying over and over in Hebrew:

"I can see!"

The boy alternately placed his hands over his ears and took them away, repeating in English:

"I can hear! I can hear!"

The research team stood in astonished silence, taking in the impromptu festivities breaking out around them.

Then Dan spoke: "They really were healed. I guess they really were healed."

"Just like the guard you saw," Joanna said.

"Now I know what I saw actually happened. There's no question."

"No question," Michael echoed, still taking in the joyous turmoil. Apparently without thinking, he had grabbed Yael affectionately by the arm.

Joanna and Dan, who were standing slightly behind the other two, immediately noticed and exchanged knowing glances. But there was no time to reflect on the Israeli and the Wheaton man because the mood on the Temple Mount had begun to change perceptibly. The few pockets of joy and thankfulness were now overshadowed by expressions of frustration. Those who had not been healed began to raise their hands up toward the light, pleading and crying. Some of the open hands even clenched into fists, and the frustration turned into anger.

Yael, always alert to danger, started to back away, toward a set of stairs that led down toward the Western Wall, the "Wailing Wall" where they had planned to meet Dudley and Geoffrey.

"It's almost 6:00 P.M.," she said, beckoning the others to follow. "If they're in the city, they should be down there by now."

When the four arrived at the base of the Western Wall, the huge, stacked blocks of the structure towered majestically over them, obscuring their view of the Dome of the Rock and the Temple Mount, which lay high above. Usually, observant Jews could be seen davening, or praying and bowing, only inches in front of the huge blocks as they recited a prescribed liturgy. But now, everyone had backed off and was staring up into the sky at the glowing object that had just caused such consternation.

Michael quickly picked out Dudley and Geoffrey, who were standing off to one side, apparently as enthralled with the recent fireworks as everyone else.

"You saw it all?" Dan asked when they reached the two astronomers.

Both men seemed a little distant, as though they would have preferred not to join the two couples. Dudley in particular seemed distracted, or perhaps embarrassed, probably because of his outburst the night before. His eyes seemed a little glazed and were shifting back and forth, not making contact with anyone. Dan wondered if he was still on medication.

"Truly incredible," Geoffrey finally said, still looking into the sky as though intent on not missing a possible part two of the fireworks display.

"Did you see any healings?" Joanna asked.

Geoffrey eyed her curiously. "No. What do you mean?"

After she described what they had seen on the Temple Mount, Geoffrey rubbed his chin silently, but Dudley expressed his usual sardonic skepticism.

"So, still believing in the powers of the Star, are you?" he said, not looking anyone in the eye.

"I'll admit I don't understand everything that's going on up there," Joanna replied. "But something extraordinary is happening."

"But miraculous healings are a little much, don't you think?" Dudley said, slurring his words slightly. "There are always rational explanations for such things, you know."

Is it medication? Or has he been drinking? Dan wondered, examining the man curiously.

"This has now gone beyond the rational," Michael said. "It will be interesting to see if your instruments measured any of this. Are they still turned on back there in the compound?"

"Yes, and I've already checked with the technicians who are monitoring them," Geoffrey replied. "Still nothing. Absolutely nothing registers."

"So where do we go from here?" asked Joanna.

"Dudley has asked two colleagues to pay us a short visit and help us conduct further experiments," Geoffrey said, pointing toward two burly men who were standing off to one side. "They're both with the SETI investigators in that site near ours."

The two men, who up to this point had escaped everyone's notice, moved up to join the group. "This is Frederick and Harold, who are trained in some highly specialized procedures we want to try," Geoffrey said. "Possible ways of determining if we're dealing with an extradimensional entity. Wormholes and all that, you know."

Although he couldn't put his feelings into words, Dan had a curious reaction to the two new men, especially the fact that no one had mentioned their last names.

"We'll have to know a little more about them before we let them get too involved with the team," Yael said. "Security matter, you know."

"We don't seem to have much time, Yael," Geoffrey said. "This light is starting to get out of hand. We need all the help we can get. Besides, this will be a short visit. We have to extend the courtesy."

"Still, my orders are to do a thorough background check on all personnel we have on the compound," she argued. "No offense, gentlemen, but it's a question of safety. Simple safety."

"Oh, come on, Yael!" Dudley objected, still not quite sounding like himself. "Don't stand on formalities. I can vouch for these men. They can help put this whole thing back on a solid scientific footing."

But Yael never had a chance to respond. Their conversation was interrupted by sporadic bursts of gunfire, which got closer and closer to where they were standing.

"Get down!" Yael shouted, as they all ran over to huddle behind a nearby stone wall.

"We've got to get out of here—fast!" she said. "Did you park in the secure area next to our van?"

"Yes," Geoffrey replied. "The driver said he'd wait there for us."

"And you know how to get back there?"

"I know the way," Frederick answered.

"Then get back there—now! We'll follow right behind you."

Geoffrey, Dudley, and their two companions immediately began moving away from the Western Wall toward Chain Street, which led to Al Wad Road, their route out of the Old City through the Damascus Gate. Yael, Michael, Dan, and Joanna left seconds later, but they quickly lost sight of the other four, as the crowds, more unruly than ever, surged around them.

"You'd think a few miracles would make people behave better," Dan barked to Joanna.

"Only if the miracles happen to you," Joanna replied. "Think about it. If you needed a healing—and you were overlooked—that could be annoying, to put it mildly."

As Dan looked around him, he saw more than one person in tears or talking angrily to friends or relatives. *Why are some healed and others not?* he found himself wondering. *Why are some chosen and others apparently ignored?*

He knew enough about the unresolved issues of his chosen field—religion—to understand that there were no easy answers. In fact, more often than not, there seemed to be no answers at all. Just events. Things happened or didn't happen, and that was that. They were rarely wrapped up with satisfying explanations. Either you accepted your fate and destiny, or you didn't. The "why" questions about life and reality seldom seemed to elicit responses that could appease human reason.

When they had finally fought their way out of the Old City through the Damascus Gate, they split up into two groups. Yael instructed Dan and Joanna to move ahead of her and Michael.

"Things are falling apart behind us," she said, apparently referring to another round of shots she had heard. "I want to be sure our backs are covered."

Dan felt his heart jump into his throat when he noticed that Yael had taken her pistol out of the holster and was holding it just under her fatigue jacket, out of public view but ready for use in case she had to execute a quick draw. He was even more shocked when he saw Michael had abruptly gone from ivory-tower Bible teacher to guerrilla fighter. From somewhere, a pistol had appeared in his hand. Assuming a combat-ready crouch, he had moved away from Yael, apparently so that they would be less likely to be hit by the same burst of hostile fire. His eyes were scanning the crowds behind them, as though searching for targets of opportunity.

Dan was amazed. *It's like Clark Kent turning into Superman.*

Sensing an emergency in the making, Dan gripped Joanna's hand tightly, and they began to jog up Nablus Road toward the small lot where he remembered they had parked the van. But as he neared the location, he realized he was lost.

"Where is it?" he said urgently to his wife. "Where's the parking area?"

Joanna stopped and looked around. "I don't know. Maybe just ahead?"

They ran a little farther up the road until they came to a walkway that led to some sort of brick buildings and walls surrounding a gardenlike park.

Ahead of them, in the midst of the trees and flowers, they saw several groups huddling together and either looking down at the ground or raising their hands up toward the sky and singing.

Hymns. Those are hymns. But in other languages. Korean. German. Spanish. And prayers. Some sort of worship service?

"This isn't it," Joanna said, now in a state of near panic. "Let's go back."

Just as they turned and headed back toward Nablus Road, Yael and Michael rounded the corner and gestured urgently for them to follow.

"You went too far!" Michael shouted. "Come on! Let's get out of here!"

As they hurried back onto Nablus Road, Joanna and Dan stepped out onto the street and a van almost ran them down.

"That was one of our vehicles!" Yael said, looking intently after the speeding car. "I thought one of our guards was supposed to be driving it, but the guy at the wheel was that new fellow, Frederick. And Dudley was sitting in the front seat."

"At least they've made it out of here," Dan said.

Those were the last words out of his mouth before the blast flattened him.

THIRTY-TWO

WHEN Dan opened his eyes, the first thing he saw was the sky and the strange light, glowing dully just above him. He blinked and tried to raise himself to a sitting position, but someone put a hand on his shoulder and gently pushed him back down.

"You have a concussion," the accented male voice said in English. "Please lie quietly."

But Dan tried to sit up again. "My wife. Where's my wife?"

"She's okay. Everyone is okay, just a little shaken up. Actually, you're the worst—and you're not so badly hurt at that. Just a bump on your head."

Dan felt his head and located a bandage on the right side of his skull. He had a dull headache, and his right shoulder was sore as well. Fortunately, he was lying on some sort of soft surface. A cot or stretcher, he surmised.

"What happened?" he asked the man who was standing over him, a person he recognized as a medic.

"Explosion. Bomb of some sort. Knocked you and the others to the ground. You took the brunt. Apparently because you were out in the road, just ahead of a woman. Your wife, I believe."

"Where was the bomb?"

"In a parking area just over there."

The medic pointed to an enclave directly across the street, which was surrounded by the twisted remains of a steel grate and rocky piles of rubble that had once been a concrete wall. It was the parking lot where they had left their van.

Despite the medic's protests, Dan managed to prop himself up on one elbow so that he could survey the scene. Joanna was hurrying toward him. A bandage on her forehead and another on her forearm didn't seem to be slowing her down. Yael and Michael were standing next to the destroyed parking lot, engaged in a serious dialogue with an older, uniformed official.

Looks like a colonel, at least.

Dan waved weakly at Joanna and then lay back on the cot. "How are you feeling?" she asked. "You got quite a bump."

"Yeah, I'm still a little dizzy," he said. "But you and the others are okay?"

"Check it out," she said, stretching her arms toward him with a smile. "Same old Joanna."

"That was some blast," he said weakly. "Could have killed us all. That's where we parked!"

"That's not the half of it," she said grimly. "They blew up our van."

"What?"

"Our van. Someone targeted us. Another few seconds, and we wouldn't be here."

"But why?"

"Yael and Michael are trying to find out."

"Thank goodness Dudley and Geoffrey got away before it went off," Dan said.

"Yes, their timing was impeccable," Joanna responded, but something about her tone made him do a double take.

"You trying to tell me something?"

"Investigators found their driver in the rubble," she said. "Dead. Shot through the back of the head."

Stunned, Dan just stared at her for a moment. "Who . . . how did it happen?" he finally asked.

"Yael called our compound and learned that Dudley and the others had already reported the man's death," she said. "Claimed he was killed by a stray bullet. Then they panicked and took off in the van."

"Without even putting the poor dead guard in the vehicle with them?"

"Right."

"Do you believe them?"

She shrugged. "Yael has a lot of questions."

"How about you?"

"It does seem a little strange that they roared off, and an explosion followed almost immediately."

"But why would they try to blow us up? And what do they know about explosives?" Dan asked, still trying to sort through this flood of disturbing new information. His headache intensified the more he thought about it.

"I don't get it either," Joanna said. "Maybe they had nothing to do with it. But that's what Yael and Michael are trying to determine." She smiled. "In any case, you're okay. That's all I care about."

Dan decided he liked this new Joanna. Even if it took a weird light in the sky, and gunshots and bomb blasts in Jerusalem to do the job. She really seemed to care about him—maybe even more than her career.

"We were lucky I couldn't find the way directly to that parking lot," he said as she squeezed his hand and rubbed his sore shoulder. "Odd, though. I immediately recognized the lot when I came to—even with the wall blown away. What was that place we walked into by mistake?"

"I'm not sure," Joanna said. "Just some private park, I suppose." She turned to the medic and pointed to the walkway they had taken up the street, which led to a little wooded park. "What's that up there? Somebody's house?"

"No," the man replied. "That's the Garden Tomb. Some people think that's the site where Jesus was buried. Farther into that alcove, you run into Gordon's Calvary, a possible location of the Crucifixion."

Neither Joanna nor Dan heard the man's last few words. They were staring at the place where they had found refuge for a few moments, just long enough to delay their departure—and save their lives.

"Yes, you were quite lucky," the medic said.

Joanna looked back down at Dan. "Lucky? I'm not so sure it's luck."

Dan, lost in thought, was already ahead of her. He was beginning to have serious doubts about whether there really was any such thing as chance or coincidence.

The four spent the night in Jerusalem at the insistence of Yael's superiors and the physicians who had examined them. Yael had pushed hard to return to the compound that night. But she was assured that the officer of the guard up there had things well under control. Finally, she received a direct order to stay put so that the medical authorities could observe all of them for at least a few more hours before they traveled.

"We'll take you up by chopper as soon as you get medical clearance," a senior military officer promised. "We should finish your checkups tonight, and if you're okay, you'll be in the air early in the morning."

Yael complied, but she was clearly worried. "I don't trust Dudley and Geoffrey, and I certainly don't trust those two new men with them," she told Michael under her breath as they waited to board the helicopter. She was so preoccupied that she didn't even seem concerned that she was within earshot of Joanna.

"Do you think they had anything to do with the bombing?" Joanna asked. "Or with the guard's death?"

"No, no, I'm not suggesting anything like that," the sabra said. "I just don't like to admit people to a high-security area without knowing more about them. And Dudley is a loose cannon at this point. Did you notice his eyes?"

"Yes," Joanna said. "A little scary. But they've probably got him on heavy doses of medication after he flipped out in our last meeting."

"He should never have been allowed to leave the compound," Michael said. "But chances are, everything is okay up there. Dan, while we're waiting, let me show you something. The Temple Mount is impressive from here. And who knows, we might see some more action down there."

As the two men walked over to an elevated knoll to one side of the chopper pad, Joanna turned to Yael. "So the two of you have got something going?"

Yael looked startled and then smiled slightly. "It's that obvious?"

"The best-known secret on the compound."

"When Dudley screamed at Michael that he was a hypocrite because the two of us were having an affair, I figured the cat must be out of the bag. Is that how you got the idea about us?"

"No, I saw the two of you together in your office. You weren't exactly talking about the Star of Bethlehem."

Yael was obviously surprised. In a rare loss of composure, she had trouble finding the right words. "We developed a strong friendship a few months ago," she finally said vaguely, careful not to disclose more than was wise.

"But isn't this a little odd?" Joanna asked, taking advantage of Yael's apparent openness to find out exactly what was going on. "I mean, you're Jewish, and he's a conservative Christian. How does that work?"

Yael sighed. "Of course, there could be complications, but we don't know where things are going at this point," she said without elaborating. "And you should know—despite what Dudley said or anyone else might think—there is no 'affair.' It's true that we do have . . . feelings . . . for each other, but we both also have our professional duties and strict moral standards. Our relationship won't go further until this political situation—and the Star issue—are resolved."

The helicopter was now landing and discharging passengers. Joanna thought she recognized a couple of Israeli cabinet members, whose pictures she had seen on the Internet in recent days. They looked particularly harried and didn't even cast a glance toward Joanna and Yael.

In only a minute or so, the four team members had boarded the helicopter, strapped on their seat belts, and been lifted off into the early morning sky. The sun was just rising in the east, and like a huge morning star, the mysterious light hung in its usual spot, just to one side of the intense dawn light.

The chopper motors were too loud to allow for much conversation during the short trip. The only way to communicate was to shout, and Yael and Michael raised their voices infrequently, mainly to point out landmarks.

The Valley of Jezreel, with the ruins of Megiddo—the biblical site of Armageddon, where some believed the last world battle was to be fought—soon appeared on the left side. The expanse of this ancient valley, a crossroads for Middle Eastern traffic over many centuries and millennia, was even more dramatic from the air. That and the recent events in the skies over Jerusalem made Dan wonder vaguely about the prophecies he had read long ago in the book of Revelation.

Soon the city of Nazareth, perched on a high cliff, came up on the left. Then the pilot chose a straight northward path toward their compound. The chopper skirted the expanse of the Sea of Galilee on the right, and headed toward looming, snowcapped Mount Hermon just ahead.

A few minutes later, the chopper settled gently on a flat area far enough away from the buildings and the research sites to prevent any disturbance from wind or blown debris from the whirring rotor blades. The four passengers piled out quickly, bending low to avoid any possible danger from the still-spinning main rotor blades overhead.

Dan and Joanna rarely flew in helicopters, so they felt rather exhilarated after the ride. But their pleasure was short-lived. Even before the chopper had lifted off to head for its next mission, the officer of the guard and Skiddy had run up to confer earnestly with Yael. Michael soon joined them, and Dan and Joanna also moved to the edge of the group.

"He was in possession of two weapons, and one of them had been fired," the officer was saying. "He resisted any attempts at questioning. Became so unruly I had to put him in custody."

"This is outrageous!" Skiddy protested. "I'm sure there's a logical, reasonable explanation. Dudley isn't a violent man. I don't think he even knows how to shoot a gun. And half the people on this compound carry weapons."

"Only those who are authorized," Yael snapped. "This is a violation of compound rules. Also Israeli law. Dudley knew that. He read and signed a statement to that effect before he ever set foot on these grounds."

"Oh, please!" Skiddy said. "We signed anything that was put in front of us. Nobody read every line. This project's left no time to read legal fine print."

"The biggest problem we face is the dead guard in Jerusalem," Yael said. "He was shot through the head. Now we learn that Dudley's weapon had been discharged. Ballistics tests will have to be done to see if it was the same weapon. In any case, he has to submit to interrogation about all this."

Skiddy turned pale. "You mean murder? You think Dudley may have murdered the guard?"

"I'm making no accusations," Yael said. "But he must be kept in custody, and we must investigate."

In what seemed a last-ditch, desperate attempt to exonerate his Harvard colleague, Skiddy pointed to Michael's waist, where the butt of a pistol was sticking out.

"What's that?" he cried. "Michael can carry a gun for protection but Dudley can't? Is this the kind of double standard we're following now? Your boyfriend is immune, but my research colleague is not?"

"Michael is a former Navy Seal, trained in more weapons than I am," Yael replied, smarting at the crack. *Why weren't we more careful?* "He was authorized to carry a pistol on our Jerusalem trip."

Surprise, surprise, Dan thought. *What won't we learn next about our Wheaton friend?*

"Look," Yael continued in a more conciliatory tone. "We just want to talk to Dudley and try to figure out what he was up to. All we're asking is for him to cooperate with us. If he won't play ball, we'll have to turn him over to the authorities in Tel Aviv."

"If Dudley goes, I go," Skiddy said stubbornly. "And if the two of us go, this project is finished. You're going to be too shorthanded to proceed."

He threw up his hands in frustration. "With Dudley out of commission, I've had to take on Geoffrey's two colleagues temporarily. Geoffrey recommends them, and the SETI team has agreed to loan them to us for a couple of days. We have to have somebody on board who can keep monitoring the spectroscopes and telescopes."

Yael blanched. "You had no authority to do that! We know nothing about these people! We have to do background checks before we bring anyone on board."

Skiddy, now feeling he was gaining the upper hand, waved her off. "Under normal conditions it may be okay to dot every *i* and cross every *t*. But these conditions aren't normal," he said forcefully. "They have to stay."

"They can't stay," Yael protested.

"You get rid of them and Dudley, and we're finished," Skiddy said. "I'll walk off the site today. I don't think that will make your dear Mr. Van Campe very happy—not to mention the Israeli authorities who are counting on us. I understand that they still regard us as one of the top investigative teams, isn't that right? What's more important—following all your little rules, or finding out the purpose and identity of that light? Besides, they were approved to be at the SETI site, weren't they? Why not here?"

Yael knew he had a point, but she wasn't willing to back down entirely. "I don't want you or Dudley to go. And I don't want this investigation to be terminated."

She thought a moment and then sighed. "Okay, the two new guys can stay on probationary visitors' status, but they'll have to be monitored closely until we can run a more extensive background check. Michael will be in charge of them for the time being. We should know what we need to know about them in twenty-four hours or less. But I want to talk to Dudley. I *must* talk to him *now*."

Skiddy grudgingly complied and followed her and the officer to a shack where Dudley was being held under guard. Meanwhile, Joanna and Dan headed toward their quarters, and Michael went to find Geoffrey and his two new colleagues.

"This is getting sticky," Dan said when they had closed their door. "Really sticky. Dudley caught with a weapon that has been fired. A guard shot through the head. Michael, a former Navy Seal. We're in the middle of a real mess."

"And then, there's the love interest," Joanna added, making signs for quotation marks with her fingers. She then proceeded to disclose what she had learned from Yael about her relationship with Michael.

"It's like a soap opera, but unfortunately, we're not on TV," Dan said. "The stakes here are sky-high."

A loud, insistent knocking interrupted them. When Dan opened the door, Yael was standing on the outside step, looking rather harried with a holstered pistol in each hand.

"Do you know how to use these?" she asked.

But then, without waiting for an answer, the Israeli pushed her way into their room. She shoved a weapon at each of them and poured some rounds out of a camouflage pouch onto one of their cots.

"I'll show you. From now on, you both must be armed."

THIRTY-THREE

Hold on, now!" Dan exclaimed. "What is this all about? You want us to carry pistols? Who are we going to be shooting at?"

"Just trust me," Yael said, obviously in no mood for long explanations or jokes. "It's very unlikely you'll have to use these. But the situation has deteriorated here in the compound, not to mention around the country. Dudley is under house arrest until we can get those ballistics tests back. Those two new guys remain a mystery—we've just started doublechecking them through our intelligence network."

"Intelligence?" Joanna asked.

"Yes," Yael said guardedly. "We've had to screen everyone on every scientific compound in the country carefully through our intelligence sources because of the sensitive nature of the work you're doing. But some questions have arisen with these two."

"What do you mean, questions?" Dan asked, now getting a little alarmed.

"I mean this: A quick additional check indicates that they aren't on all the usual lists of scientists with credentials to do SETI research. It could be they're quite innocent, just technicians whose names aren't always included. But at this early point, we can't be sure. So for now, we've had to rely on the assurances of Dudley and Geoffrey. But in the discussion I just had with Dudley, he contradicted his earlier statement—claimed he couldn't remember meeting them. Says he thinks he met them through Geoffrey. But he's still fuzzy-headed."

"Sounds real fishy," Dan said. "Maybe even dangerous. What's the exact deal with Dudley?"

Yael looked at them both for a moment and then made her decision. "Because of my position with the government, I have access to information and sources that aren't available to you. Theoretically, you're not supposed to know what I'm about to tell you."

Then she glanced at the pistols, which they had already strapped on their waists. "But you're not supposed to be armed either. So here goes. As you've heard, Dudley came onto the compound last night carrying two unauthorized pistols. He claimed one of the guards had given them to him, but he couldn't identify the guard. He said it was too dark. Also, he seemed to have trouble remembering other details."

"Liars often have trouble with details," Dan said.

"When the guards confiscated the weapons, they found that one had been fired recently," Yael continued. "Because he had just visited Jerusalem, and one of our guards had been killed down there, he was immediately taken into custody. We had to do that to investigate, just to be sure he wasn't involved in any of the shootings."

"So was he implicated?" Joanna asked.

"It's not looking good for him," Yael said. "During the questioning, he asked if any of us had been hurt or killed in the bombing of our van."

"How did he know about that?" Dan asked.

"Good question. He might have heard the explosion because they would have been only a couple of blocks away when the bomb went off. But there was no way he could have known it was our van. In the past twenty-four hours, all the calls made from Jerusalem to this compound have gone to the officer of the guard and no one else. The officer was instructed to tell no one about what had happened down there. Yet Dudley knew."

"Did anyone question him about his knowledge of our van?" Dan asked.

"Yes, extensively," Yael said. "But his responses were inconsistent and not very satisfying. On one occasion, he said he had heard someone else in his van talk about ours. Another time, he said he saw someone examining the underside of our van just before his group drove off. But when questioned later, he was vague on those statements."

"Did he see the guard, his driver, get shot?"

"He says no."

"How about Geoffrey or those two new guys?" Joanna asked. "What do they have to say?"

"They said they knew there had been an explosion," Yael said. "But during a brief inquiry we just conducted, they said they couldn't tell what direction it came from. And they claim they had no idea our van was involved."

"So Dudley seems to be the main one who is knee-deep in swamp water," Dan said.

"We certainly don't have a confession, but there is reason to suspect him of something," Yael replied. "And there have been other findings that are quite disturbing. Our guards have determined that Dudley's two pistols came from our armory here on the compound. And as they were going over the inventory, they discovered several other weapons were missing, including two automatic rifles."

"Sounds like Dudley needs to be tossed in an Israeli jail," Dan said.

"The problem is, there's no evidence he took those other weapons," Yael responded. "Also, he was heavily medicated when he arrived here. In fact, blood tests showed that he had more tranquilizers in his system than would be consistent with the prescriptions he was given."

"Does he have his own store of drugs?" Joanna asked. "Is he some sort of addict?"

"A search of his quarters revealed nothing," Yael said.

"He shouldn't have been allowed off the compound after he attacked Michael," Dan said. "He should have been turned over to the Israeli authorities."

"But the evidence was skimpy—and after all, he's a Harvard professor," Yael said. "A junior faculty member, to be sure, but still a prominent scholar. The Israeli government would always think twice before throwing a respected American scientist in jail."

"What about Skiddy?" Dan asked. "Can he shed any light on this mess?"

"No, but he's defensive. And very protective of Dudley. That's another problem we face. If we move against Dudley too soon, we'll also find ourselves fighting Skiddy. Could cause an international incident—not to mention make it impossible for this team to make any more progress with the Star."

213

"You're quite right," Dan reflected. "Even if Skiddy does know something about Dudley, he would be the last to accuse him in public. Dudley is Skiddy's anointed right-hand man, and anything that would make Dudley look bad would automatically reflect poorly on Skiddy. So Skiddy can be expected to try to cover up for Dudley to save his own skin and reputation."

"How about Geoffrey?" Joanna asked. "Can we trust him?"

"I have my doubts," Yael said. "But we have a dilemma. He's really an established expert. A recognized astrophysicist on several continents. If we start leaning on him without more evidence, the whole thing could explode in our face."

"*Your* face," Dan corrected. "*Israel's* face."

"Yes," Yael conceded. "Though I don't think any of us want to be part of an international incident. So we have to move deliberately, but at the same time protect ourselves. I've already requested backup from Tel Aviv, and we should be getting some help here shortly. But our country's military and security resources are strained to the breaking point because of the increasing social and political unrest. If you think Jerusalem was bad when we were there, you should see it now! Same with Tel Aviv. Our outpost, as important as it is for research, just doesn't rise to the same level as Jerusalem or Tel Aviv when social order breaks down."

"So what's your plan until you get help?" Dan asked.

"As a stopgap, Michael and one of our regular guards are handling surveillance on the two new people," she said. "He's seen them using Geoffrey's instruments—and also a couple of new devices they brought in. Says they seem to know what they're doing. So maybe they really are just scientific technicians with a very low profile who haven't shown up on all our initial checks. We should know more about them in a couple of hours."

"What exactly are these new devices of theirs?" Joanna asked.

"Michael couldn't tell," Yael said. "They wouldn't let him get too close. They said the instruments were sensitive to human heat."

"That doesn't sound quite right," Joanna said. "And I wouldn't expect Michael to have the expertise to evaluate the latest scientific devices we're using, even if he got right on top of them. They're too sophisticated for a layman."

"You might be surprised," Yael said. "His Seal training and covert military assignments exposed him to all sorts of advanced scientific equipment. But as I said, they wouldn't let him get close enough even to try to make a determination."

"Michael's certainly a man who's full of surprises," Joanna said noncommittally. *But I'm still going to do my own evaluation of our mysterious new colleagues,* she decided.

One of the guards came through the door just then and handed Yael a message.

"Skiddy is calling another meeting of the research team in twenty minutes," she said, looking up from the note. "From his tone, I'd suggest that we all get there on time."

Joanna wanted to change her clothes, so she told Yael and Dan to go on ahead of her. When she finally walked out of her quarters, she looked up toward Geoffrey's research site and noticed that the California astrophysicist and the two new technicians were just leaving to go to the team meeting.

Ducking back into her room, Joanna waited for them to enter the headquarters building. Then she walked quickly up to their site to do a brief, once-over reconnaissance.

Geoffrey's telescopes, computers, filming equipment, spectroscopes, and other measuring devices were all in their usual places. But when she checked two side tables where the two new men had been working, she was not at all prepared for what she found.

THIRTY-FOUR

THE entire research team—with the exception of Professor Dudley Dunster—was already assembled in the headquarters building when the tall, angular Skiddy Kirkland walked through the door. His dark expression and tense movements left little doubt that he was upset.

"I don't know what's going on around here," he began, "but I want all this silliness resolved before we leave this room. Otherwise, I'm going to resign—but that's not all. I'll schedule a press conference announcing the end of this project, and I'll name names of the people who have undermined our work."

"Exactly what silliness are you talking about?" Yael asked pointedly. She obviously wasn't willing to concede that anything she was doing, including the investigations she was conducting of Dudley, could be dismissed as "silliness."

"Unnecessary delays in our research, unfounded accusations of valued colleagues, the whole direction this investigation has been taking," he replied.

Rather vague, my friend, Dan mused.

Skiddy was clearly reluctant to make specific accusations and thus precipitate a crisis at this point.

"And who do you think might be responsible for our problems?" Geoffrey asked, again putting the project director on the spot.

"That will all come out—if, and when, there is a press conference," Skiddy said with some irritation. "But I'm hoping things won't come to that."

Dan looked over at his wife and almost imperceptibly shook his head. She knew exactly what he was thinking. His disgust was transparent to her. *Hollow threats. Skiddy will never deep-six this study unless he has absolutely no other choice. He'll rant and rave, but he knows where his next paycheck is coming from.*

Then Dan looked back at the Harvard psychologist and began to have some second thoughts.

Still, I've never seen him quite this agitated. Does he have some hidden agenda I don't know about? And why is he so intent on protecting Dudley? After all, it isn't easy to justify attacking a colleague, possessing unauthorized weapons, shooting one of them—and maybe killing your own driver. What does one Harvard man have to do to cause another to lose confidence in him?

"Okay, let's summarize where we are—and have some reports on what happened down in Jerusalem," Skiddy said, eager to change the subject. "Joanna, why don't you tell us what the four of you saw on the Temple Mount. Then we'll hear from Geoffrey, who witnessed things from another vantage point."

Joanna stood and recounted the dramatic pulsating of the light, and its streaking, east-west-east movement across the sky.

"Yes, I think we all saw the same thing, more or less," Skiddy said. "From up here, as well as other sites around the world."

"You mean regardless of where observers were around the globe, they saw precisely the same movements and changes we did?" Michael asked.

"Yes," Skiddy said. "Of course, this has characterized the light since it appeared. Everyone sees basically the same thing, regardless of the vantage point."

Then he turned back to Joanna and asked for a description of the three healings that had occurred on the Temple Mount. Joanna, relying on some notes she had jotted down after the incident, provided plenty of details.

Skiddy then studied his notes for a moment and said, "What you saw in Jerusalem has been corroborated in several news reports. Furthermore, hundreds, if not thousands, of similar healings have been confirmed in other parts of the globe."

"Same circumstances?" Dan asked.

"Yes. A blinding beam of light streams down from that object, and various diseases disappear. We can't always confirm that the people were really sick before the event. But there are enough cases of individuals with prior medical records to validate the healing power of the light."

"It goes beyond psychology?" Dan asked. "You're sure of that?"

Skiddy hesitated, then nodded.

"My initial response with the wounded guard on our compound was to be the devil's advocate," he said. "As a scientist, I have to be extremely careful. I've got to consider every possible known or identifiable cause before I turn to the unknown or abnormal. But I must say, something seems to be happening well beyond the placebo effect, hysteria, or other emotional or psychosomatic influences. I'll admit, I don't understand it."

Skiddy then turned to Geoffrey. "What did your group observe?" he asked.

"We saw the internal, pulsating changes of the light," the astrophysicist replied. "And we detected its movement across the sky. But we didn't see any healings. On the whole, the phenomena we noted seemed to be mostly negative or disruptive. What's the advantage of having a few healings if shootings and bombings accompany them?"

After consulting his notes again, Skiddy nodded. "Interesting point. Even as people are being healed around the world, I'm getting an increasing number of reports of intensified violence. According to one estimate, we've had five times the normal incidence of terrorist attacks during the past month. Hundreds of people have been injured or killed. One consequence is that some weaker governments are in jeopardy. Social and political instability are becoming a real problem."

"Even disease seems to be on the upswing," Yael said, referring to reports she was perusing on her on-line computer screen. "Hospitals in many nations are overflowing. The developed Western nations aren't immune either. Facilities in the large American cities, such as New York, are close to capacity."

"Could be stress-related," Skiddy suggested. "I know you people don't like my psychological interpretations of these things. But the anxiety and stress produced by this thing in the sky could easily result in more physical illness."

"I have no argument with that," Michael said, surprising everyone with his willingness to agree that the light might be associated with negative effects. "We can't deny the fact that mental and emotional pressures may in some way be triggering the increased violence, injuries, and sickness."

"That brings me to an important point," Geoffrey said. "There could be an even deeper connection than we've realized between the strange light and all this social and political turmoil. Our objective is still to figure out what that thing really is. I think our new colleagues, Frederick and Harold, may be able to help in this regard. They've been conducting some experiments and would like to share their findings, if that's all right."

"Certainly, certainly," Skiddy said, eager for any sign of progress in the investigation. "And, um, forgive me, gentlemen, but your last names were . . . ?"

"Hermes," Frederick replied. He half rose from the old couch against the back wall, where he had been sitting quietly with the other new man, and greeted the group with a weak wave.

"And Cadmilus," Harold said.

"Yes, unusual names, hard to remember," Skiddy said. "Sorry, but there's been so much confusion around here in the last few hours that I failed to pick them up."

They never told us their names, Dan reflected.

"So who'll be first?" Skiddy said. "Mr. Hermes?"

"Dr. Hermes," the man corrected. "But Geoffrey said in his briefing that you're on a first-name basis, so please just call us Frederick and Harold."

Frederick then walked forward and placed his computer on a nearby desk where he could refer to the screen. His large head, which seemed far too big for his medium-size frame, and his unruly mop of blond hair dominated the entire front of the room.

"We've brought some special instruments along with us," he said. "I'm afraid the SETI people we were working with at that other site down the road didn't quite understand the significance of these devices. But we believe they've made it possible for us to identify certain characteristics of the light that may have escaped notice before."

"And what exactly is this equipment used for?" Joanna asked.

"A number of purposes," Frederick replied confidently, "including the tracking and analysis of what are called 'Near Earth Objects,' or NEO's. Typically, the devices have been used to observe 'Near Earth Asteroids,' or NEA's. But we're finding that they are also useful to study the light."

"And what have you found?" Skiddy asked eagerly.

"We believe we're picking up specific messages from the light—messages that apparently are coming from another dimension of reality," Frederick said.

"Another universe?" Skiddy asked, his excitement obviously growing. "You actually have scientific evidence that this thing is from some other dimension of reality?"

"Well, yes, but it's more complicated than that," Frederick said tentatively. "You see, we're convinced that we're dealing with some sort of extraterrestrial intelligence—some ETI. The beings who are involved want to tell us something tremendously important about our culture, our world, something that could transform earth into a perfect society in the future. But we must connect with them. We must establish solid lines of communication. And we believe that this particular research effort—your project, Professor Kirkland—is ground zero for our effort to make this first contact."

"Why, this is wonderful!" Skiddy said. "But of course, we'll need to know more. We'll need more specifics . . ."

"Many more specifics," Joanna finished. "May I ask a few questions, Dr. Hermes?" She seemed to make a point of not addressing the speaker on a first-name basis.

"Of course, of course, but these things are so technical."

"I'm a technical person, Dr. Hermes," she replied—rather caustically, Dan thought. He could always tell when his wife was about to do intellectual battle.

"You see, I work with instruments all the time that measure light and heat waves," she continued. "My methods often overlap a great deal with astronomical research. I also happen to know something about the newest equipment for tracking NEO's—the special computers and cameras that scientists at the University of Michigan developed to catalog asteroids and the like."

She stood up, walked over to one of the windows, and looked out at the research sites. "But I happened to be walking past Geoffrey's equipment, the section where you've been doing your work, and I didn't see anything that looked remotely like the devices used for NEO analysis. No special computers or cameras. Nothing. Are you in touch with the Michigan scientists?"

She looked back at Frederick and paused for a moment to allow all this to sink in. The silence was so complete that when Skiddy cleared his throat, half the people in the room jumped.

"Well, we are using even later, more experimental devices than the Michigan people have developed," Frederick finally said.

"Actually, it was scientists at M.I.T., not Michigan," Joanna said with a glint in her eye.

Dan chuckled to himself. *Ah, my devious wife!*

"And what I saw in your research area didn't resemble anything a scientist might use," Joanna continued, walking back toward Frederick until she was standing only a couple of feet from him and looking him straight in the eye. "You have several prisms out there, connected to nothing in particular. A scattering of crystalline-type rocks. A chart of the heavens that looked like it might have been drafted hundreds of years ago. And some sort of laser, connected to a rather crude graph device. I almost felt as if I had entered the study area of ancient astrologers, rather than contemporary scientists."

Again, there was deafening silence.

"Sometimes, unusual methods are required for unusual scientific challenges," Geoffrey finally said, obviously trying to offer some kind of defense for the new researchers.

"I'd like to hear from Frederick and Harold about this," Michael said.

"I'll admit we're sometimes rather unconventional in our methods," Harold said, contributing for the first time to the discussion. His totally bald head, which had given him a rather dashing and distinguished look, was now glistening with a film of perspiration. "But after all, the usual scientific techniques haven't worked at all. Correct? And I'm convinced we are beginning to get a response from the light."

"Explain," Yael said.

"For one thing, the prisms and crystals seem to be filtering the rays of the light in meaningful ways. They're producing configurations on charts we've devised, which suggest possible intelligent communication. Also, the charts and some ancient texts we're using suggest that the mysterious light may in fact have particular influences on events here on earth—such as military conflicts, political changes, and physical healings. The light may also help shape other events that religious groups traditionally have regarded as miracles."

"In other words, astrology," Dan said. "You're just giving us your version of astrology. You study the movements of celestial bodies—in this case, the unexplained Star—to understand what's happening on earth."

"Well, it's more complicated than that," Frederick began, but Dan interrupted.

"No, it's not complicated. What you may not have known is that I'm an expert in the history of religion—especially spiritual movements outside the mainstream, such as cults. I've written several articles on astrology, past and present. And call it what you like, your approach fits right in."

Frederick slammed his computer top down and became visibly angry. His wild blond hair vibrated as he shook his huge head at Dan. "We had heard there was considerable dissension and bad feeling on this particular team," he said, "and I must say the reception we've received confirms the worst."

"And who might have told you we were so hard to get along with?" Yael asked, moving into her interrogation mode.

Frederick glanced at Geoffrey, a look that said more than words could ever convey. But then he responded to Yael's question. "Professor Dunster filled us in. We've known him for a while."

"Oh, have you?" Yael said. "We've been doing our usual background checks on you, Dr. Hermes and Dr. Cadmilus. And quite frankly, we haven't found any connection you might have to Dudley or anyone else on this team. Who exactly are you, and where do you come from?"

"We're independent researchers," Frederick said, clearly not disposed to be more specific. "We've had previous, intermittent contact with Professor Dunster. And we recently met Professor Gonzales. We do cutting-edge work that isn't yet common in many research institutions. But Professor Dunster thought we might be of some help, given the unusual nature of this light—and the fact that it's been impervious to the usual methods of analysis. And I think that's proving to be the case."

"Now let me see if I have this straight," Joanna said, a contentious edge now openly in her voice. "You've come onto this compound in the eleventh hour of our investigations, without credentials that are linked to any established research institution. You're using devices and techniques that seem more appropriate for the Middle Ages than twenty-first-century science. In fact, you're apparently involved in some form of astrology."

"But . . ." Frederick protested.

"Please let me finish," Joanna said. "You seemed to be unaware that the latest NEO research comes out of M.I.T., not the University of Michigan. And yet you want us to provide your conclusions with our imprimatur as established scientists and scholars. Is this correct?"

"You're being rather argumentative, I think," Harold objected.

"No, I think she's just trying to get a straight answer," Yael shot back.

"This does all seem rather irregular," Skiddy said, now beginning to realize that the two new additions to the team might not be all they were cracked up to be. "Geoffrey, what about you? Do you vouch for the good doctors here? I wish Dudley were here. He's adept at evaluating other scientists and new techniques in his field."

"Their work is certainly as promising as Michael's biblical fantasies about the shekinah glory," Geoffrey said. "As far as I can tell—and I do know astronomy at least as well as Dudley—they are making progress. Besides, what do we have to lose? I heard that question over and over when we were sitting patiently waiting for Michael's Bible studies to end. So perhaps we should be willing to exercise a little patience now."

"So do you have any more insights for us?" Skiddy asked the two new men tentatively, apparently hoping against hope that they might have come up with something. "Do you have any concrete ideas about the identity of that light?"

Joanna and Yael—knowing Skiddy was grasping at straws, given the men's unorthodox research methods—greeted his question with poorly concealed disdain. But they kept quiet to see how the men would answer.

"Clearly, we're dealing with an extradimensional entity," Frederick replied confidently. "And clearly there is intelligent, extraterrestrial life in that light or on the other side of it, maybe in another universe. It's also abundantly obvious that the alien beings up there want to make contact with us. They want to communicate."

"The appearance of the bright figure to Joanna confirms this point," Harold added, apparently trying to draw the Yale professor over to his side. "Yes, we've heard about that, Joanna. And we're sympathetic. We believe strongly that a superior alien intelligence is asserting itself."

"Also, remember the healings—another sign of the benign motives of those behind the portal," Frederick said. "Yet there are also negative forces abroad. The violence and political turmoil. The rise of diseases. Apparently, a few around the earth are open to the positive overtures from beyond, but many more are hostile and closed. Our goal should be to overcome any misunderstanding with the aliens and allow them to speak to us. Give them the freedom to merge their minds with ours."

Again, there was silence. An amazed silence this time. Then several spoke at once, with Skiddy finally managing to outshout the others.

"Am I to understand that we've gotten back into UFO's again?" he said. "I thought we had left this behind long ago! We can't conclude that that thing is a UFO! At least not unless we have much, much more proof than this."

"This is the only logical answer," Geoffrey said with such force that all eyes became riveted on him. "We must listen to Frederick and Harold. Allow them to take their investigation to its natural conclusion. Then you'll see the validity of the extradimensional ETI thesis."

"So you buy into their approach, Geoffrey?" Michael asked. "You're comfortable with their methodology?"

"Absolutely!" Geoffrey replied.

"Okay," Yael said, surprising the others with her seemingly quick capitulation to the UFO theory. "I think we've said about all we can say at this point. Why don't we break up for now and think things over? We have a lot to digest. In the meantime, Geoffrey, you and your two colleagues might continue with your approach and see where it takes you. Sound reasonable?"

"I really don't . . ." Skiddy started, but Yael raised her hand to interrupt what was obviously going to be a protest.

"Let's just allow things to proceed on this path for a little while, Skiddy," she emphasized. "I think we all have a lot to ponder. I know I have a great deal to sift through. And all this may be helping us to think more creatively."

Reluctantly, the project director acquiesced, and the meeting was adjourned. Even Michael was eyeing Yael strangely, as though he couldn't figure out her strategy.

Geoffrey, Frederick, and Harold were the first to leave the headquarters building. They were obviously in a hurry to get out of the meeting. That left the others standing around, picking up their notes and computers, looking quizzically at one another, wondering precisely what was happening with their investigation.

"I don't like this at all," Skiddy said.

"Don't feel like the Lone Ranger," Dan said.

"We're all opposed to this UFO business," Michael said. "Especially when they're apparently starting to rely on astrological charts and ancient sorcery texts. Why did you encourage those guys, Yael?"

The Israeli agent looked up with a very worried look on her face. "I had no choice. If we had pushed them any further, they might have exploded."

Then she shoved a sheet of paper toward them, which she had just printed from her computer.

"Here's an encrypted message I just received."

As the others read the short, top secret communiqué, their mouths sagged open, one by one.

"Now we know who Frederick and Harold really are," Yael said.

✦ THIRTY-FIVE

THE five team members remaining in the room—Dan, Joanna, Skiddy, Michael, and Yael—huddled anxiously around the report Yael had given them.

"These read like police rap sheets," Michael said. "I haven't seen anything like this since I worked with the navy's criminal investigation division."

"Can this all be true?" Skiddy asked.

"If it is, these guys are really dangerous," Dan said.

"It's true," Yael replied. "If there were any question about it, the reports would say so."

Still not quite believing what was on the paper, Joanna reread out loud, point by point, some of the findings on Frederick Hermes—whose real name was Frederick Carlson:

- Indictment, attempted murder, Palo Alto, California. Acquitted.

- Arrested and charged with possession of automatic weapons, Berkeley, California. Dismissed.

- Frequent psychiatric institutionalization, including two periods in hospitals for the criminally insane.

- Highly intelligent and capable of appearing quite normal for extended periods. But has a history of emotional relapse, requiring medication and other treatment.

- Member, officer, New Jerusalem Way, an apocalyptic cult. Group has tendency toward violence. One prominent doctrine is that members are justified in using violent responses against those opposing the movement. Weapons caches uncovered in northern California, Idaho, and Montana.

- Beliefs include odd mixture of biblical end-times thinking and a conviction that UFO's and aliens are real and will play an instrumental role in an end-of-the-world scenario. Also, there have been attempts to incorporate ancient Greek and Roman mythology into their belief system, with members assuming names of ancient gods according to their functions in the cult.

- Latest duties with New Jerusalem Way include a special assignment to seek out and establish contact with alien or extraterrestrial visitors.

- Goes under several pseudonyms, including "Frederick Hermes."

"The material on Harold is similar, though he doesn't have a psychiatric record," Yael said. "But both are members of this New Jerusalem Way cult. Cadmilus is also a fake last name, by the way. Harold's real name is Stucky."

"Cadmilus," Dan said, thinking out loud. "And Frederick's fake name is Hermes. What do you remember from your Greek mythology?"

"Hermes was the Greek name for the Roman Mercury, the messenger of the Olympian gods," Michael said. "But I don't recognize Cadmilus."

"Cadmilus—Harold's assumed name—was the designation for Hermes in Samothrace, a Greek island in the northern Aegean Sea," Dan explained.

"They've in effect assumed the same identity," Skiddy said. "Psychologically that's always significant. If you think about it, they act alike. Even seem to be speaking in tandem sometimes."

"Apparently they both see themselves as messengers to the gods—who they believe have arrived in that object up there in the sky," Dan suggested.

"Fascinating," Michael said.

"Impressive analysis," Joanna added.

"So finally, the Amherst religion department makes a contribution," Dan said, wearing his pride on his sleeve.

"And an important one," Michael said. "That pretty much gives us the complete picture—and tells us what these pseudoscientists are all about."

"But what about Geoffrey?" Skiddy asked, a worried look on his face. "Is he with them?"

"That's still unclear," Yael said, scanning the latest messages she had received. "I've asked for a check on any links he may have to this New Jerusalem Way bunch. So far, nothing. But something else is curious. Some of his publications have been quite inconsistent with the belief in UFO's that he's expressed to us. For instance, he's written that he believes it's highly unlikely we'd ever be visited by extraterrestrials through a wormhole or other portal."

"So he's changed his views big-time?" Joanna asked.

"Yes, and that definitely bears further investigation," Yael said. "But right now the connection of these other two with the cult is our main concern—and makes it necessary to get these people off the compound as quickly as possible. We can deal with Geoffrey after that."

"So how would you suggest that we proceed?" Michael said.

"My government contacts have already assembled a small strike force, but they're leaving the final decision up to me," Yael said. "I want to handle this in the safest way, and those guys are obviously unpredictable. I'd prefer to take them by surprise—and that may mean it will be best for us to handle the situation ourselves."

Michael at least was keeping pace with her.

"I've been evaluating our tactical situation," he said, "and there are a number of possible obstacles. For example, the missing weapons, including two automatic rifles. Have we located them?"

Yael shook her head.

"So they could be in the hands of our friendly cult members," he continued. "That's dangerous. I wouldn't want to order them off this compound, and then have them pull out their AK-47's."

Yael sighed. "I've considered all that, and I agree. We haven't found the weapons, and we do need to get them back before we make our move."

"Why don't all of us just leave and let the military come in here and deal with them?" Skiddy suggested.

"Because we'd probably never get through the compound gate before they reacted," Yael said. "We have to assume that they're unnaturally suspicious and quite paranoid. Frederick is mentally unbalanced, and both he and Harold have violent criminal records.

They could start shooting without warning. No, we need another plan."

"What if I work with the guards to overpower them and put them in custody?" Michael said.

"That might work with Harold and Frederick," Yael said. "But what about Geoffrey? He could be in cahoots with them. Then again, for all we know, he's a perfectly legitimate scientist. If we arrest him and it turns out he's done nothing, we could cause a scandal we don't need right now."

"On the other hand, if he's working with the other two and we don't arrest him, he could come at us with those concealed weapons," Michael cautioned. "We could be facing a real bloodbath."

"Also, we're shorthanded," Yael reminded them. "Remember, we've lost one man, the one who was killed in Jerusalem. Another guard is in charge of Dudley—and I don't think we can afford to loosen our grip on him at this point. For all we know, he's a part of this cult thing as well."

"I doubt that," Skiddy said.

"The ballistics tests say different," she said, studying another message that had just been transmitted by computer from her head-quarters. "Says here that the tests on the stolen pistols Dudley was carrying have just come back. The round that killed the guard at the parking lot in Jerusalem came from one of Dudley's weapons."

"One of those other guys, Frederick or Harold, could have planted the weapons on him," Dan said. "Probably did."

"But the first time they were on the compound was when they arrived here with Geoffrey and Dudley," Michael reminded him. "So the weapons must have been stolen from our armory earlier by Dudley—or Geoffrey."

"But we're not sure—and Dudley's the only one who's been caught with illegal weapons so far," Yael replied. "We can't take a chance with him. And with a guard watching him, that leaves only two others free, plus the officer of the guard and myself. And Michael."

"Five should be more than enough to neutralize the Mercury twins—and contain Geoffrey at the same time," Michael said. "You know our military training is superior to theirs."

"But surprise will be essential," Yael said. "We can't give them any chance to get their hands on those weapons."

Then Yael, gazing at her computer screen, raised her hand. "Wait. Another message is coming in. Tel Aviv is hitting me with everything at once."

Her expression resolved into a deep frown as she read. When she finally looked up, her breath was coming in short bursts.

"Apparently Geoffrey is not really Geoffrey," she said.

"What?" Skiddy cried, not fully comprehending what he had just heard.

"This message says that a body has just turned up in a northern California forest," Yael said. "Some hikers found it. And it's been identified as Professor Geoffrey Gonzales, a noted astrophysicist."

A stunned silence gripped the headquarters building.

Yael started to give them additional facts, but when she looked up into Michael's face, all she saw was a startled expression, frozen in place by the blast that ripped through the room, blowing the walls away and casting a cloak of deep, unconscious blackness over the headquarters building.

THIRTY-SIX

M I C H A E L was the first to struggle to his knees.

The air was thick with dust and the burnt-oil stench of a plastic explosive. *Probably C-4.* The thought came into his sluggish mind automatically, part of his military training. He was aware of a dull pain in his right thigh, and he also had a sharp headache. When he looked down, he saw a shard of metal sticking out of his leg.

Not too bad, he thought as he yanked the sharp shrapnel-like fragment out of his body. *I've seen worse.* He proceeded to open a wider tear in his trousers so that he could put a makeshift pressure bandage on the wound.

With his own bleeding stanched, Michael surveyed the chaos around him. The others were strewn out across what was left of the floor. Michael thought he could make out one body beyond the rear of the building, which now had no back wall. No one was moving.

Michael half crawled, half stumbled toward the closest casualty, who was lying about five yards from him, the upper body partially obscured by pieces of one of the walls. It was Yael.

He quickly dragged away the debris and checked her vital signs. Her pulse was strong, but blood blanketed her forehead, the result of a superficial head wound caused by flying wood or metal. Fortunately, she had been hit a glancing blow, without any penetration of her skull. Two other wounds, one on her left shoulder and another on her right side, also seemed to be shallow, though they were oozing blood.

Miraculously, the room's watercooler had made it unscathed

through the explosion. Michael used some of the liquid to clean Yael's head wound. The cool water immediately brought her back to consciousness. She pulled herself up abruptly and looked around at the devastation. "What . . . where . . . ?"

He put his hands firmly on her shoulders. "Conserve your strength. You may need it."

Then, he tore off part of his T-shirt and fashioned several makeshift bandages to stop the flow of blood from the minor wounds on her body. As Michael tied Yael's last bandage, he heard a groan a few feet away. One of the desks, which had been tipped over halfway, moved slightly.

He pointed to Yael, motioning to her to stay where she was, and rolled quickly in the direction of the voice. It was Skiddy. He was pinned to the ground by the desk and other refuse, and his right leg appeared to be broken. Otherwise, though, he seemed to be suffering just the temporary effects of the concussion of the blast.

When Michael finally looked up from his emergency work, he saw one of the other victims—it looked like Dan—moving toward the back of the blown-out building.

Dan regained consciousness just after Michael did. He saw the Wheaton professor laboring over someone who was lying on the floor. The clothing and hair made him think, *Yael.*

Then the thought hit him. *Where's Joanna?*

He rose too quickly and almost passed out from the dizziness. Feeling his face, he discovered multiple lacerations, but they seemed superficial. His arms and legs also appeared to be working.

Forget it! he thought. *Find Joanna!*

A quick check of the destroyed headquarters revealed nothing. Then he looked out back, beyond where the wall to Yael's office had been, and he saw Joanna, lying still on the ground.

Dan moved as quickly as he could to her side and was relieved to find that she was breathing regularly and was beginning to regain consciousness.

"What happened . . . ?"

"An explosion, but don't try to move!" Dan said. "You seem to be okay. Just knocked out, like the rest of us."

"I can't hear too well," she said, trying to sit up.

"Neither can I. The blast, I guess."

Then he put a hand on her shoulder. "You wait here. Stay down, and be very quiet. I'm going to the front of the building—to try to find out what's going on."

"You be careful!" she cautioned, holding on to his arm.

"I'll be fine. Just stay down."

Looking back into the devastated building, Dan could still see Michael working over Skiddy. But realizing that he would never get through all the splintered furniture and other wreckage, he circled around the side of the building and rushed out into the parking area in front of the ruined headquarters shack.

Dan was not at all prepared for the sight that greeted him.

Frederick and Harold, each holding an AK-47 automatic rifle, were moving deliberately toward the demolished headquarters building. When they saw Dan, they stopped, trained their weapons in his direction, and seemed on the verge of opening fire.

"Wait!" a voice behind them barked.

Dan now noticed that Geoffrey—or whatever his name was—was standing behind the other two, holding a pistol in one hand and a rifle in the other. As he scanned the area near the phony professor, Dan caught his breath. It seemed that there were bodies all over the place, littering the landscape everywhere he looked. Dan counted at least three . . . no, four . . . all in Israeli uniforms.

The guard detail.

"What have you done?" Dan said.

"What we were forced to do."

"Who are you? I know you're not Professor Geoffrey Gonzales."

The man looked surprised, but then smiled confidently. "So you know, but you've learned too late. No, I'm not Geoffrey Gonzales. He wasn't able to make it."

"You killed him. They found his body in a California forest."

That piece of information made a definite impression. Harold and Frederick looked nervously over their shoulders at "Geoffrey," who shifted uncertainly from one foot to the other.

"So you've learned a great deal. But it won't do you any good now. You or anyone else on this compound."

"What's this all about? You'll never get away with this. You and Hermes and Cadmilus. Some Greek gods! What's the point?"

Now, Harold and Frederick were quite agitated.

"Let's kill him—now!" Frederick spit out the words, a flicker of insanity creeping into his eyes.

"He knows too much," Harold said.

"Patience, patience," their leader cautioned. "Dr. Thompson may be of some use to us."

"Who are you, really?" Dan asked again.

"Let me introduce myself. I'm called Phoebus. Dr. Phoebus. In a past life, I was known as Dr. Lanski. But my colleagues at the University of California—including Geoffrey Gonzales—didn't approve of my creative research goals or methods. I knew more than any of them about astrophysics and astronomy. But they didn't appreciate my personal beliefs. Wouldn't give me the professorship I deserved."

"The New Jerusalem Way," Dan said.

Again, there was a surprised silence.

"My, you do know us well, Dan," Phoebus said. "What other interesting tidbits can you pass on? The more you tell us, the longer you'll live. We might even set you free. Are you the only survivor? Seems so. And that means that after we've departed, at least one person would remain to pass on the story of what's transpired."

Dan realized now that he had to suppress his anger and play for time. His life clearly depended on it. *These kooks obviously don't know anyone else is alive in that building. Help me, Michael! If you can hear my thoughts, help me! If You're there, God—and You really answer prayers—give me a hand!*

"One thing I know is that your cult uses names of ancient Greek gods," Dan said, blurting out the first thing that came to his mind. "You call yourself 'Phoebus.' That's another name of Apollo, the god of light. Appropriate name for one who's trying to discover the meaning of that light overhead."

"Good, good!" Phoebus said. "You're brighter than I thought you were. I was wondering about the quality of the Amherst faculty for a while, but you've restored my confidence."

"What do you think you'll gain from this?" Dan asked, gesturing at the carnage and wreckage that lay around them.

"We won't be here much longer," Phoebus said confidently. "Our prophecies and teachings make the situation quite clear. The activity of the great gateway overhead has been increasing, just as our seers have predicted. There's no doubt that today is the final day. And midnight is the final hour. On the stroke of twelve in Jerusalem, we'll be transported through the portal and into a marvelous new life with the inhabitants of the New Jerusalem."

The other two responded with goofy grins.

Is this really happening? Dan wondered. But as he watched the menacing movements they were making with their automatics, he quickly decided not to question the seriousness of the gunmen. His best strategy was to delay, delay, delay—and hope the cavalry came riding to the rescue.

"So, do you expect to be the only ones who get sucked up by that light?" Dan asked, racking his brain for questions that would elicit long answers.

"Our people, who are scattered around the earth, have also been chosen," Harold replied. "Most are still in California. The holiest people live in California."

"Right," Dan said, trying not to irritate them with the sarcasm that he was trying so hard to contain.

"But many of our keenest minds have succeeded in joining the top scientific teams studying the holy light," Phoebus said. "And when necessary, as here, we'll eliminate opposition. You see, we've become convinced that visitors from above will first contact the most intelligent beings on earth. Your team is at the top of our list. That's why I'm here."

"And us!" Frederick and Harold said, almost in unison.

"Yes, yes," Phoebus replied, waving them into silence.

But Dan knew silence could be deadly for him. So he groped for other questions to ask. "So how about those newspaper articles. Did you plant those stories Geoff—, uh . . . Phoebus?"

"Yes. Again, you're surprisingly perceptive. The *New York Times* was merely the tool that we chose to let our followers know what was happening on this compound."

"So you're the leader of this, uh, New Jerusalem Way group?"

"Let's just say I'm an elder. A cofounder."

Keep him talking about himself. These types can't resist letting you know how great they are.

"So you're one of the big shots, the guys who run the show," Dan said. "Given that you're so prominent, how did you manage to keep everyone in the dark about your identity for so long? Weren't you afraid that someone would figure out that the real Geoffrey Gonzales was missing?"

"It's easy to shield your identity if you know how to go about it," Phoebus said. "You obviously didn't notice the approach we used with the *Times* articles."

"What do you mean?"

"We used the paper rather adeptly, if I do say so myself, to get our message across. They dutifully reported in their paper, Web site, and other outlets that this was an investigation into UFO's, extraterrestrial intelligence, and the possible arrival of a portal to another universe. The reporter used terms and rhetoric I had planted with her, and our followers around the world immediately picked up those signals."

"And what better place than the *Times,* which is the premier paper not only in the United States, but in the world as well?" Harold said proudly.

"But weren't you afraid that one of Gonzales's colleagues would see his name in the paper and begin asking questions?" Dan asked.

"Again, you missed a key point," Phoebus said, waving his muzzle back and forth in Dan's direction—and increasing the Amherst professor's fear of an accidental discharge. "The name of Professor Geoffrey Gonzales was never mentioned in any of the articles," he boasted.

Dan looked at him incredulously. "Are you sure?"

"I invite you to read them again."

Then Phoebus interrupted himself with a chuckle. "But of course you won't get a chance to read them again. So I'll have to explain. You see, since I was the paper's anonymous source, based right here on the site of the investigation, they had no choice but to accept my version and my conditions—that is, if they wanted a story at all."

"We helped too," Frederick said, wanting to be sure he got some credit for the ruse.

"Yes, of course you did," Phoebus replied patiently. "Frederick and Harold were quite effective in sending messages to the paper from their site. Made it harder to identify me as the source of the stories."

Then he turned back to Dan. "So after insisting that they keep my name out of it, I named everybody but Gonzales. I had them add that there were 'also a number of other experienced astronomers, astrophysicists, and scientists' on the project."

"This reporter must have been in your pocket," Dan said, using flattery to stall for time.

Phoebus's chest seemed to expand visibly at the adulation.

"We've cultivated this reporter and many others over a number of years," he bragged. "This particular woman has grown to trust us implicitly."

"Wow—seems that you know every trick in the book," Dan said. *Where are you, Michael, when I really need you? I can't keep this up forever.*

Fortunately, Phoebus was still more interested in flaunting his superior strategy and new position of power than in finishing the job with Dan. "But the most important reason I've been protected is that the visitors above have cloaked me," he continued, pointing up toward the strange light. "They have made my identity invisible with their radiance."

Mistaking Dan's lack of a response for admiration, Phoebus continued with more practical reasons for his success. "It was also easy to assume Gonzales's identity because he was something of a recluse," he said. "He was a bachelor, and typically, he would disappear for weeks at a time, especially during the summer months. He liked to spend time kayaking in Montana or Idaho, or hiking in the Tetons. I was quite correct in assuming that no one on this team had ever seen him—not even Dudley, who is an astronomer and attends most of the conventions. Of course, Dudley knew of Gonzales and had read his papers. But he had never met him."

That reminded Dan of a question he had neglected to ask. "Where is Dudley now? I take it he's not part of your little cadre here."

"Of course he's not. He's far too unstable."

Dan glanced at Frederick. *Yeah, maybe a little unstable, but hardly in the same league as these other nut cases.*

"So where is Dudley?"

Phoebus pointed toward the astronomer's quarters. "I believe he slept through everything. His guard is dead, of course. But Dudley is well medicated."

"Your doing?" Dan asked.

"Yes. He was a fine red herring that allowed us to obtain these weapons."

"You set him up with the pistols," Dan said. "Then you drugged him so he wouldn't know what was going on. That left you free to shoot the driver down there in Jerusalem. All that remained was to frame Dudley for everything."

"You are astute, my dear Amherst colleague. If you had achieved enlightenment a little sooner, you might have become one of us . . ."

Not on your life.

". . . but unfortunately for you, this present age is fast coming to an end."

Dan now faced a split-second decision. *Should I ask more questions or make a run for it? Should I head for the fence and try to pull these guys away from Joanna and the others who are still stuck in that wreckage?*

But Michael James and Yael Sharon made his decision for him.

THIRTY-SEVEN

T H E pistol shots rang out, popping so rapidly that they sounded like automatic rifle fire.

The sharp cracks paralyzed Dan, rooting him to the spot as Yael and Michael came tumbling out of different ends of the headquarters wreckage. They rolled this way and that on the dirt, and yet somehow managed to crank out round after accurate round aimed at their adversaries. Both Frederick and Harold fell wounded to the ground before they could get off a shot.

"Hit the dirt, Dan!" a voice behind him screamed, and without thinking twice, he dived to the ground.

Automatic gunfire erupted, a deafening, rippling roar that tore up the dirt in every direction. Phoebus was on one knee, spraying rounds from his AK-47, first toward the Israeli agent and then at the Wheaton professor. Dan could see that Yael was down, evidently hurt badly. Michael was still moving, zigzagging, trying his best to stay alive. But all seemed lost now. The cult leader's firepower was obviously too much for them.

Then out of the corner of his eye Dan saw something moving in a blur toward Phoebus. Like a locomotive, the object rammed into the cult member and knocked him in one direction and his rifle in another.

It was Dudley Dunster, streaking out of nowhere like an avenging angel. Dudley's explosive entrance seemed a reprise of the unexpected surprise attack he had launched against Michael during that headquarters meeting—which had taken place only a day or so ago, but now seemed to have occurred in some distant, long-past life.

239

Dudley's charge gave Michael the opening he needed. He gathered himself up off the ground and sprinted directly toward the fallen Phoebus. It was a race for life. If Michael covered the remaining ten yards before Phoebus could recover his rifle, he would live. If he was a step late, he would die.

Phoebus shook his head, evidently to clear his mind after the collision. Then he saw Michael coming and lunged toward his weapon. It was in his hands. His trigger finger was in place. The barrel was sweeping toward the former Seal.

But he was an instant too late.

Michael crashed into the man with such ferocity that the impact by itself would probably have knocked Phoebus senseless. But the Wheaton man's training left nothing to chance. Just as he made contact, Michael delivered a heavy chop with the edge of his hand against the cult leader's neck, precisely at the carotid artery. The blow rendered "Geoffrey Gonzales" senseless and brought the brief, deadly encounter to a swift end.

The compound resembled a war zone just after the bloodiest of battles. Two helicopters had landed, and the dead had been lined up in a neat row, where they awaited the body bags that the airlifted troops and medics were bringing in.

Heavily armed light infantry—probably trained commandos—had already poured out of one of the choppers and set up a heavy perimeter defense. Other choppers were landing in the distance to provide extra security.

Dan and Joanna were hardly aware of their wounds as the Israeli field nurses worked on them. They couldn't take their eyes off Yael, who lay motionless, eyes closed, on a makeshift cot a few feet away. A medical team labored feverishly over her, as Michael leaned forward at her feet, head bowed in silent prayer. Joanna left Dan's side and hurried over to comfort Michael.

And I'd be praying, too, if that were Joanna, Dan reflected.

"Will she make it?" Dan asked his wife, who had just returned to his side.

"I don't know, but it doesn't look good," Joanna said. "The nurse told me that the wounds from the explosion weren't too bad, though they're not sure how she recovered quickly enough to launch that counterassault. But she did. And then she took two rounds from Geoffrey's automatic rifle. Both through the chest."

"Not Geoffrey—Phoebus," Dan corrected.

"I still can't wrap my mind around this," she replied, beginning to sob. "How could we have let that man fool us?"

"We were in a hurry," Dan said. "Everyone was in a hurry. Corners were cut. Security suffered."

"And Yael has paid the price."

"How is she?" a familiar voice called from behind them.

It was Skiddy Kirkland, hobbling toward them on crutches. When he reached their side, Joanna quietly explained what she had learned from the medical team.

"She saved our lives," Joanna said. "None of us would be here if she hadn't come out with Michael to defend us. He could never have managed alone, with all those weapons trained on him."

They sat in silence, contemplating what Yael had done for them.

"I wish I believed in prayer," Skiddy said, causing the other two to look at him in surprise. "I'm glad Michael does."

"It's hard to keep from believing that something beyond us is at work here," Joanna said. "Otherwise, how could we possibly have survived?"

Then she looked in Yael's direction, and her anxious expression turned to one of horror. "Oh, no! No, no!" she exclaimed, both hands covering her mouth.

The attending physician was gently pulling a canvas cover over Yael's face. Then Michael moved to the doctor's side and stayed the man's hands.

"Give me a moment," they heard him say softly.

He pulled the canvas back down from Yael's face, bent over, and brushed her lips softly with his own. Tears were streaming down his cheeks, and he could barely control the racking sobs that were welling up in his chest.

Then he bowed his head again, and they saw his lips move in a brief, silent benediction. Finally, he replaced the light canvas over her face and turned away, unable to watch the troopers who were moving in his direction, preparing to entomb his precious, unrealized love in the impersonal body bag they were carrying.

THIRTY-EIGHT

O N E *week later . . .*

The team sat quietly in a newly constructed headquarters shack, which the Israeli army had erected practically overnight with pre-fabricated materials. Their depleted ranks said it all: Once they had been seven. Now they were only five—yet five who were even more committed to working together to find the answer to the great mystery they were confronting.

In many ways, the physical surroundings were similar. Skiddy's new office was still at the back of the building on the right. The room that had been Yael's base of operations was on the left. The larger meeting area up front was furnished in almost exactly the same way as it had been in the previous building.

But of course, nothing was really the same.

Yael was gone. Nothing could change that. Nothing could erase the memory of her broken young body from their minds—especially from Michael's mind. It was little comfort that a military funeral, with full honors and the highest national decorations, had just been conducted for her in Jerusalem, with attendant praise from leading Israeli politicians. None of the accolades could bring back Yael.

Predictably, Michael's recovery from the tragedy had been slow and agonizing. Every team member had been aware, at least to some extent, of the depth of his grief. Joanna and Dan both knew that for a short time, little more than a week ago, marriage had actually begun to seem a possibility to the couple. But then, all hope had been dashed.

An accident of cruel fate?

Or some inscrutable act of divine intervention?

Michael didn't believe in accidents or coincidences in such matters. In some way, he had to grasp what had happened in terms of God's will. That was the only answer that would ultimately satisfy his aching soul. Though his inner torment was great, he couldn't dispute that it was necessary to accept what had happened. But for now, it was impossible to make the pain go away.

Even though the Wheaton professor experienced the greatest anguish from his loss, the other team members could at least participate in his burden. To some degree, they could even help him bear it. But ultimately, Michael knew that only the One with more power than any human being could heal his inner wounds.

It's up to You, Lord. I can't handle it unless You help.

It was also some comfort to all that the deceiver who had pretended to be Geoffrey Gonzales had been removed and arrested. There seemed to be an assumption among Israeli authorities that he would never be seen in public again. At the same time, no one could begin to imagine, much less articulate, the grief that they knew must have overwhelmed the family and colleagues of the real Gonzales, the astrophysicist who had actually been murdered in California.

Feedback they had received from scientists and others back in the States had painted a picture of the real scientist as a gentle, if reserved and reclusive, man. A man who, in most ways, seemed to have been the polar opposite of the pretender who had been part of their team.

"The Israeli government still plans to send a replacement for Yael?" Dan asked.

"Eventually," Skiddy replied, "though they seem in no hurry. In the meantime, our liaison will be the new head of the guard—a higher-ranking officer this time, a major."

Dan shook his head. "It's amazing. After all that's happened, they still want us to continue. The prime minister even said so. Not only that, Peter Van Campe wants to move ahead—and he's willing to fund us for additional equipment and replacement personnel as needed."

"But we must issue a report," Skiddy reminded him. "And that means we have to make some big decisions."

With that, the Harvard psychologist lapsed into an uncharacteristic silence. Dan looked at Skiddy with considerable curiosity. *He really has changed. I thought he was just temporarily stunned by the violence. But there's more going on—more than meets my eyes, anyhow.*

Dan was particularly perplexed at how much Skiddy's attitudes toward Michael James had shifted in just the past few days. He seemed to have been transformed from Michael's archenemy to what, disconcertingly, was looking more and more like the Wheaton man's most solicitous, trusting friend.

The tragic loss of Yael had obviously taken some of the edge off Michael's assertive style in presenting his views. Yet far from being relieved, Skiddy seemed to miss the adversarial voice that the Wheaton man had provided.

What caused Skiddy to change? Dan mused. *Perhaps it all started with the bombing of the van in Jerusalem . . .*

Or the obviously abnormal, extrascientific behavior of the "Star" . . .

Or his disillusionment with Dudley's mental problems and weapons violations . . .

Or the scary revelations about the two new "scientists" and the shadow of suspicion that had been cast over Geoffrey . . .

Or Michael's emerging role as perhaps Skiddy's most reasonable, levelheaded colleague—and a strong physical leader, who seemed to possess the qualities necessary to guide them through this dangerous crisis . . .

Or his strong sympathy with Michael after Yael's murder . . .

Or all of the above.

Whatever the cause, Skiddy now seemed more than willing to rely on Michael for advice, not to mention on Joanna and even Dan himself. *Even on me, his perennial whipping boy!* Dan mused. *Every day, another completely unexpected twist in this crazy situation. What could possibly be next?*

"How are you feeling, Dudley?" Michael asked, emerging from his grief for a few moments to pat the pudgy Harvard astronomer on the leg.

That's another miracle, Dan thought. *That is, if I believed in miracles. Dudley and Michael—almost buddies, certainly not enemies.*

"Better," the Harvard astronomer answered. "I'm not used to such exertion. The medic said I'd probably be suffering some aches and pains for days. It's not often I get a chance to execute a full-body block on somebody."

Dudley did look tired. But somehow, the anger, fear, and sour cynicism that had driven him since the team had arrived in Israel had dissipated, quite literally, overnight.

Dan ruminated further. *Maybe the hand-to-hand combat with "Geoffrey," a.k.a. "Phoebus," knocked the meanness out of him. Or maybe something else is going on. Something I don't quite understand.*

"Now, we have a difficult task," Skiddy said. "The Israelis have charged us with the duty of drafting a preliminary report for the public. Only two other research groups in the country have been given this honor. We can't afford to ignore such a strong request from our host country. And Peter Van Campe has been putting pressure on us too. He wants a preliminary statement as well."

"We're really not quite ready for a report, are we?" Dudley asked. "I mean, we have no scientific evidence telling anything about that light. All we have is some theories about what it might be."

"True, but let's face it—this is not your normal, garden-variety research study," Skiddy said. "I have to put my public-health hat on at this point. Public anxiety is building. Even hysteria in some places. And we just may be in a position to help quell some of the turmoil. But our only option seems to be to feed the public some intelligent guesses. Even speculate about that 'Star' up there."

He paused and looked at the Wheaton professor. "Any suggestions, Michael?"

Michael, obviously distracted, seemed a little tongue-tied at first. Everyone appeared to understand that his mind was still on Yael. More than once, the others had noticed that he was only half listening to the conversations around him.

But he had picked up some of Skiddy's comments. He was aware of his responsibility to the team, so with a visible effort, he gathered his energy and concentration to respond.

"I don't pretend to have any final answers about what's happening," he finally began. "And it's no secret that I haven't yet managed to get my mind back into our project here. But slowly, God is bringing me out of this. And now, I have a growing sense that what we're witnessing will be earthshaking in its final consequences."

He paused for effect and looked around the room so as to emphasize what he was about to say. "In a nutshell," he finally said, "events have convinced me that what we see overhead is some sort of recurrence of the light that the Magi saw more than two thousand years ago." He paused again to let his comments sink in.

"So you really have concluded that this is the Star of Bethlehem?" Joanna asked after a brief silence.

"Yes, in a sense. And ironically, my conclusion comes close to the way our former colleague Phoebus understood it—as a window on an extradimensional reality. The difference I'd have with the cult is that I think the truth about that Star, and our key to understanding it or relating to it, lies in our traditional spiritual heritage. That can only be found in the Scriptures—or in subsequent historical experiences that are consistent with the Scriptures."

"So the Star is somehow supernatural," Dan said.

Michael hesitated. "Let me respond with a tentative 'yes'—but I'd prefer to put that word on the shelf for the time being. Let's think 'extradimensional' rather than 'supernatural' for now."

"It's also the shekinah glory, the light that accompanies God's presence?" Joanna said.

"Yes again," Michael replied, and then he looked tentatively at Dudley. The eyes of the others also drifted toward the Harvard astronomer.

Dudley, who seemed more relaxed than any of the others could ever remember, actually smiled. "You're expecting me to pounce on that, aren't you?" he said. "Well, I've been through too much to pounce again—on anything or anyone. I'm actually beginning to think that maybe some things are more important than tenure at Harvard. Things like my life, which I almost lost a few days ago."

"I can identify with that," Skiddy said, fingering the cast on his leg. "I think we all feel like combat veterans."

"And for once, I'm willing to listen to you, Michael," Dudley added. "I have to admit that the light up there isn't a natural phenomenon, at least not in the sense that we scientists have been trained to measure or understand. Other tools—spiritual or philosophical or historical—will evidently be required to crack this conundrum. But I warn you, I'm not prepared to let you get away with any religious platitudes. I'm not a believer. So you'll have to convince me every step of the way."

"Fair enough," Michael said. "But let me emphasize that as far as I'm concerned, faith—which to some degree may be necessary to grasp what the Star is all about—is not contrary to reason. Matters of faith often *transcend* reason, but they don't go *against* reason. As one sage has said, a phenomenon like the Star may be *non*rational, but it's not necessarily *ir*rational."

With that, Michael picked up a marker and turned to the new melamine board that was hanging on the wall behind him. "Let's go over what we know, or what we're reasonably certain, is true."

Then he began to jot down the points.

"First, the strange light can emit a healing beam.

"Second, some sort of discernment or intelligence is involved, because the beam can seek out those in need of help. Also, Joanna reported that she encountered a shining figure that spoke words she understood in English. By the way, I accept her report as true—though I don't pretend to be able to explain exactly who the figure was.

"Third, the light also moves about, apparently when important things like healings are about to occur. When we went to Jerusalem, we saw it streak through the sky, from east to west and back again, just before those healing beams cured several people.

"Fourth, it has the power to change shape. We saw it grow considerably larger just after we arrived in Israel. In Jerusalem, we saw it pulsate dramatically—almost as though we were watching a strange, beating heart up there in the sky.

"Fifth, it's changed colors—fiery streaks of red appeared among the basic shades of cool blue and green. And it emits a blinding white light as healings are taking place, and also when it flashes across the sky.

"Sixth, despite all the activity and movement, we haven't been able to measure the object with any known human scientific instruments—though we could record it on film. The cult twins, Hermes and Cadmilus, did say they had picked up something new with their prisms and crystals. But those claims remain unsubstantiated and highly suspect. Haven't been replicated by any other tests. And quite frankly, I don't believe them."

Dudley raised his hand. "As a corollary to this sixth point, you might include something like 'possibly extradimensional,'" he said.

Michael looked at him seriously. "You really accept that possibility now?"

"Yes, I've finally come around," the Harvard astronomer said with a sigh. "I've searched my mind and my data banks for any other possible scientific answer—any scientific measuring device we might have overlooked. But I've come up empty-handed. So I think the only honest thing to do is to suggest this corollary—though I'd still like to see that word *possibly* inserted before *extradimensional*."

"Fine," Michael said, making the addition. "Now, is that it, or have we left something out?"

"The violent, negative social and political reactions," Skiddy reminded him. "And the possibility of mass hysteria and terror."

"Yes, but at the same time, we should remember that those responses don't seem to have been *caused* directly by the light," Michael replied, adding this suggestion as his seventh item. "They appear to be just how people and groups have reacted when confronted with the increased social stress and uncertainty."

"How about the possible biblical connections—the shekinah and all that?" Joanna asked. "Have you forgotten those relationships?"

"No, I certainly haven't forgotten," Michael said, jotting the number "8" on the board. "Up to this point, I've been referring to facts that we know, not interpretations. But it does seem that the time has arrived to explore historical links that might lead us to interpretations."

Then he wrote "UFO" in a separate place, in the upper right-hand corner of the board. "Geoffrey and the other cult members were convinced of their UFO interpretation. But I'm afraid I can't buy that for one simple reason—there's no historical backing that would warrant such an inference. Yet for me, the light in our skies is similar—provocatively similar—to the historical accounts of the shekinah glory and the Star of Bethlehem."

Skiddy stood up and walked to the back of the room, as if attempting to clear his head. Michael stopped and watched him expectantly, waiting for some comment.

"Quite frankly, this is getting beyond me," Skiddy finally said.

"I'm not trained to think in these terms. I'm not a religious person. And I've always believed that what goes on in the physical world—or in our minds, for that matter—can be explained by natural means. Yet I must admit, this light doesn't lend itself to the usual methods of analysis or interpretation that I understand."

"Now we're really thinking out of the box," Dan said. "And that seems the only option, doesn't it? Maybe you are onto something, Michael. Maybe this really is some sort of supernatural sign."

"You'll notice I still avoid that word—*supernatural*," Michael cautioned. "One of the reasons is that I think it can be misleading. Many times, the word suggests events that are abnormal or contrary to the laws of nature. Yet I don't think what happens in God's realm is against nature."

"Somehow they coexist, or work together?" Joanna asked.

"Well, in a sense, I see our world and God's world on a continuum," the Wheaton man replied. "His divine dimension often intersects with our more limited, space–time universe—but at the same time extends far beyond it. Furthermore, at least some of the laws of His realm may apply to our more restricted world as well—as many people know from their experiences with prayer."

"So remind me—what words are you using instead of *supernatural*?" Joanna asked.

"Oh, I might say that God's reality is in a kind of 'parallel universe,' or a 'superuniverse' that overlaps in some instances with our own," Michael said. "Or I could describe His abode as 'multidimensional' or 'extradimensional.'

"The important thing to keep in mind is that God is separate and eternal. He's infinitely beyond us and our reality, except to the extent that He chooses to interact with us. He created our universe, but He exists apart from it. At the same time, God and other conscious and willful extradimensional entities in His realm may break through into our limited reality and communicate with us—or even influence our world in some way."

"Such as angels," Dan said.

"Right."

"Or demons?" Joanna asked, seemingly a little embarrassed at her own question.

"I think so," Michael replied. "But remember, many times these names, such as angel and demon, are just limited human words. They can't tell us the whole story, even though they can be found in this book, the Bible, which contains God's ultimate written revelations to us about His 'universe.'

"Certainly, the Greek words in the text are rich in meaning—*daimon* or *daimonion* for demon, and *aggelos* for angel. By the way, *aggelos,* pronounced 'an-gel-os,' actually means 'messenger'—a fascinating tidbit for you, Joanna, since you actually received a message from that figure you saw."

A shadow of understanding passed across the Yale professor's face. "So that may actually have been an angel I saw?"

"Maybe," Michael replied. "In fact, I think you did meet an angel. But even if it was an angel who spoke, you heard the message in words, and human language can take us only so far. The *reality* you experienced went light-years beyond what any of us could ever put into words. Remember the *Flatland* story. Those two-dimensional creatures couldn't come close to grasping what a three-dimensional universe was all about.

"Similarly, we three-dimensional creatures operate in time, which many people regard as a fourth dimension. Yet we can't come close to wrapping our minds around God's multidimensional, timeless universe. It's impossible to crack this higher, infinitely more complex reality through human reason."

"As limited humans, we don't have the built-in faculties to understand or analyze," Joanna added.

"Exactly," Michael said. "So if we're going to 'get it,' the One who controls that other universe has to give us some tools and guidelines. How can we understand? Perhaps some keys can be found here in the Bible. You'll remember one of those keys we've discussed is the shekinah glory."

Dudley had been listening intently, with no trace of cynicism on his face.

But be careful! Dan thought. *You can't always tell from Dudley's expression. He'll strike with devastating sarcasm just when he appears to be at his most innocent. And who knows—violence may still be lurking inside that soft exterior.*

THIRTY-NINE

Bu t Dan soon concluded that his worries about Dudley were misplaced. Some genuine inner transformation was apparently occurring in the acerbic Harvard astronomer—just as profound changes of one sort or another seemed to be occurring in every team member.

"I guess I can buy what you're saying as a pretty good religious explanation of an extradimensional universe," Dudley finally told Michael. "I might put it in different, less religious, terms than you do. But I think I can stay with you—at least for now."

Skiddy wasn't willing to let the Wheaton man off so easily. "I still have a big problem, Michael," the psychologist said. "It sounds to me as if you might be agreeing with Geoffrey, uh, Phoebus. After all, he argued that the light was an extradimensional reality. And when he talked about UFO's and extraterrestrials, that sounded an awful lot like your references to God and angels and so forth."

Michael, who seemed to have temporarily put his preoccupation with Yael behind him, smiled engagingly, apparently quite ready to reenter the world of theological repartee that had energized him before the recent tragedy. "Actually, Skiddy, there are fundamental differences between my view and the one expressed by Phoebus," Michael responded. "It's possible that we both believe there's another reality—a parallel universe beyond our limited space–time universe. Also, we'd apparently agree that this superuniverse consists of many more dimensions than we can now experience or understand."

Then he stopped and shook his head vigorously. "But we'd differ totally on the nature of the other universe because I rely on ancient spiritual texts, the Old and New Testaments, for my authority. I also look to the historic Christian tradition, which spans more than two thousand years."

"So as you see it, the main difference is different assumptions about spiritual authority?" Skiddy asked.

"That and something else," Michael replied. "Phoebus's source of authority was less established and much weaker than that of an ancient faith such as Christianity. He was relying on a very recent hodgepodge of beliefs that he and the other cofounder of his cult had concocted. Beliefs that haven't withstood the test of time."

"I can confirm all that," Dan said. "I've managed to pull together a considerable amount of background on the New Jerusalem Way cult through my sources on the Internet. I've even read some of their texts. There's no question that Michael's characterization of their beliefs is basically true."

"Typically, these cult leaders sit down with the Bible and spiritual texts from other religions or belief systems," Michael continued. "Then they make up their own special spiritual program. The cult's doctrines often include words and terms from established faiths. But at heart, these sects are based on the leader's own peculiar mode of reasoning and emotional whims."

"Then, they do some heavy-duty proselytizing," Dan said.

"Right," Michael agreed. "They try to convince others that they, as individuals, have the line to ultimate truth. But they make it clear that cult members can't go directly to God and then make their own spiritual decisions. They must go through the cult leader and do exactly what he or she tells them to do."

Skiddy remembered some cases from his own psychological practice. "Vulnerable, often emotionally unbalanced, people join these groups," he said. "Then they come under the near-total control of the leader. That's apparently what happened with Phoebus's group, the New Jerusalem Way."

"Yes, quite true, according to my own research into cults," Dan said. "But there's more. When cult members—especially leaders like Phoebus—run into solid resistance to their beliefs, they sometimes flip out."

Michael nodded. "I believe that's the main reason he went violent and tried to kill us. He could see his interpretation of extradimensionality and UFO's was going to put him completely at odds with the rest of us. The major problem was that none of us really bought into his UFO thesis. So in his mind, there was a huge danger that we would interfere with the final, history-changing message he expected from the light."

"So where do we go from here?" Skiddy asked. "We have to put out a preliminary report. How do we tie all these loose ends together? Any suggestions?"

Dudley stood up and walked to the writing board at the front of the room. "May I suggest an approach?" he asked, picking up one of the markers.

Dan still couldn't get over Dudley's new persona. He was actually polite. His defensiveness seemed to have disappeared entirely. He appeared to truly want to be helpful.

Michael, mildly bemused by the new Dudley, gave up his spot at the front of the room. But he continued to watch the astronomer closely. *Can a leopard change his spots this quickly, Lord?* Michael asked. *Even if he hasn't developed a relationship with You?*

But even as Michael felt a nagging responsibility to keep a close eye on Dudley, he slipped back into his sorrow. Thoughts of Yael kept floating in and out of his mind. *Why, Lord? I just don't understand why!*

"As you know, I'm intent on keeping this thing scientifically respectable," Dudley was saying. "So I'll push for a reasoned, scholarly research approach to any paper we publish."

He looked around, as though expecting some rebuttal or protest. Not encountering any, he plunged on. "But with that caveat, I still think we should outline the most likely extradimensional possibilities," he said. "And let me say this: I have no objection to including or even highlighting Michael's shekinah hypothesis—especially if we can present it convincingly and acceptably in the extradimensional terms he's been using. That will make the whole thing more acceptable to the mainstream academic community—a prerequisite for me, and I think also for the other scientific professionals in this room."

He looked pointedly at Skiddy and Joanna, who nodded their

assent. Then he resumed with his line of thought. "So I'd propose that we start our report with a description of our hard science findings—various radiation and spectrum measurements, the astronomical observations, and so on. Of course, all those came back negative—but we still need to describe them in detail."

Joanna interrupted. "And remember, we're in good company here. Everybody else—research groups, the military, everybody—has come up empty-handed too."

"Right," Dudley said. "Then, at the end, we can suggest other possible explanations, including the extradimensional ideas and also what we might call the 'historical precedent hypothesis.'"

Joanna laughed. "That term certainly sounds serious enough. An acceptable smoke screen for any academic journal."

"Yes," Dudley said. "You know how we play the game. You've published enough. As long as academics hear the right buzzwords, they're satisfied. Pardon my cynicism, but that's the way it is."

Joanna grinned. "But of course, what we'd end up referring to would be the possible biblical precedents for our strange light, as well as subsequent historical reports involving similar religious or spiritual phenomena."

"That's exactly right," Dudley said.

Yes indeed, Dudley has *come a long way,* Michael reflected.

Skiddy waved his hands in an attempt to slow down the momentum of the discussion. "Hold on a minute!" he said. "We have to be cautious. We can't just end with speculation or a bunch of vague suggestions. If we're going to try to point people toward a definite conclusion—and frankly, I'm still not convinced that's such a good idea—we have to be careful. We can't let our conclusions outrun the facts. And we've got to employ terminology and concepts that will be acceptable to the scientific community. I'll be watching this draft closely just to keep you all honest."

With this plan in mind, the team split into two groups to begin the initial draft. Dudley, Joanna, and Skiddy retired to Skiddy's office to focus on the scientific aspects of the report. As for Michael and Dan, they holed up in the other office to deal with the historical, biblical, and spiritual issues—and the knotty question of extradimensionality.

Hours of discussion, sometimes loud and strident, echoed through the headquarters building. Finally, at the end of the day, they reassembled to share their findings and progress.

"The scientific issues are fairly cut-and-dried," Dudley said. He then proceeded to pass out detailed printouts with explanations from the spectroscopes and telescopes, and computer analyses.

"I've also included the results—or the lack thereof—from other astronomers and astrophysicists around the globe and in space," he said. "As you know, they've had access to large, sophisticated radio-telescope arrays, as well as the SOFIA plane and the satellite scopes. After reviewing their methodology and findings, we've concluded what you might expect. They've all come up with nothing."

Then Michael stood to summarize the work he and Dan had done. "So far, we've heard only what the Star *isn't*," he began. "So apparently it falls to Dan and me to offer suggestions about what it *is* or *may be*. So here goes.

"We've talked a great deal about the possibility that this light is an extradimensional phenomenon. I've also described in some detail my opinion that it's related to the shekinah glory. Now, hold on to your seats. In order to put this into a workable proposal that might help the public move toward some sort of practical action plan, we now have to begin to consider the question of prophecy."

Dan grinned as the group shifted and murmured uncomfortably.

"Give him an inch and he takes a mile," Skiddy said under his breath. "Remember, Michael, careful. Be careful."

"You're really getting onto shaky ground now, at least from my point of view," Dudley cautioned.

"Okay, I see the red flags," Michael said. "Now here goes. Many religions have teachings about heaven and the afterlife. But from all Dan and I can tell, the Judeo-Christian tradition comes closest to describing the phenomenon in our sky. Here are some of the details."

He moved to the melamine writing board once more and jotted down occasional short notes to make his points. "First of all, the New Testament teaches clearly that Christ will return physically to pronounce judgment on all human beings, both the living and the dead. There are many theories, or eschatological positions, about how the last times on earth will unfold, and I really don't think it's necessary to go into detail about them for our purposes.

"The important question we have to answer is this: Does that light in the sky, that Star, have anything to do with Christ's return? In other words, might it somehow signal His Second Advent, as Christians call the event?"

He wrote "Second Coming" on the board.

"Okay, don't keep us in the dark," Joanna said.

"I believe there's a connection," Michael replied, "possibly a direct link, to some teachings of Jesus known as the 'Olivet Discourse.' He passed on some detailed information to His disciples on the Mount of Olives. You might recall that the area lies just to the east of Jerusalem, within easy walking distance from the Old City wall."

He then turned back to the board and jotted down references to several New Testament verses:

Matthew 24:27
Luke 17:24
Matthew 24:30
Luke 21:11

"These passages may point us toward the answer to our problem," he said, waiting as the team members shuffled through the pages of their Bibles—replacements for those that had been destroyed in the explosion of the old headquarters building.

"Okay, look at the first reference. The passage in Matthew 24:27 says, 'For just as the lightning comes from the east, and flashes even to the west, so shall the coming of the Son of Man be.' I put that at the top of my list because I think you'll immediately see the connection I'm considering."

"The movement of the Star when we were in Jerusalem?" Joanna said.

"Right," Michael replied. "As we were watching that Star, it streaked from east to west and then back again."

"But Michael and I wanted to be extremely precise as we analyzed the Bible passages," Dan explained. "So we tried to determine exactly *when* and *how* this phenomenon that was similar to 'lightning' might occur in an end-times scenario. But from the context here in Matthew—and in a similar passage in Luke 17:24—it seemed obvious that there could be several possible interpretations."

"For example," Michael said, picking up on Dan's point, "will the lightninglike phenomenon come simultaneously with the arrival of Christ? Or will it appear beforehand, to signal the imminent onset of His second coming? And if it—whatever 'it' is—happens before Christ's arrival, how long before? It's not entirely clear from the text. So we decided that must mean Jesus wanted to leave the precise timing and details of this event up in the air."

"To put this another way," Dan said, "even if the teachings of Jesus and the prophets are entirely accurate—and for purposes of this discussion, we're assuming they are—they probably can't be used to predict many, if any, of the details in advance. We won't be able to foretell when this or that will happen. We won't know the fine points of the events until they actually occur."

"It's sort of like the Old Testament prophecies of Christ's first coming," Michael explained. "Nobody but Jesus Himself—not even His disciples—really understood immediately that there would be two advents. The First Advent is recounted in the Gospels. This involved the Christ of Isaiah 53, the Suffering Servant who would be crucified and resurrected as part of God's plan of salvation for all human beings.

"But the Second Advent—which we're now awaiting—will feature the conquering Christ, who will return to overcome all evil and establish a new heaven and earth at the end of human history."

Dan interrupted, a note of excitement creeping into his voice. "When that happens, we'll be able to recognize it and what it all means by referring back to the Scripture, but we'll only understand *after the fact*—as the early Christians did. We won't be able to predict beforehand."

"Sounds like you're buying into this prophecy business hook, line, and sinker, Dan," Skiddy said.

"Well . . ." Dan started, but Dudley interrupted.

"So you really think this passage may refer to the east-west-east movement we witnessed in the sky in Jerusalem?" the Harvard astronomer asked.

"That's a possibility," Michael said. "But now, let's move on to the second verse—Matthew 24:30. This reference says that 'the sign of the Son of Man will appear in the sky,' and then there will be mourning throughout the earth. Then, finally, everyone will see the

Son of Man coming on the clouds with power and glory. The prior verse, by the way, indicates that there will be a solar eclipse."

"We saw a kind of solar eclipse up here on the compound," Skiddy remarked.

"The same in Jerusalem," Dan said. "Everything got very dark before the Star began to streak back and forth."

"The 'Son of Man' refers to Christ?" Dudley asked.

"Yes," Michael replied.

"So you're saying that the Star up there is the 'sign of the Son of Man'?" Dudley said, intent on nailing down every detail.

"We're just suggesting possibilities," Michael replied. "No commentators have come up with a good explanation for this term, 'sign of the Son of Man'—and for good reason. Remember, no one has actually witnessed the precise sequence of end-times events."

"At least not until now," Joanna said.

"Perhaps," Michael replied.

"But I see a potential problem with your interpretation," Joanna said. "The previous verse, number 29, says that a lot of other things will happen before this sign appears. The solar eclipse is one. But the passage also refers to a lunar eclipse, a dramatic falling of the stars, and some sort of tribulation."

Michael sighed. "You have a point, of course. So far, those other celestial events, such as the lunar eclipse and the falling stars, haven't occurred. Also, many Christian eschatologists—that is, those who study the theology of the end of history—would argue that we haven't yet seen a period of great tribulation, or extremely hard times, such as the Scriptures foretell."

"Things aren't looking so great around the world right now," Dan noted. "Our big cities are falling apart. People are going crazy."

"But there's another issue here," Dudley said. "If we assume that this Star is somehow linked to an extradimensional universe—or what some religious people might call 'heaven'—then time may have an entirely different meaning in these passages. In other words, it could be wrong to assume a linear unfolding of these events, at least in terms of our space–time universe. They might all occur, but at a pace and in a sequence that's more consistent with *God's* multidimensional universe than with our own . . ."

The Harvard astronomer stopped in mid-sentence, shocked at

what he himself had just said. "I can't believe it. I said 'God's universe,' and up to now, I haven't even believed in God."

"It seems that the Star is not the only thing that may be changing before our very eyes," Joanna said with a wink.

"That's an extremely important point, Dudley," Michael observed, bringing the group back to the issue under discussion. "Time probably is quite different—maybe even meaningless or nonexistent—in the world or worlds that may lie behind that Star."

Joanna looked at Michael curiously. "Doesn't this make you a little nervous? Sounds to me like we're getting away from a straight literal reading of Scripture. I thought that was essential to you."

Michael smiled easily at her challenge. "I do take the Bible literally, in the sense that I take each section at face value, for what it purports to be. Poetry for poetry. History for history, and so on.

"As for these passages we've been discussing, every traditional biblical scholar agrees that when we read apocalyptic literature, special literary rules come into play. Symbolic language is common in these sections, and so we must watch for it and be prepared to seek interpretations."

"Give me an example," Joanna pressed.

"Okay, take Matthew 24:27," Michael said, pointing to the first reference on the board behind him. "That verse says 'as the lightning comes from the east.' That's a signal that we're not dealing with real lightning, but with something similar to lightning. In literary terms, Jesus is using a simile here. There's a great deal of metaphorical and symbolic language in the apocalyptic sections of the Gospels, as well as in the really extensive prophetic passages in the book of Daniel and also in Revelation."

"And remember the issue of time," Dudley reminded him.

"Very good point," Michael replied. "As Dudley's suggested, when we discuss these matters, we should probably be prepared to adjust our understanding of time. You'll recall that Jesus talks about events in the last days that often begin in heaven and are consummated on earth. Also, John in the book of Revelation sometimes appears to actually *be in heaven*, either through a vision or some other means, when he watches future events unfold. The prophet Daniel has some similar passages in his Old Testament book."

"So the question becomes, which time frame controls our reading?" Dudley said. "Is it the human space–time continuum, which involves a sequential, linear concept of time? Or is the writer talking to us from an extradimensional place or context, where time as we understand it doesn't really exist?"

"Exactly!" Michael said. "You explain it better than my Bible commentaries!"

"Now you're really making me nervous," Dudley said. "Just don't mention that to my friends back at Harvard."

Michael, all business again, turned back to the board and his list of verses. "Look at this final passage, Luke 21:11," he said. "There, Jesus says that the onset of the last days will be preceded by many terrible events, including wars, earthquakes, plagues, famines, and 'terrors.'"

"Interesting," Joanna said. "We already seem to be seeing some of that, with the increased levels of terrorism and other disruptions around the world, don't we?"

"And look at this," Dan said. "While Michael and I were having our discussions, I was struck by verse 24 in Matthew 24, which refers to the rise of 'false Christs' and 'false prophets.' Make you think of anybody we've encountered here recently?"

"Phoebus," Joanna said. "That passage seems a clear reference to the rise of cults, which compete with Jesus' message."

"We're beginning to put it all together now," Michael said. "But there's more in Luke 21:11. Jesus goes on to say that there will be 'great signs from heaven.' By the way, the Greek word for 'sign' in all these passages is *semeion*, which can mean a 'wonder, miracle, or sign.'"

"My head's spinning from all the Bible references," Skiddy said. "They may be pertinent, but remember, we're not going to be writing a report for theologians. Can you begin to wrap it up? What does it mean for us and that light in the sky?"

"Let me make it explicit," Dan emphasized. "We're suggesting that it's just possible that the extraordinary events we've been witnessing in the heavens may be one of the 'great signs' Jesus is referring to here in Luke."

"You said 'we,'" Joanna said, peering cautiously at her husband. "I take it that means you're on board with Michael's theories."

"I'm not just talking theory," Dan replied. "I'm talking fact." He then paused, took a deep breath, and apparently settled something in his mind before he spoke again.

"Look, you should all know something. I wanted to tell you first privately, Joanna, but this can't wait. You see, while Michael and I were discussing this material, something happened to me. I can't quite explain it, but as we were talking, I walked over to the window and looked up at that light and suddenly, I knew. I understood."

"Understood what?" Skiddy asked.

"Something seemed to grab hold of my thoughts, so that I really began to comprehend what this is all about. There was no voice. No blinding beam of light either. But I sensed something deep inside, something irresistible. I understood that everything Michael has been saying is true."

"And?" Skiddy prodded.

"And I realized at that moment that I had become a believer. I had become a follower of Jesus Christ."

✦ FORTY

N o one spoke.

Skiddy studied Dan in obvious consternation and then finally found his voice. "Let me get this straight. You're really buying into Michael's religion? I'm not sure I get it. I thought you'd been a Christian for years. In fact, you could say everybody in this room is Christian. At least, we're not Jewish or Hindu or something. I mean, I've been a Congregationalist, Episcopalian . . . and I may even become a Baptist, like Peter Van Campe."

"That's not it," Dan said. "I know more about religion than anybody in this room, except maybe Michael. And I've been a church member for years. What's happened to me goes beyond religion—or cultural Christianity. I've changed deep down in my . . . my spirit. In some way I don't completely grasp, I'm a new person. Everything seems different from a couple of hours ago."

Dudley seemed fascinated by the unexpected turn of events. "This seems a little out of character," he commented. "I thought you were the Amherst fundy-fighter."

Dan shifted uncomfortably, apparently not entirely at ease in explaining his newfound faith. But then he stuck out his jaw and leaned forward, ready to defend his new identity, regardless of the consequences.

"Okay, sure, I've always opposed Christian fundamentalists and evangelicals. But I can't deny what's happened inside me. And I can't explain it, except to say this: Apparently, what I've read and studied most of my professional career about God's grace and spiritual rebirth has actually happened to me."

"You really think that the light in the sky is one of the signs of Christ's return—a sign that was prophesied in the Bible?" Dudley said, apparently not quite willing to believe Dan.

"Let me put it this way," Dan replied. "Even if I hadn't had this experience—this total inner turnaround—I'd still be a little reluctant to challenge the power of that thing up there. It seems evident that a potent intelligence of some sort is behind it. And let's face facts: The farther we go, the more everything fits into this biblical scenario."

Then Dan leaned forward again and shook his head. "But you have to understand, none of these rational considerations or arguments are the controlling factor for me. The key thing is that somehow, in a way I can't express adequately in words—in a way that goes beyond reason—I've been totally transformed inside."

Michael leaned against the wall behind him in amazement as the others sat back quietly in their chairs. Michael had suspected something positive was going on in Dan, but he wasn't sure. And given the circumstances, he hadn't felt quite right about taking the initiative and asking the Amherst professor how he was doing on the spiritual level.

As Michael glanced around the room, he was surprised again, this time at the response of the team. There wasn't one word of protest after Dan's confession. Michael then contemplated Dan for a moment or two.

I never thought I'd see this day. Thank You, Lord. Thank You.

Finally, Skiddy broke the silence. "Well, what next! I must say every hour around here seems to bring another surprise. But now, we've got to push ahead. Bring this thing to some sort of conclusion."

He glanced at some notes he had been taking and proposed the next step. "We've got to put something down on paper, so I'd suggest this arrangement. Dudley, you write up the scientific sections. Michael, you draft the extradimensional and theological parts. And Dan, when they're finished, I'd like you to go over the whole thing. Edit it so that we have one style and voice throughout."

As they began to disperse, Skiddy, who was all nerves, couldn't help himself—he had to remind them again. "Remember, intellectually acceptable! Completely defensible! We know we'll be criticized by our scientific peers for suggesting a nonscientific possibility. It's got to be something we can all live with back at our universities. Okay?"

But at this point, Dan's disclosure seemed more on their minds than the report they were drafting. Michael felt himself wrestling with an almost overwhelming urge to rush over and hug the Amherst professor on the spot. But Joanna saved him from the impulse. She already had her husband by the arm and was dragging him out the door.

The problem for Michael came when he was finally alone, sitting in front of his computer screen in the rebuilt headquarters office, trying to focus on the report, which he knew might be the most important thing he'd ever written in his life. The problem was that he could feel her presence, as palpably as though she were right there with him.

Yael. She'd been working and planning right on this spot only a few days before.

Where are you, Yael? I know you're present, but where? Can you see me? Hear my thoughts? You must know how I miss you. God must still keep us connected in some way. If only I could hold you once more. If only I could say one last time, "I love you, Yael. I love you more than my life."

FORTY-ONE

THE Harvard research team's preliminary report caused consternation, considerable outrage, and some mockery, not only throughout the scientific community, but also among the public at large.

Leaders of non-Christian religions accused the group of narrow-mindedness and intolerance. A cadre of university scholars took out several full-page newspaper ads condemning the group's methodology and conclusions. And a *New York Times* editorial had just been published on the Internet edition of the paper suggesting darkly that quackery was afoot. The editorialists warned the team that their conclusions could foster bigotry and bad feeling in a world already racked by social and political turmoil.

But as night fell on the compound in northern Israel on the evening after the report and immediate responses had been released, a strange calm prevailed. Dudley might have been expected to lose his composure when the public and academic criticisms hit. But he just shrugged.

"Let them come up with a better answer," he said simply. "Besides, the old ideas are passing away. Something new is in the wind. And I think I want to be part of it."

Michael did a double take at that. *Sounds almost biblical.* But he decided he wouldn't press the Harvard astronomer to explain at this point.

Skiddy still appeared rather uncertain about what his attitude should be. But it did seem that he had finally given up on the notion that his entire future depended on putting together a research project that would pass muster with traditional scholarly standards.

"Peter Van Campe is pleased!" he announced after receiving the initial response of the Panoplia International director to their report. "He even wants to join us when we get back."

"Get back?" Joanna asked. "From where?"

"Oh, didn't I tell you?" he replied. "I guess not. I've been so busy, what with the reaction to the report, the television reporters crawling all over the compound and all. Yes, we'll be leaving in a couple of days to conduct some off-site research and interviewing—that is, if you all are game. We need to get some perspective from other investigators, and I think we should all get a firsthand look at the social and political problems in the outside world, which seem to be escalating."

Joanna immediately nodded her assent. "Great idea! I'd like to check further on the reports about an increase of natural disasters—earthquakes, famines, and the like," she said.

"The summer's not even half over," Dan said. "Can you believe all that's happened here in just six weeks?"

Then they remembered Michael, whose expression hadn't changed. Dan felt like biting his own tongue. They had all grown close enough to sense the pain Michael was feeling. But the Wheaton professor quickly filled the awkward silence.

"Some of it hasn't been so good," Michael said. "But I should tell you, I'm more convinced than ever that the tragedies and deaths have to be part of a broader, cosmic plan. And the Star is somehow at the center of it all."

They all looked up at the light, which was now the same size and shape as when it had erupted in the sky a few short weeks before. There was no suggestion of the incredible fireworks that had occurred up there in the sky just a few days ago. What might occur in the future? They had seen enough to not try to predict even a moment or two beyond the present.

"So everybody's on board?" Skiddy said, looking around at them with some relief. "Good! Now, I'd suggest that each of you pick your targets of opportunity abroad. Choose some research, interviews, or other contacts that might help us further our work here. We'll split up and reassemble here in three weeks."

Dudley chose to travel to some spots where he could observe

astronomical studies that were being conducted in New Mexico, at Caltech, and in Australia. "And of course, I'll drop by Cambridge, just to see if there's any point in my trying to return after my adventures here," he joked. "The people at Harvard and M.I.T. might even be making some progress with this light, though I doubt it."

Joanna wanted to focus not only on reports of natural disasters around the world; she also planned to explore any breakthroughs that scientists with the American government might have made.

"They'll be closemouthed because of national security and intelligence concerns," she said. "But I have my sources. I might be able to pry something out of them—if there's anything to pry."

Dan expected to strike out on his own to evaluate the social and political problems that seemed to be increasing. "Also, I want to check with some colleagues who monitor cult groups," he said. "It would be helpful to know if there are any other groups like the New Jerusalem Way that we need to worry about."

Michael nodded. Although the New Jerusalem Way bunch had been stopped and the leaders taken into custody, similar groups had taken their place. *False Christs and false prophets. Another possible sign for these times.*

Skiddy announced that he would continue his work evaluating instances of mass hysteria and other psychological problems that might be affecting large population groups. "If those biblical 'terrors' are indeed on the rise, we need to know the specifics," he said.

Michael looked closely at Skiddy, not sure if he was serious with that comment. But the Harvard psychologist's expression said nothing. *If that remark was tongue-in-cheek, he's subtler than I ever gave him credit for.*

As for Michael, he decided to concentrate most of his energies on intelligence he could gather within the evangelical community. If anyone claimed to be receiving prophecies or other special divine messages—and those claims were credible—he needed to know.

But he didn't want to think about that now. What he needed more than anything else was a good night's sleep. He was so tired he couldn't even recall their last conversation, just before they broke up. Or walking to his quarters. Or collapsing into his cot without even undressing.

But the dream—that was something he'd never forget.

✸ FORTY-TWO

A N all-encompassing river of exquisite sound and light enveloped Michael. Escape from the blissful flow never entered his mind, especially when he felt—not just saw—the ones who had joined him for the journey.

Time had disappeared. So had separation and alienation. Michael sensed only connection with unseen others and his surroundings. But *surroundings* wasn't the right word for the sea of soothing sounds and harmonies—like, but unlike, voices and vibrations and clarions—which moved in and out of his white-bright body, at once energizing him and infusing him with an ineffable peace.

He was still Michael James, but he was also at one—and constantly interacting—with something beyond himself. All theological preconceptions and worldly anxieties had been transformed into complete confidence and security. Now he knew, though he couldn't put what he knew into words—because words were no longer necessary.

Thoughts, moving at blinding speed, had supplanted language. In seconds—but there were no seconds—he learned twice as much as he had absorbed in a lifetime on earth.

Earth.

Where was he? Who were these beings standing, sitting, swirling around him?

Instantly, even before the questions came to mind, he knew. Caught up with him in that sea of light and sound he could see Peter.

And Dan.

And Joanna.

And Dudley.

Dudley! What's Dudley doing here? Where am I? What is this place?

The answer came even as he asked the questions: *"You shall know fully, but only when you are face-to-face."*

Then a sweet silence and rest filled him and seemed to suspend his transformed body in a motionless sea. Yet even as he was embraced in this stillness, he was moving, so it seemed, upward, higher and higher—though height had lost spatial meaning. Now "up" had been transformed to become movement that carried him not in any discernible direction, but closer and closer to the center, to the light—to the Star.

The light around him intensified. But instead of bringing pain to his eyes—*which may not even be eyes anymore,* he reflected—the luminescence empowered him to perceive everything and everyone more clearly.

Now, he could behold that special one in a brilliance far transcending earthly beauty, even though her beauty had been so exquisite and had always encompassed so much more than shiny black hair, near-perfect physical features, and challenging intellect.

Mind to mind: *Yael. You're here.*

Of course I'm here.

We're together.

God is good.

Then he opened his eyes and saw it—the Star shining more brightly than ever before through the small window in his quarters. He was still in Israel. The noises outside, colleagues stirring around the compound in the early morning, told him it was a new day, just north of the Sea of Galilee.

But today is finally a day of promise. A day of hope.

ABOUT THE AUTHOR

WILLIAM Proctor has history and law degrees from Harvard University, has studied at the Harvard Divinity School, and has written more than seventy books, including *The G-Index Diet* with Dr. Richard Podell (Warner Books, 1993). His works include a novel on a cult kidnapping; ghostwritten books on medical, scientific, and business topics; and a recent apologetic supporting the biblical account of the physical resurrection of Christ. Mr. Proctor's books have been translated into more than forty languages. He has had several national best-sellers and an eighteen-week appearance on the *New York Times* best-seller list. His previous titles with Thomas Nelson are Dr. Kenneth Cooper's *It's Better to Believe* (later published in paperback as *Faith-Based Fitness*) and Dr. Cooper's *Advanced Nutritional Therapies*.